HEIRS OF THE SECOND DAWN

THE
LIGHT
UNDER
THE
SHADOW
WING

USA TODAY BESTSELLING AUTHOR
AMANDA BOUCHET

To Séraphine and Sébastien—this is our book in so many ways. I hope you're as proud of it as I am.

To my dad—you didn't get to read this one, but I think you would have loved it.

And to my readers—for your kind words, support, and encouragement. I am so privileged to have you cheering me on.

AUTHOR'S NOTE

This book is intended for an adult audience and contains graphic content and themes that may be difficult for some readers. Sensitive material includes, but is not limited to:

- Battle violence with people and animals
- Blood and gore
- Disordered eating
- Explicit language
- Infertility
- Kidnapping
- Off-page parental neglect
- On-page sex

WYNDWOOD

Sinjar Hill

THE WHITE PALACE

Muirvale

TANTURRIFF

IVY HALL

TORRI

DRAYKE

The School of Fire and Flight

Upper Drayke Lake

Southern

Drayke Mountain

Glarraden

CITY OF DRAYKE

RUTHINOCK

THE REALM OF ELLONRIFT

Tyburn

Millburn

Porthwood

Draywood

BLOODWOLD

Hellwood Forest

BLACKROCK KEEP

DAIG

Silver Moon Mountain Range

EVERNIGHT CASTLE

Lakes

FANGHAVEN

N
NW NE
W E
SW SE
S

CHAPTER ONE

IDALLIA

Today, I turn two hundred and twenty-six, and I look *fabulous.*

My fitted fighting leathers hug my curves like a second skin, and my new, wider sword belt sits comfortably on my hips while also serving as a clear reminder that I can kill my enemies without breaking a sweat.

Alone in my quarters, I jut out a hip with enough flair to light a forest fire, then draw my new blades and give them an inaugural twirl. They're almost exactly like my other swords, so it'll be easy to adjust to their weight and feel. The only real difference is the set of matching jewels embedded in the pommels. The fire opals look just like the sharp, blazing eye of a phoenix about to dive into battle.

Delighted with my birthday presents, I take down my hair, kick off my boots, and dance barefoot through some advanced fighting moves to get a feel for my new belt and blades. My team gave them to me at lunch, and while I shouldn't wish for a fight, I also can't wait to try them out. The belt is supple and light, and the swords already feel like old friends in my hands.

Sunlight streams through my high, arched window, too tempting to ignore, and I keep up my battle dance as I move into the puddle of light. Warm stones greet my bare feet, and my long black hair soaks up the sunshine, seeming to nourish me all the way to my veins. A beautiful day, friends, and gifts. Smiling, I lift my face to the rays.

Not yet done playing with my new weapons, I accelerate, spinning and slicing until metal whistles like wind through a crack in a tree. I see past battles and counter the moves of envisioned enemies with learned precision. After a brutal jab at an imagined vampire, I finally bring my mock combat to a close and give my blades a final twirl. The fire opals glint in the sunshine as I flip the swords in my hands and sheathe them with a flourish. They slide into the leather scabbards attached to the belt so easily that I grin.

As far as birthdays go, this is a good one.

At least, it's the birthday my adoptive parents gave me. I appeared one day on their doorstep at the country house in Glarraden, an infant in a basket with a name pinned to my blanket and a bag of gold so large it could rival the fortunes of any gildenfae. The note in my basket said to take care of me, so they did.

I didn't want for a thing growing up—neither education nor training in the arts of war—but considering how little Rita and Gerard chose to interact with me, I did feel more loved for the bag of gold coins that mysteriously showed up every year on the summer solstice—Dragon's Night—than for my sparkling wit or my skill with a sword.

Reflected sunlight winks at me like party candles from the mirror on my dresser, and I dance toward it, humming a tavern tune. I blow myself a birthday kiss, my pinkened nose and cheeks from riding my warbird in the sun and wind intensified by the flush of exercise with my new swords. I smile, remembering how Fyrestar easily outpaced the other phoenixes today—as usual.

Chirps and rustling greet my ears, and I turn to the rocky caverns carved deep into my bedroom wall. "Rim! Sol!" I call, my smile growing. If they're done resting, we can go outside and enjoy the remainder of the day together.

In just seconds, my phoenixes fly to me, perching on my shoulders. They're the babies. Or rather, the reborn. At nearly sixteen years old, Rimblaze is a hefty hunk of bird and weighs heavily on my arm. I lost Embersol for the third time only a few years ago, and she can still barely cough up a fireball.

I coo and nuzzle them, stroking their colorful feathers and praising the little flames boiling in their beaks. Pretty soon, Rim will be fully trained and strong enough to come out as my wing guard. I'm not sure when I'll be able to ride him again. He seems to be growing more slowly this time around, but we all know magic has been waning in Ellonrift for decades and that Cealastra hasn't seen fit to show her presence and replenish it yet. For little Embersol, battles and carrying me on her back are both still years away, but sometimes, it's not so bad knowing she's safe inside the mountain when we go off to protect Torridaig.

"You smell like spices today." Rim chirps his words into my mind. Is his voice getting deeper? He's matured so much lately—though not enough to stop squabbling with Sol.

"I had a spicy lunch." I smooth a rebellious red feather into the orange ones on his forehead. "And a birthday cake." I don't know where it came from, but it showed up at the table, just like it does every year with the same regularity that the gold shows up at Glarraden House, even though I'm barely there. The Elite Wing ate most of it, but I still got the part with the candle to blow out. The cake had dark-red rose petals scattered across pearlescent frosting, reminding me of when I slice into enemy vampires on a moonlit winter hillside and drain them of their stolen blood.

"I want cake." Sol's baby squeak makes my heart pinch. These

two didn't make it through the battles, but they're still mine. If my phoenixes couldn't come back to me, I'd rather die with them.

"I'll throw some rodents together for you later." I tilt my head against hers. "But don't eat too many at once. You know you'll get a tummy ache."

The babies' sharp talons prick my skin, and they caw excitedly as Fyrestar lands on my window frame in a burst of sparks and wind. *"You're in a good mood today."*

I smile at my warbird, his rumbled words resonating in my head. "It's my birthday."

"So you think."

"Someone had to choose a day, so Rita did."

"Have Rita and Gerard come to visit you recently?"

I give him a bland look. Fyrestar knows very well that they have not. He just likes to remind me, because he thinks I should cut them loose and stop sending them part of my earnings, especially since their chest of gold—so big that everyone in the area started calling it "the gildenfae gold" almost from the very start—still arrives like clockwork every summer solstice. But I'll inherit Glarraden House one day, because they don't have anyone else to give it to when they finally fade from existence. I want to help with the upkeep.

I return to Glarraden sometimes, even if the people who raised me never come here. I had a home growing up, and if I survive, I'll have a home to grow old in where my birds can fly free. They'll have more than earned their peace by then—far more than I'll have ever earned mine. Despite the neglect that used to tie my stomach into knots and still comes roaring back with a remembered shock of loneliness more often than I'd like, I don't have any hard feelings toward Rita or Gerard. They did...okay. And my phoenixes give me all the love I need.

"They haven't been here since I was inducted into the Elite Wing." Nearly two centuries might've passed, but I'm still the novice of the Dragon King's personal squadron—the youngest and the last to have been chosen for the team—and everyone loves to remind me of it, especially Kellan. He hates it when I win the privilege of flying on Bale Cinderheart's right wing.

The thought of Bale makes me both shiver and heat. The potency of the Dragon King reaches me even here, floors and floors below his high lair in the mountain castle. He's been spending even more time than usual with the Elite Wing, despite the Ellonrift Council coming up soon. I crave his intense presence and dread it at the same time. I want him to look at me as much as I want him to turn away.

"What should we do this afternoon?" I ask my birds. "Survival training? War games against the team?"

"*You're a rainbow of fun,*" Fyrestar teases. "*Why isn't a picnic in the woods or a spin over the lake ever an option?*"

I toss him a mock frown. "What's more fun than beating everyone else?"

"*We don't* always *win,*" Rimblaze chimes in. "*Especially with Embersol, who can barely make fire. Or form complete sentences.*"

Sol squawks in protest. The little sparks escaping her oblong nostrils heat my ear. "Sol's fantastic. She's quick as a whip and sneaks in when no one sees her coming. She hardly ever participates in training, but she still saved your feathered behind just a few days ago, so give her some credit," I scold.

Rim huffs smoke, his beak half open in annoyance. The thirteen phoenixes of Torridaig all sprang from the same magic, and the sibling rivalry is real, especially for the birds who end up as younglings again at the same time. I've only lost Fyrestar once, and it was nearly a century ago. He's far too mature to get sucked into the younger birds' shenanigans.

"*Aren't you going to admire yourself some more?*" Fyrestar asks with a smirk in his voice. "*Blow another kiss to the mirror?*"

"You saw that from outside, did you?" I grin, not embarrassed at all.

"*It was hard to miss. The new swords and belt look good. Although I think you look better slicing through* real *enemies until you're covered in blood and painted red enough to match our feathers.*"

"Wow." I laugh. "Who's a rainbow of fun now? As long as it's not my blood. Or *yours*." I shudder, sobering.

"*It's never your fault,*" Rim says quietly, all trace of his earlier snark gone. "*You defend us well.*"

Great Cealastra, my eyes start to prick. Rim took a werebear's claws in the neck so the lethal tips didn't shred mine. And poor little Embersol. We both fell when the arrows hit her. The vampires tried to suck her everlife from her, but I fucking killed them all.

The satisfying memory of revenge doesn't stop the gut-wrenching recollection of my phoenixes' rebirths from surging up too. Of watching sparks circle sparks for agonizing days until the glowing magic finally solidified into tiny little birds right here in Drayke Mountain, where Bale first created them. Just like the phoenixes are growing more slowly now, it took longer for Sol's rebirth last time. I stood vigil for five more torturous days than usual, terrified that Ellonrift's fading magic would take her from me, from Rim, from Fyrestar.

Blinking, I clear my throat. "We defend each other," I say hoarsely. "Forever and always."

"*Forever and always.*" All three of them instantly chirp our personal motto, but instead of making me feel better and calmer, it just makes me worry about where Cealastra is and if she's ever coming back to restore magic in Ellonrift.

Torridaig's battle horn suddenly blares from the peak of Drayke Mountain, cutting through my perpetual underlying dread with its hard, sharp blast.

Or maybe adding to it.

"Bloodpit," I growl. "No training today." It'll be the real thing instead. I lift my shoulders, urging the babies off me. "Back to your roosts."

"*I can fight,*" Rim says. "*I'll be your right wing.*"

I almost wish he could. Everyone else on the team is a dragon shifter. The only fire and flight I have working in my favor comes from my birds. "Not yet, love. You haven't passed your tests." Sol's small talons leave my skin. Rim's larger ones depart more reluctantly. Even as fledglings, they recall everything about their past lives and form a bond with me immediately. Strength, reflexes, inner fire, and the ability to communicate mind-to-mind in the language of Ellonrift are slower to return.

"Come back safe," Rim says as I grab my boots and pull them on.

"Safe," Sol echoes in her little voice.

Nodding, I grab a short, fur-lined vest from the foot of my bed, slip it on, and hook it closed. My weapons are already on me, and I don't have time for more. My heart already pounding like the drums of war, I turn and race for the open window. "Fyrestar! Go!"

He launches off the sill in a whirlwind of heat, and I dive after him, blasting through the wall of searing air he left in my window frame. Outside, direct sunlight slams into my skin and eyes, the shock of it always abrupt after being inside the cool, dim mountain. Squinting, I spread my arms and legs, free-falling down the sheer mountainside until Fyrestar swoops underneath and picks me up.

Straightening, I wait for my vision to adjust as I brace my legs firmly around Fyrestar's body and grip the tough black feathers ringing his neck. Wind rushes through my loose hair, and I cringe at the oversight. The headmistress at school would've had my hide for showing up in the training ring with my hair down, and Bale is sure to do the same.

I tap my pockets, hoping I might've forgotten a leather strap inside. No luck, and I can't easily tie my hair back while flying anyway.

My stomach sinking, I press lower against Fyrestar's feathers, cursing vanity for making me take down my daily tight bun to indulge in a moment of birthday frivolity in my bedroom. It's a rookie mistake, and now, it's too late. We have a mountain to climb, and if Kellan reaches the war room before I do, he'll win right wing again.

Fyrestar ascends, the near-vertical angle forcing me to hold on tight and squeeze my legs. *"Are you all right, Idallia? Too steep?"* he asks when I slip back more than I should.

"No. Keep going. I want right wing."

"You're too competitive. It's not the wing that counts."

It's always the wing. I'm the foundling. The nobody. The youngest. I don't know who I am. *What* I am. I stopped visibly aging when I reached my prime, so Rita and Gerard eventually decided I wasn't human after all and must be strong enough to train for war. Even though I don't have fire or flight, they dumped me at the school pumping out soldiers for Torridaig and paid the headmistress enough to keep me there—the only student who wasn't a dragon shifter in the whole starsdamned place. They left with a vague goodbye before hurrying back to Glarraden where they could continue to only pay attention to each other without me around to try to gain even a scrap of their time.

My memory is too sharp for comfort, and that rush of excitement I'd felt about starting at the Drayke School of Fire and Flight hits me before souring just like my school years did. I thought maybe I'd finally make some friends. But then a student I recognized from around Glarraden lifted his hand on my first day, pointed straight at me, and said, *"Why is* she *here? She's the gildenfae-gold kid."*

I press my mouth shut against a snarl, and Fyrestar flies so fast that the high mountain air helps hammer the echoes of my time as a student off me, leaving only the need to prove myself and win.

"We're almost there, Fyrestar. Go!" Entrances to the war room open near the pinnacle of Drayke Mountain, not far below Bale's lair. We aim for the nearest window. Excelling at combat against everyone's expectations is the only reason I'm *anything*, and I want right wing.

We blast through a high entrance, and my warbird moves like a firebolt straight for the six pillars of the Elite Wing. Kellan flies in through another window at nearly the same time. His primary wing guard follows, sleek, fast, and glowing, his long tail feathers trailing fire. Grambolt is as mature and experienced as Fyrestar.

My pulse racing, I urge Fyrestar faster. Kellan's scales shimmer even in the low light of the gigantic room, the arresting mix of darkness and iridescence a distracting flash in my periphery as we both dive for the same flat-topped column rising from the stone floor next to the map of Ellonrift.

Kellan's ice-blue eyes narrow. *"Not today."* The words resonate inside my head in the same deep voice that used to suggest things like leaving the Elite Wing, settling down together, mating.

I don't answer and vault off Fyrestar, already sprinting for the coveted first spot at the right-hand side of the map. With only a few steps to go, I take a running leap and land on top of the wide pillar. Kellan hits it at the same time, instantly transforming into his fully clothed common form to get both booted feet on the surface. Skidding wildly, I thump into the rock-solid, four-hundred-year-old dragon shifter and bounce right off him. My stomach plummets.

Kellan reaches out to steady me, but it's too late. I'm already falling, and the failure is nauseating. I hit the ground on my side, a pained breath wheezing out of me. Fyrestar's worried caw rattles in my head. My hip numb, I scramble up, vault over the map, and lunge for the left-wing column, but Maia just took the front pillar because she didn't even try for right wing. I jump onto the column behind her before anyone else can take the second row. Right wing is more prestigious, but I don't want to be responsible for watching Kellan's back. I'm too incensed right now.

Seething, I scowl across the giant, raised map of Ellonrift, wishing *I* could breathe fire. Kellan winks at me, his smirk as big as he is.

"That was mine," I grind out.

"Same time, but I kept my balance," he says as the rest of the team fills in the remaining pillars, their primary warbirds already circling the cavernous room along with mine. The phoenixes brighten the yawning darkness above our heads, their luminous feathers throwing warm, reddish-gold light onto the roughly carved-out rock ceiling. The floor is smoother, worn down by centuries of dragon shifters working tirelessly to keep the peace in Ellonrift.

I don't have inner fire like the rest of the team and force myself not to shiver as I take in today's formation. Five dragon shifters and whatever-the-stars I am. Six phoenixes so far. Too many blades to count.

"We could share," Kellan offers, knowing that's patently impossible.

"Fuck you."

He gives me a heated look. "Anytime you want."

"How about never, never, never, ever," I shoot back.

His brows rise so slowly and deliberately that I want to bite them off his forehead. "You mean never again?"

Turning away, I ignore him as the younger birds arrive. They're the dragon shifters' left-wing guards. There are only two of us without—Danica and me—because our little ones are still too young to fight. She has her right-wing phoenix, and I have Fyrestar. Bale gave me three warbirds since I don't have wings of my own.

Fyrestar catches my attention with a heavy, golden gaze. He doesn't like that I'm alone—either in flight or in life. But I'm not truly alone. My warbird and I have matching eyes.

The wing guards find their principals and stick to the older birds like pitch, just like Rim will do with Fyrestar soon. But for now, it's Fyrestar who's alone, and I don't like it, but there aren't any other phoenixes in Ellonrift.

The Dragon King created thirteen phoenixes infused with everlife and his own fire from the thirteen chest scales his greatest enemy sliced through, nearly reaching his heart. Bale won the battle in the end, but the Vampire King somehow survived. With some of the strongest magic in Torridaig, Bale created the fiercest, most devoted fighting force in Ellonrift. He raised the phoenixes to their first maturity and trained them to be as loyal as they are lethal. Then he established the Elite Wing about two hundred years ago—one dragon shifter for two warbirds.

Or that's how it's supposed to work. Bale didn't fill the last pillar until he chose me straight out of school. He walked the lines of graduating students, looking us over with narrowed eyes—not that he hadn't already been watching us for years. Then he stopped in front of me and offered me a home and a team. It took half a second to realize I'd bested everyone at school, and another half a second to push my *yes* past the explosion of excitement launching my heart straight up my throat.

Rimblaze, Embersol, and Fyrestar were the last to be given a soldier. Maybe it was just luck that three remained, but it gave me a warbird to ride, and two wing guards to make us an even more formidable team. The day I met my birds, I fully understood how lucky I was—I finally had a real family after all these years.

Some say the Vampire King ripped a fourteenth scale right off Bale's chest. Bale has never confirmed, but the scar that still marks his skin after all these years makes me think it could be true. Bale removed the thirteen damaged scales to create our firebirds, and so that new scales could grow in their place. He doesn't have a warbird of his own, though Rim, Sol, and Fyrestar flew with him until I came along.

As usual, Kellan doesn't let the subject drop. "Never ever is a long time when you live as long as we do. We'll see what happens in a decade or two." His admittedly attractive blue eyes dip over me. "Or we could just go back a couple dozen years and remember the good times?"

I glare at him, hearing Maia quietly snort to my front and Arran groan softly behind me. They were good times, but they're over. Kellan needs to let go of the past and stop dragging everyone else into our business.

Our *finished* business.

"Or, I could reach my hand down your throat and yank out

your vocal cords so you'll stop bringing up ancient history," I growl.

He chuckles. "Love your fire, Idallia. Too bad it doesn't actually burn."

My nostrils flare on a sharp breath.

Not having a comeback enrages me, but it doesn't matter. Everyone goes quiet and faces forward as Bale Cinderheart explodes like a volcanic blast into the war room.

CHAPTER TWO
IDALLIA

Bale is a force of nature. Flames and wind, heat and strength. His black scales shimmer with red undertones, his inner fire seeping out on a blaze of shadows. Hot, amber eyes brighten a dark auburn face shaped by horns and spikes and scales. He flies straight at us, fangs hidden, a fiery rumble resonating in his throat. His huge, sinewy body blots out the light from the windows as he swoops toward the Elite Wing pillars. His crimson wings beat the air like a tempest on the horizon, and my heart thuds against my ribs, echoing the heavy, powerful thumping of the opaque membranes.

My breath catches as he nears. It's inevitable, and I'm not the only one. Even the warbirds stop calling, and their flight slows. Bale's line is ancient and mighty. He's the Dragon King, born of the stars and Cealastra's own choosing. He unfurls blood-red talons for landing, his tail whipping a lethally spiked line behind him. Bale touches down and transforms so smoothly he doesn't even pause as he strides toward us, smoke still curling from his nostrils.

Nerves twist in my belly, and I lift my chin as Bale takes in our formation across the pillars. His decisive footsteps echo in the huge cliffside space, our silence total. The rhythmic beat gets louder the closer he comes, and that shiver I was holding back ripples over me. He might be even more impressive in his common form because he still exudes effortless power and dominance without claws or fangs or fire.

Tawny eyes flash over us as he stops, a hint of the same deep crimson in his scales giving his dark-brown hair a smoldering undertone. My skin tingles, my blood a flash flood in my veins. At only a decade shy of six hundred years old, the Dragon King is everything he should be and more. As handsome as he is frightening. As terrifying as he is fair. As big as he is brutal.

As powerful as he should be—the king who holds the center of the world.

The whole of Ellonrift used to be one, with the six kings and queens constantly disputing the boundaries of their goddess-given territories, and who could do what and where. Now Torridaig, at the heart of it all, belongs to Bale Cinderheart, and *peace* is just the short way of saying we're not literally at war.

Clearly defining a sovereign kingdom for each ruling bloodline—human, fae, werebeast, vampire, and dragon shifter—was supposed to encourage better relations and enable the different populations of the land to gather with their own if they preferred. Centuries later, we all know how well that went—and still goes. No one was forced to leave their homes, and edicts were put into place to protect any who stayed, but separatists quickly became a problem, voicing their venom against anyone who didn't see things their way.

In the center of Ellonrift, Torridaig has always been a land of different peoples, although there are many more dragon shifters than anyone else. Vampires can live peacefully in Torridaig as long as they abide by Torridaig's laws. Same with humans, weres, and fae. Vampires who bite without consent had better move to Bloodwold, though, before edict primis catches up to them. We don't tolerate blood thieves here.

But nothing worked out as planned, and true sovereignty and equal Council votes just gave every ruler of Ellonrift more power to fight only for themselves. Now, blood-trafficking vampires plunder our villages in the northeast. Radical werebeasts slash at our northern towns. On Torridaig's eastern border, desperate fae will glamour their way through unsuspecting settlements, leaving victims aged by decades in their wake. There's mostly peace to the south, because humans are scared of the populations around them and need Bale's kingdom as a buffer between them and the nightmares everywhere else.

Personally, I don't discount the sorcerers. No one else seems nearly as scared of them as they should be, but I have dreams that tell me a human magic-wielder can do as much damage as any other beast.

Bale's posture finally relaxes, his hands settling on his hips. The phoenixes grow excited again. They chirp in greeting, and their inner glow lights their vibrant feathers, turning them into circling chandeliers. Looking up, Bale warms for them. Flames lick through his eyes, and the firm set of his mouth softens in a way it only does for his firebirds. He's breathtaking this way, unguarded and visibly proud, but when he lowers his focus back to us, his expression loses all trace of paternal softness.

His piercing gaze hits Kellan first. He nods, his dark hair sweeping forward with the sharp acknowledgment. He has his right wing, with Wade and Danica positioned behind Kellan.

He looks to the left wing next, giving Maia a cool but approving glance. His gaze slips to me behind her, and his amber eyes visibly darken. His rich, centuries-deep voice resonates inside my head. *"Do better."*

I stare back at him, heat and frustration and a chest-cramping distress tangling through me. At least he didn't say it aloud. The others can't hear what Bale says only to me, but they won't miss the tenebrosity seeping from his lightly tanned skin, and the shadows forming an almost solid layer of reddish-black dragon scales over him. The shadow scales quickly lose form and fade, though his magic still lingers in the air like ink blots on parchment.

I can't answer him without everyone hearing, so I keep my mouth shut. Besides, what would I say? Kellan pushed me? I'll die a thousand grisly deaths before I resort to tattling.

Or admit to losing because I *fell*.

My unsettled blood rushes through my body, and I force slow, steadying breaths until Bale's eyes finally shift to Arran behind me. His stare goes as icy as a werebeast's den in winter, and I swallow. At least I'm not left *and* last.

Except...his flinty gaze quickly swings back to me. "What's wrong with this picture?" he asks in a deceptively soft voice. The question is for everyone, but his eyes never leave my face, and my stomach hollows so fast it hurts.

The team stays silent. I just stare back at Bale, my pulse beating violently.

He moves so fast he's next to me in less than a heartbeat, a shadow trail marking the air he cut through. He's slow and deliberate, though, when he reaches up and slides his fingers into the hair at my nape, gripping it firmly, then steadily tips my head, bending me sideways until I'm unbalanced on the column. His free hand comes up to circle my neck, his big, hot palm over my throbbing jugular.

Our eyes lock. "Why is your hair down, Idallia?"

My lips part on a shuddering breath. I know this is going to be bad, and it's even worse when the inevitable heat of arousal thumps between my legs. I ruthlessly drive it away before anyone can scent it. I'm not sure I succeed. Bale's gaze flickers ominously as he draws us almost nose to nose.

"An oversight," I admit, wishing his nearness didn't throw my entire body into turmoil. Even in his common form, his senses are too sharp to miss the heat blasting off me, only part of which is due to being singled out in front of everyone.

I pull against his grip, gaining a measure of space between our faces.

"Do you want to give a Bloodwold vampire a convenient handle to jerk your head to the side and expose your throat?" His hand tightens in my hair, keeping me from moving again.

"No." The word vibrates against his palm, strangely intimate, and I force myself not to think about how Bale's touch might feel under other circumstances.

His focus drops to my neck. "You know the rules."

I nod, the movement jerky under his hand. We either keep our hair up or short. And if it's not up, we take the time to *put it up*. I like my long black hair too much to cut it off, and part of me is terrified that Bale is going to whip out a knife right now.

"It won't happen again," I assure him.

He's still gripping my hair and neck, bending me in a way that makes it hard to stay on the column. I try to steady myself as he leans in, his mouth so close to my neck I can feel the threat of imaginary fangs there. "See that it doesn't," he whispers in my ear.

Another hot wash of arousal quivers through me, mixing with humiliation and annoyance. Not that Bale humiliated me. I did a good job of that myself. I fight the arousal. I don't want anyone to know my secrets—especially Bale—though it's not like most people wouldn't react the same way if they'd just felt the Dragon King's breath on their neck and his hand in their hair.

Bale backs away from me, his stare volcanic and his thumb drawing a hard line down the entire throbbing vein in my neck before he finally releases me.

I lurch upright, nearly falling from the pillar. My blood pumps hot and cold—a horrible feeling. I don't know what's worse. The heat of embarrassment and reflexive arousal, or the ice of being furious with myself.

"I should've reminded you." My hard-pounding heart nearly drowns out Fyrestar's remorseful words.

Glancing up, I shake my head. I can't answer him, but it's not his fault. It's mine. Bale would say my biggest flaw is getting easily distracted and losing focus. He's wrong. It's vanity that does me in again and again.

In front of me, Maia's perfect, tight bun is a mocking reminder of the one I wore earlier today. Danica sheared her hair to spiky black curls ages ago. The men all wear their hair short. We're soldiers of Torridaig. There are rules that make us battle-ready and keep us safe. Rules I'm stupid enough to ignore.

I'm also stupid enough to harbor a fierce attraction for my king, but I'm definitely not stupid enough to act on it. I already tried romance with a teammate once and learned my lesson. Things didn't even end badly with Kellan; they just ended because my feelings changed, and I'm still caught in the middle of a complicated and awkward *something* and paying for it thirty years on. With Bale, an ending—especially a bad one—would be exponentially worse. We're not equals. He rules me and my warbirds. I'm not putting myself in a position of potentially having to leave my team and my home, and no force under the stars would make me leave my birds.

Thankfully, I have nothing to worry about. There's no evidence of the attraction going both ways, and Bale hasn't taken a lover in so long that none of us have ever even seen him walk these mountain halls with anyone by his side.

As Bale resumes his position in front of us, Maia fishes around in her pocket and pulls out a leather hair tie. She discreetly holds it out behind her, and I take it. Securing my hair back doesn't replace a tight bun, but it's better than nothing, and I'm grateful to my friend. I make quick work of a braid and tie it off at the end with Bale's amber eyes flicking over me.

"Weres struck again in the northwest," he announces darkly as my hands drop back to my sides. "The Muirvale forces answered the alert horns and countered the assault. They drove the invading weres back over the border and are guarding it now, but there were kidnappings. We need a small, fast force to penetrate Wyndwood and try to recover the children."

My tense shoulders loosen, and I take my first normal breath since Bale arrived despite the grim news. Great Cealastra, it never ends. Weres keep attacking their own kind, which somehow seems worse than attacking us.

"A were-heavy section of Muirvale?" Danica asks.

"All of Muirvale's were-heavy," Kellan mutters from his right-wing perch.

Most werebeasts who already lived close to the northern forests decided not to move across the official border when the lines were drawn by the kings and queens of Ellonrift. It was the only time the six rulers ever agreed on anything, and it still took two and a half decades to negotiate. The borders were drawn with ancestral lands in mind, as they already contained the heaviest populations of each of the peoples, and resulted in a fairly equitable split of territory and resources in the end.

No one was forced to go anywhere, and most of the weres who already lived close to the new line weren't about to move across a valley or over a hillside simply to answer to a were king rather than a dragon shifter. Their homes were already in their historical territory, or at least, close enough. They had their roots, their dens, their lives. They weren't stuck right in the middle of Ellonrift or in some hostile place far from their ancestors and traditions or the great, wild forests where they hunt and mate as their instincts demand. They lived under Bale Cinderheart's protection. So why leave?

What they didn't count on were the weres who *did* cross thinking everyone should've done the same. At first, there was shunning, shaming, and prejudice. That lasted centuries. Then a new group cropped up with a new tactic. Steal werechildren before the pups, cubs, and calves are old enough to decide for themselves—and kill anyone who gets in their way.

"These are Torridaig weres." Bale's eyes flame. "*My* weres. My tolerance for the Were King's weakness regarding these fanatics is at an end. He needs to control his people, or I will." Bale's ominous words ring of war. We all know it's rushing toward us from Bloodwold in the east, and now it could be rising in Wyndwood to the north. If the leaders of Ellonrift still can't reach any significant or satisfying agreements at the quickly approaching yearly Council, I'm almost certain Bale will finally give up on diplomacy, when he's the only ruler even keeping diplomacy alive.

His gaze sweeps over us, the bitter hardness in his expression seeming to echo my thoughts. "You know what to do. You know how to do it." Darkness wraps around him as he begins to shift. My breath shortens, the magic in the room immediately so thick it clogs my lungs and sits on my ribs. Those werebeasts chose not to leave Torridaig, which means they're Bale's. No one takes what's his, and a dragon shifter doesn't share. Fire roils in his elongated mouth, and his words thunder in my mind as he pushes off on powerful legs and thumps tremendous wings. *"To the north!"*

"To the north!" we cry, the shifters changing form and Fyrestar swooping in to pick me up.

I leap off my pillar onto Fyrestar's back, hook my legs around his body, grab his black neck feathers, and hold on as he gathers speed. We barrel out of Drayke Mountain's south-facing windows and swoop back around the giant peak, heading toward the were kingdom of Wyndwood. Quickly solidifying our formation, we fly at the speed of fire. I'm in the middle again, tucked between two of the squadron and their wing guards.

I try not to let my position irk me. I'm still one of the six elite soldiers of Torridaig, handpicked by the Dragon King himself and the only non-dragon shifter on the team. Despite this unprecedented accomplishment, apart from a pillar-race victory here and there—mainly over Kellan—the middle is my usual place.

My mouth thins, tension keeping me rigid. Not good enough to be first, but good enough not to be last.

Or maybe that's not even true. Maybe the only reason I'm not consistently bringing up the rear is because Fyrestar is so exceptional.

I grip his feathers, my fingers already chilled from the thin, cold air. Fyrestar's colorful plumage starts to glow with his inner fire, warming me all over before I start to shiver.

He knows me well—probably better than I know myself, since I don't know a thing about where I come from.

I *will* do better. And maybe when I'm the best soldier here, I'll be good enough to find the answers to the questions about my origins and abilities that have haunted me for years.

CHAPTER THREE

BALE

We fly over Muirvale and head straight across the border into Wyndwood as the long northern dusk begins to fall. It took us the entire afternoon to get here, and I worry that the marauding werebeasts have a significant lead. Fortunately for us—and hopefully the captives—the border forest is rough, hilly, and offers few paths. The difficult terrain will have slowed the kidnappers down, but we can fly right over it and search the thinner woods beyond.

"*Fan out.*" I direct the order to the entire squadron. "*There are only so many accessible paths north from Muirvale. They can't be far now.*"

The team widens their formation to cover more ground. I know they'll stay within communicating distance, but I can't help a quick look at Idallia and Fyrestar as they veer off, moving away from me. She watches the ground, searching the increasingly visible werepaths below with such absolute focus that I know a meteor could light the sky and she wouldn't even notice it hurtling down.

I look away. Knowing she can handle herself doesn't keep my gut from tightening with worry as I keep my own eyes vigilantly on the ground. Idallia of Glarraden can kill anything when she's concentrating. The problem is she can just as easily be killed when she's not, and *staying* focused is the one thing I can't seem to drill into her, even after more than one-hundred-and-eighty years.

I don't worry about the rest of my team going up against weres like I do with enemy vampires, who force us out of the sky with arrows and spears and don't burn in our firebreath thanks to their despicable king's dark magic. Werebeasts have shorter lifespans than even humans and no accelerated healing. They come in different forms and can be clawed, fanged, big, and vicious, but my dragon shifters and I are clawed, fanged, bigger, and more vicious. The trick is not swallowing any of their meat or blood as we rip into them.

Ironically, Idallia is better suited to fighting vampires. Heavy, clawed werebeasts with their big fangs and powerful hindquarters for pouncing from afar are the bigger threat to her.

I catch a hint of movement in the trees and angle lower for a better look. The kidnappers could be anyone, or more likely, a mix of werebeasts brought together by this new faction, which is solely about ideology. Wolves, foxes, bears, snow tigers, northern bulls, giant leithrats...They've never warred, but they don't have much in common either—besides their ability to shift. *This* brought a huge and powerful group together—stealing children.

The growl boiling inside me rumbles louder when I realize the movement I'm tracking is just a deer.

"There!" Wade's mind-to-mind shout carries across the distance from behind me.

Turning in a tight circle, I dive in the direction Wade is indicating. The others wheel around and start their own downward spirals. Fyrestar keeps pace with me at first, but falls behind as I near the treetops. I get a good look at the group despite the waning light. Werewolves, werebears, and weretigers.

I gather heat and magic in my throat and unleash a firebreath that cuts off the weres leading the pack and forces them to turn toward a small break in the forest. The blaze helps us see better, and Maia and Arran bank left to follow several weres who splinter off from the main group as the treetops go up in flames.

My gaze follows them for mere seconds, my focus on the larger group. I can't tell how many werebeasts we're dealing with yet, but we know it's enough to have made off with fifteen Muirvale werechildren as they woke in the early hours to use outhouses and gather water from wells. A classic snatch and run, just like we're seeing more and more of these days.

The captain who flew to Drayke Mountain to report wanted authorization to pursue them across the border with his northern unit, but sending soldiers into Wyndwood is a delicate thing. I only have permission from the Were King to recover kidnapping victims if I'm fast, discreet, and don't go too far into the northern forests. I don't have permission to send an army of dragon shifters into a sovereign kingdom. Doing that now, especially with tensions running high before the upcoming Council, would be a declaration of war.

With the Elite Wing handling the situation, we can still pass it off as politics instead of aggression, even if the latter is closer to the truth. War has an actual scent in my nostrils these days, like the smoke from an old tallow candle that's starting to go rancid and leave its black soot and strong stench in the air. The scent mostly comes from the east, fueled by vampire raiders on the hunt for blood, but the north is starting to stink of it too. The Were King had better start solving his problems if he wants to keep ruling his kingdom.

"Head for those clearings. Separate the weres from the children. Then kill the beasts." I don't have to remind them to be careful of what they ingest. Cealastra's gift of protection to weres is a curse to others if they eat their flesh or drink their blood.

Low to the trees, our long shadows chase the kidnappers through southern Wyndwood. I want to herd them toward where the forest thins so that we can stay in scales. The fight will go quicker than if we shift, and we can stop this before going any farther into Wyndwood. The Were King doesn't like this new faction of extremists any more than we do, but he hasn't been successful in controlling them so far. I'm tired of doing the work for him when I have bigger problems to the east, and he'd better not fucking come after me with some false claim of hostility during the next Council or I'll tear off his head and throw it from my mountaintop.

Now *that* would be hostility.

Below us, small paths open up, and werebeasts suddenly scatter in every direction. My snarl heats my throat. *"Get lower! Cut them off!"* Their dispersion forces us out of our already loose formation. We were herding them, but now they're separating us.

I glance to the side. Maia and Arran are already well to the west in pursuit of the group that originally veered off and crashed through the underbrush. On my right wing, Kellan, Wade, and Danica all speed off after different clusters, their wing guards following them. Fyrestar and Idallia angle down and drop below the canopy, small enough to weave through the trees and follow in flight. I lose sight of them quickly and don't like it.

Part of me still wonders why I thought she'd be better off with the Elite Wing than in the big, mostly empty halls of Glarraden House. There, no one thought twice about where she was—or thought twice about her at all. But she was too quick and ferocious and skilled to overlook, with a burning desire to *overcome*, and now I can't seem to look away, which might be the biggest problem I've had since Rannigan Bloodthief figured out how to protect his vampire raiders from our firebreath.

I scan the woods below but don't see a black-haired warrior or a burning streak of feathers. Idallia can fight, and Fyrestar will protect her with his life, so I stay my course and speed up to get in front of the weres I'm tracking, looking for a big enough opening to accommodate my size.

Landing hard in a clearing, I kick up woodland debris and crunch exposed roots under my taloned feet. Branches blow back as if trying to flee, autumn leaves trembling and dropping in fear. The werewolves of this now whittled-down pack pull up short. The five of them are in half skins—bipedal but beasts—and hauling three rope-tied children who haven't mastered changing forms yet.

I look the little ones over, trying to judge their ages. We all start out in Cealastra's image, with the five points of her hallowed star being our heads, arms, and legs. Humans, fae, and vampires stay that way. Only dragon shifters and werebeasts develop an alternate form, and that can sometimes take years. It's longer for a dragon shifter—often a few decades. A were lifetime is fleeting in comparison, and their changes happen faster and usually before adolescence, but these children still have short, common-form legs and only a handful of years.

I strike without warning and crunch down on the lead werewolf's head, ripping it from his body. I spit him out, blood seeping from between my fangs. Like all werebeasts, his goddess-given defense is to taste like death, and I use my inner fire to burn his werepoison from my mouth. *"Give me the children."*

"They're not yours," someone dares answer, a guttural voice coming from a half-skin wolf.

"Torridaig weres are *mine."* I take a heavy step forward, my claws scraping the ground. The angry rumble in my chest carries fire that I don't dare let out for fear of burning the children. *"Hand them over and I'll give you a ten-second head start."*

The three werebeasts with kids yank the children in front of them like shields. My lip curls in disgust, cool air hitting my exposed fangs in a way I don't like after the hot wash of blood followed by the scorch of inner fire in my mouth. Skin it is. I can't fight in my dragon form without risking the safety of the werechildren who are looking at me with sheer panic and hope in their eyes.

I slam shadow wings forward and sweep the two closest weres off their feet as I transform. The effort to make the darkness solid against the kidnappers but not the children costs me a measure of magic and slows my usually seamless shift into my fully dressed and armed common form, but the unexpected move allows two of the kids to wrench their ropes from their captors' hands and jump away while I lunge and grab the third child. I shove her toward the other two as I draw my sword. It's one against four, but it will be almost too easy now that the children are clear.

Two weres leap for me. I fight them off, then whip around and smash my blade through the face of the werewolf who just tried to get behind me, dragging my sword back out with a twist that leaves a hole in his misshapen, half-skin head. He drops, and the three trembling kids stumble backward.

"Go!" I snarl to the children.

A little weretiger with new whiskers and one feline ear instinctively popping out in fear grabs the other two by the hands. She gives them both an urgent tug, and they run into the forest.

I shift back into scales and whip one kidnapper into a tree with my tail. The crack of bones isn't nearly satisfying enough, and I spin, clawing him to make sure he's not just dead—he's eviscerated. Sensing movement, I open my jaws as I twist back around and bite down, ripping the entire top half off a fur-covered body and flinging the tainted meat away from me.

My eyes narrow as fire roils in my mouth, cleansing it of werepoison. There's one left, and I stalk her, enough heat seeping from beneath my scales to wilt the low vegetation between us. Blood-wet leaves smolder. I could roast her alive right now, but I hold back, hoping she'll give me more sport than the others. Why do they even bother? Only Bloodwold vampires have contrived some sort of sorcery that temporarily protects them from our firebreath. Everyone else burns.

The werewolf retreats, upright but on canine legs. She's stayed in her half-skin form—unappealing but powerful. She'd have a fighting chance if she took up a spear or a bow and arrow, but that's not the werebeast way. They fight with tooth and claw, relying heavily on their inner animal.

"There wasn't much hope of you sneaking far enough into Wyndwood to hide the children and make them disappear without a trace."

"It's worked before," she answers harshly. At least she doesn't beg for a life she knows I won't spare.

"On smaller groups, maybe. But you got greedy, and Muirvale raised the alarm so fast that you'd barely crossed the border before we were on your tail."

"Muirvale should be *in* Wyndwood. You stole a whole city of weres. We're just taking back what's ours."

Flames escape on a rasping chuckle. *"Yours? Who thinks that? Not the weres who live there. Not your own king, the leaders of Ellonrift, or Cealastra, who approved the terms."*

"How do you know what Cealastra thinks?" she grinds out.

"How do you know I don't?" Those who attend the Council have felt the goddess's presence, and there's no mistaking it. The Star of Ellonrift hasn't deigned to take physical form there in centuries, but her divine essence tells us where her favor goes. When there's a tied vote to break or a prolonged and dangerously tense disagreement, her celestial magic illuminates the ruler she chooses to side with, and not even Rannigan Bloodthief can argue with the formidable power in the room—or with the goddess's final decision. It's been that way since the second dawn of Ellonrift and the founding of the six ruling bloodlines.

Except, we haven't had a tied vote that would've forced Cealastra's appearance in more than two hundred years. Rannigan has seen to that with his murders and coercion. And Cealastra hasn't renewed magic in decades, leaving our sorcerers weaker, worried, and praying for her return.

"Where are her eclipses now?" The werewolf backs away from me. "For all we know, Cealastra is gone, and magic is next."

Magic *is* waning, which might mean Cealastra is too. The unfortunately real possibility rattles me. If the Star of Ellonrift never weighs in on another Council, even I'll give up on the six kingdoms and their increasingly false promises of nonviolent solutions. The day that happens—maybe at this very next meeting of rulers—the Vampire King will be more of a threat than ever, especially to Torridaig.

"Do you think your politics are working?" I ask in lieu of trying to convince this werebeast that Cealastra persists, despite the lack of eclipses to remind everyone of her presence and renew magic across the lands.

"Do you think *yours* are?" She trembles now, her distorted, hairy feet scraping back through moldering leaves. I smell anger and fear on her sweat. Defiance and defeat.

The next Ellonrift Council is in mere weeks. I'm hosting this time and willing to give diplomacy one last try. Officially, we're still at peace. Five different kinds of people and five leaders sharing a continent, even though there should be six sovereign rulers in place.

Cealastra gifted vampires with two starborn bloodlines and the entire east, which split into Bloodwold and Fanghaven after the border treaties came into force. She wanted to watch people moving under her starlight while the rest of Ellonrift slept. But a deceiving monster with his own kingdom stole the sovereignty of the other by massacring all but the youngest member of Fanghaven's royal family, then schemed to speak *for* her at the Ellonrift Council...as his wife.

The real enemy is the Vampire King. I need to be able to strike back at Bloodwold the same way I can against these fanatical werebeasts who don't represent Wyndwood or its king. Rannigan Bloodthief steals my people so that his people can drink them down to husks, and I *can't* cross the border without risking sanctions at the Council—a yearly meeting where the Vampire King now gets *two* fucking votes.

"I think I protect, and you terrorize." I move forward. She's

almost at the edge of the clearing, and I can't let her slip out. I'm too big to crash through the trees in my dragon form, and she could finish shifting in the blink of an eye and dart off on all fours. *"I think your own people are mostly against you, and you're alone in dark little dens planning a revolution that won't happen. I think if you weren't inedible, vampires would've sucked you dry by now. And I would've let them."*

"Your days are numbered, Bale Cinderheart. Cealastra won't protect you forever, if she even remains. Magic is dying, and when it goes, you'll be the first to lose everything."

She whirls to run, and I catch her mid-shift and mid-leap toward the line of trees in a blaze of firebreath. She burns, the stink of charred hair and scorched skin rank in my nostrils.

I turn away from the smoking puddle and blackened bark. Too easy. I'm sure the rest of the team has done much the same.

Except for Idallia. She has to find other ways to kill.

And to stay alive.

I bite down on that thought with fangs that shrink as I shift back into skin and move into the denser forest in the direction of the children. I find them quickly, mainly by scent, then lead them through the trees toward the nearest team member.

I hear my squadron throughout the woods. Each time I come across another dragon shifter, my apprehension grows. They've won their battles, just as I did. They have children in tow, just as I do. We've recovered a dozen between us, and they cling to us, not afraid even though the Elite Wing is one of the most frightening things in Ellonrift.

The werechildren aren't worried, but I am. I've found everyone except for Idallia and Fyrestar. I don't hear another fight. I don't smell her anywhere. She got lower faster than we did, weaving through trees in a way we can't with our giant wingspans. What did she see that sent her flying in a direction none of us took? How big a group did she go after?

"Where is she?" Kellan growls, listening hard.

I hold back the snarl I want to throw at him, especially as I let my dragon loose and shift again. My ability to scent is better. My hearing too. It means I can hear Kellan's heart pounding now, harder than it should for the woman he refuses to get over.

Tension and growing hostility I don't want to acknowledge sweep over me on a ripple of shadows that blend into the fast-falling night. I lift my head, dragging air deep into my nostrils. I still don't smell her, that unique mix of sunshine and ice. We all have dry, aged scents—heated rock, parched earth, windblown sand, crisp autumn leaves already on the ground—but Idallia is a spring lake about to burst, the frozen surface cracking under the strong rays and ready to transform into something else.

"I saw her head northwest," Arran says, then shifts. *"We should fly that way first."*

I tamp down the useless annoyance I feel at Arran knowing something I don't. Idallia slips out of my sight too often, but treating her differently isn't an option. She'd rebel.

Except, she *is* different. I need to tell her just how different, but I can't bring myself to do it. The moment she knows the truth, it'll change this team forever. It could change *everything*, and some truths alter people. I'm already two centuries too late in confessing what I know, but I want her where she is as much as I need her where she should be.

My silence was an absolute necessity for a long time to ensure her safety, probably her freedom, and maybe even her life. But is it now?

And would Idallia's life be better for knowing the truth? I'm wary and unsure of the answer, and it's a question I've been grappling with since the day I plucked her from school.

The snarl finally leaks out. *"Danica, Wade—keep all the wing guards with you and follow us with the children. If anything goes wrong, fly them straight to Muirvale. The wing guards can help carry them."*

I take off without waiting for a response. Fyrestar can come back if he's killed, but Idallia can't, and the too-silent forest around us makes my heart pound harder than it should.

CHAPTER FOUR
IDALLIA

Fyrestar drops below the tree line so fast I barely mark the moment we go from being above the canopy to below. The dimness is sudden, but my eyes adjust quickly. Going from dark to light usually feels like twin daggers in my eyes, but going from light to dark is easy, almost a relief sometimes. Unfortunately, now I can perfectly see the type of werebeast I'm chasing, and it doesn't look good.

"Bloodpit," I growl. "Snow tigers." Faster than bears. More dangerous than wolves. They're the worst type of weres to fight, especially alone.

"This group is bigger than I thought from above." Fyrestar is right to be wary. But everyone else took off after their own quarries, and I'm not about to let these weres get away with the kids.

The snow tigers are in half-skin to carry the children. They see Fyrestar and me closing in from above, and three of the six werebeasts fully shift and accelerate, breaking away from the group. The three carrying kids need arms and keep running in their in-between forms. I can't tell from this distance if the little ones are too young to shift, but they wouldn't anyway. The Muirvale werechildren spot us and start struggling against their kidnappers with a violence worthy of Torridaigan soldiers.

My grim smile praises their efforts to slow their captors as Fyrestar banks left and right, angling in between big trees at a breakneck pace. This part of the forest isn't as thick as the border woods, but Fyrestar's wings still clip branches, leaving a trail of smoldering leaves. In summer, I'd worry about starting a forest fire and making the Were King spitting mad, but the autumn woods are cool and damp. Not even Bale's firebreath will burn for long.

The lead weretigers move so quickly that they disappear around a bend. We gain on the ones in half-skin, and I lie flat against Fyrestar's back as he dips lower, almost skimming the ground. Fyrestar is faster than anything on two legs, and little hands reach out, stretching toward me. These kids know who's coming for them. A dragon shifter could be anyone, but a warbird only flies with the Elite Wing.

"Closer, Fyrestar!" The wind snatches the words straight from my mouth as we race along the rough werepath.

"You grab the girl. I'll distract the beast."

My answer is to grip Fyrestar even more tightly with my legs to free up my hands while he delivers an impressive burst of speed. He brings us close enough to the last weretiger and the little girl bouncing against his shoulder that I can see the gap of her two missing front teeth. What age would that make her? Six? Seven? Definitely old enough to help me rip her from his grasp.

I sit up straighter, meeting her eyes with a rock-hard stare. My expression says, *"Now!"* and she'd better understand, because Fyrestar opens his beak and scorches the snow tiger's lower back just as I pitch forward and grab her outstretched hands.

Howling in pain, the weretiger skids to a stop and whirls. He holds on to the child's waist so hard that her hands slip from my grasp as we blow past. The next weretiger on the path twists to face us and slashes out. He nearly clips Fyrestar's chest, but my warbird spins, putting the top of my head so close to the ground that my braid sweeps up dry leaves, then spits them out again as he rights us and pivots in the air to come back around.

Holding a child under one arm, the second weretiger blocks the path while the other two crash away through the forest. Concentrating on the one who stayed, we attack head on, and Fyrestar avoids lethal claws as I reach for another little girl, hoping I can hold on this time.

Her hand snaps out to meet mine, but the weretiger jerks her in tight, and I only brush cold fingertips before we're gone.

"Bloodpit," I snarl in frustration. "Circle back."

"Two," Fyrestar caws in my head as we race straight for the weretiger again.

Just one word is enough to communicate the strategy, and I somersault off his back as I draw my blades. We charge the final distance together, forcing our opponent to divide his defense between us. Not seeing an alternative, the weretiger tosses the girl aside, fully shifts, and bats a vicious paw at my warbird.

Fyrestar zips under flashing claws and rams his fire-filled beak into the werebeast's side, yanking out a burning mouthful of flesh and fur. Just a step behind, I dart in and stab the weretiger through the chest with one sword and cut off his forepaw with the other as he tries to strike. The limb drops, and blood sprays me before I can yank out my blade and spin away from him.

He stares at me, swaying on three legs. His flanks heave as the lifelight leaves his eyes. Maybe the sudden fear in his gaze should affect me, but all I feel is the rage that comes with knowing the child cowering on the edge of the path could've been lost to her Muirvale kin forever, and with time, would've probably forgotten her home, her people. The color of her mother's hair and eyes.

Fuming, I stare back at the weretiger. I don't remember anything from before Glarraden aside from snippets of dreams that might not even be real. I was just months into life and shouldn't remember anything, but the flashes and feelings are hard to discount when I know my memory doesn't work like other people's. What goes in never goes out, and ever since I was a few years old, it's all stayed so sharp that it could just as easily be yesterday as more than two hundred years ago.

I kick the dying weretiger in the shoulder and topple him. Breathing hard, I grind out, "You don't. Take kids. From their families." Especially from families who *want* them.

Blood seeps into the ground around the snow tiger's body and stains his white fur. His eyes stay open, glassy and cold, and he dies in his animal form—the choice of all weres at their end, as far as I know.

My nostrils flare as I stare at the dead werebeast, my ears pricked for any sign of those who fled. Most weres aren't raiders and live peacefully in Wyndwood or in other places, especially Torridaig. The Muirvale weres would love to live peacefully in their chosen territory, too, but fanatics like this one have been making that impossible for years.

"Idallia!" Fyrestar's warning explodes in my mind.

I whirl, lifting my blades on reflex. My warbird shoots over my head, breathing fire at a huge weretiger who springs out of the woods. The weretiger knocks me over, her fresh, phoenix-fire burns heating my skin. I hit the ground on my back, my swords crossed between us, and her weight almost buckling my arms. Before she can overpower me, I slash up and outward with both blades, drawing blood that splatters my face, but not severing her neck deeply enough to kill. Fyrestar zooms back around and slams into the snow tiger from the side, shoving her off me and sending the two of them tumbling across the ground.

I jump up, and for a moment, there's a battle of talons and claws, then they crash into a tree with Fyrestar pinned between the weretiger and the trunk. The were's huge jaws clamp down on Fyrestar's thigh with a sickening pop of feathers and flesh. I gasp as Fyrestar squawks in pain, and his inner fire surges to the surface. Leaping forward, I attack, stabbing deep into the weretiger's shoulder, twisting my blade, and yanking it up. My bird flames so violently from every feather that the werebeast abruptly spits him out and slinks away.

Blood streams down the were's bulky shoulder and strong leg. She limps sideways, her agitated gaze bouncing from me to Fyrestar and back. The child she was holding captive before she fully shifted runs to join the little girl we already freed.

I see them out of the corner of my eye, both so shaky and scared that they've shifted into odd, unintended half forms. Whiskers, clumps of fur, and animal ears poke out of their heads. If this is their first transformation, I fear it may traumatize them for life. Weres have been known to repress their animal skins if shifting makes them feel unsafe.

I sense increasing danger before I see or hear anything new. My blood goes cold, the way it does sometimes in warning. A chill bursts across the back of my neck, and a waiting silence fills me, as if even my own pulse doesn't beat anymore. My suddenly heightened senses tingle with the knowledge that we are absolutely not alone.

"Fyrestar, can you fly?" I ask quietly.

"I'm injured, not incapacitated."

He sounds offended, which wasn't my intent. Maybe he's just on edge, like I am, because he knows something bad is about to happen.

The enemy group emerges from the woods, and my heart drops like lead through my chest. They've doubled their already significant number with other werebeasts they must've gathered in the woods. There's not a single little leithrat or delicate fox among them. They're all wolves, bears, and snow tigers. Huge, lethal, and spitting mad.

"Can you fly with two werechildren?" I whisper, getting the children behind me and angling them toward a tree. I don't see the third child anywhere, and my gut tightens with worry. A dozen massive opponents and a missing kidnapping victim was not how I envisioned this going. And now Fyrestar is hurt, which worries me most of all.

Fyrestar's golden eyes cut to mine, their fiery glow lighting the dusk-dark forest. *"And you—difficult."*

I don't say to leave me behind. Fyrestar will sacrifice those kids for me if he has to, and I don't bother pretending, even to myself, that I wouldn't do the same for him.

"We can call for help," he suggests.

I press my lips together. I don't want to—I never do—but more than that, I want my warbird and these kids to make it out of this without any more damage—physical or otherwise.

I nod, my focus on our enemies as I prepare to shield Fyrestar and the children. The werebeasts stalk me, predators to the core. They move slowly, low to the ground, watching. They'll stay that way, waiting, half-crawling, until erupting in a sudden surge.

Behind me, Fyrestar starts drumming his wings, rotating them back and forth so quickly that a low, deep thumping fills the woods along with a rising billow of heat from him.

In mere seconds, the distant roaring of dragon shifters fills the forest. The team's answering calls are too far away for comfort, but at least they heard us and can determine a direction.

I urge the kids to fade into the trees as the werebeasts creep closer. Fyrestar moves forward until we're back-to-back, the weres surrounding us. We slowly circle, keeping them guessing at how best to attack. My goal is to hold them off until the team gets here, and antagonizing the enemy usually keeps them talking instead of striking.

Sneering at the gigantic werebear facing me, I keep my feet moving and my muscles warm. "You could really use a bath and a brushing—I've never seen a pelt so filthy. Since you're clearly someone's pet, you should really get your master to take better care of you."

His beady eyes narrow, and his words grate in my head. *"I have no master."*

"Oh, so you're in charge of the kidnappers? Lucky me." I

chuckle dryly. "I've met the mastermind behind the whole faction."

He doesn't answer. He's definitely not the mastermind, but he doesn't like being called someone's pet, either.

"I've heard that bears secretly have the hots for little foxes. Is it true? Seems like a bad deal for the foxes." I haven't heard anything of the sort. I just want to keep him talking.

"We don't interbreed. Everyone knows that."

"It's not necessarily about breeding," I shoot back. "I'm pretty sure the parts are compatible."

He growls. *"Maybe we'll see how compatible* our *parts are once I pin you down and hold your neck between my teeth."*

I give him a scathing look, and I mean every burning bit of it. "Maybe we'll see how fast I can kill you. I'm *really* good at it."

The werebear lunges for me, teeth bared. Just as I brace for impact, he abruptly swerves and slashes out at Fyrestar instead. Fyrestar barely evades with a startled caw, and my swords slice through thin air. Two werewolves spring at me while I'm still off balance, and I only just get my blades around in time to hold them off.

Fyrestar and I fight hard. We stay back-to-back, protecting each other and ourselves. I kill a werewolf, and another takes its place. The werebear focuses on Fyrestar, and Fyrestar's speed and flames are barely enough to avoid the werebear's thundering hits and huge, knife-sharp claws. A weretiger suddenly blasts between us, forcing us apart. I whirl and slash out, but the werebeast is fast and avoids my sword.

"I'm a heartbeat from flying you out of here," Fyrestar mutters.

I don't think Fyrestar and I have the time to mount up and take off. The werebeasts are relentless. They'd be on us in seconds. It would also mean leaving the children.

I push myself harder, killing another werewolf with a lightning-fast feint and stab. The weretiger instantly takes her place. More werebeasts wait in the wings, ready to jump into the fray. I growl a curse. I need to do more, do better. The team still isn't here, Fyrestar is injured, and I'm tiring fast.

Dread-laced heartbeats bang inside me as I fend off attack after attack, narrowly keeping deadly claws and fangs from tearing me apart. A slice burns my hip. I spin, my blades swinging. A claw rips across my lower back, and I gasp. Fyrestar bats the werewolf away from me with a burning wing. Blood stains my phoenix's thigh, and he staggers, his punctured leg hindering his balance.

Breathing hard, I fight off pain but welcome rage and panic. Fear burns through me like my own sort of inner fire, and I let it scorch. The only thing that can save us now is me fighting on a whole different level, one I'm already reaching for. I know I can do better. I just can't always make it happen.

Fyrestar suddenly squawks in pain. I spin, slam the opal-embedded pommel of my sword into a werewolf's head, and yank him off my warbird. The blood-wet, broken feathers on Fyrestar's back send a chaotic burst of terror through me, and the thunderclap only I can hear finally hits, abruptly changing everything. My strength increases, my senses sharpen, and I become a blur of speed. I can suddenly focus on everything at once—sounds, sights, smells—and make sense of every detail in the space around me. I'm powerful, precise, fast. We're still seriously outnumbered, but now we have a fighting chance.

Striking fast, I whirl and kill the snow tiger with one brutal blow. More enemies come at us, and I slice them down. They're everywhere, and the more frantic I become, pinned in this murderous circle with Fyrestar, the faster I move. I whip to the side and take down a werebear that joins the bigger one still attacking Fyrestar. I slice through his throat as he rises onto his back legs to try to maul Fyrestar, and his blood momentarily blinds me as it sprays into my face from his severed jugular.

I wipe my eyes just as razor-tipped claws sink into my shoulder from behind and tear down my back, ripping through my vest and fighting leathers. Hissing, I stumble forward. Fyrestar screeches a fierce battle cry, spitting fire, gouging with talons, and battering with his blazing wings to drive the weres away from me.

He kills two of them, giving me the time I need to steady myself. Werebeasts litter the ground around us, but now, we're both wounded, and more enemies creep out of the forest. They're layers deep. I don't see an end to them, but grip my swords, still riding the burst of strength that turns me from scary into something so dangerous I don't even recognize myself.

Pain pulses in my clawed shoulder. Hot blood drips down my back. I welcome all the terrifying thoughts of death and failure circling inside me, because they're what will give me one more strike, one more kill, one more breath.

Without warning, I go on the offensive, my blades moving so fast it feels like they're leading me instead of the other way around. I cut down a kidnapper. Another one comes. I dole out death like gold coins on Dragon's Night, my vision and mind barely keeping up with my body. Instinct drives me, and I listen in a purely physical way, my thoughts wholly focused on the worst thing I can imagine—losing Fyrestar while magic might be too weak for him to come back to me.

I kill a pair of werewolves in a snap of movement, then see the original big werebear suddenly leap over his fallen bear comrade and come down hard on Fyrestar, pinning him to the ground.

My heart stops dead, and I lunge for them as the werebear's teeth crash toward Fyrestar's throat. Screaming, I slash through his muzzle before he can bite, drenching my phoenix in blood. The bear rears back, blood gushing down his face. Turning, he swipes at me but staggers. I duck and come back up with a jab that plants my blade straight into his heart. The resistance of the vital muscle against my steel is deeply satisfying.

"Fuck you and your fucking band of kidnappers," I growl, yanking my blade out.

The lifelight leaves his eyes before he even hits the ground.

A weight suddenly slams into me from behind. I land on my stomach with a pained grunt near a slashed-up and bloody

Fyrestar. Claws sink into my upper back, digging deep into muscle and hitting bone. Agony explodes through me. The claws rip downward from my shoulder blades to my waist, and I let out a ragged cry.

A huge paw flips me over. My head spins, white-hot pain erupting as a snow tiger steps on my arms, pinning me. The harsh ache in my clawed shoulder collides with the new, vicious throbbing in my back. Blood pours out of me, warming the ground. My arms feel crushed, my fingers numb. The weretiger cages me under his gigantic body, his hot breath in my face, and his lips curling back in a snarl.

That thunderous force inside me shuts down like a lid snapping closed on a box. Everything comes crashing back to normal speed, and I stare up at the weretiger—probably the last thing I'll ever see.

"Idallia! No!" Fyrestar's desperate screech triggers a fear in me that my own death can't. He'll blame himself for lifetimes.

Fangs flash above me, and I kick my legs upward as hard as I can. The weretiger jerks back with a howl instead of ripping into my throat. I ram his balls again just as Bale appears, spiraling tightly between two tree trunks and swooping low to reach me.

The weretiger whips his focus toward Bale as relief seeps out of me on a broken sound. Bale's eyes blaze with amber fire. Shadows spill from his wings. Dusk becomes night as Bale opens his huge, firelit jaws and slams headfirst into the weretiger. He bites straight through ribs and spine. The weretiger breaks in half, his hot blood drenching me.

Bale tosses the parts aside with a flick of his head. I groan out a pained breath, turn over with difficulty, and crawl to Fyrestar. My whole back is blood-soaked, fiery torment. I start to shiver as the rest of the team converges on the werebeasts.

"Fyrestar?" He doesn't answer. My eyes burn, but he doesn't. He's so dim, so mauled, so covered in blood. "Talk to me, love." I bury my face in his feathers, tears streaming down my cheeks as all around us, the Elite Wing ends the battle in mere minutes.

"Idallia..."

My head snaps up. "Fyrestar?"

"I'm not burning into the next life yet."

A harsh breath explodes from me. If anything, I cry more, shake harder. "You scared me," I say so thickly it's more sob than words.

"You scared me too." A hint of Fyrestar's natural glow returns to his feathers, shining through the vanes and across each soft barb. His accelerated healing seems to be working.

Mine's not as immediate or as strong. My back throbs, my teeth chatter, and my vision wavers, but Fyrestar isn't facing an uncertain rebirth, so I can face anything else.

Bale swoops back around and drops like a boulder next to us, changing forms in a whirl of inky smoke. He looks at me, then at Fyrestar, flames bright in his eyes. His jaw ticks. Is he that angry? Or do we look that bad?

My heart pounds heavily, proving I've still got some blood in me. Struggling to sit up, I sniff back tears. I'm dizzy but try not to show it, determined to be stronger than the gray spots floating across my eyes. I pretend I don't have tears on my face. People don't cry in front of Bale Cinderheart. The entire Elite Wing already thinks I'm weak.

I reach out, stroking Fyrestar's slowly warming feathers. "I'm sorry." Sorry and weak aren't the same thing, and I'd trade my life for Fyrestar's a thousand times over, especially if Cealastra's continued absence means he can't be reborn.

Bale's expression veers toward something even harder. "Sorry has no place here. You accomplished an objective. You fought hard, killed many, and protected your warbird." His amber gaze flashes to the two werechildren Fyrestar and I recovered. I see more than a dozen children, including the third one I'd been tracking. I don't know how she got here, but there she is, thank the stars.

Relief weakens me even more. I sway, and Fyrestar somehow wiggles closer to brace me. "Did we get them all?" I ask.

Bale nods. "Fifteen were taken, and fifteen will go home."

I swallow the thick lump in my throat, thankful we accomplished our goal. "We had to call for help," I mumble, my words growing heavier and harder to form.

"You were fighting an army by yourselves." Bale helps me to my feet, keeping his hand around my arm to steady me. Almost under his breath, he adds, "I would've been very angry if you hadn't called for help."

My heartbeat echoes from far away, and I can't stop shaking. Fyrestar struggles to stand, swaying almost as much as I do. "Fyrestar can't carry me."

Kellan appears from out of nowhere. Well, not nowhere, but he wasn't that close before. "I'll carry Idallia home."

I gape at Kellan, stars streaking across my vision and half obscuring him. For the first time, I see Bale hesitate. He looks back and forth between us, shadows seeping from him like a storm cloud rolling over the horizon. My legs suddenly give out, and only Bale's hand on my arm keeps me standing. I swing limply toward him, and his other arm circles my waist. He holds me upright against his side, his expression questioning.

"I don't care how I get home," I rasp, my weakened pulse suddenly beating harder at his nearness. "I just need Sybil."

Bale nods. He retracts his shadows as Kellan shifts into scales. Bale and Arran hoist me onto his back, and Maia gives me her cloak, tucking it around me. Her blonde hair looks dark in the low light, but her brown eyes gleam with worried inner fire. She's the best warrior on this team besides Bale, capable of startling violence, but she's also the most attentive and thoughtful. I grip her cloak with numb fingers and murmur my thanks.

Arran gathers my new blades, which I'm too weak to hold now anyway. I know he'll take good care of them and return them to me cleaned and sharpened. Each swipe of a cloth or whetstone will be his way of burying the shock of seeing me half dead right now, and returning perfect blades to me will be his way of saying how relieved he is that I made it.

Maia moves toward Fyrestar, but Bale cuts her off, laying a protective hand on Fyrestar's forehead.

"I'll carry him." Bale doesn't take his hand off Fyrestar, and my phoenix glows even brighter, his soft coo making my heart swell. "Kellan goes immediately. Idallia needs a healer as soon as you reach Drayke Mountain. Maia, you're his right wing. Arran, you're his left. All your wing guards stay here to help carry the children."

Maia and Arran shift as Danica asks, "And us?"

"You, Wade, and the wing guards will fly the children back to Muirvale and reunite them with their families. I'll burn the werebeasts' bodies to prevent carrion eaters from ingesting werepoison. As soon as I'm done, I'll bring Fyrestar home."

With the plan set, Kellan takes off immediately. I'm pretty sure his urgency is necessary. I heal faster than humans, but I don't heal like a dragon shifter or a phoenix. Maybe if I knew what I was, I'd know my limits. As it is, I stumble along learning from trial and error, and tonight feels mostly like error.

As we lift into the sky and the treetops race by beneath us, I concentrate on staying on Kellan's back and reaching Sybil. She's human, a healer, and my best friend. Cealastra knows, Sybil's had to use her healing magic on me often enough over the last few decades. At first, I didn't want another human friend. They age so fast and die so quickly. But she was young and lonely when she arrived at Drayke Mountain, and it didn't seem right to only care about what I wanted—or feared.

My eyes prick again for reasons I don't want to think about. I'm always more emotional when I'm injured.

I shiver violently as the wind rushes past us and ices my blood-wet hair. My numb fingers and heavy legs barely keep me on Kellan's sleek back as he speeds south toward Drayke Mountain.

"So cold." My teeth clack together.

He increases his inner fire, warming his scales. *That should help.*

His heat seeps into me, and my eyes close just as the lanterns of Muirvale come into view on our right. I think I sleep. When I lift heavy lids again, I ask, "Why'd you offer to carry me?"

His chuckle is familiar and yet foreign at the same time. I don't hear it that often anymore. *"I knew you wanted me between your legs again."*

"Fuck you," I murmur without heat, the night sky so dark I wonder if I'm actually seeing anything.

I barely hear his low reply as I drift off to sleep. *"Anytime."*

CHAPTER FIVE
IDALLIA

I wake up so stiff and sore, I fleetingly fear that parts of me don't work anymore. The terrifying thought fades as I gingerly stretch and take stock of my limbs. All there, all intact, and more importantly, so are my birds.

Little Embersol sleeps tucked into the crook of my right arm. Rimblaze warms my entire left side. Fyrestar lounges at the base of the bed, keeping my feet from feeling the constant chill in my open-windowed quarters.

I know who else is in the room before I even turn my head. Sybil sits at my bedside, holding a mug of hot something between her hands. I smile at her a little warily as she looks at me through the steam rising from the cup.

My sheepish grin turns into a grimace. "I'm in for a scolding, aren't I?" The rasping words scrape my parched throat.

"That was hard to fix." She doesn't look amused, eyeing me as if she wants to do more damage than healing right now.

"It was just a few scratches."

She snorts. "Tell that to the skin on your back I had to regrow."

"Fine, really deep scratches." I try to sit up and immediately abandon the idea. Between everything hurting and my phoenixes pinning me down under my blanket, I stay where I am. "Scars?" I ask hesitantly.

"As if I'd let anything mar that skin of yours."

Relief sweeps through me—vanity striking again. I'd eventually heal on my own, but Sybil's magic both speeds it up and erases visible damage. I only have one mark on me, smallish twin scars on the inside of my right forearm that happened before my perfect memory kicked in.

"Did I almost die?" I ask.

She shakes her head, her frown accentuating the fine lines around her mouth. "You're hard to kill. Luckily."

I nod, the usual questions circling my mind like crows and pecking at where I'm the most sensitive and unsure. I carefully stretch my limbs without disturbing the phoenixes, glad to be alive and healed, but wondering what in the blazing stars I am. I've already lived about a hundred and thirty years too long for a human and still look like I'm twenty-five. My slow aging and natural healing are on par with the fae and vampires, but I don't have fae magic, and I might have a finicky appetite, but I've never once been tempted to latch on to a vein and guzzle down blood. I don't shift into anything, were or dragon. So what does that leave?

"Was healing me even harder than usual?" The dimming of magic is always a concern these days.

"It was...intense," she answers.

I don't like her cagey tone and look over sharply. "What do you mean?"

"Stuart's convinced I've lost a year off my life." She shrugs. "It just took a lot out of me."

I stare at her in shock. "Is that possible? A year?"

"I don't know. I wouldn't have thought so, but magic has never been this weak, and everything is harder now."

47

"I'm so sorry, Sybil." Tears well in my eyes. "I wish you'd left me scarred."

"Are you jesting?" Outrage lifts her voice along with her brows. "I would consider it a professional failure to leave so much as a scratch on you. Besides, I know how much you'd hate it."

My throat thickens. "I'd hate losing you more."

"That, my friend,"—she reaches out and lightly grips my hand, a still-sleeping Sol between us—"is inevitable."

I squeeze her hand back, fighting the rise of more tears. Sybil has already crossed over the halfway mark of a normal human lifetime. Healing magic only exists in humans, which is another reason the southern kingdom of Ruthinock needs the Dragon King's protection. Everyone wants a human sorcerer around—especially a healer—but not everyone wants to give them a choice about where they go or who they work for.

"Don't worry." Sybil sits back again, the steaming mug still in one hand. "Even if Cealastra doesn't see fit to replenish magic in Ellonrift, you won't have to worry about much more than decapitation, extreme blood loss, or a sword through the heart. And there will still be healers around, even if they're not as powerful as they are now."

"You're right," I say hoarsely. But they won't be my best friend.

I close my eyes, and that familiar, queasy feeling of dread hits me like a gong, vibrating the worst of my memories through me. I'd been so alone at Glarraden House. Rita and Gerard were always too wrapped up in each other to notice me. There were no other children on the estate, just a few crusty old dragon shifters on staff in an isolated country mansion—the "big house" of a small town.

Nearly forty years went by before my adoptive parents looked up from each other enough to notice I wasn't aging and wouldn't live a human lifetime and die. Being sent off to the Drayke School of Fire and Flight was going to change everything. Companions. Socializing. Normal-life stuff. It was all I wanted, and it couldn't have gone more wrong. Nothing went right until Bale offered me a job and a home.

Swallowing hard, I open my eyes. I hate my memories more than seeing the age on Sybil's face and the gray strands mixing into her brown hair. But I don't turn to her yet. I look to Fyrestar instead.

His golden gaze meets mine, compassionate and warm. *"Don't be sad, Idallia. You know humans never last, and Sybil's life is good and filled with comfort and friends."*

I clamp my mouth tight against the surge of emotion trying to emerge as an anguished sound. Leave it to Fyrestar to know exactly what I'm thinking, and leave it to being recently injured to make my reactions so raw I feel turned inside out and buffeted by rough updrafts beating at my exposed heart.

I already lost Everly to the human rot of age, and she wasn't even that old. She was a healer, too, and very different from Sybil, much quieter and more maternal. After she died, I avoided humans for a long time, furious at them for their fleetingness. I didn't talk to any of the sorcerers for years, but then Sybil showed up, young, alone, nervous, and just like me when I was at school —desperately in need of a friend.

I inhale quietly, pulling my emotions back inside.

Sybil inspects the mug, carefully swirling its contents. "Almost cool enough to drink, and you need some food."

"I'm not hungry."

"I don't care." She stares me down and, as usual, she wins.

"Fine. But I hope it's a vegetable broth and not something with meat." I usually can't stomach meat. Luckily, there's never a shortage of highly carnivorous dragon shifters around to finish what I don't eat.

"Of course. For now," she adds ominously. "And without anything that might've even remotely touched a turnip."

"Thank Cealastra," I murmur. I hate turnips.

Sybil helps me sit up straighter and tucks an extra pillow behind my back. My skin is sore, but I know the discomfort will pass. I still groan, the creaking stiffness in my muscles a mix of healing remnants and having fought so many werebeasts that I lost count somewhere along the way.

Sol barely stirs as Sybil hands me the mug. Rim clicks his beak, making sure I know he's watching me until I take a sip. Fyrestar surveys us all from the foot of the bed.

I take a few swallows of the thick soup, warm liquid soothing my dry throat. "Satisfied?" I ask the room in general.

Sybil nods but won't take the mug back when I try to hand it to her.

Fyrestar chuckles. *"Nice try."*

"Finish it or I'll tickle you," Rim says, placing his beak menacingly close to my armpit.

I instinctively pull my arms in, give him the stink eye, and take another sip.

It takes some effort, especially after my initial thirst is quenched, but I down the entire mug. The soup was dense, but at least there were no chunks. "I deserve a medal for that." Setting the empty mug on my bedside table, I settle back into my pillows, tucking Sol in close.

Sybil's exaggerated exhalation speaks to how many times we've had this same conversation after I wake up from an injury. "My biggest triumph will be the day I find something you like to eat."

"I liked my birthday cake." I made sure both Sybil and Stuart got a piece.

"I'm not talking about fruit or desserts."

Sighing, I stroke Rim's feathers, his inner fire warming my fingers. With my other hand, I gently tease the soft plumes of Sol's little yellow head crest, her small talons lightly twitching against my waist as she sleeps. Fyrestar continues to keep my feet comfortable with his pleasant glow.

I blink heavily, drowsy now that I'm toasty and fed. "Kellan flew me back," I murmur.

"I know." Sybil pitches forward, her hazel eyes gleaming with interest. "And? What was that like?"

For some reason, my chest squeezes tight. "He's big and scaly."

She laughs. "You used to enjoy riding him."

"You were young. You don't remember right."

One graying eyebrow creeps up. "I arrived here at seventeen years old and remember everything perfectly—including that the two of you couldn't keep your hands off each other."

I shrug a little painfully. "Things change."

"Not for him."

Guilt blooms in the lingering tightness of my chest. "Kellan wanted more than I can give."

Sybil sits back, her brow creasing. "He wanted to marry you. Mate. Have a family. Is that so bad?"

"Yes, when I realized I didn't want to marry him." The guilt still eats at me. For hurting Kellan. For the tension still impacting the team. Some days are fine. Some are strange and hard and so incredibly awkward I wish I could reverse time and never start something that was going to end.

That *I* was going to end.

"I know he antagonizes you, but that's only because he wants your attention."

He definitely antagonizes me. He'd also lay down his life for me in a heartbeat. "Kellan wanted all of me, and I don't even know who I am. *What* I am. I just...couldn't."

"It's more than that," Fyrestar rumbles in my mind.

"And something was missing," I add softly. "It just didn't feel right."

"It *sounded* pretty right," Sybil says saucily. "And you gave *very* detailed descriptions at the time."

I can't help smiling. Of course I did. Kellan was my first love, my first—and only—lover, and Sybil is my best friend.

"It was great," I admit. "I just didn't want what he wanted in the end."

"Which might be why Kellan can't get over it."

I bite my lip, slowly rolling it between my teeth. That—and

the fact that we're still stuck together, day in and day out. We both chose to stay with the Elite Wing, even after the breakup and all the ensuing resentment and unease. If we'd gone our separate ways, things would probably be different. Kellan would've moved on, and I could've stopped feeling irritated and guilty when nothing terrible even happened—no lying or cheating or violence. I just broke his heart. "I wish he would get over it."

"Me too—especially for his sake. A dragon shifter's life is long."

Sybil pours me a glass of water from the pitcher at my bedside, then pours herself one too. She leaves mine where it is, within easy reach of my cocoon of pillows, and sips from her glass as she sits back. Dehydration is an aftereffect of healing magic, and I worry sometimes that she doesn't put the same effort into taking care of herself as she does into taking care of me.

"But if he's not the one, he's not the one." She shrugs, draining half her glass. Then slyly, with interest she can't hide sparkling in her eyes, she asks, "What's this about Bale chomping straight through a weretiger to rescue you?"

Tension rips across my chest. I don't answer right away, seeing it all in my mind again. Those burning amber eyes. That precise, deadly spiral. The brutal bite.

Goose bumps splash over me, but the sudden shiver feels hot and settles heavily at the base of my spine.

"He got there just in time." My pulse beats hard, pushing a flush I can feel to my face.

"That's it? That's all you're giving me?" Her expression begs for more, and my take-it-or-leave-it shrug makes her huff, incredulous. "He came, he killed, I lived?"

"That's all there is to say." I don't want to bring up how Bale praised me, even when I nearly got Fyrestar and myself killed, or how he hesitated to let Kellan carry me home. There could be a hundred reasons for that.

"Your bright-red blush begs to differ," she says tartly.

I heat even more, and my heart gives a nervous thump against my ribs. Sybil is the only person to ever guess at my secret crush, but I've never confirmed it, even when she fishes for information. I don't want to admit it to anyone. Maybe I don't even want to admit it to myself, because there's nothing more stupid I can think of than getting involved with my king, the leader of the Elite Wing, and the man who holds the fate of my birds. As much as I call the three of them mine, in truth, they're also Bale's.

I turn my attention to Fyrestar to avoid Sybil's probing gaze. His everlife heals him of his injuries much faster than any human magic could heal mine. It also brings him back from the dead— something unique in Ellonrift, at least if magic endures. I can't imagine how many years Bale must've shaved off his own long life to put that gift into the warbirds. I know he did it with the help of a human sorcerer, a woman long since dead. The talented witch lived in lavish comfort here in Drayke Mountain for her remaining years, and I'm glad she did. "You okay, old friend? All healed?"

"Who are you calling old?" Fyrestar ruffles his feathers, but a soft coo follows the protest, negating its heat.

"If you're old, then I'm old, so I should watch my words." I'm roughly the same age as the warbirds of Torridaig, but since they've all burned back to their primal lifespark at least once, including Fyrestar, I'm their elder by far. "And I take it that means you're fine?"

"Fit as a dragon, but it took three days."

I gape at him. "Three days?" I whip toward Sybil, straining the tender skin on my back. "How long was I asleep?"

I don't like the way she shifts in her chair. "A while…"

My eyes narrow. "Three days is a lot longer than it should take a warbird to heal." Too long. It makes me want to reach into the night sky, pull down the Star of Ellonrift, and shake the magic out of her. "How long was I unconscious?"

She reluctantly answers, "Five days."

I snap my mouth shut. This prolonged lack of Cealastra's magic-replenishing eclipses is affecting us all now. Going by past experiences, healing should've taken a day for Fyrestar and a maximum of three for me.

Rim lifts his head, his tawny eyes reflecting my worry back at me. The phoenixes all have amber eyes like their maker, except for Fyrestar. His golden eyes match mine. *"Embersol hopped around in Fyrestar's feathers from dawn till dusk,"* he mutters. *"I'm sure that didn't help."*

Sol chirps. *"Not hop. Comfort."*

My heart melting, I smooth her little feathers as she heats with indignation, fluffing out her wings to puff herself up.

Sybil's soft chuckle ends the budding quarrel. "I love watching you talk to your birds."

I smile over at her. "Thanks for being patient. It must be strange to only hear half the conversation." Scolding a little, I tell my birds, "You could let Sybil hear what you say, you know. She's family too."

Sybil just laughs again before the phoenixes can respond. "Don't worry about it. They only have eyes for you, and it's become a bit of a game for me to try to guess what's going on. I hear one part and try to fill in the blanks."

"But they're much more interesting than I am," I protest.

Her dry look could send Torridaig into drought. "Idallia, my dear, you highly underestimate yourself."

"Okay, I'm fabulous," I say just as dryly.

Instead of the smile I expect, she shakes her head, looking irritated. "Why do you always say things like that? You *are* fabulous. And yet all you can see is that you're different. *Who am I? What am I?*" She looks upset, even angry, and I go utterly still, staring at her in shock. We don't fight. We never have. I make sure of it, because I don't want to regret some stupid argument when she's gone and there's no going back. "So what if you don't know who your parents are, or why you can't shift or glamour or do whatever else people do in Ellonrift? Your dream has been to fit in, but maybe it's better to stand out. Just be *you.*"

"Oh, it sure was fun standing out at school." I don't want this to escalate, but my anger is rising, too, along with the memories of being ostracized, tormented, and ridiculed. And before that, I was simply alone.

"Who cares about school? That was nearly two centuries ago." Sybil swipes her hand through the air, making the water still in her glass slosh to the rim. "You're always wondering why Bale chose you for the final position on the Elite Wing. It's because he's smart, and he's got an eye for what he needs."

I snort. "He didn't need me. I know I can fight—and fight well—but a dragon shifter can literally chomp a weretiger in half with one bite. It's not the same."

"What about Bloodwold vampires?" Her hard look pins me in place. "Firebreath doesn't kill them like it used to, and fights come down to people and their blades. That makes *you* the best."

Sometimes. When I can release that thunderclap inside me and focus my senses, moving so fast that I streak through the air. Unfortunately, it doesn't happen on command. Or often, at all.

I blink and see blood splattering across a moonlit sky. There are severed heads on the ground. Everything is dark and there are no specific landmarks, so I don't know if the sudden flash is something old, or something still to come. "Not better than Bale," I mutter.

She waves a hand again, this time more careful of the water in her glass. Her ire seems to wash away with the movement, her features softening once more. "It's not just about someone who can fight. Bale Cinderheart has legions of soldiers all over Torridaig for that. You *unify*. The Elite Wing fights hard for each other, and for all of us, but do you know who they'll fight for the hardest?"

"Bale," I say automatically.

She shakes her head. "You. They'll slash, burn, and claw through anything to make sure *you* live through a fight. That means they win. Always and no matter what."

I stare at her, my stomach sinking. "No wonder I almost always end up in the middle of the formation. They're *bodyguarding* me." Especially Maia and Arran. There's no way Arran couldn't regularly take a more prestigious position if he tried.

"No, don't think of it that way. And it's not as if you can't hold your own in a fight."

"Oh, great. So I'm a *cause*?"

"Stop taking this all wrong," she grumbles, setting her glass down with a thump. Her gaze shifts to the birds on my bed. "And your phoenixes? It's not like with the others, either. They're friends, allies, companions. But you four...You're fused in this circular mix of parent and child. I don't know who's who half the time, but you're a family."

Emotion jerks inside me, a rope pulling tight and anchoring me to my phoenixes. Rita and Gerard might've let me go without a backward glance, but I stopped caring the second my birds replaced them and offered a thousand times more than they ever did. "And?" I ask, the word a little shaky.

"If you want to label it—fine," Sybil says. "You're their cause. Just like they're yours."

They are, aren't they? My birds. My team. There's no length I wouldn't go to. I would burn down worlds.

I exhale loudly, shaking my head. "I'm five times your age. How are you so wise?"

"Let's not exaggerate. More like four and a half." She grins. "And humans mature faster. We have to. We have fewer years."

I sink into my bed, thoroughly depressed again. I see Sybil wither and fade before my eyes. I refocus my gaze and she's back to normal, but I can't help thinking that half her life is already gone, and at least half my time with her is already spent.

Trying to hide my sudden sadness, I ask, "How's Stuart?" They found each other here, after Bale recruited them both decades ago. Sybil joined the ranks of Drayke Mountain's prestigious healers, and Stuart has magical gifts that come in handy all the time. He has a touch of foresight, like me, and he's particularly good at dampening fae magic, which makes it harder for the fae to hoodwink anyone here with their cunning wiles. When a powerful fae puts their full magic into it, they can probably convince anyone to do anything, including Bale.

"Stuart's worried about *you*," she says. "When you arrived on Kellan's back, you gave us both a scare. We figured it must be dire."

I laugh even though my heart's not really in it. "I guess it was." *Five days.* That's terrifying. And three for Fyrestar worries me even more.

Sybil stands, stretching after what was probably a long, chilly day of keeping vigil at my bedside. She should've lit a fire in the hearth, even if I almost never do. "I need to get back to the infirmary. I've hardly been there in days, and it's probably chaos by now. We have a whole slew of new recruits who are either terrified after leaving home for the first time or flirting wildly with anything that moves. I'm not sure which is worse, but no one seems to be studying their spells."

I find a real laugh this time. "Aren't you glad you're head healer now? You get to do all the fun stuff, like endless scroll keeping and wrangling horny teenagers."

She levels a bland look at me. "*You* still give me plenty of real challenges."

She's got me there. "Thanks for everything." I pluck at my blanket. "For staying, and bringing me food..."

"Always." She flashes a cheeky grin, whispering, "*On Kellan's back!*" to me just before she turns and walks to the door.

I half-groan, half-laugh, and she chuckles on her way out, leaving me alone with my birds. My smile widens. Everly would've kissed my cheek, fussed a little, and tucked my sheets around me, but Sybil has always tried to be more of a friend than a mother to me.

My smile fades. I just hope she doesn't think I'm her cause and in need of protection. I have enough of that from the team.

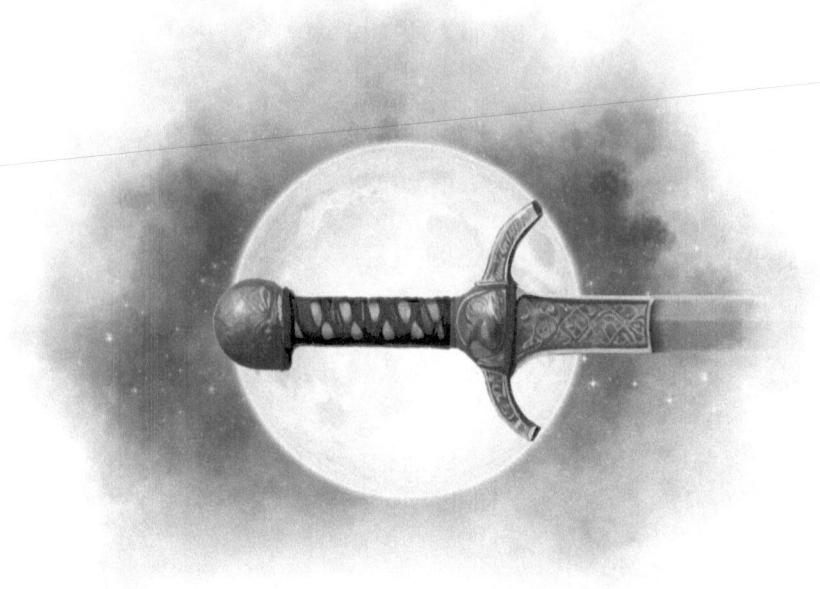

CHAPTER SIX

BALE

I'm intolerably bored without Idallia. And I'm not the only one.

Daily workouts are bland for everyone, the fighting half assed and the faces grim. Even the wing guards look like dull dots in the sky instead of deadly firebirds. Without her on the training field, it's even more obvious that she's the spark that sets the Elite Wing on fire. I knew it would be this way when I mapped the team out nearly two hundred years ago and brought her in last, but the blatant evidence of it every time she's laid up with injuries causes my chest to cramp.

I was supposed to let her go decades ago. I'd meant to.

Unease bites at my gut like buzzards picking through entrails. I don't want to hold her back, but setting her on her intended path will mean the end of everything we know. She's completely unaware that everyone looks to her for cues, too focused on her birds and on feeling isolated when that couldn't be further from the truth. The Elite Wing would follow her into an active volcano. I doubt they'd follow me.

The irony is, if I tell her everything, I might not even need the Elite Wing. Torridaig would be better off without her. But I'm convinced none of us would be, including me.

I made a plan for Idallia because I had to, but it was also a plan for me, for Torridaig, for Ellonrift. It's the only plan in my whole life that I haven't respected at all.

Or at least, not anymore.

Everything was on track until Idallia started a relationship with Kellan, and I didn't want to shoot a flaming arrow straight into their happiness. The intended strategy veered even further off course after the relationship *ended*.

When did I start spending more time with Idallia? I'm not entirely sure. It happened just as gradually as valuing her insight more than anyone else's and delaying the moment of truth.

Fyrestar suddenly bolts toward us like a shooting star. He swoops low over the training field, his wings and tail feathers trailing fire. He's the brightest thing I've seen in days, and my heart starts to pound. If he's blazing this much, it must be good news.

"Idallia's awake!" he caws out to us before circling back toward Drayke Mountain, drizzling sparks into the lake as he banks sharply and speeds away.

Relief keeps my pulse thumping hard. Five days is too long.

I sheathe my sword, knowing that's it for training today. Everyone's concentration will be shot, mine most of all.

The way the team takes off immediately, their scales aglow, both comforts and worries me. They didn't even ask for permission to go, proving once again that Idallia is the flame fusing us together, not me. But no matter my regrets when it comes to Idallia, giving her these people and the warbirds when she didn't have anyone will never be one of them. *This* is her home.

I hang back until the others disappear into Drayke Mountain

before taking off in the same direction. They'll get cleaned up and go visit her, their phoenixes perching all around on her oddly bare-bones furniture and the sole, large window frame in her room. I'll wait until later. I'm too solitary to want to join the group.

Or maybe I want her all to myself?

The idea comes from out of nowhere and leaves me reeling, that thought just as harrowing as any of the rest.

I fly back to my lair at the top of the mountain without rushing, trying to enjoy the warm autumn day, the colorful trees, and the golden light bouncing off Upper Drayke Lake. I need to clean myself up too. It was a long morning of training, even if it wasn't as intense as usual.

Swooping through my biggest window, I shift on landing and stride toward the back of my living quarters. Asking the staff to bring hot water all the way up to the peak of Drayke Mountain seemed cruel, so a few centuries ago, I devised a way to tunnel in snowmelt and rainwater, allowing it to fill a deep, natural dip in a secondary chamber far inside the mountain, beyond my study. I created a pool, but it needs regular heating.

Restless tension whips through me as I walk down a stone hallway with a sharp bend, lending privacy to the bathing area. Not that I need it. No one ever comes up here except the occasional staff member or possibly Stuart if I invite him to join me in my study to discuss something.

Once I'm in the large bathing chamber, the cold, clear pool spread out before me, I shift again. Several long firebreaths heat the water to almost boiling. As soon as it's steaming, I return to my common form, strip down to bare skin, and slip in, the water reaching my shoulders.

My groan sounds like it should come from someone else. It sounds like the groan of a man sinking into a woman, and I haven't made that kind of guttural noise in so long it feels foreign to my ears.

Heat snaps in my groin. A flash of black hair and ruby lips fills my mind before I brutally shove the thought away.

I dunk underwater. This pool is big enough for two, but I've never shared it with anyone. Privacy became a way of life for me a long time ago. It's less appealing these days.

Moving to the edge of the pool, I perch on an underwater ledge and lean against the smooth stone wall, my head back and my eyes closed. I sit there in the silence, letting the heat soak into my muscles and hoping it'll relax not only them but the pressure snarling deep inside me as well. As usual, it's deathly quiet at the top of the mountain, and I wonder when I started missing noise.

Maybe it was around the same time I stopped enjoying solitude so much. As a young, new ruler after my father died and my mother quickly followed him, I chose isolation. Keeping my own council meant no one was whispering viperous ideas in my ears. And keeping my body out of anyone's bed meant seduction wouldn't influence politics, and pillow talk couldn't alter the course of kingdoms.

I didn't want to make mistakes and learn lessons. I wanted to *prevent* them.

Five centuries on, I'm fucking lonely and starting to feel half dead even though I'm in my prime.

Idallia flickers through my mind again, and I grimace, worried about how much I single her out. It's not just her, though. It's the whole Elite Wing. If I can pinpoint one source of joy in my life, it's them.

The water starts to cool as clean, cold runoff from outside filters into the heated pool, and my hot water trickles out via another channel. I soap up, rinse, and get out. As soon as I'm dressed, I know where I'm going, even though I should be planning security for the upcoming Ellonrift Council and reading the mountain of scrolls I know must be sitting in the basket outside my door.

I could go straight to check on Idallia, but it's likely the team is still there and will be for a while. They're used to my presence during training or on missions, but Idallia is the only one I ever speak to at length in private. If I go now, there won't be anything private about it.

For now, it's enough to know she's awake, and I want a report from Sybil anyway.

Instead of flying out my window and going directly down to the lower levels of the mountain fortress, I use the stairs. It takes me a hundred times longer to get to the infirmary, but part of my job is letting people see me and asking them about their lives and families. I can only guess how the other rulers of Ellonrift act in their own homes, but I know how *I* want to act, and that's different from my parents, who were elitist and aloof.

I finally make it to the bright, airy domain of the healers, my throat parched from inquiring after health, hobbies, and children. I know the residents of Drayke Mountain, but they don't know me. I'm not sure anyone does, except for maybe a handful of people, including the one I'm about to see.

Sybil's door is open, as always, and I walk straight in. She looks up from her desk, and her eyes brighten with true welcome, making my own responding smile easy and natural.

"Fyrestar told us Idallia's awake."

Her brows lift. "Straight to the point, aren't we?"

I brush off the sharp jolt that darts through me. "Always, but I'm not only here about that." I step farther into the room, feeling as though all the objects crowding her space are going to topple over and bury me. Sybil has never gotten rid of a single gift from a grateful patient, and part of me can understand. Dragon shifters collect and keep their treasures too. "I'm curious about the new recruits."

"What should I start with?"

"Idallia. Why did it take her so long to recover?"

Sybil settles back in her chair with a sigh. "You know why. What I could accomplish in a day a few years ago now takes me three. And her natural healing is slower now, too, just like

Fyrestar's. We need an eclipse to blanket Ellonrift in magic. The covering we've got is threadbare at this point."

Her words don't surprise me, but they amplify the constant dread gnawing at my stomach. "Idallia isn't healing as well on her own, then?"

"A human would've died on the battlefield, but she was still up and talking and made it home. She heals better than a lot of people, but she doesn't heal like you do, or even your phoenixes. You're starborn and heal instantly when you change forms. That doesn't mean you can't get hurt"—her eyes dip to my chest, where my only scar remains—"but the weakening magic can't impact your healing because it's physical for you—the shift triggers it. Idallia doesn't have that."

Neither do other dragon shifters. Their shift might be physical, but their healing doesn't work like mine does—a starborn gift from Cealastra herself. For everyone else, a hole in one form leaves a hole in the other, and I've seen too many of my soldiers die on the tips of Bloodwold lances and arrows.

"But why didn't she at least wake up sooner? Even if she wasn't ready to jump out of bed, she should've regained consciousness before now."

Sybil shakes her head, seeming at a loss. "The same thing happened to a lesser extent the last time she got hurt."

"It wasn't *five* days." I realize I'm almost growling and modulate my voice. "That's a long time without food or water."

"That doesn't appear to bother her like it would a dragon shifter or a human. It seems to me that as soon as she knows she's safe and in good hands, she shuts down to heal. Kind of like hibernation."

"So she's sleeping it off in her own bed?"

"Basically, yes. It took five days this time, but there's not a scratch on her now. Not a scrape, not a scar."

Her delicate features whip through my mind along with a shimmer of golden eyes. My skin warms, and my dragon crawls through me, the heated, smoky shadows wanting to seep out, take form, and see Idallia *now*. "So she's fine?" I ask gruffly.

Sybil snorts. "She'll *be* fine. But again, she's not you and can't race straight back into battle—or training. I'd recommend several more days of rest."

Easier said than done. As soon as Idallia is on her feet, she'll want to be sparring again.

"She doesn't fit the profile of any known people in Ellonrift," I say cautiously. "Do you know what she is?"

Sybil looks steadily back at me. "Do *you*?"

Her blunt question sounds almost accusing. It makes it harder to force a lie to my tongue, so I shake my head.

Sybil folds her hands on her desk in the one place that isn't buried by scrolls. "No, I don't know. Just try to get her to rest."

My mouth thins. "It won't be easy."

"Make it about her birds," she suggests. "If it's better for them, she'll do whatever you ask."

I swipe a hand down my face, grimacing beneath my palm. "That's infuriatingly true."

"Oh, don't grumble like that." Sybil laughs. "You have it easy. If I could use that same argument to get her to eat something, I'd do it in a heartbeat."

The grimace freezes on my face. That's because Idallia is better suited to a diet far different from our carnivorous ways.

"And the new recruits?" I ask, abruptly changing the subject.

"An interesting batch. Even with magic waning, there's some real power that just needs honing, and there are some others that'll do fine out and about in the different cities and townships."

"Anyone good enough to stay here? Or go to the Drayke School of Fire and Flight?" The headmistress keeps almost as big a permanent healing staff on hand as I do.

Her lips pursing, she wobbles her head back and forth in a that-remains-to-be-seen kind of way. "Give me until after the Ellonrift Council to decide. You'll be too busy until then anyway to deal with dispatching new employees all over the place."

Some say I'm too much of a hands-on ruler, approving every soldier, healer, and sorcerer placement around Torridaig. No one gets one of those jobs unless I approve it. This is one of the few things I don't do alone, though. The headmistress gives me input on the soldiers finishing their schooling, Sybil offers opinions on the capacities of the healers, and her husband, Stuart, assesses all the other sorcerers who come through Drayke Mountain before applying for open positions around the kingdom.

We recruit as many human sorcerers graduating from the magic schools in Ruthinock as we can. Most Torridaigans have fire and flight and accelerated healing, and I might've called down the power of the very stars to make our warbirds, but dragon shifters don't have magic like humans do. Human spell weaving is a whole different game with so many players and tricks and tactics that it's impossible to counter every strategy unless you have an army of sorcerers of your own.

"Take as much time as you need," I tell her. "There are several healers around Torridaig applying for retirement." That probably accounts for half the parchments awaiting my attention. "We've got more positions to fill than you have new recruits, so it's just going to be a question of sending the best where they're needed the most."

"Couples are already forming. They might want to stay together."

I look at her, bemused. "Humans move so fast. It's only been a few months."

She laughs. "Maybe you move too slowly, Your Majesty."

Maybe I don't move at all. And I definitely don't like the pressure I'm getting from the regional governors to finally produce an heir. If I die without one, Torridaig won't have a legitimate ruler unless Cealastra chooses a new one herself and gifts them with starborn magic, and that's unlikely, seeing as she isn't even showing up for eclipses anymore.

"Don't *Your Majesty* me. You know my name is Bale." I soften the reproach with a smile as I move toward the door. "Ask Stuart to come to my study before dinner. We need to discuss security for the upcoming Council. I'm pretty sure Marissa Turin won't risk breaking the non-aggression pact herself while she's here, but I don't trust the Fae Queen's entourage with so many tempting humans and dragon shifters around."

True dislike hardens Sybil's features. It's not an expression I'm accustomed to from her, but I understand. Humans aren't people to the fae. They're prey. "Fluttering eyelashes and a few pretty words are all it takes for those parasites to glamour their way into your personal space and steal your life away," she says bitterly. "They claim consent, but it's deceit."

Not all fae take too much or do it deceitfully, but the problem is undeniably growing with the weakening of magic. Just like Sybil needs three days now to do what she used to do in one, the fae need three times as much lifeforce from others to maintain their health. Fear has been making them greedy. And for too many of them, lack of funds to pay for what they need to survive is driving them to steal it instead.

Mere kisses and touches will strip years off a human existence, and sex will basically leave a human on their deathbed, so the orgasm had better be worth it. But fae glamour magic masks the reality of what's happening until it's too late. Dragon shifters live long enough that a fae encounter or two barely makes a difference. Same for vampires. The fae reject weres unless they're truly desperate, and they're physically unable to siphon lifeforce from their own kind—including the gildenfae, who don't need to siphon from the living at all. It's my humans I have to protect.

"I need some kind of spell that'll diminish fae magic all over Drayke while they're here. At least give people a fighting chance of seeing through their trickery until the fae leave again."

"That'll take a lot of power." She looks skeptical.

"That's why I need to talk to Stuart. To see if it can even be done."

She nods. "I'll tell him."

I nod back, as satisfied as ever with this capable woman whose kindness and potential jumped out at me from her very first days inside Drayke Mountain. It saddens me to know I can't save her from the fate that takes all my favorite humans away.

I climb back up the stairs, going through greetings and questions again with any residents and staff I encounter, but stop halfway up the mountain where the Elite Wing lives. I linger in the hallway leading to their quarters, not wanting to bother Idallia if she's sleeping again, but not willing to let the whole day go by without seeing with my own eyes that she's out of that terrifying state of dormancy.

I don't know if she could get any direct sunlight through her perpetually open window. It would've helped.

I stand outside her door, still debating like an indecisive fool instead of a king with nearly six hundred years under my scales. A squawk and a spurt of laughter eventually confirm that she's awake and so are her birds. I don't hear any other voices and lift my hand to knock, hoping to all the stars that Kellan isn't inside making her laugh.

If he is, I might not be able to resist the burning desire I've had to throw him out a window ever since he carried Idallia home.

CHAPTER SEVEN
IDALLIA

My head snaps around. Another knock can only be Bale. Everyone from the Elite Wing has already stopped by. Sybil was here when I woke up. Stuart might come back with her later, but they'd wait until after his workday is over. Unless...

My stomach drops.

Unless it's Kellan again.

I nervously chew my lip. He came by earlier with a bucket of late-season wild blueberries he must've picked in the valley we found together ages ago. He knows they're my favorite.

But they didn't come for free. They came with a conversation that made the blueberries curdle one by one in my stomach.

"You know we could finally leave the Elite Wing together. Build a life."

My heart suddenly pounding, I shake my head at him. "I don't want to leave the team. I like it here."

His blue eyes flick up, meeting mine. "Maybe just think about it?"

My jaw slowly drops. "Kellan, we're not even together anymore. I don't know why you're bringing this up."

He stares at me for so long that I itch to fill the silence, but I don't have anything else to say. I'm afraid even confirming that I care about him, about our friendship, will just keep this discussion going for another thirty years.

"I hated seeing you hurt," he eventually says. "It made me realize..." He trails off, and my chest cinches tight. I'm grateful that he cares about me, but he needs to care differently now. Things have changed, and I'm not going back. "Do you love someone else?" he asks quietly.

I huff an instant denial, but amber eyes and a deadly spiral abruptly fill my mind. The remembered wash of weretiger blood is so real that I can feel the wet heat all over me again. "No."

His hard, sad smile stabs right through me. "I'm glad you're awake." He stands to leave. "I'll see you at training, I guess."

I nod. "Yeah. See you around."

The knock sounds again, a little louder this time, and I gingerly sit up in bed, making sure I'm decently covered. The nightgown Sybil put me in after getting rid of my bloody clothes is loose at the top, and the thin straps keep sliding down my shoulders.

"Come in," I call out. I'm awake but frankly not motivated to get out of bed, especially if it's Kellan again.

The door swings open to reveal Bale Cinderheart in the hallway. Awareness ripples over me, and I quietly steady my breathing. He looks grim and stiff, but maybe that's because the only times he ever seeks me out in my chambers are after I've been seriously injured.

"Fyrestar told us the good news. It took you long enough to wake up," he says sternly.

"So sorry my self-healing skills aren't up to dragon shifter standards," I shoot back acerbically.

Frowning, he clasps his hands behind his back. "Yes, well, everything's harder these days."

My eyes narrow. He'd better not criticize Sybil, or I *will* get out of bed. "I'm fine now. I'll probably be up for training tomorrow."

The crease between his brows deepening, he shifts his gaze from me to Fyrestar at my feet. The babies have gone back to their roosts. "Fyrestar was badly injured. Let's give him a few more days of rest."

Worry rises like a swollen river inside me. Fyrestar seems fine now, but was he in even worse condition than I thought? Three days is a long time for him to recover.

"Okay. Maybe we'll just gently stretch our wings tomorrow. Rim and Sol can fly with us."

Bale's lips lift in a slight smile when I say *our wings*. "That could work."

He still hasn't moved into the room. His broad shoulders fill most of the doorway, his tall body tapering to a narrow waist encircled by a worn leather belt that holds a set of double blades. His white shirt gapes wide below his neck, the laces loose, while supple black leather pants encase his long legs, leaving little to the imagination. There are muscles for days.

I pretend not to look. I mean, I *don't* look. Not really.

"But what if there's an emergency?" I ask. "More werebeast kidnappings? Or Bloodwold vampires?" They kidnap too. A dragon shifter will sell for hundreds of gold coins at their blood markets. Humans don't last as long and sell for less.

"There won't be."

I laugh without humor. "Because you can control even that?"

He doesn't answer. He cocks his head, his jaw stiff, and the cherry-dark tattoos racing down one side of his neck seem to bulge with tension. They're a series of small stars, moons, and eclipses—a homage to Cealastra that I know continues straight down over the scarred skin across his heart and disappears into his waistband. On sweltering summer days, sometimes Bale's shirt comes off on the training field. Those days are distracting, and if I didn't have Fyrestar's help, I'd probably have been decapitated.

"Are you going to loom in my doorway like a giant bat or come in?" I ask tartly.

Bemusement flits across his features. "You have an odd way of speaking to your king."

I laugh for real this time. "Are you going to loom in my doorway, Your Big Shadowy Majesty, or come in so I don't have to shout across the room?"

Bale's mouth twitches. When the battle horn blows, he's all business and fully in charge. In training, it's mostly that way too. Otherwise, he always seems happiest when none of us treats him any differently from anyone else on the Elite Wing. The warbirds and the team are like family to me, and I'm pretty sure Bale feels the same way.

He moves inside and shuts the door on the chilly cross breeze from the open window, but instead of sitting in one of the chairs Sybil left next to me, he stops at the foot of my bed and puts a hand on Fyrestar.

Fyrestar's feathers warm, and so does my heart. A soft, internal sigh echoes bleakly inside me. Bale really doesn't make it easy to get over this infatuation.

I wiggle up a little more, sitting straighter against my pillows. His eyes flick up, then quickly away, and I glance down, seeing that the neckline of my nightgown has slipped dangerously low again. I tug it back up, my face flaming. I try to pull the sheet up, too, but Fyrestar's weight pins it down.

I clear my throat. "Can I offer you..." Glancing around, I realize the only things I have in here are weapons, clothes in a free-standing dresser, a screen hiding a bathing and personal needs area, two chairs, and a bed and bedside table. Warmth crawls up my neck again. "A glass of water?" There's one clean glass left.

"You keep very sparse quarters," Bale remarks, scowling as he looks around my spacious but mostly empty bedroom. "The others have set up their lairs more..." He hesitates, his amber eyes swinging back to me. "Comfortably."

That's something he knows from checking on team members

after injuries. Otherwise, he's never on the Elite Wing level inside the mountain and hasn't once in almost two hundred years tried to join us in our lounge in the evenings. I can count on one hand the number of times he's joined us in the Drayke Mountain dining hall for dinner, most of them in the last few years. The only time Bale doesn't choose isolation is when we're out on missions and he's truly part of the team, not something inherently separate.

It's not that he and I don't talk. But usually, he finds me on one of the open, south-facing sun porches or pulls me aside for extra training. And I need it. I'm sure he knows my room best since I'm always the one getting hurt.

I shrug. "I'm not a dragon shifter. I don't need a lair."

"You need a home."

"This is a home." I nod toward the roosting wall with the deep, built-in cavities for my phoenixes and their nests. "And I have my birds."

Bale's expression darkens. "This is basically what prisoners have in my dungeon, and even they ask for more. There's not even a rug. Or a fire in the hearth. Is this what you were used to at Glarraden House?" His frown deepens. "Cealastra knows there was gold enough to provide."

Taunting voices fill my head. *Gildenfae-gold kid.* I shove the remembered jeering aside.

"I've never been deprived in my life," I answer honestly. Except of answers. Of attention. Of friendship. Anything material I ever wanted or needed, I had.

And of course, everyone knows about the gold arriving systematically on Dragon's Night. My known history is an open book, just like Bale's, Maia's, Arran's, Wade's, Kellan's, and Danica's. We're famous in Torridaig. And infamous everywhere else.

One of Bale's eyes narrows, pinching with a quick twitch. He continues gently stroking Fyrestar's head. "My garrisons in the northeast say Bloodwold vampires are getting bolder by the day.

Torridaigans in the border cities keep disappearing without a trace."

I can only assume the change in subject means Bale is over his indignation at my plain living space. I feel my body temperature rise again, this time in pleasure that he's bringing the affairs and concerns of the kingdom to me. Bale doesn't keep advisors on staff, so if he needs to bounce ideas around or work on strategies, it's usually with me, Stuart, or Sybil. We all realize how unique that is.

"Should we retaliate?" I ask.

"If we don't, I fear they'll only grow bolder."

"But we'll have to do it on our side of the border, which means waiting for them to attack."

"And more Torridaigans could get caught in the crossfire."

"But if we cross the border, even in pursuit, Rannigan Bloodthief will go after you at the upcoming Council for aggression. You know the Were King will side with him just to keep Rannigan from looking his way, and the fae could easily side with him too." The fae kingdom of Tanturriff is safely across the continent from Bloodwold, with the whole of Torridaig in between, and the fae can suck down vampire years just as easily as vampires can suck down fae blood. It's led to a stalemate of sorts —and an alliance at times.

"The Were King will only openly side with me in exchange for something huge. He's too scared of the Vampire King to do otherwise, even if werebeasts are inedible. We all know Rannigan will murder for a throne and the Council vote that comes with it."

"Something huge? Like integrating all of Muirvale into Wyndwood?" Bale nods, and I feel ill. Anyone from Muirvale who wants to be in Wyndwood is already there. "Will the new Fae Queen keep up the old one's politics?" I ask. She and the Vampire King aligned against us in the past because they were out of each other's reach, and they both wanted to feed off dragon shifters in their own ways.

Bale's mouth thins, his expression unsure. "That remains to be seen. The upcoming Council could change a lot, and I have plans to try to get the new queen on friendly terms with us."

"Plans?"

"She's young, her magic is weak, and she's under continual attack by her own people. Until she marries and produces an heir, she's in constant danger. Half the fae nobility want to force themselves on her and hope for a child who'll be the next undisputable, starborn ruler, and the other half want to murder her, hoping it'll force Cealastra to show up again, renew magic, and choose a new ruling bloodline for Tanturriff. If I offer Marissa true protection, I'm hoping she'll be my ally."

Jealousy darts through me at Bale's use of the Fae Queen's given name. "How close an ally?"

"As close as I can get."

The jealousy bursts in my chest like an exploding star. What if Bale decides to marry this woman? Together, they'd rule a huge portion of Ellonrift, and a half-dragon shifter, half-fae heir would be a powerful force securing a merger of the two kingdoms.

Great stars, I feel sick.

"Are you all right?" Bale hurries to my side. "Your heartbeat just accelerated like you took off at a sprint." He frowns down at me, almost reaching out.

"I'm fine," I say hoarsely, wishing I could sink under my covers and disappear. "Your hearing must be old and deteriorating —like the rest of you." Hopefully the teasing insult distracts him from my racing pulse and the heat blasting off me like a forge.

A chuckle rises from deep in his throat. "Now I can't wait until you're better. One afternoon of training, and I'll have you eating those words."

His challenge only makes my pulse thump harder. Sparring with Bale is the only time we touch.

"How will you protect her?" I ask, almost reluctantly bringing us back to politics. *Please don't answer, "With myself."*

I watch him, waiting for the worst.

"I'm still debating. I have a few ideas in mind."

I wait for more, but Bale seems done with the subject of the Fae Queen. He glances at the door, but I stupidly want to keep him with me, so I ask, "If Rannigan Bloodthief can somehow paint us as the aggressors and get the other rulers to vote in favor of sanctions, he'll demand we hand people from Torridaig over to him for his blood markets."

Fyrestar's golden gaze swings toward me, as if he knows exactly what I'm doing. I look away from him, flushing.

"Rannigan can demand all he wants. I'll never do that," Bale says harshly.

Every year, we get closer to all-out war with Bloodwold as Rannigan manipulates Council votes in his favor and Bale retaliates in whatever way he can to protect his people while still trying to keep diplomacy alive. There used to at least be tied votes, but Rannigan found a way to eliminate those—along with one of Bale's long-standing allies.

"But you have a plan." I know that dark heat in his eyes, the shadow scales lightly coating his skin. "A last effort to avoid the war breathing down our necks?" We might not have courted this already bloody conflict with Bloodwold, but we're ready for it—and Bale seems ready to exchange words for blades and be done with endless useless Councils. I'm frankly surprised he's giving the system another chance, but I think his devotion to Cealastra makes it hard to let go of what she put into place.

He nods. "We get undeniable proof that they're the aggressors. We capture his blood traffickers on our soil before they can cross the border again."

"But can we prove they were on our soil?"

"We'll need to get the prisoners to testify truthfully during the Council, even with the threat of Rannigan looming over them."

I grimace. That would mean cutting a deal with traffickers, promising them safety and blood.

Or threatening them worse than the Vampire King.

"We've countered blood raids before, but taking prisoners is never easy," I point out. "The traffickers take their own lives rather than risk exactly what you're talking about." Sol peeks her beak out of the roosting wall, and I reach for her as she flutters down. She settles near my hip, drawing affectionate glances from both Bale and Fyrestar. "We'll need to already be in the right place to act fast enough. But how can we know where they'll attack?"

"We can't. We can only guess at it and hope we're right."

I stroke the angle of Sol's wing bone, thinking. "The northeast is getting hit hardest now, so it would be logical to start there. Where do you want to go?"

"As soon as you're better, I think we should take up position in and around Porthwood. See if a raid happens."

My spirits immediately lift at the idea of a stakeout. I hope Bale will pair me with Maia or Danica. No one sleeps. We sharpen blades and laugh about past ill-advised flirting after too many mugs of dragon's brew down at our favorite tavern. The fun comes to a crashing halt when the violence starts, but as long as we're winning, that's usually fun too.

"Why Porthwood?" I ask. "They could hit Draywood just as easily—or any of the lesser towns near the border with Bloodwold."

"They already hit Draywood twice in a row. I'm just guessing they'll change it up and raid Porthwood instead."

"I hate to delay us. What if we miss a raid?" I purse my lips, wondering how quickly I can get back into fighting shape.

Bale's eyes dip to my mouth. It's quick enough to mean absolutely nothing, but heat still drips through me like a bead of sweat.

"I'd rather wait. We'll need Fyrestar at full strength."

I glance at Fyrestar. He seems tired now, but does he really need that much rest? He was fine earlier when he was roughhousing with Rim and chasing Embersol, who zipped around like a spark.

"Have you answered the Fanghaven pretender about the Council yet?" I ask. Rexton Hale has sent so many messages to

Drayke Mountain to request an invitation to the meeting of Ellonrift's rulers that people are taking bets on when the next request will arrive and how loud Bale's roar of frustration will be.

Bale sits heavily in the chair by my bedside and drops his head into his hands. His fingers spear through his short, dark hair, gripping his head in a way that makes me want to soothe his scalp with a softer touch. "No. And that man is just asking for me to bite him in half," he growls.

I giggle. The sound is silly and girlish, but it just pops out. Bale looks back up, suddenly smiling. Our eyes lock, and my chest squeezes painfully, hurting like it was just clamped in a werebear's jaws.

"Don't do that," I say, still smiling despite all the reasons I shouldn't. "But you're probably right to exclude Hale from the Council. If Rannigan's Fanghaven wife ever manages to kill her husband and escape, she won't appreciate you giving her rival her seat at the table."

"Rannigan captured an infant and legally bound her to him in marriage after he murdered her entire family. Now he represents them both at the Council, claiming he has her full confidence and that she prefers not to leave Blackrock Keep."

I snort. "She's not a wife. She's a prisoner." And since consent means nothing in Bloodwold, Rannigan did whatever he wanted without hers.

Bale nods. "He stole her, and he stole her vote." His bitterness seeps out on an inky wave of darkness. His shadows wash over my hand and forearm, and I shiver even though they're not cold. They're warm and living, the essence of his dragon.

Tensing, Bale pulls his shadows away from me, and I shiver again, this time from the loss of his heat. "At least Fanghaven vampires have stayed true to their original starborn ruler's edicts. They don't bite without consent." Fanghaven vampires established nonviolent feeding and a thriving blood commerce far before my time, but Rannigan's regicidal rampage took place when I was just a child. Ellonrift has been dealing with the political fallout ever since because now the Vampire King gets two votes at the Council—one for his own kingdom of Bloodwold, and another for Fanghaven—his jailed-up wife's kingdom by starborn right.

No one can prove Rannigan doesn't have her full confidence, as he claims. No one can even prove she's alive, but Cealastra never replaced her with a new starborn ruler for Fanghaven, so chances are, she is.

Unless Cealastra is just as dead as the Fanghaven queen. But that's a whole different crisis to deal with.

"Do you think the Vampire Queen is still alive?" I welcome Rim to the pile of phoenixes on the bed. He must've woken up, realized Sol had left the roost, and had to find a spot here too. Rim's very real fear of missing out gets him into trouble all the time. In training, he already barrels into fights he can barely handle simply because almost everyone else is there. "No one ever sees this woman, and she hasn't produced Rannigan's heir." I don't even know her given name. Something Bruhane, since that was the family name of the Fanghaven royals. "What if she's dead but Cealastra either can't or won't replace her?"

Bale looks at me oddly. I'm sure he has thoughts about this— both are huge concerns. "The Star of Ellonrift still shines in the night sky."

My brow pinches. That's not exactly an answer. "What about Rexton Hale, then?"

"There's nothing starborn about him. He wouldn't be Cealastra's choice even if the Fanghaven queen is dead." Scooping up Embersol, Bale settles her on his lap. She nestles into him, her feathers shining with happy warmth. He absently strokes her little butter-colored head crest, and I wonder if he misses having birds of his own. "But I think she lives." His gaze flicks up from Sol, searching mine. "If we free her from Rannigan, do you think she'd be an ally if she could vote?"

I'm almost too distracted by Sol's adorable warbling and Rim's envious stink eye in her direction to answer. Fyrestar pins

Rim with a warning look, and the younger phoenix sidles closer to me. Putting my arm around him, I say, "If someone killed my whole family, held me captive my entire life, and stole my goddess-given vote at the table of Ellonrift's kings and queens for himself, I'm pretty sure I'd ally with anyone else—especially with someone who helped me."

Bale slowly nods, still stroking Sol's head. "You're a good strategist, Idallia. I'm glad I came to talk."

Just my name on Bale's lips sends my insides into a heady spiral. But treating me like an equal? Listening to my advice and thoughts? Those might be the sexiest things I've ever known. Add in the affection he shows my birds, and I'm pretty sure my decades-long secret infatuation just got kicked aside by my own thrashing heart and catapulted into something worse.

Standing, Bale gently deposits Sol on my lap. He suddenly lifts a hand and touches my neck. The movement is controlled, just quick and unexpected, and I swallow as his fire-bright amber eyes meet mine, his fingers lightly pressing into my skin.

"If we're going after blood thieves next, we have to make sure no vampire can get near this neck of yours." His hand drops away, but I'll feel his touch for hours. "I'll ask Stuart what he can contrive."

I nod, incapable of answering. My hammering pulse steals my breath, and there's no way Bale doesn't hear the blood storming through my veins. Abruptly, he turns and leaves without a backward glance.

CHAPTER EIGHT

IDALLIA

I've already been up and training again for three days when Bale tells us all to meet after lunch in the large field by Upper Drayke Lake. Fyrestar and I land in the already scorched meadow, and Rimblaze and Embersol perch in nearby trees. It's our usual training venue, and the terrain reflects the abuse, the dirt churned up and the grass rough and burned. The autumn day is hotter than most, making the huge, meandering lake look tempting for a swim. If I didn't know the clear, cold mountain water would freeze an instant scream out of me, I'd dive in.

Once we've gathered, the wing guards all watching from close by, Bale looks us over with a critical eye. We've been training hard with vampire tactics in mind, knowing the Porthwood stakeout approaches.

"Bloodwold raiders don't burn and always attack in groups." Bale's amber eyes cut to me, assessing. I stare back at him, my chin high. Does he think I'm not ready for a hard workout? I can't wait to prove him wrong. "As usual, today we train in skin instead of scales so that we're skilled enough to beat them at their own game. It'll be swords, knives, feet, and hands. Fight dirty if you have to. Fight to win."

It was the same when I was at school. Students almost always trained in their common form—which definitely helped me—but the switch from scales to skin only happened a few years before I got there, just after the Vampire King's human sorcerers accomplished the one thing that could even the odds between vampires and dragon shifters.

Rannigan Bloodthief's sorcerers somehow created a magical shield against firebreath. That kind of magic is too taxing to maintain over long periods or cover too many people, so Rannigan limits it to protecting his raiders. In, out, then the magic wears off. In the meantime, dragon shifters have to get out of the air, or be picked off by arrows and spears. Fangs don't even really help because dragon shifters can't get close enough to bite before they're riddled with holes or a sword is driven straight into their softer underbelly scales.

After the initial losses, Bale and his captains around Torridaig quickly understood they had to fight Bloodwold vampires differently—on two legs and without mercy.

"What are the teams?" Kellan asks. His blue eyes flick to me. I look away from him.

"You're in pairs against Idallia."

I pivot toward Bale so fast that wind whistles in my ears. "How is that fair?"

His eyes glint, seeming to answer my earlier, chin-lift challenge. "I didn't say it was fair. I said we're doing it. Besides... do you not think you can win?"

I snap my mouth shut. Maybe I can. It depends on how desperate the others make me. If I don't feel a true sense of danger —or fury—I can't always accelerate and focus like I should. I fight my best when I'm the underdog, especially when winning is the only way my birds and I can survive. It's harder to unlock that blast of violence in training. Sometimes, I'm not sure I should.

Bale's gaze returns to the rest of the team. "All of you are going to savagely attack Idallia like you are vampires who want to pierce her flesh and drink her blood until the husk of her lifeless body falls to the ground."

"Thanks for the visual," I mutter.

Bale's lips almost seem to twitch, but I know he wants to push them into pushing *me*. "Just motivating them."

Good. The more vicious my opponents, the better I fight. The dragon shifters of the Elite Wing are highly skilled, dangerous, and not afraid of drawing—or losing—blood. Training with them is brutal, just the way I like it.

Fyrestar hops to my side. His eyes brighten, and flames roll in his beak. *"We'll savagely attack back."* He sounds as eager as I am for some real sparring. Everyone's been going easy on us for days.

Bale shakes his head. "Not you this time, Fyrestar. Idallia fights on her own."

I glare at the Dragon King in outrage, and Fyrestar's shrill squawk of protest attacks my ears. *"That will never happen in a real fight,"* my warbird heatedly chirps.

"It could," Bale answers solemnly. "You might be eternal, but that doesn't mean you can't die and leave Idallia on a battlefield while your primal lifespark returns here to be reborn."

Fyrestar almost argues, then claps his beak shut. Smoke coils from his nostrils, and he takes off to join the other wing guards without a word. His disgruntled sparking says it all.

I watch Fyrestar go, angry now that I'm truly alone. I recognize this as Bale's second motivation attempt—direct and effective. I preferred the dead-husk visual to losing the help of my warbird, and I give Bale the side-eye, letting him know I'm not fooled. This time, his lips really do twitch.

"Wade and Danica—you team up first." Bale turns to me, his expression hard. "And you—fight like you're going to die. Then I know you'll win."

"Thanks for the vote of confidence, Bale," Wade tosses across the sparring field as he starts limbering up. His good-natured smile takes the sourness from his words, but I don't let his affable nature fool me. He's a beast in any form once the fighting starts.

Danica unsheathes lethally long daggers and twirls them in her hands. "It's so much more fun fighting like this. It's always over too fast when we're in scales."

I get my hands comfortable around the hilts of my twin blades as I move forward into the sparring area. "I guess we should thank Rannigan Bloodthief for finding a human sorcerer skilled enough to come up with a spell to counter firebreath. Chomp, chomp, and it's done might've turned you all into lazy dragon shifters a long time ago."

We start to circle. Two against one means I have to watch all sides and move faster than either of them.

"Is that your best trash talk, Idallia?" Danica chuckles menacingly as she edges forward. "It needs some work." Quick as the beat of a dragon's wing, she leaps in and strikes hard.

I counter her attack, hold Wade off with my other sword, then kick Danica in the hip, sending her stumbling back. "So does your footwork. I'd suggest keeping your legs under you in a fight."

Sensing more than seeing the menace from behind, I duck Wade's swing, and his blade sails over my head. Instead of popping up, I drop low and sweep a kick around to hit his legs. He jumps at the last second, and momentum carries me around. I twist and roll, coming back up into a defensive stance.

Wade takes another swing at me, coming in high while Danica goes low. Deflecting them both at once isn't easy, but the challenge is just what I need for strength to surge inside me with that thunderclap only I can hear. I speed up, but they're fast and relentless, pounding at me in quick succession and looking for ways to disarm me. The harder they try, the better I fight back, my movements faster and harder to track. My assets are speed and reactivity. I'll never hammer with the brute strength of a dragon shifter, but I don't need to if I can get in just the right hit.

The longer we spar, the more my reflexes come alive, and my senses sharpen. Then suddenly, I can hear everyone's breath, the grinding of insects, the rustle of leaves, the fluttering of our warbirds in the trees. I can even sense a ripple of wind on the lake, feel each ray of sunshine sinking into my skin, and hear Bale's soft inhalations through his nostrils as he evaluates my moves.

Instead of helping, the overload of information starts to distract me. Wade gets in a kick, and I stagger to the side, my ribs aching fiercely. Clenching my jaw against the pain, I regroup, filtering out the excess and sharpening my focus on what counts —my opponents. Wade's next swing doesn't even come near me as I leap back, avoiding Danica's next attack just as fast.

"Is that all you've got?" I taunt, grinning viciously.

Danica's unspoken answer is to bring her blades in close to her body and spin at me with a flying kick that hits my middle so hard I skid backward through the dirt. The impact of her foot ejects all the air from me, and I can't breathe, a howling ache in my abdomen almost making me double over and vomit. She lands, still turning, and swings at me as Wade lunges in with a downward strike to match hers.

Sensing their imminent win as sharply as the pain in my stomach, I react on pure instinct and speed up with a second thunderclap, louder than the first. I move so fast I don't even see or comprehend my own retaliation until the flurry of hits and ringing steel suddenly stops, and I have to pull up short or else run my blade straight through Danica's chest.

I back off, my eyes widening. Neither of them holds a weapon anymore. "Sorry."

She shrugs, smiling. "No one's dead. We're all good."

I huff a laugh, then see the blood pouring down Wade's arm and sober. "Did I do that?"

"I'll be fine. You're a terrifying small person, though." His smile reaches his eyes, so I believe him—about both things—and turn my attention to my next match.

I want to get started before my speed and focus wither like the autumn leaves around us. Momentum can be a real problem for me. Even if I can find it, I often can't keep it.

Wade heads back toward the lake with Danica, who's fussing over his injured shoulder, and Kellan and Maia step forward to take their place. They'll be harder to beat, and I've barely had time to breathe, but both disadvantages will keep me motivated. These two are usually right and left wing to the Dragon King, always fastest to the pillars—and they keep their balance. That means they're the best of us, but I'm up for the challenge.

Maia comes in swinging so fast her blade is a metallic smear. Just a quick break from fighting drained the sharpest of my focus, and I have to build up speed and intensity again. She swings nonstop and knocks one blade out of my hand. I ignore the vibration ringing painfully up my arm and scurry after my lost sword while barely defending my fleeing backside. I pick up the blade on the run and spin to face her.

Do better. My mind supplies Bale's voice in my head, and I strike back hard, making Maia back away this time. I accelerate with whirlwind precision, soon getting in as many hits as Maia does.

Kellan hangs back, barely engaging, but Maia fights like the powerful warrior she is, in skin or scales. He's moping—or else afraid I'm incapable and frail—so I'm glad she's hammering at me like this. It's exactly what forces me to battle back hard.

I fight Maia off enough for a break from her relentless attacks. As she shakes off my kick to the outer thigh that leaves her struggling for balance, I whirl and turn my full violence on Kellan. He's not playing the game, so he needs to quit the field.

Snarling, I lunge, forcing him to at least defend himself. He increases his speed and the strength of his hits, but it's not enough. I disarm him and kick him away from me before I mockingly let down my guard and show him how he's been acting—useless. His nostrils flare.

Keeping an eye on Maia, I say, "That was pathetic. Don't do that again."

Kellan's face reddens. "You were just unconscious for *five days.*"

"So?" My brows fly up.

"So maybe I don't like beating on you right after that."

"That's your job," I snap.

"That is *not* my job," he snaps back. "We defend each other."

"This is training to do just that!"

"I concur," Bale growls, stepping between us. He turns a dark glare on Kellan. "Gather your warbirds and go home."

"What? Now?" Kellan's voice rises, incredulous.

"You heard me. And yes, *now*," Bale thunders ominously. "Get out of my sight and don't come back until you're ready to act like a member of this team instead of a—" He cuts himself off.

Kellan's jaw bulges on a chewed-up response. Without a word, he gathers his blades, his face tight and blank. He shifts and flies away, heading toward Drayke Mountain. Grambolt and Featherspear follow him.

Maia doesn't wait for any sign from me or permission from Bale to restart the match. She's a terror on the field and keeps me on the scrambling defensive enough to almost win not once, but twice, in mere seconds. I barely keep upright or my blades in my hands. My focus isn't coming back after the stunt Kellan pulled, and I can't seem to dredge up any of the movement-blurring quickness and purely instinctual reactions I need.

Then it happens all at once. Maia knocks me over, and I lose a sword as I hit the ground on my back, her brutal kick still thundering through my shoulder. She drops to one knee and circles my throat with her hand as she yanks my remaining blade from me.

She grins. I groan.

"And you're dead," Bale mutters from the sidelines.

I turn my head and scowl at him. "Thanks for the commentary."

"Happy to oblige," he murmurs.

"You just spit fire. I saw it." Rim's cheeky comment from a nearby branch isn't just for my ears, and I hear chuckles all around me, including from the other warbirds. Trying to catch

my breath and shake off Maia's final blow is all that keeps me from smiling along with them.

Maia's grin widens as she pulls her hand off my throat and sits back on her heels. Her hair is making an admirable escape attempt from the tight prison of its bun, so I must've given her a real challenge despite feeling sluggish compared to my first round. Her light-brown eyes simmer with inner fire, and the scar on her cheek elevates her face from beautiful to interesting.

"I want a rematch," I grumble up at her.

She holds out her hand and helps me to my feet. "It'll happen soon enough. Right now, Arran's waiting for his turn."

Arran's waiting for a lot of things. Like telling Maia he's in love with her.

It's clearly reciprocal, but she's not saying anything, either. I'm pretty sure Kellan and I were a cautionary tale for the whole Elite Wing. No one wants what we have now.

I know I learned *my* lesson. Lovers and work don't mix, especially when retirement won't come around for centuries.

Shaking myself out, I gather my blades. I'm definitely fatigued after the first two matches, and if I can't wake up my own inner beast again—whatever that might be—there's a good chance Arran will win.

Arran moves forward to take his turn, and my stomach sinks when Bale joins him.

Bale sees the look on my face and shrugs. "I told you it was going to be two against one."

"But you're..." I flap a hand at him.

His dark eyebrows creep up. "I'm?" he prompts when I don't finish.

My mouth thinning, I lift my blades and try to connect with them like they're claws or fangs—extensions of my own body—as I cast about for a reply. *Worth fifteen people in a fight. Faster, stronger, craftier. Star touched and shadow gifted. More powerful than any of us.* Yeah, I'm not going to say any of that. "Big."

A corner of his mouth curls up. "Then I guess you need to

fight harder. You're not getting any bigger, so you'd better get better if you don't want to end up flat on the ground again."

"Maybe *you'll* end up flat on the ground," I mutter. My trash talk really does need work, but Bale's challenge catapults my need to win straight up my spine. Competitive energy builds inside me, sharpening my focus and heightening my senses again.

But then Bale waits on the sidelines, letting Arran try to get the better of me first. The unexpected turnaround drains my motivation, and I have to keep repeating *do better* in my head just to concentrate on Arran rather than on all the sounds and smells and slanting rays of sunshine. Or on Bale hovering in the background and doing nothing—just like Kellan.

It's a test. I know it is, and I'm determined not to fall headfirst into Bale's trap.

Just when I find a steady rhythm that's going to keep Arran and me in a stalemate for the next decade, Bale swoops in and attacks.

I come alive with a bang, acceleration as natural as a heartbeat. Sounds pop out at me, but only the ones I need, helping me duck strikes and avoid kicks. Moving faster, I tap into unused power and somehow neutralize Arran in seconds. I barely see his brows rise in surprise, his hands suddenly empty of weapons, before I spin on Bale, staying just as aggressive and whip-crack fast so I don't lose my momentum.

Bale still gains the upper hand after only a few exchanges. I skitter back, regrouping. Trying to think instead of just move, I steer him toward the rockier terrain at the edge of the lake. He doesn't overwhelm me as quickly as I feared, but it's also difficult to know how hard he's trying. My desire to win remains high, helping me. Logic tells me I *can't* win, but my heart and body aren't complying with the negative message.

I kick small, sharp lake stones at him, forcing him to throw an arm in front of his face to protect his eyes. Following up instantly, I lunge. The tip of one blade nearly hits his torso before he spins out of the way, leaving a trail of shadow.

I snarl in frustration.

To my amazement, Bale snarls back. His jaw tight, he comes at me with fevered speed, forcing me backward until one boot splashes into the water. He keeps pushing, and I step back again, sliding on silt-covered stones. Cold water seeps into my boots. Gritting my teeth, I push in the other direction, but he shoves back with strength that far outmatches mine. He follows up with a strike I barely block. My feet slip, and I lose my balance on the uneven surface. Panic zips through me as I fall, crashing into the frigid shallows on my backside.

The shock of ice-cold water slows me down, and I barely lurch sideways in time to avoid Bale's blade. It slices the water as I hook a leg around his knee and bring him down with me. His splash sends freezing water over me, but I don't pause this time and pounce, maneuvering on top of him. The triumph of putting my blade to his throat lasts only a split second before he throws me off him, pushes me down, and straddles me.

I gasp, barely keeping my head above water. His expression dark, his eyes on fire, Bale holds both my shoulders in a steely grip so I can't use my blades and pushes me under the surface.

I stare up at him through clear lake water. The sunny blue sky beyond him mocks me. The look on his face doesn't. He holds me under until I start thrashing. I scream his name, the little air I have left bubbling out of me.

He scoots back and hauls on my arms, pulling my upper body free.

Bent at the waist with Bale still pinning my legs, I drag in a huge breath, my lungs aching.

He pulls me closer, lowers his head, and whispers against my neck, "And you're dead."

Arousal snaps through me, jerking a tight, hot ribbon of sensation from my chest to between my legs. Cold lake, warm breath. Hard hands, soft lips. Goose bumps sprout all over me. "Then why am I still here?" I ask roughly.

He draws back, his amber eyes brighter than Cealastra's star in the night sky. They hold me enthralled, and I wish I could fight their spell on me with feet and fists and blades, just like I fight everything else. "Because you would've killed fifteen of them before they got anywhere near you or your warbirds."

"Twenty," I counter sharply.

A slow smile spreads across his face, warming me like sunshine on my skin. I stare at the way his lips move. He's always so stern and reserved. His smiles are as powerful as an eclipse—and almost as rare. I swallow, a fire kindling inside me despite the glacial lake.

Bale's expression abruptly shutters, and he releases me, rising to splash up the shore. Disappointment hits me as I lurch to my feet. And relief. Bale leaving my personal space feels like a star dying inside me, the heat and power snuffing out.

I shake off sensations I wish I didn't feel and desires I'm too smart to give in to, and grope around with icy hands for my dropped blades. As soon as I have them, I follow him out of the lake.

The others surround me, offering cloaks and extra tunics and cutting off my view of Bale. My teeth chatter as the autumn breeze pins my wet clothing to my skin, and for once, it's not so bad being the youngest who everyone coddles.

CHAPTER NINE

BALE

You'd think someone who'd lived for nearly six hundred years and ruled a kingdom for most of them would be smarter than this. But who am I kidding? The only time I was ever able to ignore Idallia was when she was a child. I didn't lay eyes on her again until she turned up at the Drayke School of Fire and Flight, fully grown and already quicker and smarter than everyone else.

It came as no surprise that Rita and Gerard of Glarraden got rid of her the second they could. They were only in it for the money and too caught up in themselves to notice the incandescent force they were hiding. That was the point, although I didn't realize at the time that my choice would have such a lasting impact on Idallia, or how it would bind her to her birds. At least I ensured a legal adoption went through so she would inherit their house, the land, and the gold.

And that she'd be a true Torridaigan.

I summon Stuart to my study before dinner. I usually eat

alone, but I think I might join the team after Stuart and I finish. He arrives, his graying hair damp at the temples from the long climb to the top of Drayke Mountain.

I offer him one of the chairs in front of the gently crackling fire. "I should've gone to the sorcerers' level instead of making you come all the way up here," I say apologetically as I sit across from him. It seems like only yesterday that Stuart was bounding up the stairs.

He waves a hand. "I'm still spry enough, and I have to keep in shape for my wife. Sybil enjoys my youthful vigor."

I outright laugh for the first time in ages. Stuart has already passed the half-century mark and looks twice as old as I do, but I wouldn't discount him in a fight—especially a magical one.

"Have you made progress on the neck protection for Idallia that I asked for?" I pour us both mugs of dragon's brew. I rarely imbibe, but the sparring match with Idallia earlier rattled me— and not only because she almost skewered me a few times. I can still smell her—sunshine and ice—and maybe something else. She smelled...excited. Aroused. Especially in the lake.

Heat surges inside me, and I inhale the frothy scent of the brew and take a sip, chasing the fire from my throat.

Violence can bring out lust in people. I've smelled it on her before. It's probably just that.

"I'm working on a torque she can wear around her neck. It won't protect her whole throat, but if a vampire fang touches it, the fang will disintegrate and never grow back."

I lift impressed brows. "No fangs mean no feeding the way they like."

"Those vampires will still consume blood, but they'll never be able to steal directly from a vein again." Stuart holds his mug without drinking. "The torque is new and unproven, but if it works, we could try producing them in larger quantities and handing them out to people, starting with the border towns in the northeast."

"What's to keep vampires from ripping off the torque? Or breaking or cutting through even a closed necklace?"

"Nothing, I suppose." He frowns. "And I guess once word spreads about the magic, they'll just bite people wherever there isn't protection."

"Hmm." I sit back in my chair, the plush fabric worn from centuries of solitary evenings keeping my own council in this room. That's somehow happening less these days. The formation of the Elite Wing changed something here. Or maybe in me. Letting myself trust and count on a few people hasn't gotten me killed or Torridaig invaded, and it's a lot less lonely than trusting and counting on no one. "It doesn't sound like a long-term solution. Let's just see how it works for Idallia during the stakeout."

Stuart nods. "You know you could just kill Rannigan Bloodthief and take over Bloodwold."

I laugh again, my humor laced with bitterness this time. "As much as I'd love to, he's of starborn descent, and risking Cealastra's wrath isn't something I want to do—even if Rannigan already got away with slaughtering starborn royals." He clearly didn't care about his people enough to be concerned. *I* care, and I'm convinced Rannigan's treachery is what made Cealastra turn from us in the first place. She's either shining her magic elsewhere or truly in decline, but whichever it is, it began with the murder of her Fanghaven royals in cold blood. If I kill Rannigan now, premeditated and outside of a battle he incited, we might lose the Star of Ellonrift entirely, and all magic will fade with her light.

"Is Cealastra even around to care anymore?" Stuart asks with a frown. "Making this torque is hard work—like pulling sweat from a corpse."

I sigh. That's the question, isn't it? "I hope so."

We both take a drink of our dragon's brew. Except for with the team out on missions, Stuart is the only person I've sat and had brews with since I was young and my father still ruled the kingdom. Sometimes I wonder what's worse: being alone or inevitably grieving the loss of Stuart's company.

"What about dampening fae magic all over Drayke while the Fae Queen and her entourage are here?" I ask. Stuart is already on that task, too, with the help of Drayke Mountain's resident sorcerers and any new recruits who are skilled with that kind of magic.

His grimace isn't promising. "No plan seems feasible so far. We've never tried something this big before. I can dampen fae magic in individual rooms or for specific people, but I've never tried to blanket a whole swath of land and a large city before. It's a tall order," he says, stretching his feet toward the burning logs.

Standing, I walk to a window and look out over the city of Drayke in the river-cut basin below. The city is longer than it is wide, stretching the length of the valley at the base of Drayke Mountain and creeping up the slopes on either side. "It's not an order." I turn back to Stuart. "It's an idea." I need my human sorcerers to protect all my people from fae glamouring while the Tanturriff entourage is here. "If Torridaigans—especially humans—can't see through fae magic, they could have their years stolen away."

"If the fae go too far, it's murder." Stuart leans forward, his mug between his hands. "Do you really think the new queen will allow her people to do that right under your nose?"

"I have no idea what Marissa Turin will do." I've only ever seen her walk fleetingly down corridors or slip into what she probably hoped were empty rooms, never involved in her predecessor's politics or allowed into Council meetings hosted in Tanturriff's white marble halls. "But the fae are getting frantic. Waning magic means the years they siphon off others aren't as effective or long-lasting anymore."

Most fae purchase years, just like Fanghaven vampires purchase blood. There's a robust commerce, especially in the west along Tanturriff's borders with Torridaig and Ruthinock. People need money? They go into the Tanturriff city markets and wait for some weakening fae to pay them for any years they're willing to part with. Plenty of dragon shifters have gotten rich selling their seeming eternalness to fae parasites. They probably figure they have enough years not to notice the difference, and that's likely true until the end comes, and then maybe they'll regret cutting their lives short for riches.

But the youth-and-health prolonging years the fae are buying aren't lasting like they used to, and most fae are neither rich enough to keep up the endless purchasing, nor part of the traditionally nomadic gildenfae, for whom finding and mining gold—and to a lesser extent, the act of crafting items out of the precious metal—is all they need for rejuvenation.

Their clan-based society has taken them all over Ellonrift, and especially into gold-rich Torridaig. Physically working with gold provides the gildenfae with the swell of lifeforce they need to stay strong and young, and Torridaig gets its cut of the unearthed riches. But the gildenfae are a minority among the fae, disliked by many of their brethren for their independence from the cost and burden of parasitic ways. For decades now, they've been finding their native land of Tanturriff increasingly unwelcoming as many fae struggle to buy the lifeforce they need, and some turn to nefarious means.

"There's a lot more thieving going on in the west now, just like along our Bloodwold border," Stuart says sourly. "And the new queen seems powerless to stop it."

Nodding, I lean against the window ledge, the sharp bite of the evening air at my back and the warmth of my fire in front. "What's been a successful and consensual commerce since the second dawn of Ellonrift could quickly turn into as big a problem as blood raiders out for crimson gold." Once again, the blame lies with Rannigan Bloodthief triggering the decline of magic. The waning started with his murderous maneuvering to control two votes at the Ellonrift Council. If this next Council is as much of a failure as the rest, my only option is war, and if he doesn't think

I'll invade a sovereign kingdom over the people he kidnaps, he's wrong.

"I don't think I can do it," Stuart says regretfully. "I can protect you or certain individuals at a specific time, but not all of Drayke at once and for days—or even all of Drayke Mountain. Countering fae magic is a rare power to begin with. I can't spread my own magic too thin, or it won't be effective for anyone, and I don't have enough strong sorcerers with the right kind of power to make a difference."

I take another sip, absorbing that bad news along with the strong drink that helps soften the blow. "Then Marissa Turin will come to the Ellonrift Council alone."

"You'd deny the Fae Queen her entourage?" Stuart asks in shock. "Send them home at the border?"

"I'll give her a better alternative right from her own doorstep all the way to Drayke Mountain." A new plan is forming, a feasible one, and I like it. Something close to glee expands inside me. I'd already planned on offering Marissa protection in return for an alliance. "She probably can't trust her nobles anyway, especially outside her castle, where she might actually have some friends."

"So you'll give her someone she can trust?" Stuart sips his brew, leaving a hint of foam on his upper lip.

I nod. "And hopefully solidify a new friendship in the process." I could use all the allies I can get.

Unease sinks through me. If only I'd take my own advice.

"In that case, I'll put my full effort into the torque and stop worrying about anything other than dampening the Fae Queen's magic while she's here."

I nod, the scents of hearthside fires and dinners cooking down in Drayke reaching me even in my high lair. I shut the window against the mountain breeze, cutting off the smell of granite cliffs, tall pines, and the cold lake as well. The last triggers images from today's training, of shiny black hair and fierce golden eyes. The scent of spring sunshine hitting frosted ice ghosts through my nostrils, and I stop breathing for a moment, holding on to the phantom fragrance.

Reluctantly exhaling, I return to the fireside chairs with Stuart, and we finish our mugs in companionable silence, my friend lost in his own musings, and me wishing my every stray thought didn't bring me back to Idallia. Half the time, it feels like she's in the room with me, even though she's never even set foot in my lair.

Stuart stands just as the dinner bells chime far down the mountain, calling everyone to tables long and wide. I stand with him. I shouldn't still plan on eating with the team right after wishing I could distance my thoughts from Idallia, but I move toward the doorway with Stuart anyway.

"The torque is almost done. I'll give it my full attention now and have it ready by tomorrow evening." Stuart's mouth pulls down in a frown as he opens the door. I know he worries that sorcerers soon won't be able to accomplish anything of significance. He's a protector, and magic is his tool. Watching it disappear little by little must be like losing my fangs one by one and feeling my fire gradually turn cold.

"We plan on leaving the morning after tomorrow, so that's perfect," I say, following him out into the stone corridor and shutting the door behind us.

Giving me an odd look, he starts down the torchlit stairs. "Did you need something else?"

The creak in his knees makes me wince. Many dragon shifters see humans as fleeting and replaceable. They are fleeting. Never replaceable.

"Dinner." I don't add that the company tempts me more than the food.

Maybe next time, I'll dine with Stuart and Sybil.

THE TEAM'S CHATTER STOPS THE MOMENT I APPROACH the table. We've shared plenty of meals over many decades, but almost exclusively when we're away. At Drayke Mountain, everyone knows I eat alone in my lair.

Trying not to feel uncomfortable about their startled glances, I pull up a chair and sit at one end of the rectangular table. Idallia, Danica, and Wade complete the side to my right, with Idallia next to me. Maia, Arran, and Kellan take up the chairs on my left, with Kellan as far from Idallia as possible.

Annoyance rumbles through me. I know Kellan has somehow orchestrated a formation putting the men in one group and the women in another, creating a separation that only seems to exist when he's sulking over Idallia. I've disrupted his efforts by sitting at the women's side of the Elite Wing. I hope he notices.

I wave over a nearby server and ask for a platter of tonight's fare—slabs of mountain bear by the looks of Idallia's untouched dinner.

"Not hungry?" I ask her, although I know she rarely eats meat.

"I'm waiting for the cheese and fruit. Does anyone want this?" She pushes her plate toward the center of the table.

Maia, Arran, and Danica all stick forks into the thick slices of meat, leaving nothing but sauce on the platter.

"Is something going on?" Maia asks with a frown as she cuts into her extra portion.

I shake my head, feeling even more awkward about having joined them without any warning. We leave for Porthwood soon, and I'll accompany them for meals there without anyone thinking it's different. I probably should've waited.

"Nothing's wrong." I sit back in my chair, hoping my dinner arrives soon to occupy me. "Just had the urge for some company."

Wade looks down the table at me. "You'll probably be seeing too much of us soon. Who knows how long we'll have to stay in Porthwood before something actually happens."

"Could be a while," I agree, already feeling the group's focus shift to the mission and away from my odd behavior. "It could also come quickly."

"Hopefully not too quickly," Wade says with a grin. "Porthwood has excellent ale and handsome men."

Everyone chuckles, including me. Wade's good-natured disposition and natural ability to diffuse tension are two of the things I like most about him. He's not the best fighter on the team, but he plays an important role: ease maker.

"It can't take too long." Arran reaches for the bread, wordlessly giving Maia a piece before taking one for himself. She immediately starts soaking up sauce with it, just like he does. "Not with the Ellonrift Council meeting here in just a few weeks."

"That's going to be..." Danica trails off, half grimacing.

I arch a brow. "Exciting?"

"Interesting," she says with a huff of laughter. "The Council is only in Torridaig every six years, and you always send us away when it happens. I want to see what the new Fae Queen looks like. And Rexton Hale." She grins.

My hands curl into fists under the table. That man will get a seat at the Council over my dead body.

With this being what I suspect is the decisive Council—for me anyway—maybe I should consider keeping the team in residence. Either our plan to sway Rannigan's usual allies with hard evidence works or it doesn't, but my gut still tells me that our next meeting will bring the downfall of an already failing system.

"All the other kings and queens of Ellonrift bring advisors and nobles and soldiers with them." Idallia pivots in her chair, looking at me. "Why don't you?"

That might be the most direct question she's ever asked me— and maybe her way of saying she doesn't want me to send her off somewhere like I usually do. She's talking about the meetings *outside* Torridaig, though, so I answer in kind. "It's safest for everyone if I go alone."

"Not safest for *you*," she argues.

My lips curl in an unexpected smile. "Worried about me?"

She frowns. "Of course. Why not? Or do you think you're invincible?"

I shrug. "I have been so far."

"That's the worst argument I've ever heard." Irritation flits across her features just as my dinner arrives. "Besides, there's a first time for everything."

"Like you downing a plate of meat?" Arran shoots over at her with a grin.

"One's a personal—and digestive—preference," she shoots back. "The other is life or death."

"None of those advisors or nobles or soldiers attends the actual Council. They're just useless additions—like this green thing on my plate." I move the leafy intruder off my meat and set it aside. "No dragon shifter wants that."

Idallia snatches it and pops it into her mouth. "Whatever I am does."

"I've seen a lot in nearly six hundred years," I tell her with utter seriousness. "But you're the first to enjoy the garnish more than the meal."

"Maybe it's a sign of refined taste." Her golden eyes sparkle as she chews.

Her effervescence bubbles alarmingly in my chest. "Well, then, Your Supreme Tastefulness, was it good?"

"Nope." She swallows with difficulty. "I think it was grass."

The whole table bursts out laughing except for Kellan. He stares at his plate.

My smile feels like it grows from an untended garden, blooming across my face. "Thank the stars, I finally know what to feed you. Grass it is."

Idallia does her best to look aghast, barely keeping her grin from sneaking out and lighting up the room. "Don't tell me you're growing a sense of humor, Bale. It'll be like a third horn that doesn't fit your head."

Her teasing heats me like a thermal bath hitting my night-chilled scales. She finally lets her smile loose, and my mind blanks of all witty replies.

Luckily, Arran saves the silence from lasting too long. "I'll look for that third horn when we fly to Porthwood," he jokes.

"Look too closely, and you might poke out an eye," I grumble.

Arran just smiles wider, and everyone laughs, including Kellan, so I must've done something right.

After a lull in the conversation that I worry I'm supposed to fill, Danica turns the subject to Fanghaven, which might worry me even more. The second vampire kingdom is heavier in everyone's thoughts right now because of the upcoming Council. It's the same every year. "How can the Vampire Queen not have escaped Rannigan and Bloodwold by now? She's had more than two hundred years."

"What makes you think she can?" Arran asks.

"She's starborn. She must be powerful. She's a legitimate ruler from a goddess-chosen bloodline..." Danica shrugs. "Do you need more?"

All talking stops as servers arrive to clear what's left of the main course and bring platters of fruits, breads, and cheeses to the table. Idallia immediately grabs some of everything as she says, "Rannigan took her as a baby. If she's even still alive, Cealastra only knows what lies he's put in her head. She might adore him and have been so isolated from the rest of the world that she thinks he saved her from..." Her gaze flicks to me. "You, probably."

My heart thumps so hard there can't be a dragon shifter in the room who doesn't hear it. Then again, there's a lot of noise in the dining hall.

"Ugh, that's probably true." Maia's face falls as she turns to me. "If she ever appears, she might be your other number one enemy."

"Or she might learn the truth and turn on Rannigan," I counter. That would be ideal.

"*If* she's even alive—like Idallia said. I'm not convinced."

Danica takes only bread and cheese and ignores the fruit, which is mainly offered for the non-dragon shifter residents of Drayke Mountain.

"The next Council should tell you more, right?" Idallia asks me. "If there's a tied vote or violence among the rulers and Cealastra doesn't show up to weigh in, we'll know she's really gone. In that case, maybe the Fanghaven survivor is too."

"A starborn successor can't be chosen for Fanghaven if Cealastra isn't there to choose," I cautiously agree.

"Then maybe Rexton Hale will finally get what he wants," Kellan says from the far side of the table. "He can claim the throne without being starborn or Cealastra's choice."

"As long as the person upholds Fanghaven's traditions, I don't really care who's on the throne." Idallia's color has improved after eating. She looked even paler than usual before. "Blood violence isn't tolerated there, and that's what matters. They should be our allies, like they were before."

Her *our* sends an unexpected thrill through me. And I agree with her. I have no more issue with the way Fanghaven vampires procure their blood, whether it's from a vein or a cup, than I do with how the vampires in Torridaig get their food. The problem is Bloodwold, where consent doesn't matter, and kidnapping victims are sold to the highest bidders at underground blood markets and taken to households where they're fed upon until they die.

"If the Fanghaven heir ever emerges, I hope she'll be our ally," I murmur. "She and I would have a chance of keeping Rannigan Bloodthief in a cage."

"Wouldn't that be nice?" Arran sighs, handing off his empty plate.

I haven't eaten much of the dessert course and pick up a fat, purple-black fig. I hand it to Idallia, then reach for the cheese and bread.

She gives me an odd look, and my inner heat rises, flushing my neck. "Did you know I like figs?"

I don't know if I did. I just figured she would because of the color and texture. I shrug.

"Why didn't you kill Rannigan Bloodthief all those years ago?" Kellan looks right down the table at me and asks the question no one ever asks. I give him a *what-the-fuck* look, but he doesn't stop there. "He wasn't protected from firebreath back then. How did he get close enough to slice through your chest scales when you could've burned him to a crisp or bitten him clean in half?"

Even Wade gapes at Kellan, finding nothing to ease the tension this time.

"I was injured," I say flatly.

"That *was* the injury," Kellan insists. "How did he get that close? You're not like Idallia. You don't get distracted and stop paying attention in the middle of a fight."

While his statement is unfortunately true, my pulse shoots off in anger just as I hear Idallia's sharp inhalation.

"I kicked your ass today, Kellan," she snaps. "Even when I was bored to death."

He cuts her a stony look. "I didn't fight back."

"Well, then I guess that makes *you* the one not paying attention. The goal was to give me a challenge, not leave me yawning and annoyed."

His chair scrapes back, and he stands. "I have things to do tomorrow. I'll see you all the morning after for the race to the pillars."

Kellan turns to leave, and I can't help the words that catapult from my mouth. "There won't be a race. Maia flies right wing, since she was the only one to best Idallia. Idallia flies left wing, since she bested everyone else. The rest of you can work yourselves out." I lean back in my chair and cross my hands behind my head, not sure if I'm pleased with myself for stunning them all silent, or worried I'm making unprecedented decisions I can't fully explain even to myself.

I strive for humor, if only to calm my own racing heart.

"Come now. I know we're carnivores, but let's not catch flies in those open mouths."

Everyone snaps their mouth shut except for Idallia. She laughs, and I instantly crave more of the spontaneous, soul-lightening sound. She's the real reason I'm here tonight, isn't she? The reason I don't like solitude nearly as much as I used to.

Sensations from earlier today flood back to me again on a hard rush of blood. The throbbing heat of her pulse jumping up to reach me when my lips don't even touch her throat. Her scent, like bright sunshine on crisp new snow. The cold lake around us, and her battle-hot body under mine, shapely and strong.

A sense of doom settles over me as everyone finishes their meal, and I start to wish I'd just stayed alone in my lair tonight. I wonder if there's a name for a card player who keeps an ace up his sleeve for so long that he forgets what part of the game the card is meant for, and now just wants to keep it close to his skin, where it's already been for years.

CHAPTER TEN
IDALLIA

"What do you know about the fourteenth scale?" I ask my firebirds as we fly over the lake on our own after a morning training session without Bale. He told us to "get in a good workout" before disappearing somewhere, which really meant to run our asses off but not pick up a sword.

Our wing guards followed us from the sky, but our running pace is nothing compared to their speed. After a long jog around Upper Drayke Lake, my birds and I went back to our quarters so I could get cleaned up, but Embersol kept driving us all crazy with her zipping around the room. As soon as I'd bathed and put on fresh clothes, we went back out to zig and zag over the forest and lake instead of watching her bounce off the walls.

"There was no fourteenth scale," Rim answers. His reddish-gold feathers ruffle in the wind, and sparks stream off him, leaving a glowing trail. Next to him, Sol is just one little fireball, blazing from beak to tail. The joy on her face makes my heart swell.

Fyrestar banks left to follow the natural curve at the end of the lake, and I grip his sides harder with my legs to keep from sliding but leave my hands loose at my sides. The younger birds follow his lead, and the high towers of the Drayke School of Fire and Flight come into view over the treetops between us and the city of Drayke.

I hold back a shudder and look away.

"But wouldn't there have been a scale where Rannigan Bloodthief actually punctured Bale's chest? The Vampire King shredded thirteen scales, but they were still there, just too damaged to properly heal. Bale removed those scales and used them to create you birds—thirteen phoenixes. But what about right where the Vampire King pierced his chest? What about that scale?"

"The Vampire King probably destroyed it," Fyrestar says.

I grimace, a vivid image of red blood dripping from sharp, black nails suddenly invading my mind. It's real and intense, and I somehow know it's Rannigan's hand, even though I've never seen the Vampire King myself. Only Maia and Arran, the two senior members of the Elite Wing, have ever remained in Drayke during a Council meeting or have even seen the other starborn rulers of Ellonrift.

"Yeah...maybe there was just nothing left." But what if there was? If Bale and his sorcerers could make our warbirds from his thirteen damaged scales, what could the Vampire King and his sorcerers make with one?

"Would like another phoenix," Sol chirps. *"There's room in the roost."*

I think about it and decide I'm utterly complete. But love isn't finite, so I imagine I'd have loved a fourth firebird just as much as I love these three. "I'm happy just the way we are."

But being happy doesn't stop the usual questions from pushing into my head. Having a real family now doesn't mean I won't continue to wonder who and *what* my birth parents were, and why they gave me up.

We fly around Upper Drayke Lake and the forest beyond

Drayke Mountain until Embersol cools down. When she finally does, she goes from a baby's boundless energy to barely keeping her eyes open, and Fyrestar and I have to carry her home.

I'M ON THE MID-MOUNTAIN TERRACE ENJOYING THE sunshine, autumn views, and a bit of alone time. It's quiet and peaceful until Bale flies over the stone railing, scaring me half to death.

"Blazing stars." My hand flies to my chest. "One second there's nothing but blue sky and then..." I wave my hand at the huge black-and-crimson dragon in front of me. "You."

Bale transforms with a frown already firmly in place, his booted feet carrying him toward me after his scales and fangs recede. "Stay vigilant, and nothing will startle you."

"This is literally the safest place in Ellonrift," I toss back, my pulse still thumping like dragon wings. "I thought I could let my guard down."

"You were half asleep out in the open. That's never a good idea."

"Fine. Sorry, Your Majesty. It won't happen again."

His eyes narrow at my tone, and shadows swirl over his skin like thunderclouds creeping over a mountain.

"Bring Rimblaze with you to Porthwood tomorrow. He'll be your wing guard."

I gape in shock. "He's not ready. He hasn't passed his tests." Did I think my heart was pounding before? Now it's *violent*. "And who'll look after Sol while Fyrestar and I are gone?"

"Embersol is perfectly capable of hunting by herself and flying back through the right window to go home." His expression softens. "But don't worry. Rimblaze isn't coming to fight. I just want him to stretch his wings and see how he does on a substantial flight."

My throat tight with expanding fear, I rasp, "Because you think he's almost ready to fly into battle again?"

"We'll see." Bale looks past my shoulder, his expression hardening again, and whoever just walked out onto the sun terrace must turn around and leave. I hear the footsteps fade.

"Convincing Rim *not* to join a fight that's right in front of him is going to be nearly impossible." I'm supposed to have nerves of steel—and usually do—but right now, I quake like a reed. It's been almost sixteen years since I had to worry about Rim, and three since I had to worry about Sol. As much as they could help me in battle, I'd rather not see them fight at all.

I hide my trembling hands behind my back, but I doubt there's any hiding the dread and panic lancing through me, my skin suddenly bloodless and cold.

Bale's sharp gaze flicks over me. "You know they can come back." He might almost reach for me. I'm not sure. All I know is that even the *potential* of a touch from his big, capable hand doesn't help my thrashing heart.

"Can they? What if Cealastra is really gone, and that kind of magic went with her?" My fear is so real that stars splatter across my vision. Abruptly, I sit, but the only seats on the terrace are low, lounging chairs, and I pop up again, swaying. I'm not going to recline while the Dragon King looms over me.

"Sit." Bale pushes me back down with a firm but gentle hand. He steps to the side so he's not shading me. "Get some sunlight. It'll help."

I nod jerkily as I swing my legs up and lie back in the chair. The afternoon rays warm my iced-over skin and do seem to help. "I know I should be excited for Rim and encourage him. You think he's almost ready. *He* thinks he's ready. I don't know why I don't."

"It's normal to want to protect those you love. It's..." He trails off, his mouth thinning.

"Human?" I supply sarcastically. "Because we all know I'm not."

"Universal," he finishes, his gaze shifting away from me.

My frustration rises like a flash flood. "You're ancient. You've really never encountered anyone like me? I look human, but I'm too fast, strong, and old. I have no magic, no shifting ability, no thirst for blood..."

He swivels back to me, scowling. "I'm not ancient. And isn't there magic in the way you fight? When you're focused, you're nearly unbeatable."

"*When* I'm focused," I grumble. "And *nearly* doesn't count. If you were my enemy, you could still burn me up from a distance unless I had some of that Bloodwold magic."

"Why would I be your enemy?" he mutters.

"I don't know. I just want to know where I come from. I want to know why I'm...alone in the world."

Fire glints in his eyes. "You're not alone. Just because you're different doesn't mean you're by yourself. As for the rest, I'm sure you'll find out someday, and then we'll see how your stars align."

I stare at him, all sound except his slightly accelerated breathing becoming a low hum in my ears. "Why would you be sure? It's been two hundred and twenty-six years. I think I'd already know something about my origins if I was ever going to."

He sits across from me, perching on the edge of another lounging chair. His knees come up too far, and he looks uncomfortable. Terraces like this were built for the human population of the mountain to get outdoors and enjoy the fresh air. "Life is long, Idallia. There's still time for surprises—good and bad."

Huffing, I turn away from him. "Cryptic and depressing. I see you haven't lost your touch."

His low growl washes over me, raising goose bumps. I probably shouldn't talk to Bale the way I do. He's my king and my team leader. My inability to be passive or blindly obedient didn't do me any favors at school, but it got me into the Elite Wing. Bale has never told me to bite my tongue, so I've just kept saying what I wanted and swinging for blood. This might be the first time I've come close to truly insulting him, though, and guilt rises along with embarrassed heat.

I turn back to him, my lips rolled in.

"I've been called a lot of things, but cryptic and depressing is a first." He doesn't look pleased.

"I call you cryptic all the time." I pause. "In my head."

Bale's dark eyebrows creep up his forehead. "In your head?"

Oh, damn the stars. Did I just admit to thinking about Bale more than I should? "You know...passing thoughts. What's for dinner? Where are my swords? Bale's cryptic..." Ugh, I'm just making this worse.

"And depressing," he adds wryly.

I sit up straighter. "You just smiled. I saw it, and you can't take it back."

His white teeth flash just before he turns his head. "Maybe there's another kind of people in Ellonrift."

Dragon shifters, humans, vampires, werebeasts, and fae. "Wait." I swing my legs off the lounge chair and face Bale. "What if whatever I am survived the meteors? What if my lineage goes back to the first dawn of Ellonrift?" Cealastra doesn't just create. She burns to the ground. "Bones still turn up sometimes from before the destruction. They all look human, but maybe they were whatever I am?"

Bale shakes his head. "And where would this whole group of unknown beings have been hiding for all this time?"

"I don't know. Maybe wherever I'm from."

His expression darkens. "You're from Torridaig. Why isn't that ever enough?" His rough tone surprises me, and he abruptly stands.

"That's easy for you to say. You know exactly who you are." I stand, too, and gesture wildly with my arms as if showing him every last corner of Torridaig. "Your grandfather was the first starborn ruler of the dragon-shifter clans. Your father came after him and united the people at the heart of Ellonrift. Then you came—very late in your parents' lives, just when everyone was starting to panic about there not being a starborn heir—and got to draw the lines of your own kingdom. It's all recorded history. Where's *my* recorded history? I want to know!"

"So easily angered." Bale reaches out and pins my still flailing arms to my sides. I gasp when he steps right up to me, and I tilt my head back to find him staring down at me with hard eyes. "Why don't you save your flapping hands and endless abandonment rage for someone who deserves it. All I did was give you a job and a home."

"Give me?" I snarl back. "Didn't I earn my place?"

His whole face shuts down. "And your other home is Glarraden. You want your recorded history? It starts there, and maybe you don't want to know anything else. Maybe there's no one left to find."

My jaw drops as he lets go and turns away from me. In an eddy of shadows, he shifts and leaps over the wall. His tail thumps the air near my face, and I flinch away from it. There's no way he didn't control that precise action and wouldn't have hit me, but I feel the sharp warning cut through me nonetheless. When we dig too deep, sometimes all we uncover are bones.

I stumble back and sit again, shaken. *Endless abandonment rage.* Tears prick my eyes.

Abandoned? Or the last of my kind?

And why do Bale's angry guesses always sound like information I should already have?

CHAPTER ELEVEN
IDALLIA

After dinner, I flop down on my bed, arms out, an apple in my hand. It rolls from my slack fingers and thuds to the ground.

Fyrestar is the first to poke his beak out of the roosting wall. *"What did you do now?"*

I lift my head. He looks sleepy. None of his feathers glow. "Why is it my fault?"

"Is it?"

Sighing, I let my head fall back, a weight in my chest and uncomfortable memories stirring. "Maybe."

Rim hops forward and launches off the ledge. He flies to the bed. *"I doubt it."*

Smiling with a mixture of melancholy and comfort, I wrap an arm around his solid body as he settles next to me. "That's kind of you to say, but I wasn't very nice to Bale earlier." I chew the inside of my lip. "In my defense, he was being weird."

Little Embersol staggers to the edge of the roosts, and Fyrestar unfolds a wing to keep her from falling. Her amber eyes only half open, she croaks a sleepy sound.

Love strikes my chest like a lightning bolt. "You should've stayed in your nest."

Ignoring that, she flutters down to me and settles into the crook of my other arm. What Rim has, Sol wants—and vice versa most of the time. *"Bale. Good king. Dad."* Her eyes immediately close again.

Mine widen. That's the first time any of my birds have referred to the Dragon King as *Dad*. "Why did you say that?" I ask.

"I hear the other little ones talking," she mumble-coos, her words slowing down. *"They have dads."*

By "other little ones," I know she means the residents of Drayke Mountain and not the other warbirds. Only Danica has a young phoenix right now anyway, and her youngest is closer to Rim's age than to Sol's.

"I didn't," I murmur. Gerard was something, but he wasn't a dad. Dads praise your efforts and sit you on their knees. Dads are interested when you talk to them and don't look right over your head or vaguely tell you to come back later when they're not busy.

A familiar ache spreads through me. I wish it wasn't so real, that hole where all sorts of good memories should be. I have everything I need now, so why do I even care? And despite Rita and Gerard seeing straight through me most of the time, they never abandoned me like my birth parents did.

I squeeze both birds a little closer. Sol's already asleep again, and Rim tucks his beak into the fold of his wing, closing his eyes.

Fyrestar lands at the foot of the bed. *"What did you argue about?"*

It takes a moment to pull it all together in my head. I'm not even sure why those raised voices and heated words even happened now, but I think I didn't help. "It was all really sudden." I sigh. I want more from Bale than I can have, so maybe

I tend to lash out at him unfairly sometimes. "What I am, I guess."

"What *you are doesn't matter. It's* who *you are that counts.*"

My throat thickens. "I know that's what I'm supposed to think, but somehow, I can never convince myself."

"*What did Bale say?*"

It's hard to answer at first. Finally, in a hoarse voice, I manage, "He told me to get over my abandonment rage."

Flames flare in Fyrestar's eyes. He clicks his beak, angrier than I've seen him in a long time. "*You might not need the people who left you, but that doesn't mean some answers wouldn't be nice.*"

I nod. That sums it up perfectly. I stare at the ceiling and its rough, jagged rock. The floor and walls are rock, too, but smoother. The whole room is a big cave carved into the mountainside, with elaborate roosts carved even deeper into the thick peak. It's getting cold now that autumn has set in.

I shiver, even with three phoenixes surrounding me and providing their inner heat. Maybe Bale is right, and I should get a rug or two. Glarraden House is full of them. Rugs, tapestries, knick-knacks, paintings, sculptures...So many sculptures. The collection is Gerard's pride and joy, but I always hated all those expressionless faces and empty eyes staring me down when I could barely get a real person to look at me.

I don't want extra stuff here because there was always too much there. If I'm still alive when Rita and Gerard finally fade from life and return to the stars, I'm going to empty the whole house and start over with just my birds.

From out of nowhere, the feel of Bale on top of me in the shallows of the lake rushes back and heats my blood.

Closing my eyes, I push out a frustrated groan. It's not as easy to expel the memory of his warm breath on my neck, his big hands circling my arms, his body holding mine down, or the almost teasing rumble in his voice. *And you're dead.*

Just what every woman wants to hear.

The thought of retiring to Glarraden House one day with my

phoenixes used to be enough, but now Bale—with his smoldering eyes, rescuing ways, and spirited conversations—keeps pushing into my long-term dreams like someone knocking on the door who just won't give up.

A knock sounds at the door right on the heels of that thought, and I twitch, my eyes flying open. Sol tweets a little snore.

I carefully extract myself from the tangle of birds on my bed, not wanting to wake her or Rim. Rim especially needs his sleep before the big flight tomorrow morning. Fyrestar watches me move across the room.

Quietly opening the door, I find Sybil on the other side, looking winded and holding out a wide silver neck cuff. It's not a full circle and leaves an opening, the metal sturdy but thin enough to bend.

"I know it's late." She dabs sweat from her forehead, breathing hard from the steep climb up to the Elite Wing level. "But Stuart just finished your torque and fell into an exhausted sleep, so I brought it up for him as fast as I could."

I frown. "What do you mean? I don't think I know what you're talking about."

She looks as startled as I feel. "Bale asked him to make something to protect your neck from Bloodwold vampires, and we know you leave tomorrow at dawn. The magic was taxing, and Stuart only just finished."

Worry thumps inside me. "Is Stuart all right?"

She waves off my concern. "He just needs a good night's sleep. He'll be fine tomorrow. The important thing was getting this done in time for the stakeout."

I motion her inside and shut the door. "Bale asked him to make this?" Bale mentioned protecting my neck but hadn't said anything since. I hadn't really thought about it again, but I should've known Bale wouldn't forget, and I hate the hot shock that arcs across my chest. The giddy explosion feels like the impending death of good intentions and smart decisions as Sybil and I walk over to my two chairs and sit.

She leans toward me with the torque, and I lift my hair so she can slip it around my neck. She squeezes the shiny metal band closed to lock it into place, then settles back in her chair. "I thought Bale would've told you. It's a start. If it works like it should, we'll probably make similar torques for the whole Elite Wing."

Lifting my hand, I touch the metal. It's about three fingers wide and should protect a good portion of my neck without inhibiting movement. "The silver feels warm." And a little jarring and unpleasantly tingly, though I don't add that. I don't want her to think I'm ungrateful, especially if making this protection wore Stuart out so much that he collapsed into bed. Besides, the discomfort isn't anything I can't live with, and I'm all for shielding my neck. "So how does it work?"

She looks smug, though I know it's on Stuart's behalf. "If a vampire fang even touches this, it'll disintegrate and never grow back."

I grin, still rubbing my fingertips over the heated metal. "Well done, Stuart." That sounds fantastic, though it's going to take some time to settle into the feel of the cursed silver around my neck. "No fangs, no bites."

Sybil's face loses the elasticity of its earlier smile. "It won't really change anything," she says softly. "They can still drain their blood captives, just not the same way."

I reach over and grip her hand. She looks older this way, but that's what grief does to you, even after decades. Not long after Sybil came to Drayke Mountain, her youngest sister was taken from their hometown in Ruthinock in a blood-trafficking raid. The poor girl was still a child. She was never seen again.

"How can they get away with it?" Sybil asks angrily. "Everyone knows what's happening, and yet time and again, Bloodwold vampires take what they want."

"Only if they don't get caught," I say darkly. Torridaig has a fierce army protecting its borders. Soldiers from the local garrisons often kill raiding vampires and retrieve the prisoners. But sometimes, the vampires slip over the border and into their elaborate tunnel system leading into Hellwood Forest before anyone even knows they came and went.

As for raids into Ruthinock, the blood-thieving vampires usually move back and forth through Fanghaven. Rexton Hale's army isn't consolidated or big enough to cover the whole road system, and the rough terrain along the Silver Moon Mountains leaves more holes and hiding places than a werefox's den for the predatory vampires to sneak around in.

Hopefully, the upcoming stakeout will put us ahead of a raid and earn us some Bloodwold prisoners. The cowardly Were King will have a harder time throwing his vote into Rannigan's lap with hard evidence of Rannigan's crimes staring the Ellonrift Council in the face.

"Why doesn't Cealastra react?" Sybil asks—mostly a rhetorical question. I don't know more than she does.

Because she's dead, my gut whispers to me, anxiety abruptly tightening everything under my skin. "Cealastra hasn't done anything obvious in decades. And even before that, eclipses were increasingly spaced out."

"It started with the Fanghaven murders."

I nod. Rannigan Bloodthief now votes for himself *and* his wife, and the Were King votes with Rannigan to be left in peace. The fae do the same, knowing Bale's not an unhinged monster who'll come after them for no reason, which leaves him—and all of Torridaig—in the lurch. Torridaig and Ruthinock always ally, but they can't counter that bigger block, and Cealastra doesn't weigh in unless there's a tied vote.

Maybe there's hope with the new Fae Queen coming to her first Council. If Bale can get her on his side and force a tied vote, Cealastra will either show up—or prove to everyone that she's really gone.

"I'm pretty sure the usefulness of the Ellonrift Council is

coming to an end." I rub a finger over the torque again. The magic in it feels like a hot-cold current pricking at my skin. "It's about intimidation instead of fairness now, and Cealastra clearly isn't keeping Rannigan's lies and bullying in check. The only reason the Council ever worked was because the Star of Ellonrift was watching and guiding, but now, she either isn't around or doesn't care."

Slowly nodding, Sybil agrees with a long, troubled sigh. "If things keep up this way, Bale will retaliate. He'll do what needs to be done, with or without the Council's support."

"I don't know why he doesn't back Rexton Hale's claim to the Fanghaven throne. He'd get that historic alliance back and force a tied vote." Wouldn't that be better than all-out war?

"And force Cealastra to appear," Sybil adds.

I press my lips together, not wanting to scare her with my dire feeling about the goddess. No one really knows if she's still with us or not. Up until a couple of centuries ago, the often-tied votes used to compel Cealastra to choose sides. Ever since the Vampire King orchestrated for that to never happen, Bloodwold does what it wants.

Maybe Cealastra is dead. Or maybe she deserted us.

The echo of Bale's voice shudders through me, tearing a frayed edge off my heart. *Endless abandonment rage.* I clear my throat.

"What are your plans while I'm gone?" I ask, changing the subject.

Sybil seems to perk up, the worry of war easily lifted from her shoulders. "Just teaching and sorting the new recruits. Magic isn't as strong in anyone these days, but at least they all want to come to Torridaig if they're willing to leave home."

I nod, still bothered by the odd, prickly feel of the silver torque but not willing to show it. The lessening of magic all over Ellonrift has already been impacting Ruthinock for a long time. Humans rely on sorcery to protect their kingdom. With less and weaker magic overall, the people of Ruthinock are more cooperative than ever with Bale, relying on him to keep them safe from fae parasites and vampire thirst.

"Will you and Stuart keep the newcomers here or spread them out?" I ask.

Yawning, Sybil leans her head against the back of the chair. "A bit of both. We'll decide with Bale after the Council is over."

At least Bale doesn't seem as alone in ruling as when I first got here.

I finally can't help it and tug at the cuff around my neck, loosening it.

"Is the torque bothering you?" Sybil frowns.

"It was just a little tight." The looser band is still prickly and warm, but since I was verging on cold, I decide to take the heat where I can get it. I also pull my bare feet up off the floor. The stones feel icier than usual, probably because a certain someone put the idea in my head that I need rugs and other things around. If Bale had just minded his own business, my feet wouldn't be cold.

Sybil spots the apple I dropped and leans down to pick it up off the floor. "Did you want this?"

I shake my head. "It's probably one big bruise now."

"I'll get rid of it on my way out."

"Thanks." I'd offer it to my birds, but they're hearty carnivores, just like their *dad*.

Grimacing, I sit up straighter, a stray thought hitting me like a battering ram. "Can I ask you something?"

She cocks her head. "Of course."

"I don't seem to fit the profile of anyone else in Ellonrift. What if I'm all alone? As in, *the only one* like me. Do you think that means I can't reproduce if I want to?"

Her graying brows arch in surprise. "Are you feeling the urge to nest?"

I laugh. "I'm not a bird."

"To mate, then?"

I think Sybil's been at Drayke Mountain too long. She sounds like a true Torridaigan. "I'm clearly not a dragon shifter, either. I think we'd know by now."

Her lips twitch at my tone. Smoothing her thumb over the red skin of the apple, she asks, "All right, then, tell me this. How careful were you when you were with Kellan?"

I glance at Fyrestar—the only one still awake. He closes his golden eyes and tucks his beak under his wing, clearly trying to give me privacy. It doesn't change a thing, but I appreciate the effort.

"Careful enough," I finally answer.

Sybil's snort makes Rim jolt in his sleep. "*Careful enough* isn't usually what I suggest when people come to the healer's level for protection. And before Kellan?"

I shake my head. "There wasn't anyone else."

"Even at school?"

Now it's *my* snort that makes all the birds jump. Fyrestar lifts his head, his gaze conveying sympathy and love. "You know I was a pariah. The gildenfae-gold kid."

Sybil's expression hardens on my behalf, my past no secret to her. "Well, that's their loss. As for the rest, I honestly don't know. You seem physically compatible with anyone in Ellonrift, in my opinion, but unless you decide you want to be a mother and actively start trying to make that happen, it's hard to know. And sometimes, even when you're compatible and trying, children just don't come along."

Blazing heat sets my face on fire and makes the odd tingle from the torque even worse. "I'm so sorry, Sybil. That was insensitive of me. I shouldn't have asked."

She waves off my apology. "I don't expect you to never talk about maybe wanting or having children just because I couldn't have them."

I nod but still feel terrible. I lived through all the years of false hope and disappointment with her. "I'm lucky to have a friend like you." My eyes suddenly sting, but when I shut them to stave off tears, I see a flash of Sybil turning to wrinkles and then to dust.

I jerk my eyes open. I don't know why I have these visions, but I never tell Sybil how often I see her death, just like I saw Everly's every day until it came to pass.

They feel like my nightmares, only I'm awake, and instead of showing me odd shadows of the past mixed with things I don't recognize, I see a future I can't change. At least Sybil is old in my visions, unlike Everly, who died too young.

Sybil stands. "It's late, and I'm ready for bed. You should rest too. I know you leave at dawn."

I get up and follow her to the door. "Take care while I'm gone. And tell Stuart thank you." I touch the torque again, finally getting used to it. It's less hot and stinging now.

"I will, but it was Bale's idea."

My chest contracts, squeezing my heart. "Why start with me? Against Bloodwold raiders, everyone fights in skin."

She gives me a penetrating look. "Why, indeed?"

Heat sweeps through me. "Are you implying something?"

"*Should* I be?" I must look like a rodent caught in a hungry phoenix's gaze, because she shakes her head, laughing softly. "It's just my wishful thinking. Bale is too alone and barely willing to lean on anyone. And you're highly capable and every single male dragon shifter's dream."

I huff a laugh, ignoring the fire building inside me like a fever burning through my veins. "They can keep on dreaming. It's the single life for me."

"You won't be testing any compatibility theories with that attitude," she teases as she opens the door.

Grinning, I playfully roll my eyes at her. My face falls the second she's gone, not only because she's right, but because my now wildly beating heart is drumming Bale's name in my ears.

CHAPTER TWELVE

BALE

The Elite Wing is more subdued than usual as we set out for the northeast of Torridaig. Did I make a mistake by eliminating the usual race to the pillars? No challenge, no pumping blood, no rivalry? For my right and left wings today, it probably feels boring and undeserved to step into a position without fighting for it, and while Maia probably isn't bothered, we all know Idallia loses interest when she isn't *losing*.

Flying on my left wing, Idallia is quiet and visibly troubled this morning. As usual, the team takes its cues from her. If she's quiet, they're quiet. If she's worked up, their energy reflects her mood. She holds out the palm of her hand, and everyone jumps into it.

Including me.

My lips pull back in irritation, baring my fangs to the cold wind. I call forth more inner heat to counter the high mountain air, since my expression remains grim.

Isn't that what I trained her for? Leadership?

But what about the hard decisions? The ones your heart doesn't want to make but your head knows you must.

I glance at Rimblaze. His feathers glow hot and bright, and he looks overjoyed to finally be flying at Fyrestar's side again.

Idallia looks the opposite. Is she angry? She's definitely upset. Rimblaze is flying out on a mission with us for the first time since his rebirth, and she obviously didn't like my imposing that yesterday, panic surging across her face like a wildfire she couldn't put out. But Rimblaze is ready, and I've already been holding back on giving him his final tests simply to avoid that awful look on Idallia's face.

Because we've all seen it before—and far worse. When Embersol took so long to come back three years ago, and we all started to doubt, I think she nearly died of grief.

Her vampire-repelling torque flashes in my eyes, but she hasn't looked at me once. The way she paled on the mountain terrace yesterday twists inside me again, but these are warbirds, and war is one more failed Council meeting away. I need everyone who can fight, and Rimblaze is ready.

I glance behind me at the rest of the team. It doesn't help that Kellan is throwing his renewed sullenness into everything. He'll be off on a mission by himself soon, though, and I'm counting on the break helping to calm the tension that's been growing ever since he carried Idallia home.

The memory of her wrapping herself around his dragon's body and clinging to his back slices through me. I quickly push the stab of jealousy aside, hoping to actually be rid of it this time. The last thing I need right now is to think like a man instead of a king. I've already been doing too much of that for too long.

My frustrated, fire-licked snarl is loud enough to make Fyrestar turn his head. Our gazes meet, his igniting in question. The wind whistling past shouts at me to answer, even as my gut and the dragon I am both tell me to shut the fuck up and not lose what I have.

Sick with the same indecision that's plagued me for decades, I break eye contact with Fyrestar and turn back to the horizon. Bloodwold is dead ahead.

Those golden eyes—the only phoenix to have them. Does Idallia never suspect why? Does Fyrestar?

The early morning sun blazing in my eyes might not burn away my worries, but it helps drive them to the back of my mind. So does the beauty of Torridaig as the central mountainous forests give way to a moorland terrain of snaking, silver rivers and wild, gorse-and-heather-dotted hillsides. Hamlets break up the landscape, few and far between. Southern Torridaig is much tamer and more populated, especially around the lake country. Today's flight to the east will soon take us toward cultivated land and larger settlements as these rough uplands turn into grassy valleys and swaths of trees, but here, the craggy, wild terrain rolls endlessly below, the air stirs the soul, the light fills it, and the warm, bright sunshine feels far holier than any distant, cold light of the stars.

We reach the city of Porthwood by midday and land at the local garrison. Rimblaze shows signs of fatigue, but that's to be expected. He hasn't flown this far in one go in his current lifetime, and our pace was the same as usual—blistering.

I meet with Titan James, the commander of Porthwood's soldiers, and explain our mission to him while the team settles their wing guards into a large inner courtyard with several good perching trees.

Titan's office feels small and confined after being in the sky all morning. "I know you usually pursue instantly if you think you can recover any of our people before blood traffickers cross into Bloodwold, but I need you to hold off this time—at least while we're here."

"Hold off?" He frowns at me.

"Have your soldiers keep close watch at night, as usual, but if they see anything suspicious, they need to go straight to the nearest member of the Elite Wing." I tell him where the team will be positioned around the city, waiting in case of news. "Don't raise the alarm. Whatever you do, keep quiet and be discreet. We want to catch thieving vampires in the act and take them prisoner before they reach the border."

He nods, understanding the strategy. "Got it. Don't let them know we're coming."

"*We're* coming," I emphasize. "All you and your soldiers need to do is keep a sharp eye out and alert the squadron to anything worrisome, even if it's just a hunch."

"I don't enjoy raising false alarms," he says hesitantly.

"I don't enjoy losing my people to bloodsucking thieves. I don't care how many false alarms you might raise. There will be one that's real, and that's all we need."

I wonder for a moment if I've offended Titan with my tone and the clear exclusion of his garrison, who've been dealing with this problem for a long time, but his jaw just firms in determination. "I'll let my soldiers know. But if you need us to step in, we'll be ready."

Grateful, I grip his shoulder. "I know you will be. You've saved many lives over the years." At least half the time, local garrisons along the Bloodwold border recover the victims before it's too late, through battle or otherwise. If it's a question of getting caught or killed by dragon shifters—or by the rising sun—blood traffickers will often abandon their captives and run.

"We captured two Bloodwold scum recently, but they killed themselves before we could get them into prison." His mouth thinning, Titan shakes his head. "They're more afraid of their own king's wrath than of yours."

Huffing sourly, I wonder when I stopped being the most terrifying thing around. Not that I enjoyed the reputation, but it was mine.

Actually, I know when. The change happened a bit more than two centuries ago, when I started trying to protect fucking *everyone* after the Vampire King murdered an entire starborn royal family in cold blood.

Except for one. He spared her life to steal her vote. *The Bloodthief Bride.* A hard smile almost curves my mouth.

"Taking prisoners is our focus now," I reiterate. "Capture—and make sure they don't kill themselves."

We don't even know if a raid will happen in Porthwood or anywhere else. Incidents are irregular, unpredictable, and happen in different places—sometimes not even in Torridaig. Coming here is nothing more than a logical guess as to where blood traffickers might strike next, one I hope will pan out and help us stand against Rannigan Bloodthief at the upcoming Council.

Or...My stomach dives to the floor. There *is* another way to thwart him. The best way of all.

The dragon in me instantly roars in protest. Shadows creep under my skin—hot, feral magic reminding me that dragons gather and keep. We don't let our treasures go.

Torn straight down the middle, I gruffly add, "We can stay in Porthwood for several days, but not indefinitely. If something doesn't happen soon, we'll have to move on."

Titan's expression turns grimmer than ever, and I fear I look the same. "I've never hoped for a raid before. It doesn't feel right."

"I know what you mean." I start toward the door, wanting to get back to the team. "But I don't plan on letting anyone cross the border and slip into the tunnels. If traffickers come, we'll stop them."

"Those fucking tunnels," Titan growls.

I couldn't agree more, an answering growl rumbling in my throat. Not long after Rannigan introduced the magic to counter our firebreath, he began riddling the whole border on his side from northeastern Torridaig to Fanghaven with tunnels he claims are "a mining operation" and that open again under the cover of Hellwood Forest. It's absurd. Gildenfae brave enough to cross the border and sniff around have confirmed there's nothing of value under that land. The real purpose of Rannigan's tunnels is to get his raiders and their captives underground and behind locked doors the second they reach Bloodwold. Safe from the sun, and safe from my army.

Though not for much longer. I'll be making my own demands during the Council, whether I have the votes to back me or not. He stops all blood raids, or I stop respecting our goddess-approved borders. Then we'll see who's more terrifying.

I give Titan a parting nod, and he nods back, confident in me and the Elite Wing. As I leave his office, that hard smile finally curves my mouth, so devoid of humor it makes me wonder to what depths I could fall if I let myself. I don't think I've ever felt more hate in my nearly six-hundred-year life than when that smug bastard dug his tunnels right in front of my face. Rannigan Bloodthief must know I could've killed him the night he murdered the Fanghaven royals, and maybe I should have.

Instead, I made a choice that gave me the worst injury of my existence and gave Rannigan the precious seconds he needed to slither away. It was all instinct and reaction, preservation more important than punishing. I saved a life instead of taking two.

That's the exact moment he became the more fearsome beast. I'm itching to take the title back.

I FIND THE TEAM AGAIN, AND WHILE WE WON'T GO OUR separate ways yet, I want to pair them off for later. I need to spread us out around Porthwood without leaving anyone alone or vulnerable.

Standing in a sunny patch of the courtyard, Idallia seems in a better mood, maybe because Rimblaze is undeniably cheerful and fluttering around her and Fyrestar with energy that can only come from sheer excitement.

The tension in my jaw unlocks. Seeing the three of them, her smiling and her birds glowing, makes my chest pull tight.

The desire to be a part of that draws me toward them, but

then reality hits, and I remember I've been keeping all the secrets she wants to know, and flat-out lying to her when she asks.

I don't regret even half these years of silence. Anonymity was key to her safety, and no one knowing the truth meant that no one could slip up and put her in danger, not even Idallia herself. But what's my reason now? Still? She's mature, skilled, ready, and wants to know.

The sharp twist in my chest knows the answer. I don't want to lose her.

Stopping, I turn away and clear my throat to get everyone's attention. The team moves toward me, waiting for orders. The warbirds fly into the trees and listen from above.

"Maia and Arran, you and your wing guards will hide out in the bell tower over the market square. You'll have a good view of central Porthwood and can see anything that moves in the main part of the city." I pair them together because they're so in tune with each other that they fight better as a duo than they do with anyone else on the team.

"Wade and Danica," I continue. "You and your warbirds will take the south entrance of the city, but don't go into the tower with the local soldiers. Find a spot not too far outside the city walls and hide out, watching for movement." They're also a natural pairing, not because of any repressed feelings, but because they're as thick as thieves and always have been. Danica's dark-brown skin and black hair will blend into the night even better away from the city torches, though Wade will just have to hope no one spots his lighter hair and features.

I turn to the two who are left and feel an odd thump of satisfaction when Idallia looks as though her stomach just dropped straight through her and hit the ground. She glances nervously at Kellan, but she doesn't need to worry. There's no way under the stars I'd pair her with him, especially with the way he's been acting.

"Kellan, you take the mid-city lookout point on the east wall facing Bloodwold with your wing guards and the local soldiers positioned there." Kellan looks disappointed but nods. He glances furtively at Idallia.

If anything, she looks just as distressed as before. "You're with me on the upper outskirts of the city," I tell her. "I want us stationed in the woods in case anyone tries to circle down from the north, and I also want to keep an eye on Rimblaze." This is his first mission and chance of real combat in this lifetime. I need him where I can see him.

Biting her lip, Idallia nods once and turns away. The surroundings suddenly seem dull without her golden eyes watching me.

I take in the team, wondering if I'm keeping Idallia away from Kellan, or keeping her with me.

Shoving the uncomfortable thought aside, I say, "We won't have much to do during the days, so this'll be a good occasion for some one-on-one training. Keep sharp and keep in shape. Kellan, you can spar with the local soldiers. They'll be honored."

Kellan's eyes narrow. He looks back and forth between Idallia and me, but what does he expect? I paired her with me, so she'll train with me.

"Sounds good." Maia tucks some hair back into her bun. It's rare she has a lock out of place, a testament to how fast we flew here.

"We have hours until sundown." Idallia turns back to me, her brows lifting in question. "What should we do until then?"

"Eat." Wade grabs his stomach, and it rumbles loudly to punctuate. He grins.

Idallia's spontaneous laughter heats me all over. "I could use some food," she agrees, grinning back at him.

I nod, a dragon-deep rasp slipping into my voice. "A meal, then rest." As intensely aware of Idallia as ever, I'm only cautiously optimistic at this point about my ability to eat, sleep, and train normally over the upcoming days. "We'll be awake all night keeping watch, so some daytime sleep should be a priority for everyone. I know of an inn with a tavern and rooms above the restaurant."

"What about the warbirds?" Idallia asks, her gaze flitting to the branches the phoenixes occupy.

"They can stay here in the garrison courtyard and clear the place of rodents for their lunches. We'll come back for them at sunset."

Everyone seems satisfied with the plan, if not with the pairings, and we leave the garrison and make our way toward the inn. Walking through the streets of Porthwood takes twice as long as it should as crowds gather. I doubt I'd go unnoticed, and I definitely don't with the entire Elite Wing. We draw gazes that range from curious to proud to fearful. They don't fear *us*, but our presence here suggests lurking danger and possible violence. Hopefully, it also speaks of my commitment to my people, to protect and avenge.

Porthwood is a city mostly of dragon shifters, humans, and weres. There are vampires too—ones who live by rules *I* can live with. The fae are scarce here, though with the gold mines of Tyburn and Millburn nearby, some gildenfae regularly travel in and out, buying supplies or selling jewelry and other decorative items they've crafted out of gold.

More and more gildenfae choosing to migrate to Torridaig instead of digging up and increasing Tanturriff's wealth didn't help my efforts to make a fae alliance at the Ellonrift Council. But now, we've just had our first death among the starborn rulers since the Fanghaven massacre. The previous Fae Queen is gone, and her daughter might need my protection more than she wants her kingdom's untapped gold.

If I can get Marissa Turin to align with me at the next Council, there's sure to be a tied vote on something that'll heat the room to violence and force Cealastra out of her isolation. Even if the Star of Ellonrift doesn't side with me, maybe it'll at least rouse an eclipse from her and renew magic across the continent.

Embersol's last rebirth sneaks into my thoughts again, those sparks circling endlessly without condensing into living form. I'll never not feel a pit of dread open inside me at the memory of Idallia during that time, her fear, her desperate tears, Fyrestar and Rimblaze with her every second of the ordeal. And I remember thinking no one in my entire existence has ever loved me the way she loves those birds. Or the way they love her.

Doubt twists my insides, fully ruining my appetite as the inn comes into view. Maybe I should've left Rimblaze at home?

We step into the tavern, leaving the curious stares of passersby behind and gaining new ones from the people inside. The slate board mostly advertises dishes a dragon shifter would want, but it's the meatless meals I specifically came here for.

Idallia's eyes brighten at the choices, and she immediately orders her meal along with a mug of ale. Salad greens and cheesy potatoes. As I expected.

My earlier worries lessen, and I order braised bear. Not werebear. We're carnivores, not cannibals. Plus, there's the werepoison to worry about.

Finding a table, we wait for our food in companionable silence, mugs of ale already in hand. Unsurprisingly, it's Kellan who speaks first, a hint of challenge in his tone.

"If we're spread out, we're not fighting as a team." He slowly sips from his mug. "The last time we were separated, it didn't go well."

Idallia drops her gaze and fidgets with the spoon in front of her. I suddenly see her pinned down, about to have her throat ripped out by that weretiger, and I barely stifle a snarl.

"We can't cover the whole city without dividing up." I sip from my mug just as deliberately as he did. "Remember, our goal isn't to stop blood thieves from rounding people up. It's to catch them before they make it into the Bloodwold tunnels. If you see something suspicious, send your wing guards to alert the others. Then we'll work as a team."

"So people are bait?" Danica wrinkles her nose.

Idallia lifts her gaze. "We're not baiting a trap, we're just waiting to see if a raid happens, and if one does, whoever is taken will be in less danger with us here than without us. But we'll need to move fast to catch them on the way out before they get over the border and drop into the tunnels with the captives."

Her answer mirrors the one I would've given so perfectly that I'm both pleased with her assessment and painfully aware of holding her back. With every day that goes by, I might be damaging the future I've spent a third of my life building because I don't want *now* to change.

Keep. Protect. My dragon rumbles seductively inside me, and there's no telling it to shut up because its essence permeates my whole body. The beast is more honest than the man, pushing thoughts of golden eyes, silky black hair, and red lips to my mind. It whispers to me through every pumping vein why I choose to spar with Idallia the most—because I know I'll win, I can pin her underneath me, and murmur something against her neck without anyone suspecting I crave her scent and want to inhale it deep into my lungs and keep it there until I can do it again.

My starborn magic latches on to my thoughts, wanting to seep out and wrap shadowy heat around the woman next to me. Contracting every muscle, I wage an internal battle and leash myself just as the food arrives. Other dragon shifters take one form or the other—a conscious choice of skin or scales. I'm both at once, which makes me stronger, faster, and more feral. What that feral part doesn't understand, or care about, is that Idallia doesn't know the truth—and that I'm the one keeping it from her.

"What's to stop the vampires from killing their captives as soon as we attack?" Arran asks, cutting into meat that drips red. "They can bolster their strength and start healing from injuries just by sucking someone down in seconds."

Leaning back in my chair, I scrub a hand down my face. "We'll just have to do our best to protect them." It seems that's all I can promise these days.

"What if we're the ones who spot something?" Idallia asks as she pokes at a potato. They steam, still too hot to eat. "You don't have wing guards to carry the message."

"We'll send Fyrestar and Rimblaze to alert the others."

My words must be sour, because she makes a face. No argument leaves her mouth, though.

Idallia goes quiet, so everyone else does too. Or maybe it's because I'm here—and barely eating. I try to show interest in my meal.

"So..." Wade's humor-laced tone cuts through an extended silence. "What do you call a vampire who can't get their fangs to come out?" He looks around the table expectantly. I shake my head, miserable at jokes. Everyone else has an *Oh great Cealastra* expression on their face, and Wade looks even more pleased with himself. "Poor sucker," he finally says when no one answers.

My groan isn't the only one. Danica rolls her eyes.

"Wait, wait." Wade grins wider. "I have another one. What do you call an old and wrinkly fae nearing their end?"

"Poor sucker?" Maia ventures.

Wade scowls at her, chuckling underneath. "Anyone else?"

"Broke?" Danica suggests.

Wade shakes his head.

"Well?" Kellan says. "Spit it out."

"Unglamorous," Wade answers with a shrug.

I laugh despite Wade's ridiculousness and the very real and increasingly worrisome amount of fae using their seductive glamour magic to change the way people perceive their intentions and deafen them to the warning bells that should be clanging in their heads.

"Got one about dragon shifters?" I ask.

Wade lifts his mug, hiding a smile behind a sip of ale. "I wouldn't dare."

"Humans?" Idallia asks.

He shakes his head. "And risk some Drayke Mountain sorcerer cursing me? Not a chance."

"Phoenixes?" Arran arches his brows.

Wade looks aghast. "Surely, you jest."

"There are only werebeasts left." Maia points her knife at Wade, her eyes narrowing. "*Please* tell me you have a good one I can use the next time we fight a pack of raiders in the north."

Wade chews his meat, his expression turning thoughtful and vague. "What do you call a werebeast who can't shift?" he finally asks.

"Poor sucker," Kellan tosses across the table with a grin. We all laugh, and for the first time in weeks, I don't want to physically remove him from my presence.

"I know." Danica halts her fork halfway to her mouth, her eyes sparkling with mischief. "Unglamorous."

Wade thumps his mug down with a huff. "Not every joke has the same punch line."

"What's the answer, then?" Idallia asks, her throaty chuckle made to haunt me.

"Human." Wade looks around the table, his brows rising expectantly. "If they can't shift, they're not a shifter. They're human."

"Yeah, that one doesn't work." Maia's flat assessment leaves Arran's lips twitching as he tries not to laugh.

Kellan spreads his hands. "It's not false."

"It's not funny, either," Danica says around a mouthful of her lunch.

"Ah! Well!" Wade lifts his mug, signaling for more ale. "They can't all be winners."

"You should've led with the worst one, not the best." Idallia pokes at her meal without eating it, even now that it's cooled off. Her mug sits on the table, almost untouched.

Leaning toward her, I frown. "I thought you were hungry." Her frost-and-sunshine scent fills my nostrils. Greedy for another breath of her, I stay close.

She gazes at her bowl of cheesy potatoes like she wants to eat but just can't. She tugs at the silver band around her neck. "I'm still...thinking."

"Would soup help?" She seems to accept liquids better than anything else.

"I don't know." She turns to me, our gazes colliding. She's so close that I see the starbursts in her eyes. "Everything tastes weird, especially since I put on the torque."

My pulse takes off with a thud. I was trying to help her, but what if I made things worse?

I lean back when my dragon reaches for her with shadows that nearly cross my skin. "Sometimes spells go wrong. If it doesn't feel right, take it off."

"I think I just need to get used to it." She touches the torque, one finger sliding over the silver. Her nail is tinged blue with cold, like in the dead of winter. "It's got to stop prickling at some point." Her eyes meet mine again, her worried frown making me want to lay answers at her feet. "Right?"

I nod, though I don't know. Another day, another lie. My meal turns to lead in my stomach as she lowers her hand and flexes her visibly stiff fingers.

"Why don't you go outside and get some sunshine?" I suggest. "It'll help. After, you can come back and finish your meal."

Nodding, she looks at me oddly as she stands, something suspicious flickering in her gaze. Unease drops through me like a rockslide, but when she shivers in the hot tavern, her body confused and her stomach rebelling, I know I did the right thing.

CHAPTER THIRTEEN

IDALLIA

Bale was right. A walk in the sun did me good. I was able to eat after that, then sleep, just like everyone else, though I'd have preferred to be with my birds.

Fyrestar, Rim, and I are back together now, though, and Bale asks me to choose the location for our stakeout north of Porthwood. I'm not sure why. Is it a test?

Do better.

We explore from above, and I look down at the treetops, searching for the perfect place to hide out and wait. We need a slight clearing to land in without too much open space, or else disappearing into the forest becomes difficult. I have to choose before nightfall when any Bloodwold vampires might emerge from their hideouts—likely the tunnels just over the border—and time is running short.

I glance east, scowling at the visible scars on the land, earth dug up with no care and obviously no intention of mining if the lack of equipment is anything to go by. From talks with Bale, I already know the gildenfae say that any nearby ore goes north into Wyndwood and not east toward Bloodwold. I don't think Bale has told the Were King about it, though.

After a few large circles that don't take us too far from Porthwood, I pick a less dense section of the deciduous woods that thicken to the north. There are paths, mostly animal tracks, but no roads going through here, which makes it accessible but not truly open, and a good way for marauding blood thieves to sneak up on the city.

We land in a clearing big enough to accommodate Bale in his dragon form. He shifts as he lands, a man again looking at me with an odd expression. I slide off Fyrestar's back, suddenly wary. Rim lands next to us.

"What?" My hand flies to my hair. I did the second-tightest bun of my life at the inn earlier. The first tightest was this morning's. After a whole day like this, my head hurts.

A red leaf flutters down from the thinning canopy, dropping between us. The bright autumn shade at dusk reminds me of Bale's coloring in both skin and scales—crimson burning through the dark.

He tilts his head toward the east. "I would've chosen the next clearing over."

My stomach drops. I reach for Fyrestar. "We can go there. There's still time before the sun sets."

"No, stop." He holds out a hand. "I was...It was a poor attempt at humor. This is fine."

"I don't want *fine*," I grumble. "I want the best." I start climbing back onto Fyrestar. Rim's wings unfold. We're almost ready to go when a firm hand abruptly tugs the back of my cloak hard enough to pull me down.

I don't know what Bale thought would happen, but I lose my balance and pitch backward. My startled cry mixes with the worried click of Fyrestar's beak.

Bale catches me against his body, holding me there, my back pressed to his chest, while I get my feet under me. His breath whispers over my hair, and my heart kicks savagely against my ribs, probably thudding into the arm banded around me. Shadow wings suddenly encircle us, going from hot magic to solid in an instant and holding me against Bale. A low, almost irritated growl resonates in Bale's throat, and the wings melt into shadow again.

I gasp, the heat of his magic dragging through me. The sensation raises goose bumps everywhere. I'm certain I don't know the extent of Bale's starborn magic, and he doesn't often show it. No other dragon shifter can mix forms, and I wish I'd gotten a look at the man with wings, but my back is to him, and his grip is firm.

My voice low and husky, I ask, "Do you ever fly in skin?"

His arms drop away, and he steps back, leaving me freezing. I turn, swallowing. Shadows swirl around him.

"I didn't mean to yank you down like that, and I said I was teasing." Walking away without answering my question, he sets down his pack. "This clearing is good."

"Good...fine..." I can still feel the heat of his shadow wings inside me and shiver like a teasing finger just trailed down my spine. "Words to strive for," I say hoarsely. "Thanks."

He swings back to me, spearing a hand through his dark hair. The way he drags it back makes the fiery highlights at the roots even more obvious. "Are you trying to cure me of any need to ever attempt teasing again?" he asks testily.

I clamp my mouth shut, instantly sorry. "No. This was kind of a first."

"Kind of a first?" He prowls closer, his amber eyes glinting. "What you should've said to me is 'do better.' Works every time." A slow smile curves his lips, and my breath stalls in my throat.

"I really wish I'd thought of that."

He chuckles. "Next time."

Is Bale implying he'll try teasing me again? My heart holds a riot in my chest.

My neck and face heating, I move toward a thick tree and set down my pack. I need to get over this infatuation. Time was supposed to make it better, not worse.

My pulse beats loudly, and my skin stays hot, but the trilling thrushes and darkening clearing do me the favor of drowning out my heartbeat and masking my blush.

Fyrestar and Rim take off to hunt for their dinners once they see that I've settled in. The team had dinner at the inn before leaving, though my appetite turned difficult again. Bale disappears to one side of the clearing, and I go into the woods on the other to relieve myself and give my obsession with the Dragon King a stern talking to. When I come back, Bale's there again, it's almost fully dark, and it's time to keep watch during vampire hours.

As the night progresses, we both take short forays into the woods. My birds watch from above, flying in low circles, their feathers fully dimmed. Everything is quiet, only native animals moving around until they finally give up on their endeavors and find rest somewhere. By the time the small hours roll around, Bale and I converge in the clearing again, and Fyrestar and Rim find a nearby tree to roost in.

"There's no one left on the streets of Porthwood to try to kidnap at this hour." I sit, settling my back against the tree where I left my pack and stretching out my legs.

"If anything happens now, which I doubt, it's more likely to be a pre-dawn raid when people are moving around again." Bale sits opposite me, his back against another tree.

"Dawn is more dangerous for vampires—the rising sun doesn't wait." I sigh. "Do you think we came here for nothing?"

He tips his head against the trunk, closing his eyes. The hot, amber glitter snuffs out, plunging his face into darkness. "It's only the first night, Idallia. Patience."

I shiver at my name on his lips. He has a way of saying it like he *owns* it. Or maybe I'm just wishing I could be his.

I inwardly grimace, hating even having that thought. Maybe in another life, another time... *This* life and time have proven that's not a path I want to take with my teammate, let alone my king. If the feelings turned out to be mutual, it could be great. Until it isn't. And then the consequences would be Kellan times a million. I might have to leave my job and home. I could lose my birds.

Sighing, I pull an extra cloak from my pack. Now that I'm not moving, I'm cold.

"Rest if you want," Bale rumbles. "I'll keep watch until dawn."

He's right in front of me, a familiar outline in the dark. I get an odd flash of him in a night-shadowed room I don't recognize. He's in his dragon form, his eyes ablaze. He looms over me, my arm throbs, and terror overwhelms me. I blink, and the vision is gone.

Alarmed, I stifle a gasp and cross my arms over my chest, wishing I could stifle my suddenly thrashing heartbeat too. Blinking rapidly chases the echo of fear from my mind, but I don't think it was only Bale who frightened me. Someone else was there. I just don't know who.

Bale's eyes open, a frown narrowing the slight glow of his gaze on me. *Great.* He definitely heard my heart crack like thunder against my ribs.

I fake a breezy tone. "Thanks, but I'm fine. I rested at the inn." There's no way I can sleep with Bale Cinderheart so close his inner heat warms my feet, his legs stretched out next to mine.

Something fiery erupts in my chest, not helping my racing pulse. Did he sit this way on purpose? He knows I get cold, especially my feet and hands. He saw it at lunch and sent me outside to warm up in the sunshine.

"Why do you always say sunlight helps?" I ask in sudden confusion. "I don't spend any more or less time in the sun than anyone else."

He takes a long time to respond and, as usual, it's with a question instead of an answer. "Why do you ask?"

"Because it *does* help. I always feel better, regain my appetite, stop shivering...But I don't tan. I never have. Isn't that strange?"

"I don't tan much, either."

"But you *do* tan." I tug at the fang-decaying torque, momentarily lifting the silver band off my skin. "Do you know something I don't? Something about me?"

He crosses his legs at the ankles, taking his heat a little farther from me. "Why would I?"

Frustrated with another question, I pull my second cloak more thoroughly over me and cross my ankles too. Where there'd been a hand's width between our feet, now there are three. "The whole sunlight thing—like I just said."

Bale shakes his head. "I'm just a keen observer. I've known you for a while—long enough to notice things."

I barely noticed or put the two together. But maybe that's what makes Bale a powerful, centuries-old starborn king and me a much younger...something.

"It might be dark," he says softly, "but I can still see the look on your face."

I flatten my expression. "What look?"

"The questions. *Who am I? Where am I from? Is there anyone else like me?*" There's no humor in his voice. "Am I close?"

I shake my head. "Way off."

He huffs. "You're an open book. Except you don't realize you can write your own pages."

Scowling, I digest that as poorly as I digest most food. Does Bale think it's that easy? "My quill ran out of ink."

Bale huffs again. I can't tell if there's humor in it this time or not.

Already feeling the tips of my toes going numb, I move my feet closer to his again. "How can I write when I don't know anything about myself? There's nowhere to start the story."

His eyes blaze, twin embers in the night. "You know exactly who you are. You've had more than two hundred years to figure it out. Just be *that* person. Write *that* story."

"I know *who* I am." My tone rises to match his. "It's *what* I am that's the problem."

"Why is it a problem?" he snaps.

"Because there's no one else like me," I snap back. "I'm alone."

He pitches forward. "How the fuck are you alone, Idallia?" The low thunder in his voice raises goose bumps on my arms and sets my hair on end. "Everyone circles you like you're the starsdamned sun, and you don't even notice because you're so busy isolating yourself with your warbirds."

My jaw drops. I snap it shut. Sybil's voice slips like a river current through my head, telling me that I unify, that I'm their cause. "That's not true. I eat meals with the team. We train together. I spend time with Sybil and Stuart."

"Yes. You've lived two hundred and twenty-six years and have seven friends. Ten with your birds."

My eyes start to sting. Seven means he's not even counting himself. Or maybe he's not counting Kellan. "How many friends do *you* have?" I challenge.

He stares at me, no heat in his gaze. "Absolutely none."

I inhale sharply. I guess he wasn't counting himself then. "Stuart would be disappointed you feel that way."

Bale closes his eyes again. Shadows swirl around him, darkening the night. "We train tomorrow morning, first thing," he rumbles, utterly changing the subject. "You need to practice."

My eyes don't sting again from his criticism. They do not. "Why am I even here if I'm so useless?"

Blazing eyes pierce the gloom again, brightening Bale's whole face. I can't tear my eyes from him—his corded neck, square jaw, strong nose, and hard gaze, staring straight back at me. His inner fire seethes like it wants to roll out of his mouth and burn me alive. Voice a flat menace, he tightly utters, "Don't ever say that again."

Glaring at him, I drag my legs up under me. I can keep myself warm. "I don't know what to make of that. You just told me I need the practice."

"*Everyone* needs practice. That's how you get better, stay sharp, *win*. You want to win, don't you?"

"Of course I want to win," I grind out. "Who doesn't?"

He grunts in answer. He doesn't speak again, and the silence feels so thick it coats my skin.

We sit there, the night stars crawling overhead, the moon small and bright. I'm too aware of Bale and stupidly try to guess his thoughts. My body confines me like a prison I need to escape, and my mind races, going back over our conversation enough times that I start to regret certain things I said.

Near dawn, my stomach rumbles. I ignore it because I don't have any food. I'd assumed we'd go back to the inn for breakfast and rest, but now it seems we'll be sparring in the morning, and I'll have to do it on an empty stomach.

I close my eyes. Maybe I can at least get a few minutes of sleep before I get my ass kicked by the Dragon King.

A swirling of crisp autumn leaves and fiery wind teases my nostrils, and my gut tenses. Those dry, woodsy scents always cling to Bale like a second skin, and I open my eyes, finding him right in front of me. He holds out an apple, arching his brows as if daring me to take it, and my heart flips wildly. The fruit looks black in the pre-dawn light, but I know it's red. I only eat red apples because green ones make my tongue feel numb.

Has Bale noticed that preference too?

My mouth waters, and my insides rumble again. "Why do you have that?"

He eyes the apple with exaggerated longing. "It was for me, but I think you need it more."

I snort, smiling. "Never in your life."

He smiles back, and damn if the sun doesn't crest the horizon at the exact same time.

"Fine, it was for you," he reluctantly admits. "Just in case."

A little fire blooms beneath my ribs. "I wish I could eat like everyone else." Maybe it's a family trait that I can't.

"Being like everyone else is overvalued. The best thing you can be is you."

A lump rises in my throat as I take the apple from him. "How do you always say the right thing? Years of diplomatic training?"

"I don't know about that," he says wryly, sitting back on his heels with his arms draped casually over his knees. "We argue a lot."

"That's all right." I shrug. "We're not friends."

His mouth thins. "Idallia..."

I wave off whatever he's going to say—or not say—and take a bite. I can't help the face I make. I can barely chew and have the strong urge to spit it out.

"What's wrong?" Bale leans toward me again. "Is the apple bad?"

Shaking my head, I force down the mouthful. "I don't think so. It's me. Nothing tasted right yesterday, either."

Frowning, he reaches out. "Do you mind?" His hands hover near my neck over the torque.

I shake my head, my pulse surging. I hope he doesn't hear the difference. Bale grips the metal, his warm fingers sliding against my skin as he gently tugs the torque open enough to slip it off my neck. He sets it aside, and I touch my throat. My deep breath feels like the first I've taken since putting it on.

"Great stars, that's a relief." The prickling heat instantly fades.

Bale nods to the fruit in my hand. "Try the apple now."

I take a cautious bite and then groan, dabbing at the juice on my lip. "It's good. *Finally.*" His eyes dip to my mouth, and embers pop in my belly. My breathing speeds up. "No wonder the potatoes yesterday tasted like rust."

He quirks a brow. "Have you eaten a lot of rust lately?"

"Oh, bucketfuls." I take another bite. "Good stuff."

He chuckles. The sound dies when he glances at the torque. "Put it back on at nightfall. For now, leave it off."

I nod, happy to oblige, and rub my neck, erasing the lingering feel of the enchanted silver from my skin. "Why would the torque make food taste strange?"

He moves back to his position against the tree across from me, his brow creasing in thought. He stretches his legs out again, his feet just next to mine. "The magic in that metal is strong. It has a bite—just like vampire teeth. It could be like when someone wears too much perfume. The strong smell leaves you nauseous and suppresses your appetite, but it's not so bad that you'll actually be sick."

I despise strong smells and understand what Bale means. "Like that fae emissary? The one who came to announce the old queen's death?" I smile even though it wasn't funny at the time. My headache lasted for days, and my birds barely left their roosts. "We could smell her all over the mountain for a month after she left."

Bale's low laughter feels like an extra blanket when he's already close enough to heat me through. "She was nauseating for several reasons."

"She was especially obnoxious after she realized she wasn't getting into your pants." Mortification fills me. I can't believe I just said that.

His eyes flash with humor. "You noticed that, did you?" His easy reply lessens my embarrassment. His smile helps too.

"I'm pretty sure everyone did."

"I could barely stand the smell of her in the cavernous throne room. Imagine contaminating my bed with that much perfume? I'd have to throw it down the mountain and get a new one."

Laughing, I bite into my apple again.

Fyrestar and Rimblaze swoop down from the branches above, their plumage glowing the same fiery colors as the dawn.

"Going hunting," Rim says. One warm, bright-red feather on his head is askew from sleep. Reaching out, I smooth it back into place.

I quickly lower my hand and resist patting him longer than necessary. He'll want to look all grown up in front of Bale. "Happy hunting. Don't bring me back anything."

Rim warbles a laugh, his expression shining with delight. He's on a mission, going hunting with Fyrestar, and getting extra time with Bale. Life is good.

"I'll keep him in sight," Fyrestar assures me.

I nod and wave them off, taking my last bites of apple as I watch them clear the treetops and disappear.

When I turn back around, Bale is taking a basket of figs and a small wheel of cheese from his pack.

My chewing slows. "Why do you have all that?"

"I think we've established it's not for me."

The way my chest tightens should be considered a grave medical condition in all six kingdoms of Ellonrift. "Thank you."

He leaves the food at my feet and stands. "I take care of what's mine."

My belly swoops violently. All food forgotten, I murmur, "You take care of everyone." I shouldn't feel special. I shouldn't wonder. I should eat my breakfast and stop staring at Bale like he's made of stars.

Except...isn't he?

Bale shifts into scales. *"Eat up, Sunshine, because after I hunt, we cross swords."*

Sunshine? The dam holding my denial in place breaks inside me, and there's no way the dragon in front of me doesn't hear my suddenly scorching blood rush through my veins.

Rooted in place, I watch as Bale lifts into the sky and angles in the direction Rim and Fyrestar took. If he hunts with them, I'll hear about it for months. It'll be the highlight of their year.

My held breath seeps out of me once I lose sight of him. I don't know what Bale's craving for breakfast, but my stomach sinks with the awareness of what *I* want and maybe can't resist.

I'm pretty sure the only thing that can save me from a terrible mistake is Bale not wanting me the way I want him. But for the first time, true doubt sneaks in. Maybe he doesn't.

But what in the blazing stars happens if he does?

CHAPTER FOURTEEN
IDALLIA

Bale doesn't return for a long time. I know he doesn't go far. I can feel him nearby like an ember on my skin. He's the start of something hot, burning to ignite. As I wait for him, a decent meal finally in my stomach but nerves cramping my belly, I tell myself all the reasons this infatuation with Bale Cinderheart is a terrible thing.

He's the Dragon King.

I'm old, but he's *really* old. It's all relative, though, isn't it? He's a healthy adult dragon shifter, and I'm a healthy adult... whatever I am.

He's solitary and always has been. He accused me of isolating myself, but he's worse. Didn't he just proclaim himself friendless? It's not true, but if that's the way he feels, it must be a lonely existence.

Most of our conversations of any length turn into arguments.

He's the leader. He makes the decisions. He's the one in

charge. I get to weigh in, and Bale often asks for my opinion, but apart from that, the power dynamics are troubling.

How *mine* are my birds? If I no longer want to be part of the Elite Wing or work for Bale, what happens to them? Their everlife is tied to Drayke Mountain, to Bale. He created them, so aren't they really *his*, no matter how *mine* they feel?

Unease swoops through me like a host of sparrows. If I'm to have a witch's hope of living normally as part of the Elite Wing and with my warbirds, I need to get over my starstruck obsession with Bale.

But what if something *were* to happen? Would it really be so bad? Would I reject what I secretly long for just because Bale is Torridaig's king, and he can tell me what to do, and I'm supposed to listen?

How well do I listen now? We usually talk as equals—or at least I feel that way, even if it's not true. Bale *makes* me feel that way. Isn't that good?

Sighing, I put a stop to my circular thoughts and remind myself that Bale has not—in any way, shape, or form—asked me to be with him.

Not long after, Fyrestar returns to the tree above. Rim follows him in.

"How was breakfast?" I ask, looking up.

"Plentiful." Fyrestar's golden eyes match the tree's golden leaves.

Rim trills a satisfied sound, fluffing his wings as he settles on a branch. My phoenixes blend so perfectly into the autumn woods with the blazing yellows, pink-tipped greens, startling reds, and fiery oranges, that only the glinting of their bright eyes and sharp talons gives them away. *"Rabbits everywhere."*

I smile. "How many did you eat?"

"Enough to not need lunch." Fyrestar gives Rim a proud look. *"And Rimblaze caught two more than I did."*

"Hopefully not so many that a stomachache is on the way."

"Only too many rats give me a stomachache," Rim says. He's just like Sol that way.

"I trust you ate your breakfast too?" Bale's deep, slightly rasping voice emerges from the woods before he does.

I pivot to face him. After all my racing thoughts and nervous pacing, the shock of him is brutal.

I nod, my breath locked in my lungs. His lightly tanned skin is flushed, as if he's still warm from being in his dragon form, but his hair is damp and slicked back, the softly curling, dark-brown ends dripping beads of water that catch the morning sunlight and glitter like gems.

I swallow hard. "And you?" I finally manage.

Bale nods. "But I'm not the one turning my nose up at meals half the time." He glances into the tree. "The warbirds are right—rabbits everywhere."

"It must take a hundred to fill you," I murmur.

He shrugs, his gaze coming back to me. "There are fewer rabbits now."

A laugh unfreezes my lungs. Bale looks startled by the sound, as though he can't imagine being funny. Maybe that's what happens when you don't have any friends.

"My difficult relationship with food isn't by choice. I'd love to be normal." His expression darkens, and I suppress a groan. I forgot. I'm supposed to embrace my individuality. "I just mean, my head says *eat,* and my stomach says *no thank you.*"

Rita and Gerard used to have fits about me going for days without eating anything, so maybe they did care about me in their own way. Or maybe they just worried their gold would stop coming if I accidentally starved to death. It became less of an issue after everyone determined I wasn't human.

"Eating outdoors is always easier," I say thoughtfully. "Maybe it's the sunshine?" I'm absolutely fishing for clues, but Bale doesn't seem to notice. Or else ignores me.

Looking up, he calls softly to Rim and Fyrestar. They swoop

down and land beside us in the clearing. Bale lays an affectionate hand on both, and I take advantage of their nearness to praise how well they kept watch with us last night when they could've rested.

"Do you want to sleep now while we spar?" I ask them.

"Unless you plan on training in silence, I doubt that'll happen," Fyrestar answers.

Half-laughing, I ask, "Are we so loud?" That can't be good. At least no Bloodwold vampires will be out and about during daylight hours.

"Clashing swords don't exactly offer the same level of peace as the roosting wall," Fyrestar answers dryly.

Rim clicks his beak, narrowing his amber eyes on the tree they just vacated. *"And those branches don't feel anything like my nest."*

I chuckle. "Do you think you might be a little spoiled by your big, cozy roosts back home?"

"More like spoiled by you," Bale rumbles.

I look over sharply, but there's no reproof in his expression. It's...warm.

I turn back to my birds, blushing. "Don't they deserve some spoiling?"

"I suppose everyone does," Bale acknowledges more easily than I would've expected. When was the last time someone spoiled Bale Cinderheart? Probably never.

From what I've heard about his parents, and especially his father, they weren't generous with anything—gold, protection, or affection. Bale didn't turn out anything like them.

A lump lodges in my chest, but it's not gold or protection that makes the feeling mushroom into something that sits achingly on my heart. It's my unexpected breakfast, food left at my feet without any warning or expectation. It's the attention he gives the warbirds that they soak up like sunshine, making their inner fire glow even brighter with happiness.

"Let's hope the Bloodwold scum don't take too long to make a raid on Porthwood," Bale says, smoothing a wayward feather on

Rim's neck. "Then you can get back to your comfortable nests and Embersol."

Rim tweets a protest even as he leans into Bale's hand. *"I wasn't complaining. Just...observing."*

Bale's lips curve into a smile that's only for the thirteen phoenixes—indulgent, caring, and proud. This side of him always makes me melt like butter in the sun.

Suppressing a sigh, I drink in the sight of them together. Do I want a raid to come sooner? Or later? I'm conflicted about spending this much time alone with Bale. I crave it, but I know it's not good for me.

"Rest or watch," Bale says with a final stroke down Rim's fire-warm neck. His hands drop away from both phoenixes and move to the hilts of his swords. "Just stay back and don't interfere on Idallia's behalf. She trains solo today."

"Solo?" I arch challenging brows. "I thought I was training with you."

Something almost eager brightens his features as he draws one sword, leaving the other at his hip. "If you think semantics will save you from getting your hide handed to you, you're wrong."

I smirk. He smirks back, and I feel his wordless dare all the way down to the marrow of my bones.

Fyrestar and Rimblaze flutter back into the tree they seem to have chosen, despite the reportedly uncomfortable branches, and I unsheathe the swords at my hips and twirl them in my hands. My blades sing as they cut through the air. Speed. Precision. Strength. I have it all. So does Bale.

I don't even try to hold back my grin as I start a slow circle, forcing the Dragon King to turn with me. "You can shift. I'll still fight you."

Bale huffs, a slightly mocking bend to his lips. "You don't need to know how to fight a dragon. You need to know how to fight things your own size and strength."

"You want to shrink, then?"

His smile turns more genuine. "Cealastra made me this way." He transfers his blade to his nondominant hand.

My eyes narrow. "Don't you dare."

"I give the orders here."

My mind jumps back to my earlier thoughts about our balance of power. Or *imbalance*. I lift my chin. "A weretiger isn't my size or strength. A werebear is even worse."

A sudden wave of shadows spills from him, the inky outline of a huge dragon nearly taking form.

I arch a brow. "Looks like your dragon wants to come out to play."

Something flickers in Bale's expression as he draws the darkness back inside. "You don't want to play with him."

"Why not?" I cock my head. "Afraid of me?"

His lips twitch. "You're lucky I'm in charge and not the animal in me."

My legs turn heavy, slowing my footsteps. The unexpected purr in his voice drags like a weight through my belly. "Why is that?" I ask.

"Because I let you be who you want to be. He wants to snatch you up and lock you in a tower for safekeeping."

My jaw slowly drops. "Let me?" I say hoarsely.

His eyes narrow. "Figure of speech."

I manage to keep slowly circling without tripping over my own feet. "Dragons *are* natural hoarders."

"We only keep the good stuff," he promises in a husky voice.

A shiver chases his words through me. "You chose me for the Elite Wing. Not exactly the safest job," I point out.

"Which is why we train."

I can't argue with that. "And we can start as soon as you stop patronizing me." I look pointedly at his sword, and he reluctantly switches his blade back to his dominant hand.

"Satisfied?" he asks.

Not in the least. The flirtatiousness of our exchange terrifies me.

Instead of answering, I attack. Bale parries easily, and I counter his simple reflexive move with an aggressive strike that drives him back a step. I try going all in immediately, wanting to force that thunderclap of power and speed inside me, but after a flurry of hits, I know it's not going to happen. I back off, reassessing.

"Not scared enough to unlock *your* beast yet?" Bale mocks.

I scowl. That abrupt heightening of my senses, focus, and strength usually needs real danger in order to come out in me—and it doesn't always last. "Stop sparring like I'm made of glass, then we'll see what happens."

His features harden. "How about you do better when you're not on the brink of death?"

"Do *fucking* better," I growl, slashing at him. "I'm sick of hearing that."

He easily dodges my messy hit. "Not *fucking* that," he growls back.

My nostrils flare, dragging in his scent of hot wind and dry leaves. Slowing my breathing, I consciously settle my emotions and launch into a more controlled attack. My double blades hum through the air and clang against Bale's with a cadence that gradually speeds up. Faster, harder, the rhythm of battle rings in my ears. The more aggressive Bale gets, the better I fight. My steel becomes a blur—a whirlwind of hits, twists, and thrusts.

Bale's still always one step ahead. He spins out of a sudden deadlock and sweeps around, knocking me over. I barely scramble up and away from what would probably be a killing blow in a real confrontation. Bale's on me again in seconds. His next hit vibrates up my arm as I block a strike that nearly knocks my sword from my hand.

A spurt of panic finally unlocks the strength and speed I need. I leap out of his reach as he abruptly comes into such sharp focus that I can see every twitch at the corner of his mouth, every subtle flick of his amber eyes, every dot of sweat lining his brow.

Revitalized, I launch into an all-out assault. My next hit

vibrates up *his* arm, and my heightened senses soak up his sharp inhalation like a victory.

Bale fights me off, then rolls his shoulders, eyeing me with increased vigilance. We circle again. I stay focused, my body coiled for action. In a real battle, my utter concentration on Bale would make me vulnerable to attacks coming from elsewhere. I'd have to widen my perception, but right now, he's my only opponent.

"What changed?" He draws his second blade, and satisfaction thumps harder than my whomping heart.

"I'm pretending you're the only thing that goes bump in the night."

His steps unexpectedly slow, and I nearly skewer him. I twist away as he strikes back, his blade whistling past me.

His breathing is labored—more so than usual. I must be making him work, and that makes me absurdly happy.

"If I were your enemy, would you be scared of me?" he asks.

"Why would you be my enemy?" I counter with words and powerful hits, driving him back until he uses brute strength to throw me off him.

"Hypothetically," he grinds out.

"I know you. It's hard to be hypothetical."

"Why? Aren't I scary?"

"Do you *want* to be?"

He barks a loud laugh, the rare sound engaging all my senses. He jumps in, his blade at my throat before I even see it coming. I go utterly still, my eyes widening.

"Don't get distracted by conversation," he says sharply.

Bloodpit. Was that a lesson? "You asked me a question," I grumble.

"So could a werebear. Or a vampire."

Fair enough. Gripping my blades until my knuckles ache, I get back down to business.

We spar like we want to cut each other to ribbons, but neither of us lands a hit. Avoiding injuring each other is also part of training—the precision part, knowing your intent. The harder

Bale pounds at me, the more I know I can't match his strength, even at my best. His constant hits rattle up my arms, numbing me to the shoulders. He knocks one sword from my hand, throws his second blade aside, and continues with one, coming at me so hard he forces me backward.

Our clashing swords heat the air. We both move so fast we blur. He drives me across the clearing until my back hits a tree, the hard thud knocking a grunt from me. His free hand shoots out and grips my neck, holding me against the trunk and forcing my chin up. His other hand pins my sword arm against the bark at my side, squeezing my wrist until I drop my blade.

His eyes burn. He smells like a lightning strike, and shadows bleed from him. The dark tendrils swirl over me, soft and warm. Bale's starborn magic seems to draw us close, linking our bodies, and arousal thumps low inside me.

Breathing hard, he stares at me. "And you're dead."

My lips part, my chest rising and falling so violently it brushes his with every breath. *I don't think I've lived yet.* The thought comes from out of nowhere as Bale abruptly backs off, ripping his shadows from me. Shivering from the loss of both, I don't move, even after I'm free.

Bale watches me from under lowered brows. He rakes his fingers through his hair, shoving it back. I think he shoves his shadows, too, because they disappear entirely. "I thought you'd last longer."

I can't tell if he's teasing and decide to take that badly, his gruff words like a winter storm dropping cold rain on my head. "That was just the warm-up." I look him up and down like he's mediocre instead of the most powerful and captivating man I've ever seen. "And I thought you needed a confidence boost."

His teeth flash in a predatory grin. "Now that you're warmed up, are you going to stand there all day, or fight like you want to win?"

"Win?" I scoff. "No one beats you." Everyone knows Bale is the best—in any form. The only one who's ever come close to defeating him was the Vampire King, and no one knows how Rannigan Bloodthief managed to get close enough to rip through those chest scales.

My body cooling in a way that's good for my heart but not good for my fighting focus, I step away from the tree and retrieve my blades.

"What did I do wrong?" I still feel the weight of Bale's hand around my throat and his chest pressed against mine. I want to ignore the lingering sensations and bursts of heat, but I can't. If he scented my desire when he pushed me up against the tree, his shadows licking over me—or if he reciprocates it—he doesn't show it. Maybe he'll chalk it up to danger lust.

Ugh, I hope so.

"You're not using all your weapons. Your two swords aren't everything. You have feet. You have hands. You have a mouth," he says. I snort, and he gives me a hard look. "Get me off balance with your blades, then try something unexpected."

"Like biting?"

His gaze holds mine. "Not unless you want me to bite you back."

Warmth clenches deep in my belly. "Then why the mouth?"

"Conversation, Sunshine." His voice a velvet rumble of fire in his throat, he says, "Use it to distract."

My insides tumble at the nickname he's used twice now. While I slowly melt, he starts circling. Exhaling tension that has nothing to do with sparring, I try to focus, gripping my weapons and waiting for him to make the first move.

It takes a long time for the nearly six-hundred-year-old Dragon King to grow impatient, but he finally does and strikes out with incredible speed and total silence. I spring into action on pure instinct and counter his attack with crossed blades, tapping into every bit of strength I have to throw him back.

"You weigh a ton." I shake out my aching arms.

"All muscle."

His cocky answer draws a reflexive smile from me as I drop, spin, and slice lower.

He jumps over my blade. His eyes glitter on landing, igniting with interest. "Do that ten times faster, and someone might lose a foot."

"Exactly. You," I mutter.

He chuckles, and I suddenly get a strong image of me riding Bale, the wind streaming past me, his powerful wings beating the air, and his fire-warm scales between my legs.

Heat roars through me as Bale strikes out, nearly slicing my abdomen. His shocked inhalation hisses loudly in the sudden silence. We both pull up short, staring at each other. I hear my warbirds click their beaks.

"What the fuck, Idallia?" Smoke curls from Bale's nostrils. His amber eyes thunder with condemnation. Sword lowered, he steps in, looking me over with a fierceness that's both worried and furious.

I exhale shakily. Bale's inner fire is volcanic and pounds at my skin. The vision was just a flash, as much sensation as thought, but it's seared into my mind now. It's not the past, so does that mean...it's the future?

My heart hits my ribs like a battering ram. "Sorry." I swallow hard.

"Don't be sorry," he snarls. "Be *focused*."

Nodding, I square my shoulders and get ready to start again. Wanting to drive the intense vision away, I go on the offensive first this time, my blades glinting in the morning light filtering through the trees. Bale only uses one sword now—like vampires —but he's so fast that I still can't find an opening.

"Are you already bored? Thinking about other things?" He strikes violently, tawny heat boiling in his eyes. "Because this isn't a real fight? Because your warbirds aren't in danger? Your team? Your *life*?" He hammers harder with every word. "Because you're not scared of me?" The blade he just hit flies from my hand. My fingers howl in shock. "You *should* be. I could eat you alive. Maybe one day, I will."

Shaking my numb fingers out, I scramble away from him. *What the fuck does that mean?* "Who's the one yapping now?" I snarl back at him. "Trying to distract me? Too bad. I'm on to your tricks."

"I can hold a conversation and still win." He lunges for me. I drop, roll, grab the blade I lost, and come up swinging with both swords again.

Bale nearly knocks the same weapon from my hand with his next blow. I double my efforts, but that rush of strength and focus I had earlier doesn't come back to me now. I hold him off, but don't advance at all. This is about to go from bad to worse, and I don't have any hope of lasting in a bang-it-out sword fight with Bale.

Try something unexpected.

Keeping all intention from my expression, I stop alternating with rapid but predictable hits and suddenly strike hard twice in a row with the same blade. While he holds off that assault, I turn the angle of my other hand and ram the hilt of my sword into Bale's lower ribs with a blow that would snap a human bone in half.

His nostrils flare. I follow up with a kick to the gut. He barely moves. *Fucking dragon shifter.*

He strikes back, adding a fast, hard twist of his wrist that sends the blade in my dominant hand flying across the clearing. I hold him off with my second sword for mere seconds before he rattles that one from my grip too. I duck his swing and lurch out of his path. He stalks after me.

I back away, weaponless and done. I know it. He knows it. I don't have a dagger on me to throw at him—a mistake I won't make again.

Bale surges for me in a hot rush of speed. I leap back, but my heel catches on a root. I tilt over backward with a gasp just as his body slams into mine. He probably expected resistance, and when there is none, we both go down.

Bale's hand wraps around the back of my head just before we hit the ground. His weight drives the air from my lungs. We stare at each other in shock, then a fiery blush explodes across my skin. I'm completely pinned, unable to move. A root pokes into my lower back. I wince, and he lifts his weight to his elbows, freeing my torso and lungs. I drag in a breath and arch to relieve the pressure of the hard knot under me.

His jaw tenses. His eyes sweep over my face, then snag on the pounding pulse at the base of my throat. Slowly, he lowers his head and whispers, "And you're dead." He inhales against my neck, sending a river of goose bumps cascading over me. I could swear his teeth graze my skin.

"Didn't we say no biting?" I ask roughly.

"I'll bet you taste good."

His fast, guttural response sends a shot of heat through me that could rival dragon fire. Wild desires smash through my defenses. *Kiss me. Strip me. Fuck me.* I shove them all back across the threshold of good sense and somehow ask, "How'd I do this time?"

Lifting his head, he rasps, "Better."

The glittering, starborn wheels in his eyes are so beautiful and distracting this close up that I can barely form words. "Really?" I huff. "Because that was my second death today."

He looks straight into my eyes, his voice rolling with smoke and danger. "Your death is not an option." His gaze dips to my mouth, then he lifts off me with fluid strength, already turning away.

I'm too weighed down by liquid heat and uncertainty to follow him up at first. When I finally stand, neither of us tries to spar again. We gather our belongings and head to the inn, silent tension hanging loudly between us.

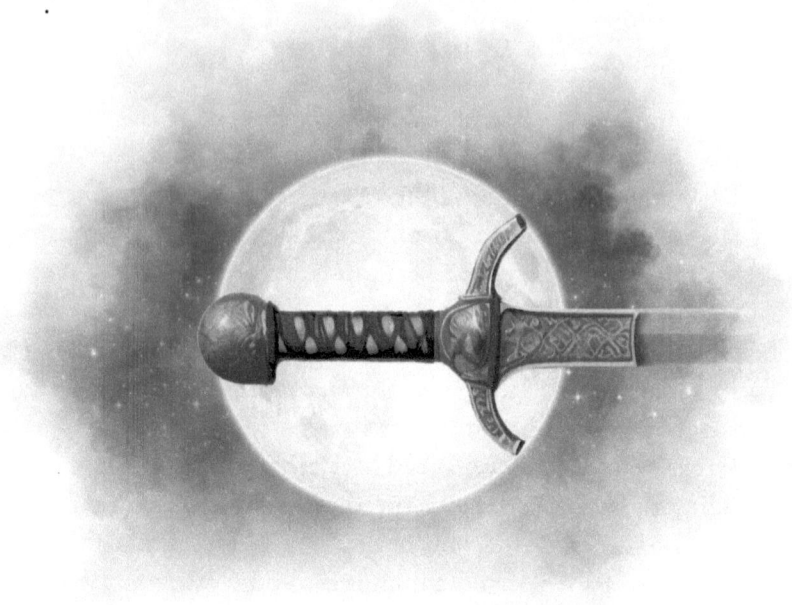

CHAPTER FIFTEEN

BALE

There must be something wrong with me. A life that had been on track for nearly six hundred years suddenly feels like it veered over a cliff.

And the cliff has a name.

I scrub a hand down my face, staring at the inn's dark ceiling. My team occupies each of the rooms on this floor. Idallia is in the one right next to mine.

I groan, the sound a rasping mix of frustration and despair. I'm supposed to be sleeping, but too many questions and a gut-deep worry plague me. I've always managed to attribute Idallia's flushed skin, pounding heartbeat, and sweet scent of arousal to something else. Violence can cause it, and we engage in plenty of that. But for the first time, I let myself believe it might be *me*.

And if it's me, then everything just got harder.

At nightfall, I'll find myself alone with her again, and if she makes me laugh one more time, I might break down and do something stupid.

Sunshine.

What the fuck was I thinking?

The way that slipped out wasn't just telling. It was *telling*. And she's so full of questions...

I force myself to breathe calmly and relax. I need to sleep now and be vigilant tonight. My efforts aren't very effective, but I know I doze off at least once because my dreams are filled with black hair, golden eyes, Rannigan's cold, angry stare, and hot blood everywhere.

We're all subdued at dinner. I don't know why. Nothing is different except that I've turned inward to muse over my own thoughts, and that seems to keep everyone else from expressing theirs. Wade doesn't tell a single terrible joke. Danica, Maia, and Arran eat quietly. Kellan furtively watches Idallia as much as I do. And Idallia just pushes her food around her plate and gazes out the window. She doesn't look in the direction of where we were earlier or where we'll go tonight. She looks in the direction of her warbirds.

Sighing, I rise. "Let's go get the phoenixes. Then it's back to our posts."

Everyone stands without grumbling, even though no one's had a chance to order a second round of food yet.

I go straight to the clearing. Idallia retrieves Fyrestar and Rimblaze from the local barracks and then joins me in the woods.

As night falls, we begin patrolling. Conversation is slim. She talks quietly with her birds, but unless I'm right there, Fyrestar and Rimblaze don't include me in their thoughts, and I can only hear Idallia's whispered replies snaking through the trees like a teasing thread I can barely grasp before it jumps away from me again.

Irritated, I move deeper into the woods. I liked it better when I craved solitude and happily isolated myself. No one to influence me. No one to try to please. Individuals are distracting. I learned that a long time ago and kept them at a distance. Then Idallia erupted into my life, and I had to figure out a way to keep her alive and train her for what comes next. The Elite Wing was a great idea—to help her, me, and Torridaig. But training them, flying with them, fighting alongside them... It's given me something I never expected—the urge to *join* instead of avoid.

Kellan was a bump in the road I didn't expect, either, even though I should have. Wade is interested in men, Arran is in love with Maia, and that left Kellan to see Idallia and get stars in his eyes. I keep waiting for his feelings to fade, but we live with centuries as our reference point, not years or even decades.

And do feelings always fade? Sometimes they grow so slowly you don't even see them coming until it's too late.

My gut tightens uncomfortably. Everything seems uncomfortable these days.

Kellan's persistent feelings are another good reason for his upcoming mission. He's a protector, so I'll give him someone who needs a lot more protection than Idallia. His knight-in-shining-armor syndrome will kick in, and maybe I'll accomplish two goals in one.

Rolling my shoulders, I let my shadows seep out, reddish-black scales building over me and wings unfurling without substance. I could turn them solid in a heartbeat and still hold on to my common form—my gift from Cealastra, along with my wounds healing when I shift.

Half-letting my dragon out relieves some of the tension snapping inside me, but gives free rein to another source of conflict. Dragons gather. We don't relinquish. We don't ignore. We don't do *nothing*. The dragon seeping from me immediately wants to collect Idallia, Fyrestar, and Rimblaze and keep them next to me, where I can see, protect, *smell*. Know they're here. Know they're well. Know they're *mine*.

My breath hisses through my teeth, and I force the thickening shadows back inside me.

I collected a very valuable girl a long time ago, and the dragon in me doesn't understand the idea of letting her go—even if it's to give her back to herself now that she's a grown woman. The man in me wants to argue less and less now.

Wary of my own thoughts—and the increasing clarity of them —I move toward one of the deer tracks but remain off to one side. My back against a tree, I listen and watch, keeping my focus where it should be—on the lookout for night raiders. I stay fully in skin, not letting the shadow of my dragon back out to tempt me with primal instincts I barely want to deny anymore.

Kellan's Featherspear suddenly caws above me. My head snaps up, my pulse accelerating. There's only one phoenix. Grambolt must've gone to gather other team members.

"Mount up!" I call to Idallia, knowing she'll hear. I shift and rise toward Featherspear. *"What's happening?"* I demand just as Fyrestar and Idallia join us above the forest, Rimblaze on their wing.

"Alarm bells are ringing in Draywood. You can't hear them from here." I cock my head, listening. Even my dragon doesn't hear. *"Everyone else is already headed to Draywood. Wade and Danica warned us. They were closest and heard the bells. Kellan sent me to tell you,"* Featherspear says.

Fire rolls between my fangs as I turn south and speed up. The information relay worked, but the attack happened leagues from here.

Catching up to us, Idallia calls out, "Wade and Danica might already be fighting? By themselves?"

"I don't know." Featherspear's plumage burns with worry, fire trailing from his wings.

"Rim's not supposed to go into battle yet," Idallia shouts across the night sky to me.

I glance over, glad to see the torque Stuart made for her back around her neck. *"Rimblaze will do what needs to be done. We'll see what that is when we get there."*

She pales to starlight white and glares at me like she just might hate my royal guts. I don't like it, but the condemnation in her cold stare isn't enough to make me set aside an asset in a fight.

Rimblaze glows brighter, excitement sparking from him. I want him ready but cautious, and say, *"Stay with Fyrestar and follow his lead. Don't get in above your head."* I'd hoped my warning would appease Idallia, but she doesn't look impressed.

Rim chirps his agreement. Fyrestar gives the younger bird a stern look, emphasizing the message.

Idallia's jaw hardens. She turns away from me, looking straight ahead.

"If they raised the alarm in Draywood, the soldiers there must be fighting the vampires," Fyrestar caws. *"The local garrison didn't know to alert us instead of engaging. We might not be able to take the prisoners we need."*

"We don't even know if there are vampires," I say. *"It might be something else."*

"Like *what?*" Idallia's acid-and-ice tone matches the cutting look she gives me, her golden eyes like chips of colored glass.

I let my inner fire heat mine—a warning. *"We'll know when we get there."*

"If it's a raid, and it's anything like usual," Featherspear chirps over to us, *"half the vampires will be dragging their catches straight for the border while the other half holds off the town's soldiers."*

"If that's the case, do we help the soldiers or try to cut off the traffickers?" Idallia asks.

I grind my fangs. Porthwood was an educated guess, and it angers me that I guessed wrong. *"We cut off the traffickers. If they cross the border into Bloodwold, we lose them and the people they took."*

An enormous, bright glow illuminating the horizon comes into view before Draywood does.

"Great Cealastra." Idallia stares in shock. "Half of Draywood is on fire."

My heart seems to drop dead in my chest. Keen vision and our view from above allow me to see a large band of blood thieves racing toward the border, as well as the inferno engulfing my town.

"*That's a new tactic,*" Fyrestar rattles angrily. Rimblaze squawks his shock.

"What do they hope to gain by that?" Idallia's face scrunches up as the first hint of smoke bites our nostrils. "That's not kidnapping. It's destruction."

"*Maybe it wasn't meant to happen,*" Fyrestar says. "*An accident.*"

"*I doubt it. That looks like a diversion—and an attempt to divide us,*" I grate out.

We weren't exactly discreet arriving in Porthwood, and I feared it might scare raiders off if they got wind of our presence. Now I think it did the opposite. They've used the cover of the tunnels to quickly gather a significant force from up and down the border and organize a raid of unprecedented proportions. *Divide us? Or kill us?* Something tells me the people they must've taken from Draywood aren't even the real targets tonight.

Kellan's Grambolt flies toward us along with Maia's Cinderblaze and Arran's Glimmerwing. All three of them glow, their heated bodies outlined by the light of the blaze consuming Draywood.

Grambolt banks around to fly with me. "*Kellan, Maia, Arran, and their other wing guards are helping the townsfolk and local soldiers contain the fire. Wade and Danica went to cut off the vampires with their warbirds. The bloodsuckers set the fire to distract the Draywood soldiers and then took off with their spoils.*"

"How many vampires?" The movement I saw from above looked like a considerable group—too many for only two dragon shifters and their phoenixes. The vampires will be protected by Rannigan's sorcerers and employ their usual tactics to make our fire and flight terrible options. And just like Idallia, Danica is down a young bird back at Drayke Mountain.

"*Forty?*" Grambolt answers. "*Not an exact count.*"

My insides twist sharply. *"You three stay with us,"* I order the newcomers. *"We head for the vampires."*

"What about the fire?" Idallia shouts above the wind of our breakneck pace toward the woods between Draywood and the border. "More people are in danger from that inferno than however many the vampires took."

"Three of the Elite Wing, half their wing guards, and the local soldiers are already on it." I angle toward where I know the woods thin and then taper off entirely—just a stone's throw from the border and those damn tunnels. The thick canopy is still all I see for now, but my guess is that the open field is where Wade and Danica will make their stand against the vampires. I hope this guess is better than my last one. *"If the bloodsuckers get away again, anyone who dies in that fire will have died in vain. We need to stop them before they cross the border."*

Idallia looks like she might argue. Finally, she settles on, "Can I send Rim to help in town with the fire?"

My lips thin, pulling over my fangs. I can't reasonably deny her. *"Rimblaze can go into town. He's big enough to help lift smaller people to safety."*

"Go, Rim!" She points him toward Draywood. "Be careful!"

Rimblaze doesn't look as pleased with this outcome as Idallia, but he goes without argument, peeling off to head dead south to Draywood.

"Where are they? Can you hear anything?" Idallia peers into the woods.

"I don't hear fighting yet. Just wagon wheels and people calling for help. I think Wade and Danica are waiting for them to emerge from the woods and hoping we'll get there quickly."

A roar of firebreath hits my ears, followed by the clash of metal.

"They'll be forced to go straight to skin and swords." Fyrestar accelerates, his burst of speed leaving the other wing guards behind.

Idallia and I barrel past the woods side by side and come out above the border clearing. My eyes widen. It's hard to get an instant count, but there are more vampires than I've ever seen making a blood raid. It's a fucking army.

"Bloodpit," Idallia curses under her breath. She whips her head toward me, her expression worried and questioning.

Wade, Danica, and their three wing guards form a small blockade on the border side, but the vampire horde will quickly overwhelm them. Rage fills me, along with a violent firebreath I wish could still burn these bloodsuckers to a crisp. *"Let's hit them from the back and make them fight on two fronts."*

We fly lower, faster. The screams from the captives in the wagon cages and the harsh clanging of swords fill my ears as the first arrows whistle past us. We evade the volley. Another one comes, and Cinderblaze screeches. I turn, dread seizing me. She wobbles, then rights herself. The arrow tore straight through her wing, but she keeps flying.

We're nearly on top of the vampires when they start launching spears at us. Fyrestar banks hard, narrowly avoiding a skewering. I glance over my shoulder. The other four wing guards are still out of reach of the throwing lances, but won't be for long. Cinderblaze takes up the rear now, her expression pained but determined.

Arrows fly at us again. I expel a furious firebreath, burning the bolts before they can hit us or the wing guards. My fire also coats a good many of the closest vampires. Another round of spears surges out of what should be a deadly inferno. One comes straight at me.

"Bale!" Idallia's shout garbles in my ears as I shift in flight, rapidly decreasing my body size.

The spear whistles past me, tearing through shadow remnants instead of hitting my fleshy underbelly. I shift again, pumping my wings hard to keep from crashing as the ground comes up to meet me. I land running and instantly transform into skin as more spears fly past. I whip out my swords and deflect the lance about to pierce my chest, then charge straight into the vampires.

Idallia swoops in just behind me with Fyrestar. I fight my way forward, hearing Wade and Danica doing the same from the other side of the battle with new vigor. They're not alone anymore against what must be at least sixty enemies. There are four of us now, several wing guards, and Fyrestar. If we can meet in the middle, we'll crush them.

The wing guards attack from above, plunging down to claw, peck, and burn. Their talons tear through scalps and eyes and throats. They wreak havoc on the middle of the vampire horde, but they're vulnerable to spears and arrows. I hear a pained caw and glance up to see a long slice bleeding along Glimmerwing's side. Cinderblaze is already injured. I call them both to me.

"Find the prisoners. Start working on opening the cages. Burn through them if you have to, then get those people back to Draywood." I use mind-to-mind speech despite my common form, keeping my words from vampire ears.

"We can fight." Glimmerwing's blood hisses and steams where it hits his burning feathers.

"This is what I need." I never slow my swords and bring my full attention back to the vampires.

The injured warbirds do as I ask without a backward glance. *Good.* I'll be twice as effective if I'm not worried about them.

To my right, Fyrestar and Idallia move like a violent wind on this edge of the battle. They leave glowing streaks in the air, using wings and swords and sheer savagery to tear through vampires. She's found her focus, and when she's on fire, the two of them burn as hot as I do.

"The captives are in a trio of wagon cages still in the woods," Grambolt caws as he swoops by and takes one of my opponents off me. He grips the vampire by his head, talons gouging into eye sockets, and flings the screaming man into a foe trying to circle around behind us.

Another vampire takes the previous one's place. They have dozens of reserves hovering between us and Wade and Danica. Vampires wait in the center, battle-ready and still shooting arrows and throwing lances to keep the remaining wing guards occupied and in danger.

I want to shift and crush these bloodsuckers with teeth and tail and talons, but a severed head will kill me just as it will a vampire. While I shred one with my fangs, five more would attack from the sides, and we've learned the hard way from our ravaged garrisons along this border that it's better to fight vampires in skin if we can't burn through them with fire.

It makes us smaller and more nimble opponents, but still physically stronger than they are. Even in skin, a skilled dragon shifter is worth several vampires.

Which is why the seven of us are usually enough to put the fear of the stars into blood raiders.

But right now, we're only four, and the vampires are dozens more than usual.

"Have the raiders noticed Glimmerwing and Cinderblaze trying to free the prisoners?" I ask Grambolt in mind-to-mind speech.

"Not yet." He spins abruptly to avoid an arrow, then swoops back to me. *"Wade and Danica are struggling."*

My dread intensifies as I fight off waves of relentless vampires. Idallia and I are struggling too. The numbers are heavily against us.

"We need the rest of the Elite Wing here," I mind-to-mind shout to Fyrestar, allowing Idallia to hear too. Seconds could make a life-or-death difference soon. *"Leave Idallia and retrieve the squadron as fast as possible. The locals will need to manage the fire alone."*

I hear Idallia's heart hammer out a hard beat despite the deafening battle. "Fight without Fyrestar? We're a team. Bale—"

I cut her off. "None of us can use fire or flight. You're on equal ground."

She scowls at me as the two of them whip toward a new threat, her legs gripping Fyrestar's body. She deflects a blow on one side and slices off a head on the other. Fyrestar hammers a heavy wing into a vampire's stomach and uses the resistance to whip around so fast they plow into another and knock her over from behind. Grambolt speeds down and drives burning talons through the vampire's neck, ripping it open.

"Equal ground?" Idallia shouts as they circle past me to attack again. "We're so outnumbered, I can't even count them!"

"Then everyone else had better get here now!" I soundlessly snarl. And that means sending the fastest warbird in our arsenal. *"Fyrestar, go!"*

CHAPTER SIXTEEN
IDALLIA

Panic gouges a hole in my stomach, but we don't have a choice. Neither of us has ever disobeyed a direct order, and I understand Bale's reasoning. Sol's the fastest phoenix alive, but she's not here. Fyrestar is far and away the next fastest, and he'll reach the Elite Wing before anyone else can.

"Let's do this," I mutter.

"Fight as hard for yourself as you would for me."

My throat constricts. I instinctively picture Fyrestar, Rim, Sol, and me all together again in our quarters, and I know I'll move the stars in the sky to make that happen. "Come back fast."

Fyrestar swoops low enough for me to vault off his back. I land spinning, my swords out, and both blades slice through a vampire's neck. The bloodsuckers next to them turn in shock. I grin viciously and strike out.

I kill two more vampires in seconds, but then a spear almost hits Fyrestar because he's looking back at *me*, and my heart plummets like a rock. He neatly evades and continues on his mission, but I abruptly lose the concentration, speed, and strength I'd found. My swords drop from a blur back to normal. I stop being able to isolate sounds and hear too many. Nothing comes into sharp enough focus. The difference is sudden and merciless, and I gasp, jumping back when a vampire nearly slices me in half. I leap back into the battle, swinging fiercely and trying to unlock my version of magic again.

"He's the fastest," Bale growls over the din of swords. Mine crashes without ceasing, but feels horrifically slow compared to before. "It was the right choice."

I ignore him. Separating me from my warbird is *never* the right choice. I'll turn into a fucking animal for my phoenixes. Nothing else can pull the same savagery and strength from me. Nothing else will make me win, no matter what. Not even my own impending death—and things are looking pretty grim.

With that thought, my rhythm breaks. I end up with a vampire boot to the sternum and stumble back.

"Do better!" Bale roars.

"Shut up!" I roar back as soon as I can breathe.

He starts fighting his way toward me. Grambolt has my back. I think Featherspear is helping Wade and Danica on the other side of the battle. Bale closes the distance between us, alternating between fighting off vampires on his side and picking off some on mine. I don't know whether to be annoyed or grateful. Maybe I should just fucking do better.

Too much of my concentration goes into straining to hit that moment when everything changes. When I'm not just good, I'm terrifying. When I can kill like a dragon and hunt like a warbird. When *I* don't even see myself coming, my body moving so fast my skin leaves a trail of light in the air, and my swords don't make a sound until I've already killed.

But no matter how hard I push, the change won't ignite like the oil-drenched torch I know is inside me, and I back away the second I have an opening. Frustrated and nervous, I stay on the fringe of the battle, taking on any blood traffickers who try to circle behind Bale and Grambolt.

"What's wrong?" Bale shouts.

Everything? I don't have a second to regroup. Bloodwold vampires swarm past Bale to reach me again. Mounting fear helps my ingrained combat skills kick in. I'm a survivor. I'll fight to my last breath, but it's with the furious knowledge that I could do so much better if that thunderclap would just hit.

I kill two more vampires. I'm still deadly, just feeling as if I'm fighting at half speed instead of moving like a meteor. Is it because my body isn't made to keep up the pace I sometimes have? Without my warbird here to pick up the slack, it's more obvious than ever when I can't find my momentum.

Five vampires organize an attack and jump at me at once. Terror always helps, and I kick into action. I wish it were daytime. I always fight better then.

Eat up, Sunshine.

Get some sunlight. It'll help.

My eyes narrow, and not only because my enemies are suddenly way too close. What the fuck does Bale know that I don't?

Distraction is the last thing I need, and I falter, nearly losing an arm. Cursing myself and Bale, I kill three of the five before one gets close enough to slice his blade across my thigh. Burning pain erupts in my leg, but I keep fighting, not letting the gash slow me down. The smell of blood seems to attract more vampires to me. One by one, they turn from everything else and converge on me like I'm the juiciest morsel they've ever seen.

I whip my blades as fast as they'll go. An army just turned on me—and me alone. I'm surrounded in seconds. Fear finally rips the thunderclap from me. The totally silent internal surge of strength and concentration helps me fight like a demon and kill, kill, kill. My swords blur and blood flies. Heads roll, but not mine, so I keep fighting while the others shout for me, trying to push their way through.

Grambolt caws out a warning too late, and a violent hit from the side leaves me reeling. A gigantic vampire uses the split second I'm off balance to jump on me, fangs out. Holding me in a vice grip, he goes straight for the juncture between my neck and shoulder before I can get my weapons between us, his hands clamping down on my shoulders and squeezing so hard my arms go numb.

I scream as his fangs sink in, the pop of skin the ugliest sound I've ever heard. He bites viciously, gulps loudly. He's close enough to the base of the torque that his fangs must touch it, because he suddenly drops me and rears back, his eyes shooting wide in shock.

My blood drips down his chin. I stagger, swinging again to keep others off me as feeling comes back to my arms. His fangs blacken and fall from his mouth. His hand flies to his face. He roars in terrified fury, but I'm too busy trying to stay alive to appreciate the moment.

"Idallia!" Bale shouts for me. I don't see him through the horde.

He suddenly rises in dragon form, locks eyes with me, and moves like a cyclone, crashing down hard by my side. The bloodsuckers immediately slash at his softer-scaled throat and chest, but Bale shifts back, leaving only his tail to sweep enemies out of the way and make room for Wade and Danica to land.

They all shift back to skin too fast for the vampires to land a solid hit, and then they're next to me, helping me drive the predators away. Wade and Danica are covered in blood, slashes, and bruises, but they fight the onslaught alongside us. Featherspear and Grambolt attack from above, burning and clawing, but we're still surrounded and hopelessly outnumbered.

The rest of the team needs to get here *now*.

"What happened? What changed?" Bale shouts.

"I don't know." I think back to when this battle went from bad to worse. "I bled?" In all our years of facing vampires, we've never been outnumbered this badly, and I don't think I've ever actually bled before. Scrapes, bruises, and even broken bones—I've done it all. But gushing blood—never.

"What the fuck is wrong with these bloodsuckers?" Wade growls as we take in the frenzied battle.

"Never seen anything like it," Danica yells back.

The vampires are feral. We kill or injure them, and they don't even care. They crawl over each other, over bodies—alive and dead—to get to me, their focus total, their fangs out, and their eyes seeming to see nothing but my blood.

I stumble back, breathing hard. "Bale, we have to retreat."

His eyes flash to me. "If we try to fly out of here, they'll fill us with spears and arrows."

He can shift and heal, but the others can't. And what about the warbirds? "There are too many. And they're fighting in a way that doesn't make any sense."

"The others will be here soon." Bale pins me with a stern look. "Just stay one strike ahead."

I nod, but I'm not the blur I was before. I'm injured and tiring, and I'm not the only one in danger. Danica is bleeding from a gash on her forehead, although the vampires are still focused on me, and Wade is slowing down, grunting with effort.

Sweat stings my eyes. Fatigue and constant effort send a wave of shakiness through me. Having lost a few deep pulls of blood straight from my jugular can't help, and blood still drips down my thigh. My pant leg is soaked through, my boot squishing. And the more I bleed, the more the vampires go into a frenzy. They finally manage to get between me and the rest of the team again when the bigger, stronger ones start killing their own in order to reach me.

My pulse thrashing, I keep my blades moving and my feet under me. Where's the team? Where's Bale? All I see are vampires.

"Fyrestar!" I don't know where he is, but I scream anyway. "Fyrestar!"

"Idallia!" Bale shouts back. How did he get so far from me?

I kick a bloodsucker off me, and my sliced leg almost gives

out. While I wobble, another vampire dives straight for my middle and knocks me over. I land with a grunt, dread lurching through me. The vampire on top of me twists, and his fangs sink into my bleeding thigh. I cry out, the pain searing. Danica charges in, tears him off me, and throws him into another.

She disappears, swallowed by the writhing horde. A woman with the longest fangs I've ever seen jumps on me before I can get up. She bites down the second she hits me, sinking her dagger-like teeth straight into my breast. I shriek and pound at her head with the hilts of my swords. She doesn't even seem to feel them and keeps dragging down long gulps of my blood like it's a drug.

A huge crimson-and-black dragon surges above me. Bale's powerful jaws clamp down on the woman sucking from my chest. He bites straight through her, blood spilling over me. He lifts his head and tosses what's left of her aside. A vampire lunges in and sinks his blade into Bale's exposed chest, shoving it to the hilt.

Bale roars, and panic hits me. *Did that reach his heart?*

"Bale?"

"Take the blade out," he snarls.

I stagger to my feet, lightheaded from blood loss. While Wade and Danica and the two wing guards try to defend us, I grab the heavy blade and yank it from Bale's chest. Blood gushes from the wound, but he instantly shifts. He's a man again, his amber eyes holding mine and blazing like burning coals. Under his battle-stained shirt, there'll be unmarred skin, healed during his transformation. It's how he gave everlife to our birds.

Bale pivots and starts fighting again, keeping me behind him. I hold on to the vampire's sword. Mine are on the ground somewhere, trampled and slick with blood.

"Why do they want me like this? What's happening?" Every vampire here wants a bite of me, and I don't know why. They pound at my circle of defense while I try to recover enough strength to join the fight. Bale doesn't answer. Wade might not hear me. Danica simply shakes her head.

A sharp, familiar caw is my only warning before Fyrestar

swoops over me and slams into the two closest vampires. He flies between them, and his hard-burning wings slice right through their necks.

I sob once in relief, the sound breaking from me like a cloudburst.

Rim swoops in right after him and tries to do the same. He cuts through one neck, but not the other, his blazing wing not hot or strong enough to do more than knock the bloodsucker over. My eyes widen in horror as the falling vampire snaps up a hand and grabs one of Rim's feet, yanking my phoenix to the ground. The vampire twists, and his fangs instantly find Rim's neck, digging through feathers to reach his jugular.

"No!" Terror shatters me from the inside out. I leap between Wade and Danica and skid to the ground. I drop the heavy sword and use both hands to pry the vampire's jaws apart. He's working hard to suck Rim's everlife from him, to take his chance at rebirth. Ferocious and unimaginable strength fills me, and I pull so hard I dislocate the vampire's jaw, then tear it right off his face. He falls away from me, gushing blood from his ruined neck, and I hurl his mandible at an approaching vampire with enough force to lodge it in her face.

The second Rim is free, he flops weakly away from his attacker, his eyes glazed over.

The vampire claws at me. I heave the sword up and lop off his head just as a warning prickle explodes up my spine.

Dropping the heavy sword, I jerk my dagger from my boot and whip around on one knee. The vampire grabs me before I can blink and viciously bites my neck. She uses her fangs and her hard grip on my arms to drag me up until my feet don't even touch the ground. Rim squawks weakly. I can't get my dagger around. She holds me against her in a vile embrace, taking long, deep, heavy drags of blood. She drains far too much before Fyrestar knocks into her, screeching his fury and burning her head.

I fall as the vampire reels away, her hand flying to her mouth. Her fangs darken and crumble. My head spinning, I slowly rise, dragging my dagger and the heavy vampire sword up from the blood-wet ground. My skin feels thin, my veins fragile. While she's still in shock, I plant my dagger in her neck and rip it sideways, severing the vein. She gurgles, her eyes bulging. As she gushes stolen blood from the jugular, I heave the sword around and slice off her head.

Rim cries a warning behind me. I spin. More bloodsuckers pounce. Fyrestar dives in with violent rage. He doesn't just burn them; he incinerates.

To the side, I see Bale again—a torrent of power and fury.

Digging up buried strength, I somehow lift the vampire blade and run it through an attacker before her outstretched hands and sharp fangs clamp down on me. The strike doesn't kill her, but it's enough to slow her down while Wade leaps in from behind and splits her in half.

Wade's eyes meet mine, questioning, as she drops between us.

I shake my head. I wish I knew.

Breathing hard but sluggishly, I stagger when my feet don't feel like they're under me. The sword slips from my fingers. My vision swims. I keel over and land next to Rimblaze. He blinks at me. I blink back at him.

Groaning, I turn enough to look up. Fyrestar is a storm above us, wings and fire and blazing ferocity. No one can touch us with my warbird's protection and three of the Elite Wing fighting furiously. Bale roars my name. The deep sound echoes like it comes from far inside Drayke Mountain. It makes me want to go home to my room with the roosting wall and my phoenixes.

I know the moment the rest of the squadron and their wing guards arrive, slower than either Fyrestar or Rimblaze. The vampires trying to get at me suddenly find themselves fighting for their lives. From somewhere in the heart of the battle, Kellan calls for me, so frantic, so frightened.

I can't answer. I've lost too much blood. I barely feel it pumping through my veins. My head feels thick. I shiver.

He needs to move on. His pain breaks my heart. I wish I

could've loved him the way he loved me. I just didn't. It would've made things easier.

Maybe I'm not capable of feeling that much. My heart pounds slowly, heavily. *Hurting*. Except...I know I can.

"I love you, Rim," I whisper, reaching out to touch him.

"I love you too."

I wriggle closer to him because he's warm, though not burning into another life, and I'm cold, maybe losing mine.

CHAPTER SEVENTEEN
IDALLIA

I sense where I am before I open my eyes. Three warm, heavy bodies surround me, and the air smells of cold rock, pine-wrapped mountains, and brisk autumn air. I take a deep breath, savoring the feel and scents of home.

"I knew you were alive. And now I know you're awake." Sybil's voice pulls a weak smile from me.

"Let her be," Stuart chides softly.

I open my eyes to find them seated in the chairs by my bedside. My birds occupy their usual positions, with Rim and Sol on either side of me and Fyrestar warming my feet. To my instant relief, they look fine. Fyrestar appears uninjured, and there are no marks on Rim's neck.

But then, they heal faster than I do.

"How long has it been this time?" I croak in a scratchy whisper. "Water?" I struggle to sit up.

"Long enough that someone was going to have to force broth

down your throat pretty soon." Sybil pours me some water from the pitcher on my night table.

I take the cup she offers, barely able to close my fingers around it. I can't remember being this weak in a long time—maybe ever. The daylight streaming through my open window shocks my eyes, and I squint at my friends. "You know I can go ages without food."

Water is different, and I eagerly sip down the cool liquid. I just wish my hands didn't shake. Sybil and Stuart both notice and exchange worried glances. Fyrestar's eyes narrow, and his plumage grows even warmer. I do like toasty feet and smile in gratitude, though I'm not sure that warm toes will help my strength return —or melt the cold nugget of fear lodged deep in my chest.

"Maybe you can go without food when you're healthy," Sybil says, "but when vampires drink half your blood, it's a whole different story."

"Half, huh?" I drain the rest of my cup, but even my own throat working reminds me of vampires forcing pointed teeth through my skin and sucking out my blood in great, thieving gulps. "Are you sure you're not exaggerating?"

"A lot, then." She frowns at me. "Too much."

I shrug. "Must not have been too much, or I wouldn't be waking up."

She huffs in impatience, her tone sharpening. "And how do you feel?"

"Like utter shit," I admit. "Awful." Inside and out. I shouldn't have been flippant. Guilt gnawing at me, I say, "I'm sorry."

Her expression softens. "Like I said, too much. You *are* lucky to be waking up." Her voice wavers, and I feel even worse for being a pain in the ass. I just hated the way they were looking at me. So scared. I'm scared enough right now as it is.

Stuart leans in and puts his arm around his wife. "I'm sorry the torque didn't work better. Maybe it needs to be thicker. Cover more of your neck."

I shake my head. "No, it was amazing. It totally disintegrated two bloodsuckers' teeth."

"It didn't stop the rest." With his free arm, he waves a vague hand toward my body. I instantly feel a stabbing twinge in my thigh and at the top of my breast.

The knot gripping my stomach tightens, and every horrible, too-sharp memory of the battle comes flooding back. Frenzied vampires. Me. Rim.

I clutch my cup so hard the pottery shatters in my hand. I stare at the chunks in my lap. "Good thing that was empty."

"At least a few sips of water are already helping you regain your strength," Sybil says archly as she stands and helps me pick the pieces off my blanket. She dumps them into the basket I use for trash before sitting again, her expression somewhat less anxious.

I guess my show of renewed vigor helped ease her worries. I don't tell her it was more about fear than strength, but my birds seem to know. Fyrestar watches me closely. Rim and Sol snuggle in.

"Is everyone else okay?" I ask. "What happened?"

"Everyone is all right now," Stuart answers. "Wade and Danica were pretty beat up."

"They gave my new apprentice healers some of their very first post-battle work. No vampire bites, but more slashes and bruises than I even wanted to count." Sybil leans back in her chair, and I realize how tired she looks. Not only did she certainly work hard to heal me herself, but she had to supervise everyone else.

"And the wing guards?" I glance at Rim. "Rim?"

"The injured wing guards are fine now. They all healed relatively quickly, especially Rim." She gives my phoenix a fond look. "He was motivated to get back to your side as quickly as possible."

"The healing room wasn't for you, Rim?" I ask.

"This is my room." His immediate answer is all I need to feel a huge lump rise in my throat.

I swallow it down, but my eyes brim as my gaze skates over my birds. All three look back at me, their eyes bright, their lifelight strong.

"What *really* happened?" Stuart asks gently. He leans forward to rest his elbows on his knees. Worry clouds his expression, forcing deep lines between his brows and aging him by ten years. "No one else was bitten like that."

The shudder that runs through me is wholly involuntary and impossible to hide. "I don't know. We were severely outnumbered, but we were holding our own. Then one of the blood traffickers got in a slice to my thigh. As soon as they scented my blood, they all went berserk. The battle didn't seem to matter anymore—not the prisoners they took, or even their own injured or dead. They just wanted *me*." The shock of being held down, bitten, my blood rushing violently through my veins and into someone else, rattles me all over again.

"But why?" Stuart doesn't understand any more than I do.

"I have no idea." Unnerved, I reach out and touch the yellow-orange fluff around Sol's ear. I smooth it, the contact soothing me. "Does my blood look any different to you?"

Sybil shakes her head. "It's just blood. And if you can stomach eating some meat, it might help you recover faster."

I feel sick at the thought, bile already stinging the back of my throat. But I hate being this shaky and reluctantly nod. "Can you mash it up and put it in some soup?"

She smiles. "You won't even know it's there."

Unlike the vampire bites that still throb insistently. The top of my breast aches, just like the column of my throat and front of my thigh. I discreetly feel my leg through my blanket. The skin is flat and smooth except for where the pain lingers. I touch my neck, finding raised lumps there too. If they haven't disappeared yet, there's a good chance they aren't going to.

"Scars?" I ask, wincing.

Sybil winces back at me. "Only the bite marks. I don't know

why. They should've disappeared along with the leg wound and bruises."

I slowly exhale, the breath as unsteady as the rest of me. Maia wears the scar on her cheek like a badge of honor, and it suits her, enhancing her beauty. My starsdamned vanity means I don't want anything lasting on me, even in places other people don't see.

I might enjoy flirting when we head out to our usual tavern down in Drayke, but only Kellan has ever actually seen me naked. The idea of baring myself to anyone again just gets scarier the more time goes by, and having these puncture wounds to explain isn't going to help.

"If Bloodwold vampires couldn't repel firebreath, we'd have won in seconds, and no one would've gotten hurt." We'd win every time. Blood traffickers wouldn't be a problem, because they wouldn't dare. They'd die.

"Magic like that isn't limitless. You know Rannigan Bloodthief must be sanctioning every single raid because he's getting his sorcerers to cover those vampires in that magic before they cross the border." Stuart shakes his head in anger, his mouth a grim line.

"You mean it'll wear off?" Sybil asks. "Like on the ones Bale captured?"

I look over sharply. "He got some?" They both nod.

"And it'll definitely wear off," Stuart confirms. "The Vampire King's sorcerers will have to recover their strength and then concentrate the same magic on the next batch of blood traffickers. It would have to be internalized—in an object, for example—to last indefinitely."

"Like the torque?" Sybil asks.

He nods. "And someone could steal an object. Or die with it in enemy territory. It's harder to make a spell permanent than temporary, and this magic is too valuable to them to risk wasting it that way on expendable minions."

"Makes sense," Sybil says.

I agree. I hadn't thought about the fact that blood traffickers die all the time, which is probably why Rannigan hasn't invested dwindling magic in more than a temporary solution to their firebreath problem.

Sybil and Stuart exchange a warm glance. I know he admires her healing skills, just like she admires his knowledge and talent with other types of magic.

The obvious affection and appreciation between them whisper to me that something is missing from my life. I don't like the thought, and I dislike how Bale instantly comes to mind even more. The sensation of loneliness deepens with the shadow of Bale in my head, and I snuggle Rim and Sol closer.

Stuart scrubs a hand down his grizzled chin, his late-day stubble rasping. The light through my window is thinning, and Stuart is always clean-shaven in the morning.

"It must be near dinnertime. You two should eat and rest." They both look like they need it.

Stuart's face brightens at the idea of dinner.

"We'll let you rest too." Sybil stands, pulling a somewhat creaky Stuart up with her. "But I'll order your meat soup and come back with it after dinner."

The words *meat soup* make me shudder. Turning my instinctual grimace into a syrupy smile, I say, "Sounds divine."

Sybil laughs. "Now I know you're fine."

"Sarcasm as proof of health?" I ask, grinning.

"It's a good start." Her eyes tell me how pleased she is.

I keep mine wide open until she leaves, still holding hands with Stuart. I know if I blink, I'll see her death, and that's more than I can handle right now.

I ask Fyrestar exactly what happened after I lost consciousness next to Rim on the battlefield.

"Everyone fought like it was the end of the world. They tore

through the vampires and, at the last second, stopped killing to take a few prisoners."

"The vampires weren't attacking in any normal way. Did that at least help?" One of the last things I remember seeing was them fighting *each other* to get to me.

Fyrestar clicks his beak in confirmation. *"They were chaotic and reckless and definitely not working as a team."*

"You didn't get hurt?" I ask warily.

He shrugs his wings. *"Besides the heart failure you and Rim gave me, not really."*

My face crumples. Tears spill from my eyes. There's no real reason for it except for too much emotion and real fear still lurking so heavily in my chest that it presses on every heartbeat. "Could Rim fly home?"

Rim lifts his head for the first time in several minutes. *"Kellan carried me."*

My heart turns over hard. "I thought you were asleep."

"Sleepy." He tucks his beak back under his wing, adding a muffled, *"Not sleeping."*

"Me either," Sol chirps groggily. She won't be left out, even of the who's-sleeping-or-not conversation.

I keep my arms around them both, my eyes on Fyrestar. "How did I get home? I couldn't ride you."

"Bale."

Heat floods me, making the glowing phoenixes on either side suddenly feel excessively warm. My mind jumps back to the battle and Bale crashing down next to me, his eyes firelit and savage. He bit into that vampire drinking from my chest like she was a raw steak. He took a sword in the chest for me.

A little to the left, a little deeper...That blow could've killed him.

A heavy swallow works its way down my throat. "Bale doesn't carry anyone."

"He carried you."

"How? I was unconscious."

"In his talons."

I stare at Fyrestar. "Well, that news must've made the rounds inside the mountain already." What would the inhabitants of Drayke Mountain make of it? What did *I* make of it?

And how like me to be unconscious during something I would really have liked to remember.

Fyrestar slants me a cautious look. *"Kellan came by every day to check on you."*

My heart sinks. "Don't. I can't." Fyrestar loves Kellan, and no doubt wanted us to stay together and have little half-dragon shifter babies he could tuck under his wings and coo over. All my birds loved him. Kellan treated them like family.

Sol looks up. *"Kellan brought us snakes to eat. Then we could stay with you and not go out hunting. I like snakes. Better than rats. No tummy aches."*

I bite my lip. "That was nice of him." I appreciate his thoughtfulness toward me and my birds. "And Bale?" I ask almost hesitantly.

"Bale too," Fyrestar answers. *"Every day—just like the rest of the team and their wing guards."*

Is that answer meant to caution me?

I sigh. "I should get over it, shouldn't I?" Fyrestar knows exactly what—*who*—I'm talking about, even if we've never had a single outright conversation about my hopeless fascination with the Dragon King. He knows me too well to have missed the signs, and he understands people better than most.

"That would require him getting over it too."

My eyes widen, my pulse thumping so hard that the fresh vampire bites throb along with it. "No." I shake my head. "He's never said anything."

"Neither have you."

Ridiculously hot all of a sudden, my heart knocking at my ribs like an unwanted guest, I roll my lips in and slowly sink down in bed. Between my uncontrollable self and the heat of my birds, I start to sweat. Fyrestar cools his inner warmth in response and moves off my feet. The other two don't stir at my sides, and I keep an arm around each, two thick bundles of heated feathers that I love more than life itself.

"I can't do it," I whisper, suspecting Rim and Sol are now truly asleep. "If things end like they did with Kellan, I don't think I could stay here. I'd lose our home, the team...Maybe even you birds. You're as much Bale's as mine, and your everlife is tied to Drayke Mountain."

Fyrestar's golden eyes get brighter as the room dims. *"Why would things end?"*

"Don't they always?"

"In your vast experience, yes."

I huff a dry laugh. "I'm supposed to be the sarcastic one."

"I learned from the best."

I can't help smiling, even though I feel more heartsick than anything else. "I can't risk it. I won't. I can't risk our life here."

"I don't think that's the right outlook. If you never risk anything, are you truly living?" His gaze slides to Rim, and I get the feeling Fyrestar didn't try to keep him away from the battle outside Draywood. Maybe he even told him to come. *"And Bale's different with you."*

I frown down the bed at him. "Different how?"

"For a self-proclaimed friendless, lone dragon shifter, he sure spends a lot of time with you. Can't seem to help himself."

Fyrestar's seemingly casual words are anything but, and they blaze through me like an inferno that could burn my resistance to ash. "Are you telling me to risk it?"

"I'm telling you to look to the future instead of the past. And problems don't always repeat themselves."

"Or they might, and then I could lose everything, including you."

"That won't happen," Fyrestar says evenly.

Fear still churns inside me. "I don't think you can guarantee that."

"If you leave, we'll leave with you. I guarantee it."

Raw emotion clogs my throat. I don't think Bale would try to keep the warbirds against their will, but who really knows what someone will do? And if what Fyrestar says is true, then my decisions will have a huge impact on them. They love the life we have here as much as I do. If my actions ruin that for them, I'll never forgive myself. I don't want to ruin it for any of us.

I expel a long, heavy breath. "I think I'm a mess right now and shouldn't make any important decisions." Fatigue drags at me. I'm also starving.

Where in the stars is my meat soup?

A knock comes just seconds after that thought, and I groan in relief. I can't shout for Sybil to come in without waking the babies, so I wiggle out of bed and stand. The second I'm upright, I sway like I'm at my drunkest after too many mugs of dragon's brew. My low-necked nightgown practically falls off me, but it's only Sybil, so I don't reach for a robe. I was too hot anyway, and the smack of cool air feels good.

I stumble toward my door, the cold stones under my bare feet wicking away my heat in seconds. Fyrestar warbles a worried sound from the foot of the bed. I try to smile at him over my shoulder, but it must be more of a grimace. He doesn't look convinced.

Tugging at my drooping shoulder strap, I revise my earlier thought about only Kellan having seen me naked. Romantically, that's true. But as my healer, Sybil has the fun task of cutting me out of bloody clothes, cleaning me up, and getting me into a fresh nightgown to recover in. I'm usually unaware of the process. Before her, Everly did the same.

I blink as I reach for the door, the split second of darkness revealing Sybil's snow-white hair, parchment-thin, age-speckled skin, and milky, unseeing eyes as blindness makes her last years more difficult. I angrily shove the future aside and yank open the door with the violence of grief already inside me.

I gape in shock. Bale is on the other side.

CHAPTER EIGHTEEN

BALE

I nearly crush the bowl of soup in my hand as I stare at a half-dressed Idallia, my inner heat blazing to life. My mouth goes dry. *Great fucking stars.* She's magnificent.

She stares back at me, her golden eyes round with surprise. She pulls up the little strap falling down her shoulder. The second she lets go, it falls down again. That strap sliding down her smooth skin holds my absolute focus. I want to bite it in half and replace everything she's wearing with *me*.

"I thought you were Sybil." My gaze snaps back up at her words. She seems out of breath and unsteady on her feet.

"Sorry to disappoint. I brought your soup." I hold out the miraculously still-intact bowl, hoping she doesn't notice the fire-scorched rasp in my voice.

Taking it, she cradles it against her chest. She visibly shivers, and the dark peaks of her nipples press against her white nightgown. I stifle a groan and focus on her face. What I see sobers me. She's gaunt and pale, and the dragon in me howls to pick her up and warm her against me, getting her bare feet off this cold floor for once.

"No, I'm glad you did. Thank you." Her gaze warms, a smile touching her lips. "It's a long climb up the stairs for Sybil. Now she can just go back to her quarters and rest." Idallia steps back, inviting me in.

I stay where I am. Sparing Sybil the climb to the Elite Wing quarters did factor into my decision to carry up the soup. But was it the only reason? My gut knows the truth, and I try never to lie to myself. That seems like a fool's way out.

Idallia's other shoulder strap slides down, and I track the narrow strip of material like prey.

She blushes, seeming to realize the bowl of soup crushed to her chest is the only thing holding her nightgown up. Turning, she walks across the room to the chairs near her bedside, the very last of the day's sunlight illuminating her curving silhouette through the thin white gown.

Riveted, I hover in the doorway. I know her shape already—combat clothes aren't exactly loose—but seeing her like this is something I try not to even let myself imagine. There's too much history between us that she isn't aware of.

I shouldn't be here. I probably *wouldn't* be if I hadn't let myself believe in the desire spilling off her in waves before everything blew up in Porthwood. Thinking she might actually want me as much as I want her is clouding my decisions.

I force myself back a step, the chilly dimness of the mountain corridor helping to slap some sense into me.

Idallia sets her dinner on her night table, then reaches for the thick robe draped over her bed frame. She pulls it tightly around herself, belts it, and then sits awkwardly, the teetering drop into the chair seeming to startle her as much as it does me.

Concerned, I step back into the room. "That bad?" I ask, my feeble resolve to leave dissipating like smoke on the wind as the door snicks shut behind me.

She groans, tilting her head back against the chair and closing her eyes. "Worse."

Two sets of round bite wounds on her neck glare at me accusingly. If she knew who she was—*what*—maybe she could've avoided that. Maybe she'd have known what she was up against.

It feels too forward to sit with her, so I move toward her open window and look down at Drayke as dusk colors settle over the capital of Torridaig. Lights already twinkle in the sprawling city nestled in the valley below, its serpentine shape following the river cutting through the central mountains. Steep hillsides rise on all sides, the dark pines almost black, and the granite cliffs sheer and imposing. Upper Drayke Lake shines like a polished sword on a plateau above the city. The towers of the military school rise in the distance beyond that, hundreds of dormitory windows reflecting the orange light of the setting sun. Idallia hated it there, and I think her pain goes far beyond the incidents I know about.

I turn back to her, a woodsmoke-scented breeze whispering over me from behind. "Things got out of hand near Draywood." I clear my throat. If that's my apology, it needs work. "I'm sorry I asked Fyrestar to leave you."

Her eyes widen, and she tugs at her robe. "I'm sorry too. But I understand why you did it. He's the fastest."

"It broke your rhythm."

Shrugging, she glances down. "A lot of things break my rhythm." Her eyes abruptly lift again, and she throws me a cutting look. "Do better, right?"

Regret sinks through me. I wish I'd never uttered those words. "You're already one of the best."

Her expression sours. "Maia beats me all the time."

"It's about even," I concede. But if Maia were Idallia's enemy, I know who I'd bet on—a small, lithe, incredibly powerful black-haired blur who hasn't tapped into even a fraction of her strength and abilities.

"*You* beat me."

I puff out my chest. "*I am* the best."

Her reluctant laughter heals something deep inside me that broke as she hung lifeless from my talons during the frantic flight home.

"I heard you got the prisoners you wanted." She reaches for her soup and lifts a spoonful in toast. If the face she makes after her first swallow is any indication, I might have to coerce her into eating the rest.

Exhaling heavily, I lean against the window frame. "I did, but Draywood is half gone. Twelve people are dead."

Looking even more sick to her stomach, she lowers the bowl to her lap. "I'm so sorry, Bale."

Nodding, I scrub a hand down my face, wishing I could scrub away the guilt. "It's my fault."

"How is it your fault?" Frowning, she eats again. At least she knows what's good for her, even if she doesn't like it.

"I'm sure someone tipped the Bloodwold vampires off to us being in Porthwood. And it turns out Rannigan himself was just over the border—probably at that stronghold not far into Hellwood Forest where a lot of his tunnels connect." She nods, knowing the one I mean. We see its dark towers from the air when we fly along the border. "Raiders usually go out in smaller, more discreet groups, but I think Rannigan must've gotten wind of the Elite Wing being in Porthwood and sent everyone he had in the area out as a big show of force." I pause. "Maybe even to try to eliminate us."

Her too-thin face goes flat with shock. "That's why there were so many of them?"

"There was ample time for the in-house sorcerers to coat them all in protective magic. The blood thieves must've gathered underground during the day to attack the second night. We should've gone to the border in secret. We shouldn't have been so visible." My mouth twists in disgust.

Her grip on her bowl turns her knuckles white. "How do you know Rannigan was there?"

"My spies hidden throughout Hellwood Forest spotted him

traveling northeast toward Blackrock Keep *after* the raid. He was at the border when we arrived. He sanctioned the whole thing himself."

Slowly, carefully, she lifts another spoonful to her mouth. "It didn't work out for him."

"No." I sigh deeply. "But it didn't work out for us, either." And there's no way a few vampires didn't make it back over the border and into the tunnels again. They'll have reported on the blood frenzy, which means Rannigan will know what I have in the Elite Wing. Likely even *who*.

Idallia bites her lip, the soup once again forgotten. "We took back the people they captured. And we got your prisoners. We all made it back alive."

"Eat," I rumble more harshly than I intend, not willing to reason away my role in the destruction of my city.

She swallows another spoonful. "In the bigger picture, I don't think it's as much of a failure as you think. We killed a lot of blood traffickers. It'll take Rannigan a long time to build up that much of a force again."

"And I won't let him."

She cocks her head, her expression sharpening. "Is it finally war, then?"

"It might be," I acknowledge. "I still want to see what happens at the upcoming Council, but even if I can force a tied vote, I don't have high hopes."

"For Rannigan or for Cealastra?" she asks warily.

I chuckle without humor. "Both."

She shivers and looks at her birds, worry creasing her brow. If magic dies, a phoenix can too.

Swallowing, she turns back to me. "We'll deal with whatever comes next. We'll figure it out, even if it means eliminating one of the ruling bloodlines."

Up until now, I'd hesitated to do just that out of respect for Cealastra, but if the Star of Ellonrift isn't going to help maintain peace and balance between the kingdoms—the very role of the Council she guided us to establish—then I'll do it.

"We?" I ask roughly.

Her gaze drops to her soup. "You."

Suddenly overheated, I welcome the breeze at my back. I like the idea of *we* too much, but I can't tell her why. Or how.

Reality pokes holes in my reasoning. I can. I *should*. I just... don't.

I watch her as she picks at her soup, slowly eating. Telling Idallia everything she wants to know would likely help me. It's the political move I've been waiting to spring on that sorry excuse for a Vampire King. But my vengeful anticipation morphed into bone-deep dread somewhere along the line, and the political move became less important to me than the person.

I know Idallia. I doubt she'd suddenly hate me. We'd hopefully be allies. But we wouldn't be teammates, and maybe not even friends. I proclaimed myself friendless, but the thought of her pounded away at that with such intensity I had to reevaluate. Except, once she knows, she won't have to put up with me, or stay here, or do anything I ask. And I won't just lose her. I'll lose Fyrestar, Rimblaze, and Embersol.

I push off from the window frame, half-wondering who I am anymore. Clarity was the one thing I had for so long that losing it feels like losing myself.

"I don't mind the idea of *we*," I say impulsively. "I value your counsel."

The spoonful of soup halfway to her mouth hovers forgotten as she stares at me. "Thank you," she finally says, lifting it the rest of the way to her mouth.

Still too warm, I clear my throat. "Is the soup good?"

She makes a face I know all too well. "It doesn't matter as long as it helps me be able to stand up tomorrow."

"I wish we could find something you actually like." But that's the problem with her kind, and why they're so rare. Unheard of, really. Hunted, unsatisfied, unable to reach their true potential... It's the choice of no parent for their child. But when the time came, Idallia didn't have natural parents to choose the usual path for her. She had a bloodbath and then Rita and Gerard in one of the most isolated places in Torridaig.

It took finally knowing Idallia to realize how lacking my choice in homes for her was. Or maybe the lacking home *formed* Idallia, making her who she is now.

Either way, Glarraden was better than Bloodwold.

"Me too. I like fruit, though. Especially red or black ones." She grimaces, as if knowing that preference is revealing but not understanding why.

"Figs," I say absently. It's no surprise, with their thin but firm skins and fleshy red insides.

She nods, still slightly frowning, and I turn again, looking out the window as she finishes her soup. I've stayed this long, lingering when I shouldn't. I might as well wait and take the empty bowl away. Rimblaze and Embersol are sound asleep. Fyrestar pretends to sleep, but I don't think he ever truly rests unless Idallia does.

I hear her set the empty bowl aside and turn back around, ready to take it—and my leave of her.

A hot pang erupts in my chest. She's sitting there in her robe, a little color back in her cheeks, and my mind instantly puts her in my lair, in one of my chairs, instead of here in hers.

She tucks her feet up under her. "I've been thinking about what you said."

"Oh?" I move closer, curious.

"Some rugs might be nice." She glances around, her long black hair sliding over her shoulders. Even in the dusk-dark room, it shines like a starlit waterfall.

"Rugs?" I rasp.

"The floor does get cold, especially in the winter. It's only autumn, and I'm already feeling the bite."

I round the bed, drawn to her as if the gold shining in her eyes is the summit of my treasures. "Shall I provide some?"

Her brows snap together. "That's not what I meant. I can buy my own rugs. I'm just...glad you suggested it."

"Always so independent," I murmur, stopping next to her.

Her eyes flash, her chin already high. "What does that mean?"

As usual, her combativeness excites me. My dragon especially wants to join the fun, and shadows push at my skin, hot and demanding. Both parts of me sense the challenge that is Idallia and reach for it with talons and hands. "You refuse to rely on anyone."

"I rely on my birds." Her immediate reply cools my enthusiasm. Her phoenixes always come first, and good luck to anyone who tries to join their tight circle. She lifts a hand in my direction. "And you pay me wages. I might as well use them."

"What if I said you should get a raise?"

"Then everyone gets a raise. We're all paid the same."

An almost melancholy smile slips out. Idallia is a team player to the core. I should let that guide me, instead of my doubts. "I think raises are in order. It's been at least a year."

She arches black brows. "Great. Then we can literally swim in gold instead of just rolling around in it."

I bark a sudden laugh, startling a snuffle from Embersol. Idallia leans forward and lays a reassuring hand on the young bird, scowling at me to be quiet.

Sitting next to her, I lower my voice. "Dragons have a particular relationship with gold." Maybe that's why her eyes captivate me.

She leans back once Embersol settles. "There's no dragon in me."

"Which is why you don't care about hoarding gold."

Her expression turns pensive. "No, I do hoard it. When Rita and Gerard are gone, I'm going to gut Glarraden House, throw everything away, and start over. The place is huge. It'll cost me a fortune."

I nod thoughtfully. I can already picture what she'll do to the country mansion just from knowing her. It'll be unpretentious and clean-lined, unembellished without being bleak. There'll be ample space for huge wingspans in every room and down every corridor, nothing to easily catch fire from stray sparks, and good roosting spots all over the place.

Longing spreads through me for inclusion in that comfortable home she'll create. "Will you be sad when they're gone, even if it gives you Glarraden House and all that land?" Rita and Gerard are long-lived, like all dragon shifters. And they're not warriors, giving them a good chance of lasting a very long time. However, they already weren't young when I dropped Idallia on their doorstep, and I estimate they've now lived about three-quarters of their natural lives. Barring a tragedy, Idallia should outlive them by far.

She seems to think about my question, those golden eyes growing distant and a little unsure. Her gaze sweeps down, and she plucks at the belt of her robe, making my mind jump back to the thin scrap of a nightgown underneath. The outline of her body against the fading daylight hits me in a scorching flash of memory, and desire thumps in my groin. Inside me, instinct growls with feral intensity, urging me to slake a need that's been building for years.

I breathe slowly, evenly, forcing calm over the man and asserting control over the dragon.

"I'll miss them in a way," she finally answers.

"In a way?"

She shrugs. "I spent so long trying to get them to notice me that I imagine I'll feel a little lost when I don't have that impulse anymore, especially when I'm at Glarraden House."

Her confession strikes like a dagger through my chest. Worse, her pain is my fault—partially, at least. "I hope you're not lonely anymore."

Her gaze immediately swings to her birds, and that dagger twists. Has she ever turned to me first? "Not at all. But my memory is too good. Nothing ever fades, so my whole life feels like yesterday."

"You know you're exceptional in that way?" I lean a little closer, keeping my voice low. "It's the same in combat. You remember every move anyone makes, which means you can anticipate just about anything from the slightest twitch."

She swivels in her chair to face me. Her feet are still up, her arms around her shins. She looks young this way. Or maybe it's the doubt clouding her expression, taking away decades of the skills and confidence she's built with the Elite Wing. "That only helps when I'm really concentrating. Otherwise, I'm too slow."

"You're not too slow. You just feel that way because you're so fast when you're truly focused and...*free*." I can't think of a better way to say it. She's either free or caged, and there's a real difference. Except Idallia's *caged* is what most highly skilled warriors can only strive for. She's comparing herself to the five best fighters in the kingdom and *me*. I chose the Elite Wing for a reason. Her *free* is the most extraordinary thing I've ever seen, and if she wasn't hindered by the circumstances keeping her from reaching for the stars, there's a good chance she'd even beat me.

Unless I shifted against her.

She sighs. "Too bad my *free* isn't guaranteed."

"I know." And being the one to know why it isn't makes me very uncomfortable with this conversation. I try to find the positive. "But when that moment hits and you just go, you can be hard to see, even for me," I admit, wedging myself sideways to face her.

She seems pleased with that, though her smile turns into a grimace. "Sometimes I go too fast, and I don't know what I'm doing until it's already done."

I wave that off. "So far, you haven't stuck a sword in a friend instead of a foe, so I think you're more aware of yourself than you realize."

"Let's hope." Her focus strays back to her birds.

My gaze following hers, I ask, "How do you find room on

your bed?" Her bed's made for two, but there's definitely no space for another person in it. There's barely room for her.

Her low laugh warms my blood. "They don't usually sleep with me. They'll snuggle up for a bedtime chat but then go to their roosts. They're just staying close to help me recover."

I nod. They're all she needs. That much is clear.

"Bale?" Her oddly cautious tone makes my heart flip uncomfortably. I turn back to her, wishing I could take the sudden fragility out of her expression, crush it in my fist, and hand it back to her as the rock-hard diamond I know she is.

"I'm here," I say hoarsely.

"What happened near Draywood really scared me. I keep seeing it over and over." She gingerly touches one of the bite marks on her neck. "And I have this knot in my stomach that won't go away. And Rim." Her voice wavers, and she clamps her mouth shut.

I reach out and grip her hand, bringing it toward me before I know what I'm doing. "Rim's fine." Her eyes widen, then dip to our joined hands. "You're fine."

"Am I? We all know what happened wasn't normal. They were killing *each other* to get to me."

My mouth quirks. "Made our work easier."

"It's not funny."

Her tremble goes all the way to her fingertips, and I squeeze her hand. "No, it's not. But things turned out all right, so now we have to concentrate on what comes next, not look behind us."

Shaking her head like that's impossible, she pulls her hand away. "I think I'll be looking over my shoulder for a hundred years."

"If you do that, then they win, even if they didn't kill you."

Her irritated huff proves, at least to me, how much fight she still has in her. "That's a little dramatic."

"So is being paranoid for a century."

"So...what?" She sits back, scowling. "Get over it?"

I nod. "Get over it. Move on."

She purses her lips, then smacks them in a way that conveys utter annoyance. "Maybe that's how you work. *Getting over it* isn't exactly my strong suit—as you point out all the time."

My own mouth puckers, my now-empty hand still feeling the warmth of hers. "You won't always have the luxury of wallowing. Believe me."

Her jaw drops. "Wallowing? Are you fucking kidding me? I just woke up a few hours ago after nearly *dying*." She stands abruptly, making Fyrestar look up from his fake sleep. "I'm sorry I confided in you. I won't bother you with any more *wallowing*." She walks surprisingly steadily toward the door and flings it open, clearly inviting me to leave.

I regret everything I said immediately. "Close the door. You're making a draft, and it's already cold in here." No wonder she doesn't mind sleeping with three firebirds hemming her in. I'd suffocate in seconds.

"Fine. If you won't leave, I will." She pulls her robe more firmly around her, looking at Fyrestar.

I stand. I'll be damned if I'll let her fly out in the dark, weak and undressed. "Close the door, Idallia." My voice rumbles as my dragon seeps out, coating me in shadows. "I'll leave you in peace."

Something darts across her expression. Regret maybe? It's hard to tell. She shuts the door but doesn't move away from it. She watches me, head high, eyes wary.

Emotion jerks inside me. I think she says the wrong things as often as I do when we're together, and then we fight.

Does she realize how similar we are? Because I do—in more ways than she knows.

"It's okay to be afraid. Just don't let it stop you from living your life." I almost cringe at my own words. Isn't fear the very thing stopping me from reaching for what I so clearly want?

The object of my hesitation looks back at me. Finally, she says, "Let's just...call it a night. I need to rest." The hand I gripped earlier presses against her stomach, seeming to push back against that knot of fear she told me had lodged there.

I move toward the window, heavy with regret. I'm heavier still with the knowledge that I don't want to leave. I want to comfort her, but I can't.

"Sleep well, Sunshine." Her lips part on a sharp breath I hear like it's right in my ear as I turn, vault over the window frame, and let my dragon loose.

CHAPTER NINETEEN
IDALLIA

I can't sleep. I slept, but then I woke up, and now my mind won't stop churning like river rapids after a torrential downpour. The skin on my hand still remembers the warmth of Bale's even though it's been hours since he touched me. Is that something a friend would do? No matter what Bale says, I think we're friends. Fyrestar seems to think we're more.

I rub my fingers against my palm, rekindling the sensation of skin on skin. That's the first time Bale's ever touched me in a way that wasn't related to combat or training. Even his hand in my hair that day at the pillars or his menacing whispers against my neck were to teach me a lesson. This...This was offering comfort and reassurance.

My insides tighten and heat, and I swallow down the longing trying to overtake my more reasonable thoughts. Don't risk it. Don't invite change that probably won't work out for the better. Don't set yourself up for another disaster. Though I bet it would be different than it was with Kellan. With Bale, my heart tells me *I'd* be the one left devastated and wishing it hadn't ended.

I curl in on myself, goose bumpy and chilled even with my birds surrounding me. Despite what I told Bale, half the time they don't go to their roosts, especially when I'm injured or unhappy.

The open windowpanes thump gently against the wall as a cold wind scrapes over me. I'd vaguely thought about lighting a fire in the hearth but lost my motivation the moment I curled up with my birds. Now the room is frigid, and it's either shiver the night away or get up and close the window.

Groaning, I drag myself out of bed and half-stumble across the room. Another chilly breeze blows in, and I lift my head, breathe deeply, and embrace the shock of it almost as a punishment. I feel like such a failure right now that a wind-lashing seems entirely appropriate. I allowed Rim to fly into danger. I let vampires draw my blood for the first time in two hundred and twenty-six years of existence. The team had to rescue me and fly me home—again. I can't shake my feelings for Bale. Instead of crushing them into nothing, they continue to grow.

I stare out the window, disappointed in myself and shaking with cold. The night sky is clear and full of stars, Cealastra's constellation the biggest and brightest. It's shaped like a giant bird —wings flared, beak sharp and dangerous, talons reaching, its shining eye the Star of Ellonrift. I think it's where Bale got the idea for creating our phoenixes. They were as much an enduring army for him as a homage to her. It pleased the goddess at first, the warbirds' everlife so strong with her blessing and the light of her star that no one could ever have imagined an uncertain rebirth.

Now it's a worry that never leaves me.

Sighing, I lower my gaze to Drayke. A few lights still flicker far below, but the city mostly sleeps, just as I should be doing. To the right of the city, the forest and lake are dark, but the School of Fire and Flight sits off to the far side of the Upper Valley, its high towers blazing with light.

I stare at the beacons, my jaw hardening until my teeth grind.

Always lit. Always bright. Those towers are a symbol of strength and power. The soldiers of Torridaig all train there before either applying to be stationed somewhere around the kingdom or returning to protect their homes. Rita and Gerard must've expected me to go back to Glarraden once I'd finished school, if not exactly to the house—where I'm sure they didn't want me anyway. Even I expected it. I never thought I'd catch the eye of the Dragon King or become a member of the Elite Wing.

Yet here I am. And it's the best thing that ever happened to me. It gave me my phoenixes. My family. My friends.

Bale.

I reach out and close the two wide, mullioned-glass panels to hold in the heat my firebirds will generate. I don't latch them, always aware of my birds and their need to go out—to hunt, to see to their personal needs, to fly. I'll never put a lock between them and freedom. But I don't need a cold wind blowing over me, either.

Turning, I hurry back to bed. I slip under the covers, angling between Rim and Sol and giving Fyrestar my icy feet. I keep shivering despite their warmth and don't close my eyes. If I do, I know I'll see vampire fangs and frenzied eyes.

Fyrestar increases his inner heat, slowly taking the frozen edge off my feet. *"I think you swayed all the way back to bed,"* he remarks.

"I was dancing." It's a bald-faced lie he's not supposed to believe. Blood loss is no joke, though I do feel steadier since that soup Bale brought me.

I bite my lip and try not to think about the rest, but I feel Bale's hand on mine again, his amber eyes steady and encouraging.

"You're not funny," Fyrestar grumbles.

"I'm hilarious."

A mind-to-mind snort is an odd sound, and one Fyrestar doesn't make often. He stares at me from the foot of the bed, the liquid gold of his eyes our only light. *"You don't have to be alone, you know. We won't think you love us any less just because you let someone else in."*

My heart yanks sharply across my chest. "I don't know what you're talking about." All I did was close the window.

And not sleep for hours.

And maybe cry a tiny bit. I thought he was asleep.

"I'm talking about Bale. He looks at you and can't look away. He doesn't want to leave. It was never more obvious than today. And he carried you. Kellan wanted to bring you home, and Bale just about ripped off his head."

I roll my lips in, pressing hard. Voice low with emotion, I rasp, "You're all I need."

"Life's not just about what you need. You should have what you want. I can hear your heart pound when Bale is near—and I'm sure he can too."

Stupid, unruly muscle. It pummels my ribs right now.

At least I'm abruptly warmer. "Please stop."

"Because talking about it makes it real?"

I nod, tears like thorny spikes behind my eyes. I swallow down the heat in my throat. "If I can ignore it, I can just live. I was doing a good job of ignoring it before. I think I can again, as long as you stop bringing it up like this."

"'Just living' isn't much of a life, especially when it's as long as yours."

I curl my hands into my blanket. "I'm not ready for anything to change."

"Change is inevitable. You shouldn't fear it. It's what makes up a life—and makes it interesting."

"Change isn't always for the better."

"You're no coward, Idallia. It's okay to fear change, but don't run away from happiness."

Closing my burning eyes, I wrap an arm around Rim and another around Sol, my toes under Fyrestar's wing. "All I want is for us to be together until I die. Nothing else will ever matter more than that."

Fyrestar is quiet for a long time. *"I wish I could give you my everlife."*

I squeeze my whole face, stifling a wild sob. "No, Fyrestar. The only reason I can face every day is because I know I can't lose you." Except, that might not even be true anymore.

There's another long pause. *"But how am I supposed to face every day? What's there to come back to if you're taken from me?"*

Hot, fat tears leak from my eyes and roll toward my pillow. I don't know how long I'll live. And something or someone might kill me.

"Rim and Sol." But it's true. And it's terrible. Unless magic continues to fade from Ellonrift, the warbirds are eternal, and that'll be a curse in the end, because they're as linked to me as I am to them.

"Time heals, but it'll take a million years, and I don't want to live that long." His golden eyes close, snuffing the light from our room.

I turn onto my side, quietly crying. I don't care how or when, but I know right then what I have to do for Fyrestar, Rim, and Sol. I'll leave them a child. That will be the safest child in all the world, and my phoenixes will have someone to love utterly again. To burn for, over and over, until that child leaves them another child and so on, because eternity is no gift unless you have someone to love so much, you'd die for them.

A LIGHT BECKONS ME IN THE DARK. I KNOW I'M dreaming, so I don't hesitate to chase the strong glow toward the open door at the end of a long corridor, even though the huge hallway is shrouded in shadows and slightly intimidating. Tall, open windows let in a warm summer breeze that makes the series of long, sheer drapes billow toward me. The dim skyline beyond the openings is gently hilly, with a clear, star-studded sky hanging over the rolling silhouettes of moderate slopes I don't recognize. They're not spiny and rugged like the mountains of Torridaig.

I keep moving forward, not aware of my feet touching the ground. The fluttering curtains brush my skin, and their ghostly touch makes me shiver. Music wafts from the room ahead. I think there might be dancing, and I hurry, wanting to join in.

After a strangely long time, I finally reach the end of the corridor and peek into a richly decorated, candlelit room. It's full of beautifully dressed people, most of them dancing, their jewels flashing as they pass. Others stand off to the side, holding conversations over goblets of red wine.

I smile. It's beautiful. Festive. The night is dark, but the ballroom is blazing and happy and alive. I stare in wonder. We never have parties like this at Drayke Mountain. Bale is too busy and somber to give this much thought or space to frivolity. That's why the team and I go into Drayke sometimes, to drink and flirt and sway to music with strangers we can leave behind.

The music calls to me, a little foreign, though not entirely. My heart still wants to dance, but I'm suddenly worried. My birds aren't here.

I look over my shoulder, but no glowing phoenixes swoop down the endless corridor. Frowning, I turn back around. I don't like being here without them.

Somewhat shy, especially without my birds to keep me company, I stay in the doorway as I watch the revelers dance and laugh and tip their goblets to their lips. There's a timelessness to the scene. Maybe this is now. Maybe it's later, or before, or never. I don't recognize any of this, and yet it feels achingly familiar.

A big hand clamps down on my mouth, stifling my startled cry as I'm yanked away from the party so fast I fly backward down the long corridor, the light and party and music fading to a pinpoint before snuffing out.

The hand abruptly releases me, and I'm in Glarraden House.

Confused, my heart pounding, I look around. It takes a moment to shake off the remnants of the party and the sudden fear of being forcibly ripped away. I'm in my bedroom, the veranda doors wide open and letting in a splash of bright sunshine that I know has warmed the dark patio stones to burning. I still step outside, letting the heat blaze against the bottoms of my bare feet and the sun crash into my face and eyes.

I cock my head. Why am I here?

Squinting, I look to the right and see Rita and Gerard in the rose garden. They're at their usual table and in their usual chairs, an awning shading them. There have only ever been two chairs at the table where they spend most of their time, season permitting. She reads and sews. He reads and draws. They play games sometimes.

I can obviously go into the rose garden if I want to, but I don't have a chair at that table, and the awning only covers the two of them, so I know I don't belong.

I look to my left across the grounds and into the woods leading to the big pond and the wild marsh beyond. I should go that way. It's my domain. There's nothing there. No one.

But the heat and sun are bothering me, too bright, so maybe I should go up into the attic with all the discarded furniture and other forgotten items and play dragon shifters versus vampires. No one ever hears me crashing around under the eaves, and no one cares if I stab old couches with the sticks I've sharpened into knives and swords. Things that go into the attic never come back down.

Except for me.

I slowly back into my room, escaping the midday heat. I feel like me—the *me* I am now—and wonder again where my birds are. But these memories are old, from when I still grew like a human child, changing every year, and Rita still thought she'd marry me off to some Glarraden well-to-do who'd finally take me off her hands while leaving her the gold.

With a blink, I'm not in my bedroom anymore. I head toward the stairs, ignoring the statues lining the walls. That's Gerard's doing. He likes them, but I just see blank eyes that don't notice me any more than anyone else does.

I'm headed for the attic when abruptly, I'm at school. My stomach plummets with a sickening downward pull. The Drayke School of Fire and Flight should've been the best five years of my life. I couldn't wait to have friends.

My dormitory building gets closer, then sucks me inside with a giant breath. High up in one of the shared rooms, students surround me. My pulse races, my insides churning in dread. One-on-one in the training yards and with the instructors watching, I almost always win. The other students don't like that, and sometimes I throw a fight, hoping it might change something when school hours are done. It never does. Outside the training yard, with no one watching, they gang up on me. I think I could probably still win, but I don't want to kill anyone by accident. This isn't much of a life, but prison would be worse.

They close in on me, backing me toward the rounded wall. Their individual faces are sharp in my mind. I remember everyone.

The heel of my boot hits stone. Then my shoulder blades. The wall at my back is cold. Students are hot and angry and jealous in front of me. Pressed up against the rough stones, I could still land a few punches and kicks, but what good would it do? They're going to overpower me, dangle me out the window, and demand their share of gildenfae gold.

I'm suddenly upside down, hanging out the soaring window, the stone courtyard far below. They hold me by the ankles and give me a good shake. A single gold coin falls from my pocket. A greedy hand lets go of my ankle to grab for it, and I wake with a scream.

I struggle up in bed, breathing hard. My shout still rings in my ears. Fyrestar's eyes are my only light in the dark. Then Rim's blink open. Then Sol's. They know my sleep can be agitated, but I don't usually scream.

Cold air sweeps over my bare shoulders, the annoying straps

of my nightgown halfway down my arms again. I yank them up as I glance at the window. It's blown open, and I really want it closed. Trembling, I swing my legs out of bed and stand just as Bale bursts through the open window, his horned, black-and-crimson head leading the way before he shifts into skin and stands in my room, shadows spilling from him.

Gasping, I jump the height of Drayke Mountain. "Bloodpit!" My pulse takes off violently, my hand flying to my heart.

Bale sweeps me behind him, looking for threats. "What's wrong?"

Startled shock mixes with the still-vivid feeling of being shaken out a window. I gape at Bale's wide back, a few shadow scales continuing to darken his neck between his shirt and hair. "Why would something be wrong?" The fact that I'm shaking like a leaf means nothing. Nothing at all.

"I heard you scream." He turns to me, his brow drawing low.

I shuffle back, putting more distance between us. His inner warmth blasts over me, and I don't hate it. I fear leaning in. "From the top of the mountain?" I smooth the mess of hair back from my face, my blood still beating like a storm. "Even if your hearing is *that* good, how did you get here so fast?"

"I was flying around." He waves a vague hand toward the chasm outside the window.

I swallow. Flying around outside my room? Heat pricks me all over. Bale feels like a wash of sparks blowing over me from a bonfire that I can't brush off my skin. They just keep burning deeper and deeper. Short of breath, iced over but somehow burning up, I almost feel as if I'm coming down with something. Maybe it's dragonkingitis. Bale is a force. He might also be a disease.

"I didn't scream." I glance at Fyrestar, who narrows his eyes. "I mean, I might've made a noise..."

I see Bale's expression darken just from the light of the stars. "You screamed," he counters bluntly, "so what's wrong?"

His gruff concern catapults my heart right into my throat. So does the hard edge in his voice. "Nothing. Really. Just a weird dream." I shuffle toward my bed and grab my robe, knowing he can hear every absurdly loud beat of my pulse.

Fyrestar gets up and ruffles his feathers. *"It's almost dawn. Let's go stretch our wings and hunt for breakfast."* Rim and Sol immediately stand.

My lips part in shock. Did our conversation during the night mean nothing to him? I stare in disbelief as he takes off, Rim and Sol hot on his tail feathers. Judging by the complete absence of sunlight, it's not close to dawn, and Fyrestar just left me alone with Bale because apparently, he's a hopeless matchmaker.

Bale watches them fade into the darkness. "I don't think I've ever seen the young ones move so fast."

My voice sours. "They'll follow Fyrestar anywhere."

"And you." He turns back to me.

The echo of my conversation with Fyrestar is louder than ever as I nod. Shivering again, I decide it's my room, and I can do what I want. I hop back into bed, fluff my pillows so I can sit up, and pull the still-warm covers over me. "Now that you crashed through my window like a falling star only to discover that I'm fine, you can carry on with your flying around."

Bale pushes the windows most of the way closed, then follows me to my bedside. "Trying to get rid of me?"

"Is it working?"

His eyes like two smoldering coins, he watches me attempt to get comfortable—impossible with him standing there. "What happened? Why the shout?"

"What if there was someone else in here?" I ask in lieu of answering. "Not all shouts are bad."

His hands curl into fists. The darkness around him deepens, shadows creeping from his skin. "You can admit to having nightmares, Idallia. It's not the end of the world."

"And you can admit to having friends. It's not the end of the world."

He sits on the side of my bed, making the mattress dip. "We're not talking about me." His gaze roams my face. "Are you all right?"

No. The tenderness in his voice makes me want to cry. And no, because the thing I want most right now is to crawl into his arms.

"I'm fine." I lift my chin. "Nightmares are for children."

"Nightmares are for anyone."

"Why? Do you have them?"

Bale shrugs. "Sometimes."

If even the Dragon King has nightmares, what chance do I have of escaping them?

"It really was just a strange dream," I finally say. "Things I recognized. Things I didn't."

"And the scream?"

The sickening feeling of dangling from that high-up dormitory window swoops over me again. None of the Elite Wing were at school with me; I'm much younger than they are. They were already seasoned warriors before I was dumped on the doorstep of Glarraden House with only a bag of gold and a name. I'm not sure exactly what they know about my years at the Drayke School of Fire and Flight, though rumors fly as fast as dragon shifters, and I've no doubt they've heard some. Bale too. But I'm not interested in digging for sympathy, and the idea of telling Bale that I was mercilessly bullied for five years tempts me about as much as pricking open a vein and sauntering into Bloodwold. "I dreamt I was falling."

"Off your warbird?" He frowns.

"Out a window."

"At Glarraden House?"

I exhale sharply. "Can we just stop? It doesn't matter now."

He moves closer. I think he's about to reach for my hand, but then my heart thumps ferociously, and he stops. Dragon heat ignites in his eyes. "Who do I punish?"

My chest lurches. "Punish?"

"Who tried to throw you out a window? Who do *I* throw out a window now?"

Staring at him, I barely breathe, my pulse pounding harder than dragon wings. I glance at Bale's hand, wishing it would move toward mine again as much as I wish he wasn't even here. He used to keep to himself all the time. That was so much easier. I never knew how much I wanted him with me until he *was*.

"I don't have fire or flight." My voice not steady at all, I add, "If someone had tossed me out a window, I'd be dead."

The fire rolling in his eyes doesn't dim. "So it was at school."

It's not a question. "And a long time ago, Bale. It doesn't matter anymore." I don't mention the *multiple* times. Or the times they almost dropped me. He might already know.

"You took revenge all on your own." There's pride in his voice. It helps repair my frayed nerves.

I nod. I took the last, coveted spot in the Dragon King's personal squadron. The Elite Wing was my revenge.

"Why didn't you fight back? At school, I mean. You would've won."

I sigh. Once I had a bit of official training under my belt, it usually took a real effort to lose. Losing didn't win me any points with the other students, though, especially when they just complained about having to fight in skin all the time because of Bloodwold vampires, so I went back to winning. Skin was all I had, and I was happier winning than trying to make friends with people who didn't even want me there.

"I was afraid I'd kill someone," I admit. "You know how it is when I'm *free*, as you said before. My mind is a few steps behind my body sometimes, and I didn't want a dead student—or ten—on my hands."

"So you let them do what they wanted?"

From his questions, it's obvious Bale already knows most of what I'm not saying. I wonder who reported to him and why. The headmistress? She was kind enough to me, but still couldn't wait until I left. "They just wanted my gold. The dragon in them..." I shrug, and the half-smile that touches my mouth actually feels real.

His expression softens, his slight smile echoing mine, and the icy nugget of fear still lodged in my chest melts. The one in my stomach—blood thief central—doesn't budge.

I almost scratch the fresh scabs on my neck before forcing my hand down.

"Are you ready for the Council?" I ask. "It's getting close."

Bale's eyes glint in the dark. "Not many people change the subject on me as boldly as you."

"I like to keep you on your toes." I spread my hands. "Or talons."

"Or both." His low chuckle doesn't last. "As ready as I'll ever be. At least we have those Bloodwold prisoners."

"Will they turn on Rannigan?" It seems unlikely. None have before. They've preferred death.

"Probably not, but I've got our sorcerers working on a truth spell. I'm hoping I can pull honesty from them."

"But it could just as easily be a *lie* spell. The other Council members might not trust it."

Sighing, Bale briefly closes his eyes. "Not what I wanted to hear."

"Sorry." I grimace.

"Don't be. It's a good point." His shoulders hunch like an invisible weight bears down on him. "I guess it'll be good, old-fashioned coercion then."

"Unfortunately, the same logic applies. They could lie under duress."

A frustrated sound rumbles in his throat. "Options are limited. It's going to be hard enough keeping them alive until the Council. One chewed through a vein yesterday. The others seem more interested in survival—for now." He scrubs a hand down his face, and the mattress groans as he shifts his weight.

My heart squeezes at seeing him so discouraged. "You could offer asylum," I suggest.

"Fuck that," he growls. "I'm not going to reward blood thieves with a place to live in peace."

I nod. I wouldn't either. "Are you going to send us away again? I know you don't like it when we're here for the Council." I don't even think I'd mind leaving this time. The hostility will be thick enough to cut with a knife, and everyone will be on edge. Besides, the thought of having the Vampire King here, in Drayke Mountain, turns my stomach, especially after what happened outside of Draywood. *To* Draywood. To *me*.

"I'm not sure yet," he answers. "We'll see."

My gaze on him sharpens. That's a first—potentially. Only Maia and Arran have ever been in residence at Drayke Mountain during a Council meeting that took place here. "What about Fanghaven? There must be a way to stop the Vampire King from proxy voting for his wife. Can you insist she votes in person, or her vote won't count?"

Bale's lips twist in a wry smile. "We can vote on it."

I snort. "That sounds like a serpent biting its tail. The vote will be a tie at best. Or a flat-out loss."

"Trying could at least force Cealastra to appear." He scoots back to lean against my footboard, lifting his legs and crossing them at the ankles on my bed. If I reached to the side, I could lay a hand on his foot.

I fold my hands in my lap. "And if she doesn't?"

"Then we'll know Cealastra is gone, magic will be next, and Rexton Hale can claim the Fanghaven throne with impunity unless Rannigan Bloodthief can prove his wife still lives."

The weight of a millstone drops through me. If magic goes, my birds can't come back.

"He's a cousin of some sort to the Fanghaven royals, right? Rexton Hale?"

Bale nods. "Not starborn, but the closest living relative to the murdered king."

"Except the Vampire Queen. It's her vote Rannigan keeps tossing around."

He nods again. "Except the Vampire Queen."

"*If* she exists. For all we know, she's as dead as the rest of her family, and Rannigan has been lying in her name ever since the massacre."

"We can't know," Bale murmurs from the foot of the bed.

"*This* long, and only Rannigan's inner circle has ever seen her? They could be lying—all of them." I shake my head. "Maybe you should just support Hale's claim. Fanghaven will ally with you. With that vote, you're a block of three."

"Torridaig, Ruthinock, and Fanghaven, as it was for more than half my reign." Bale looks at me, his gaze heavy. "I can't support his claim."

"Why not? It would solve a lot of problems."

"Because he's not starborn."

"That's very elitist of you," I snap, pulling my legs up under me and sitting forward. "From what we know, he's competent, cares about his people, and upholds Fanghaven's traditions. Besides, we don't even know if Cealastra is still around to choose her next pet."

Bale's eyes widen. Mine too. "Pet?" he grinds out.

I wince. I should apologize. Instead, I ask, "What if Cealastra is gone and you die without an heir? Who rules Torridaig then?"

Bale's expression cools. So does his tone. "I don't plan to die without an heir."

I wave that off. "No one *plans* to die. You need to get on that, or Torridaig is in big trouble." Heat crawls up my neck. It's too late to take that back, so I just own it and stare at him, my gaze as stony as his.

"Since you're so concerned, perhaps you can suggest a mate?" His overly smooth question grates on my nerves.

"Forget it, Your Passive-Aggressiveness. I'm sorry I brought it up."

Bale doesn't look amused. "Rannigan doesn't have an heir yet, either."

"Hopefully his poor wife is fighting him off," I say dryly.

"Especially because that child would rightfully inherit both vampire kingdoms."

"True." Bale sighs loudly. "I've never wanted a Council meeting less."

He sounds so weary, clearly sensing an end to a system that was bound to fail. "I'm sorry I said *pet*. I didn't mean it."

His eyes flick to mine. He nods, then changes the subject. "When they burned my city, I wanted to cross the border and burn one of theirs."

And I would've helped him. But... "Do you really think that would make things better?"

He slowly shakes his head, his amber eyes like burning stones. "Not every Bloodwold vampire is a monster, just like not every dragon shifter is good and noble."

I instantly see students dangling me out a window and jeering about gold. "That's very wise of you."

His lips jerk up in a smile, but the sound he makes is as brittle as winter leaves. "You should get some rest. You're still recovering. I'll stay until your birds return."

The moment Bale mentions rest, fatigue slams into me, and I almost wonder if he hasn't added the power of persuasion to his charms.

Slipping deeper into bed, I pull up my covers and close my eyes. I relax surprisingly quickly despite Bale's presence, and drift in an in-between state, not quite ready to leave this moment behind.

Bale confiding in me.

The two of us talking in the dark.

I'm not cold, even with the window still slightly open, and I don't actively miss my birds. With everything else quiet and calm, even my heartbeat for once, I can hear Bale breathing. I can smell him, too, that combination of dry leaves, woodsmoke, and wind. His scent reminds me of that huge pile of autumn leaves old Gus used to rake up for me behind Glarraden House. Gus was already ancient when I was a child, but he'd still find the strength to hoist me up and toss me into the pile. I loved it. And I wasn't alone. He died and returned to the stars when I was only five. I was sad for months, and nobody noticed.

I lift heavy lids and see Bale watching over me from the foot of my bed. I'm not alone, even without my birds.

I don't wake until morning. My phoenixes are back, and Bale is gone.

CHAPTER TWENTY

IDALLIA

The following afternoon, Bale summons us all to training at our usual location next to Upper Drayke Lake. Fyrestar and Rimblaze get to participate, but I'm told in no uncertain terms to sit aside with Sol. It's fine. I don't love everyone else getting to keep in shape and learn while I have to sit on a rock and watch, but I also know my limits. I might not be staggering around anymore, but I'm not up for a fight against the best warriors in Torridaig.

A little rest can't hurt. And the sunshine feels wonderful.

I tilt my head back, soaking it in. I won't tan, but the rays feel nourishing on my skin, and like they're sinking into my black hair and feeding me as much strength as that meat soup Sybil keeps bringing.

It was meat soup for breakfast and lunch today. It'll probably be meat soup for dinner.

My stomach always feels a bit off after eating it, but it must be doing me good. I'm getting stronger by the hour.

A blaze roars, drawing my gaze back to the combat scorching up the field. Watching the team train in scales is impressive. The ferocity. The pure instinct. The fire and flight. It's a dragon shifter's natural way to fight, and they only get to use this part of themselves against marauding werebeasts now. Too bad marauding blood thieves don't burn like weres.

The fae are a whole other trouble, but they don't tangle with Torridaig on an organized level. And maybe the new queen won't tangle with Torridaig at all.

Bale flies over me in a whoosh of heat and wind, his shadow covering me for a split second before he's gone.

I shiver, goose bumps spreading down my arms.

Since you're so concerned, perhaps you can suggest a mate?

Mortification jabs needles of regret straight into me. My stupid question and Bale's flat-toned reply bring heat to my face all over again. I've heard Marissa Turin is exceptionally beautiful. Worse, she's desperately in need of protection. What if Bale sees the new Fae Queen and decides *he* should be the one to protect her? And as more than just an ally.

Dread settles heavily in my stomach. Torridaig and Tanturriff joined by marriage? A starborn child to eventually inherit both? The territory would be colossal. The populations too. Bloodwold would tremble, even if Rannigan Bloodthief still controls two thrones.

Consciously shedding my dire thoughts, I square my shoulders, inhale deeply, and concentrate on drawing the warm sunshine into my lungs. Above me, the team goes at each other like beasts. They use all their tools. Flames and wings. Claws and fangs. The fire is constant, heating the air so much that sweat dots my brow. Dragon scales provide protection against firebreath, but strong enough blasts will still scorch. Everyone is going to have reddened skin when this is done—except Bale.

Sol watches with me, entranced.

"They are a sight, aren't they?" I murmur.

She bobs her head, then chirps worriedly when Fyrestar darts under a slashing claw, trying to help distract Maia away from Bale. Bale forms a team with Fyrestar, Rim, Wade, Danica, and their wing guards against Arran, Maia, Kellan, and theirs. Sol tweets in triumph when Fyrestar twists in the air, surges upward, and bangs his beak into Maia's sensitive lower-chest scales. Maia growls fire at him and spirals out of the way as her wing guards swoop in to force Fyrestar back.

"Too close," Sol mutters.

"He had it under control," I say as Fyrestar circles around to regroup with Rim. They hover for a moment, then Rim dives in like a flaming arrow and uses almost the same move on Kellan, zipping away before either Grambolt or Featherspear can attack. Kellan gives Rim a fiery side-eye, and I smile.

"Fyrestar is a good teacher." Sol's feathers spark and warm, and she hops excitedly on the rock next to me. She wants to join the training, but she's far too young and small.

"He'll teach you soon." Sol might be the size of a small lynx already, but she still has a lot of growing to do. She's half Rim's size and a quarter of Fyrestar's. The Elite Wing lets her in on training sessions sometimes, but never when it's a full-blown mock battle in scales.

"I remember things," she chirps with confidence, already too grown up for her own good.

"You remember. That doesn't mean you have the strength, reflexes, or skills."

"I'm fast."

"That you are," I agree. At her peak, Embersol was even faster than Fyrestar. "But you have to follow Bale's rules, which means no combat until you pass your tests. He's the king, and he knows what's best for the warbirds."

"You don't listen to Bale."

I nearly choke on a laugh. "Yes I do."

"Not like the others. Not like Bale is in charge of you."

I glance at her, frowning. "Why do you say that?" Bale is

definitely in charge of me, so I don't know what Sol is talking about. But the young often spring truths on unsuspecting adults.

"I'm not always as sleepy as you think." She gives me a cheeky look, her soft, yellow head crest bobbing from her constant movement. *"He likes to talk to you."*

My eyes widen, then I laugh. "You sneaky little phoenix. Well, I like talking to him too," I say a little wistfully. I feel the impulse to add that he talks to everyone on the team, but I know he doesn't really. I think the only other person he confides in is Stuart.

And I know that from *Stuart*. Bale doesn't say a thing.

"He seeks you out. Can't stay away."

"Okay, that's enough," I say, my chuckle strained this time because of the almost painful explosion of heat crashing through my body. "I'll bet you listen in on a lot of my conversations with Fyrestar, don't you?" Ears pricked, eyes closed, little beak tucked under her wing.

"Rim does too," she chitters, fluffing her wings.

Smiling, I shake my head. It doesn't matter. We don't have secrets. But I don't know if she's old enough to understand that us forming a family with "Dad" is extremely unlikely and probably not good for anyone, especially me.

Sol jumps closer, and I loop an arm around her barrel of a body, enjoying the warmth of her feathers and the sunshine on my skin. It's almost too bright and hot, though, reminding me of my dream from last night and how I backed off the patio, the flat, dark-gray stones burning my feet.

"Maybe we should visit Glarraden House. I can't train for a few days anyway—not like that." I nod toward the Elite Wing, fire roaring, tails thumping, fangs and talons slicing the air. The warbirds streak in and out, twisting and burning. Rim almost hits Arran's wing, and my heart jerks, but they pass each other without colliding. Maia whips her tail around, aiming for Fyrestar. She only misses because Fyrestar calls up a burst of speed that surprises even me. I exhale in relief as he darts away from her, gathers Rim, and they come back again, ready.

Grambolt and Featherspear veer off from Kellan's wings and dive as one. They skim low to the ground, then pull up abruptly, their feet punching into Danica's flank in unison as she heads for Arran. The phoenixes would've punctured an enemy's flesh with their talons and ripped it away, spilling blood and intestines. Danica is only knocked off course. Bale and Wade dive in to protect her while she readjusts and comes back roaring.

"Rita and Gerard don't keep rats. Always hungry there." Sol's sullen little comment speaks volumes about how much my adoptive parents care about me and my warbirds.

"But you could really stretch your wings on a flight to Glarraden. And the hunting is good around the pond and the marsh. Lots of beavers." The last time we went, the flight to southwestern Torridaig was too much for Sol to handle in one go. She should be fine this time. It's been months, and she's grown. "Besides, most places don't keep rats on purpose. Bale does that especially for you."

"You're always nice to them," Sol says, and I know exactly who she's talking about. *"Why aren't they nice to you?"*

Ah. From the mouths of babes. "Rita and Gerard aren't *un*kind to me. They just don't really think about me at all."

"That is unkind."

I stroke her feathers. Sol has the brightest yellow plumes of all the warbirds, with a smattering of fiery orange mixed in that reminds me of the best sunsets behind Drayke Mountain. "What they do or say or think doesn't really matter now. I have you and Rim and Fyrestar. I have the team. I have a home—with a great big roosting wall for you," I add. "I have all the family I need."

And it's true. Wondering *what* I am doesn't mean I'm interested in finding a long-lost family—the people who abandoned me. I'll never know if they left me on the doorstep of Glarraden House out of necessity or simply because they didn't want me, and while a small part of me *does* care, it's not the question that haunts me.

Why gold still shows up on every Dragon's Night is also a good question. Whoever left me there hasn't forgotten about me in two hundred and twenty-six years. Now that's dedication. Except...not to me.

Rita and Gerard are among the richest people in all Torridaig now, and the only work they've ever done in their lives was making sure I didn't die for the first thirty-five years of mine. When everyone realized I hadn't changed at all in about ten years, my adoptive parents declared me something other than human and shipped me off to school. We'd known I was fast and strong, which is why they chose soldiering instead of scholarly pursuits, but I had no idea *how* fast and strong until a teacher put a sword in my hand and showed me a few moves.

"Idallia!" Bale's somewhat more guttural dragon's voice cuts like a rusty knife through my thoughts. *"Run a lap around the lake. Start building up your strength. Embersol flies with you."*

Groaning, I turn to Sol. "You've got the better part of this deal."

"Good deal," she chirps.

"That'll take me two hours!" I call back. The lake is huge.

"Then you'd better get started if you want to have dinner with the crew." The flat look in Bale's eyes as he flies past us does *not* invite argument.

"I told you Bale was in charge of me," I mutter to Sol as I slip off the rock and start stretching.

"In charge," she trills far too cheerfully.

I give her a sour look that somehow turns into a huge smile and take off at a slow jog. She joins me, her jaunty little face turned to the wind and happy sparks trailing behind her.

Sol makes my heart sing and my feet move faster. The lap around the sun-dappled lake goes quicker than I expected, and I do feel stronger afterward.

CHAPTER TWENTY-ONE

BALE

I shouldn't, but I can't help following Idallia when I see her and Fyrestar fly past my mountaintop lair flanked by Rimblaze and Embersol. I still haven't let her get back to training yet, although she's been diligent about building up her strength and was probably ready a few days ago. Now she's getting restless, and that'll turn into aggression before long—especially toward me.

She hears me land in the meadow next to Upper Drayke Lake and cracks open an eye as I shift into skin, but then she goes back to sunbathing as if I'm not even there.

The irritation rising in me at her apparent indifference fades like an eagle's cry on the wind as I move closer. She's lying in the grass with her warbirds surrounding her. Her hair is down, the long black locks a silken pillow. My breath hitches. The sheer beauty of them together. Idallia so cool and pale and dark-haired, and the birds so bright and colorful and burning.

The phoenixes watch me approach, even if Idallia doesn't. My affection for these birds is boundless. Not only did I create them, but they're the ones I know best. They flew with me until Idallia was ready for them. My feelings for her are more complicated. There's affection, but that doesn't account for the tumble in my stomach when I see her or the ever-increasing need to seek her out.

"Do you know the origin of your name?" I ask, sitting beside her. I lean back on my elbows and cross my legs at the ankles, soaking up the same rays as Idallia.

"No." She turns her head toward me, her golden eyes opening. She shades them with a hand, adding, "I've never really thought about it. I know I came with a name. I didn't think about it having a meaning."

"You never looked it up?"

She shrugs. "My early schooling was an odd mix—whatever an available private tutor knew or wanted to teach me. My later schooling was all about weapons and war and protecting Torridaig. If you want, I can list every border city and give their approximate population and the specific dangers they face. But I didn't know my name meant anything and never thought to look it up."

"It means *behold the sun*." I glance up, squinting. Today is one of those bright autumn days when not even a wisp of a cloud streaks the sky, and the sharp, dry air warmed by the still-strong sun feels like a glorious contradiction.

"Is that why you're always telling me to get some sunshine?" Her question is clearly baited, but I don't bite.

"Sunshine is good for everyone."

"Not for vampires," she says dryly.

I grunt a nonanswer, my gaze straying to the still-healing bite marks on her neck. "Are you up for sparring?" I ask. I might be changing the subject. I might also be trying to get my hands on her.

She frowns up at me, her eyes narrowing under the shadow of her hand. "You're the one who won't let me join training."

"You're ready now, though. Aren't you?"

She sits up so fast I barely see her move, intensely eager. She's intense about everything, which makes me wonder how Rita and Gerard could so easily ignore her. I didn't know about their indifference—not until their role was mostly finished, and it was too late to undo the damage. Formative years stick—I know that better than anyone. "I was ready days ago. Now I'm just bored."

Laughter rumbles out of me. "I didn't want to rush it."

Her face suddenly falls. "But I don't have a hair tie or pins. I'll..." She glances at Fyrestar.

"Don't worry about it. I'll make an exception." I harden my voice. "*This* time."

She stands, already bouncing on the balls of her feet, itching to fight. "I only have knives."

She was expecting a lazy afternoon at the lake with her phoenixes. Instead, she got me—and likely an invitation to disaster.

"Knives it is, then." I stand with her, then nod to her birds. "You three can go hunt for lunch. I'll bring Idallia home."

She goes still, gaping at me. "*Flying*?"

My heart cramps impressively. "Did you want to walk?" I ask gruffly, my chest tight enough to strangle my voice.

She shakes her head, her eyes so wide they swallow me whole. I hear her heart pound. At least she can't hear mine.

Fyrestar glances at Idallia. It takes her reassuring nod for the phoenixes to actually leave.

I unwind a little once they disappear into the trees. It borders on childish, but I had her all to myself that night after her scream, and I've been craving her companionship ever since. If her birds are here, I'll come last. I want to come first, even if it's only for an hour.

She rolls her shoulders and unsheathes her knives. "I might be a little rusty."

And I might be suffering from highly distracting thoughts and feelings.

I infuse my expression with wolfish aggression, trying to hide my turbulent mood. "I'll go easy on you, Sunshine."

She looks over sharply. "I've never had a nickname before."

"Never?" My blood heats.

She shakes her head. "Not even something ridiculous, like shortening Idallia to Dally."

I laugh without meaning to. "Would you have wanted that?"

She twirls her knives, looking thoughtful. "Yes and no. I'd hate it, but at least it would make me feel special." She slows, her eyes widening as she seems to realize what she just revealed. Color splashes across her cheeks, and I do my best not to react and make her feel more awkward.

Great fucking stars. I need to stop. Or else...commit to the course. The way her blood rushes in her veins, her heartbeat thunders in my ears, and her flushed skin heats the air around us, spreading her scent, overloads my senses. She's clearly affected by me—there's no doubt in my mind now—and I don't want to resist anymore. But don't I have to? Especially while I still hold her most vital truths.

Withhold them.

Tension gripping me down to my deepest layer, I clench my jaw and start circling her like a predator. The analogy is apt. I *am* a hunter, and she's everyone's prey. She just doesn't know it.

Idallia circles, wary of my slow steps. Her mind might be trying to concentrate on sparring, but her body is exactly where mine is—utterly aware of the person in front of her. Her usual scents of sunshine and ice fade under something warmer and muskier. Heat floods my groin. My nostrils flare on a long inhalation, drawing the perfume of her arousal deep inside.

Confusion darts across her face, and she swallows. Does she know her body is throwing off mating scents that drive me wild?

"What's working so hard in that mind of yours?" I ask softly. Shadows seep from me, my dragon reaching for her. I let the darkness surround me and nearly touch her.

She shivers, her gaze snagging on the manifestation of my

dragon. "Your shadows always look like they should be empty and cold, but they're not. They're hot and alive."

And I want her to walk right into them. "I thought you'd be planning your strategy."

She steadies her breathing, her focus returning to my face. "I am. Just trying to decide the best way to put you at a disadvantage."

I think she meant to toss that at me, taunting. She purrs it instead, and heat sinks through me like molten lead, turning my limbs heavy.

My voice a deepening rasp, I say, "I think you've already done that." My gaze flicks over her. She's small compared to dragon shifters. Her body is strong and lithe, making her curves almost a surprise and impossible to ignore. Her features are delicate but well defined, and her golden eyes are highly unusual and pure starlight, but maybe only I see that because I know what to look for. The truth is, Idallia is as starborn as I am.

She seems almost shaken by my answer and watches me warily. I watch her back with intensity, absorbing every detail of the woman who should be ruling her own kingdom right now. Her pale skin contrasts with jet-black hair, lashes, and brows, and she has the reddest lips in all Ellonrift, as if her body knows they should be stained red with the blood she'd be drinking if I hadn't stolen her from Rannigan and thrust her into the sun.

Those blood-red lips part on a shallow inhalation that stirs a lustful hunger deep within me. "How so?" she asks huskily.

"Your hair is so shiny it blinds me. Shiny and black and smooth."

"Dragons like shiny things," she murmurs, more sweet-scented warmth billowing off her.

"Exactly." I hear the roughness in my voice, my dragon deepening it as fire climbs up my throat. I don't usually have trouble keeping the two parts of me separate, but right now I barely feel in control. "When I pounce on you, I'm going to grab hold of that shiny hair, and I might not let go."

She forgets to circle, letting me get close enough to smell her deepening musk so strongly my cock twitches in my pants.

She clears her throat, remembering to move again. "Hair pulling is for school children."

My mouth lifts in a predatory smile. "Then I guess I'm about to school you."

I lunge so fast that she barely has time to bring up both knives and stop my downward strike. She stumbles back from the ringing blow, and I follow up so quickly that I get in a hit with the flat of my blade.

Her eyes narrow as she backs out of my reach. But my reach can be longer than an arm, and I let my dragon out little by little until there's a full shadow dragon looming over her.

She watches, her golden eyes riveted. "You never said it was two against one."

"I never said it wasn't." I lash out with my shadow tail, firming it up at the last second, and sweep her off her feet.

She lands with a grunt. "I guess that's solid."

So is something else. I refrain from the comment and attack while I pull my dragon back in. The man needs to be in control of the beast, and if that's too hard, I need to leave.

Idallia holds me off without making any progress. She finally sees an opening and kicks out, but she projects the move too far ahead of time. I grab her foot in the air, lift, and twist, launching her toward a grassier spot than where we're sparring.

She drops her knives and gets her hands under her, breaking her fall. The look she throws me over her shoulder promises the combat I'm looking for.

Excitement hums in my veins. She comes at me, and we engage in a flurry of hard, fast moves, but then she ends up on the ground again. I swoop in, the tip of my blade at her throat. "And you're dead."

Fury ignites on her face. "I'm getting sick of hearing that."

"Then do better." For the first time, those words are teasing, my tone light. I back off, but just as she starts to sit up, I instinctively leap for her again, grab a small lock of her loose hair, and sheer it off.

Her hand flies to the now chin-length piece, her eyes flaring in shock. "What the fuck, Bale?"

"Trophy for the victor." I spring up, tucking her hair into my pocket. My heart punches my ribs. *What the fuck?* is right. That's not just dragon hoarding behavior. That's courtship.

She pops up and lunges at me. Her punch is hard—almost too hard to block. I catch her fist at the last second and narrowly avoid the uppercut she throws with her other hand. I shove her away from me.

"A fist fight?" I chuckle deeply, my dragon clawing up my throat. "You're dreaming." She growls in rage, and I arch a mocking brow. "At least that sound was scarier than your punch."

My provocation must ignite her inner motivation because she goes feral in an instant. She speeds up to a blur, uses the blinding sun to her advantage, and attacks lightning fast. Her elbow collides with my jaw, her foot with my ribs, and then she fucking stomps on my foot before I even get a good enough look at her to get out of her path of fury.

Smirking, she dances back a split second before I can retaliate.

"Made you mad, did I?" I smirk back.

"Made me something," she mutters.

She lunges again, fire-snap quick, but I'm ready for her this time and sidestep, sweep her feet out from under her, and reach for her as she goes down. I catch her mid-fall and yank her back up, crushing her against my chest. She struggles, and I keep one arm banded around her back as I grab a handful of her hair, wrap it around my fist, and tug her head back, baring her neck.

She inhales sharply, going rigid in my arms.

"So quick. So strong." I trace my thumb down her neck, avoiding the wounds and stopping over her fluttering pulse.

She breathes hard, her parted lips entrancing me. Idallia's arousal tinged with rage is the most delicious thing I've ever scented.

Her voice low, almost trembling, she tells me, "If you say, 'And you're dead,' I'll do everything in my power to knee you in the balls."

I smile. How long has she desired me? "You can't move, Sunshine. Not unless I let you go."

Her jaw firms, and she doesn't say anything else. My hand loosens in her hair. I resist stroking the fantastically smooth locks, but can't help gently brushing the healing wounds on her neck. She softens at my light touch, and a physical ache throbs low in my abdomen. Can she feel my half-hard cock?

Her eyes start to change. The angry fire dims. Uncertainty replaces it, and she pushes at me. It's a clear message and has nothing to do with sparring. My dragon roars in protest, but I let her go.

She runs a shaky hand through her hair, stepping back.

I don't move, rooted to the spot as if standing still will make her come back into my arms. "You're a different creature altogether when you're angry or scared." My eyes snag on the blunt end of the hair I sheared off. My skin burns where my new treasure is hidden in my pocket.

"I wish I could be that fast and strong all the time," she says.

I step to the side, not wanting to shade her from the sun. "Sometimes unlocking full potential is dangerous. And changes everything."

I hear her heart thud like slow but heavy footsteps. "What do you know, Bale? If you know something, then tell me."

My heart thuds too. My tongue burns with everything she should know, but instead of answering, I shift into my dragon form, tucking skin inside scales and answers under subterfuge. *"Behold the sun, Idallia. It suits you better than the shadows."*

I move toward the rock she likes to sit on and wait. She'll need the height to climb onto my back for the flight home. I don't care who sees us fly in. Maybe Kellan will, and this time he'll be the one who can't stand seeing her gripping scales that aren't his.

She clambers up, and I take off with a strong leap, forcing her to squeeze her legs around me. Instead of bringing relief, her tight grip just unleashes more cravings, more pressure, more desire.

The land races beneath us, bold and beautiful. I barely see it, all my focus on Idallia. She's supposed to be the ace up my sleeve, and right now—when I no longer think I can protect Torridaig without launching my kingdom into war—is my last chance to whip her out and fling her at Rannigan Bloodthief.

Cold air hits my fangs from my own mocking smile. Hasn't time proven I'd rather keep Idallia in the dark and endanger my border towns just to keep her with me? I'm no better than Rannigan in this, but at least the darkness I keep her in comes with sunlight.

CHAPTER TWENTY-TWO
IDALLIA

I don't see Bale over the next few days, which is probably good for me. He's busy with the final preparations for the Ellonrift Council, and no emergency calls us to the war room. My heart still explodes every time I even think he's around a corner, and my sleep has been terrible, leaving me irritable and with dark smudges under my eyes.

I keep dreaming about a marble floor slicked with red, black nails on blood-covered fingers, and crimson talons that look just like Bale's. I wake up with a sharp pain in my right arm every time, just under the one scar I've always had. Two actually. They're round and identical and not far apart on my inner wrist. Rita and Gerard told me that I was bitten by a dog when I was little, but I don't remember that at all, and I remember almost everything. And now that I have matching marks on my neck, thigh, and upper breast, I'm pretty sure it wasn't a dog.

My natural healing ability didn't do away with those old

marks any more than with these new ones, but why would I scar when other people heal from vampire bites?

With these disturbing dreams, unsettling questions, and lasting scars, I want to know more than ever what in the blazing stars happened to me in the early months of my life before my perfect memory kicked in. How did vampires get to me? Did they get to my family? Is that why they sent me away?

I don't ask my questions because no one has answers. Sometimes I think Bale might, but I'm not certain enough to outright accuse him of anything, and I'm not sure I want to. Things have already changed enough between us. Everything I wanted to avoid seems to be barreling toward me like an unstoppable storm on the horizon, and I'm starting to think I can't hold off this need to seek him out and be with him any more than I can an inevitable tempest.

The first deep breath in days fills my lungs when Wade suggests heading into Drayke after dinner. Getting away is just what I need. Bale's overwhelming essence permeates the entire mountain and reaches me wherever I am, and I can't shake the feeling that we're teetering on a precipice.

One of us acts, and everything will be different.

Or we both ignore whatever's happening between us, and things might be tense for a while, but nothing fundamentally changes.

The problem is...I don't like either option.

Hurrying to my dresser, I get ready for a night out in Drayke, utterly unsuccessful in ignoring that my head and my heart are at war over Bale. I let them keep fighting and put the finishing touches on my outfit. The form-fitting leather is meant to attract, but I never follow through. Whoever I flirt with tonight might call me a tease, but I don't care. I want to blow off steam, especially after three rainy days without training.

Well after nightfall, we meet in the lounge on the Elite Wing level of Drayke Mountain. The tavern is no place for Fyrestar, so I know one of the team will fly me down.

Kellan intercepts me before I make it across the room. "How are you feeling?"

"Fine." I glance past him toward the others. "Back to full strength." I don't mention the sinking feeling that regularly swoops through me, that whoosh of dread as the frenzied vampire attack comes back to me in such vivid detail that for a split second, I think it's happening all over again.

"How do you know?" He frowns. "You weren't able to train with us, and then it started raining."

"I worked out with..." I stop. I shouldn't have to. It's been literal decades since Kellan and I were together. He needs to get over it, but something in me doesn't want to say Bale's name—for both Kellan's sake and my own.

"Bale?" He does it for me. I nod, my stomach dropping. "I heard about the flight back to the mountain." His tone is almost neutral.

"It would've been a long walk," I murmur.

He chuckles under his breath. There's no humor in it. "I'm guessing you need a ride down to Drayke." My heart starts to pound—and not in a good way. Sweat prickles my nape. "How about it?" he asks. "For old time's sake."

I stare at him, not breathing. I do need a ride. But I'd rather stay home than fly with Kellan, especially just after feeling the sleek muscle of Bale's dragon form between my legs.

Maia makes a beeline for us and slings a proprietary arm around my shoulders. "Idallia is flying down and back with me. We already talked about it." Relief floods me as she jerks her chin at Kellan, adding, "That way you're free to stay in town if you get an offer you don't want to refuse."

Kellan's eyes narrow. He looks back and forth between Maia and me, offering a tight smile. "Fantastic. Thank you." He pivots, shifts, and takes off through one of the big open windows without waiting for the rest of us.

An uneasy laugh leaks out of me along with the breath I was holding. "Thank you."

She squeezes my shoulders before letting go. "You've made yourself clear. He needs to respect it."

"If I'd known what this was going to be like, I'd never have gone down that path to begin with." I instantly think of Bale—another wrong path just waiting to happen.

Danica joins us. "Kellan needs to figure himself out. This is getting old for everyone."

I sigh in utter agreement as Arran comes over and echoes Danica's words, adding, "He's not being fair to you, always making you uncomfortable."

"Was I fair to him?" I glance out the window Kellan flew from. "He thought we were forever."

"Things don't always work out." Arran shrugs, his gaze flitting to Maia. "You can never know what'll happen."

"Hmm." I nod, but I also know that if you don't try, *nothing* will happen.

I'm not about to take my own advice, so I keep my mouth shut, even in the face of Arran and Maia's barely disguised mutual pining.

Wade joins us, his exaggerated swagger instantly lightening the mood. "The look on your face says you'd rather go back to your room right now and be with your birds, but I'm not letting that happen. It's dragon's brew tonight, and the first round is on me." He smiles widely.

I grin back, letting Wade nudge me toward the windows, but deep down, worry still churns inside me. How does one live and work with an ex-lover—or potentially *two*—for centuries? For the first time, I almost envy humans their short lifetimes.

I look around at the rest of the team as we gather to take off. We've all watched Maia and Arran circling each other for decades, but they're smart. They learned from Kellan and me. The question is, did *I* learn anything?

My head says *yes*. My heart and my body say *fuck no* the second Bale is near me.

My stomach rolls over hard, and I place a hand on my

middle. I might be a mess on the inside for more reasons than just my dinner sitting as precariously as ever, but I'm dressed to impress, in black leather pants and a sleeveless black leather top that laces up the front to tie in a bow at the center of my cleavage. A black leather choker covers the fading bite marks, though it's clear now that they won't disappear entirely. My long hair feels hot on my back, as if it soaked up the sunshine at the lake that afternoon and kept it there for these cloudy days when I'd need it.

Shiny and black and smooth.

Bale slicing off a lock and pocketing it as a victory trophy rushes back to me with striking vividness, and the hot shock in my chest makes it hard to breathe.

Steadying myself, I turn to Maia. Escape is what I need, even if Kellan will be there.

"Ready?" she asks, starting to shift.

I nod, knowing exactly where this night will lead. Some drinking, flirting, dancing, and a disappointed man or two. Offers are appreciated but never taken, at least by me.

Arran helps me onto Maia's back, then shifts, too, along with Wade and Danica. We fly out the big windows, ready for a night on the town.

WE GO STRAIGHT TO OUR USUAL TAVERN, THE FORK IN the Tail. It's big, with several rooms, all of them crowded and noisy. We're greeted like old friends, even though our visits are occasional. For the owners, it's a coup to be the local watering hole of the Elite Wing. For the other patrons, it's exciting to catch a glimpse of us up close—their lucky night, since no one ever knows when we're coming. And for us, it's nice to feel connected to a more normal life every now and then.

For me, these nights out feel like one of those school-aged

social experiences I should've had but didn't. No one ever invited me.

Drayke is a melting pot, though dragon shifters are the most numerous of the many peoples who call the capital of Torridaig home. The next biggest group is humans, but we also have vampires from Fanghaven, and refugees from Bloodwold who rebelled against the blood violence in their kingdom. Unless they want to risk a long prison sentence, Torridaig's vampires only feed off the willing, and it's no secret that when it's consensual, pleasure blossoms instead of pain.

I still shudder at the idea. I've never been tempted to allow a consensual bite, and now, less so than ever.

We also have werebeasts who hold all sorts of jobs and raise families among us. It's rarer, but some fae are mated to dragon shifters or vampires, sparingly absorbing enough years and vigor from their partners to sustain their lives and ethereal beauty. Gildenfae are as welcome as anyone else who obeys the law, but they mostly roam around Ellonrift at their own pace, finding and mining gold until tunnels run dry, then packing up and moving on to their next source of ore and lifeforce.

Enjoying the energy of the tavern, I do just as I planned for a couple of hours—drink, flirt, and dance. Kellan never shows up, making everything so much easier. There are no piercing comments or long, heavy stares. No innuendo or insults. I do what I want, and if a conversation gets too personal or I sense an invitation to go somewhere more private coming, I saunter off for another mug, leaving the flirtation behind.

There are already one too many brews in me when I decide I absolutely need to use the washroom. I walk a little unsteadily toward the back of the tavern and hate the way my head spins. I should've known better. This is when everything slows down instead of speeding up, and the hot, crowded rooms suddenly hold no appeal for me. People reel to the live music, and I squint against the lantern light flashing in my eyes as they jump and twirl and spin each other around. The aftertaste of all that dragon's brew strikes me as bitter now, and I grimace, swallowing it down.

I have to cross three rooms, and each one feels interminable. Finally slipping into the washroom, I take a second to breathe and clear my head. It's cooler and quieter here. I relieve myself, then go to the basin and spout to wash my hands and splash cold water over my face. Water drips from my nose and chin as I look at myself in the old, speckled mirror, already feeling steadier. I usually stop before the dragon's brew that puts me over the edge, but tonight, I guess I just...didn't.

I swipe the remaining water from my face. Kellan still hasn't appeared, and none of us know where he is. At first, I enjoyed the freedom from the constant pressure of his focus on me, but now I'm worried about him.

Everyone else seems to be having a good time. Wade found a battle-scarred, slightly older dragon shifter to go home with a few minutes ago. I wasn't surprised by the choice after seeing Wade's face light up when talking to the man. I have a feeling Danica is close to making a decision about the tall, blond dragon shifter who's been sniffing around her all night. And Maia and Arran only talk to each other in this place. I never worry about having a ride back to Drayke Mountain because I know they'll be right where I left them when I'm done flirting and dancing and want to go home.

The terrible mirror isn't so cloudy that I can't see the wry smile on my face. Tonight, it's been a little harder than usual to extricate myself from conversations once I'm done with them. Kellan's glowering presence usually helps drive men away from me. It's been more work without him, and the realization makes me wish he was here almost as much as I'm glad he's not. I've wondered sometimes if I'd actually leave with someone if Kellan wasn't watching my every move, but tonight is proof that I wouldn't.

Then again, no one compares to Bale Cinderheart.

Sighing, I give myself a sour look in the mirror, frustrated by my persistent obsession. Since there's no solving it—or dissolving it—tonight, I leave the washroom and plunge into the dim corridor. A man peels himself off the wall and blocks my path, the narrow back hallway empty except for the two of us and one flickering lantern.

My pulse hammers out a warning beat, and my senses sharpen. Scowling, I try to slip past him and leave him access to the now-empty washroom, but he slides with me.

"Don't be afraid." He holds out his hands. His dark eyes don't look menacing, but anyone blocking me in a tight corridor isn't my friend.

"Get out of the way," I snap.

"I need to talk to you." He's bigger than I am, tall, wide-shouldered, and sturdy with more muscle than most regular people pack on. I don't see even a hint of exposed fangs, but every instinct in me screams vampire.

My heartbeat accelerates, and my recent wounds suddenly throb. Worse is the fear that freezes me solid. I back away from him as my mind turns into a tangle of too-sharp memories. Piercing fangs, lancing pain, terror, Rim.

"I don't know you. We have no reason to talk." I lift my chin, pretending panic isn't rampaging through me.

"I can hear the blood hurtling through your veins."

"Well, that's reassuring." Shuddering, I try to push past him.

"Idallia." He grabs my arm, his tight hold pulling me close. "You're in danger."

Gasping, I rip myself from his grip and lurch back so hard I bump the wall. The lantern sways precariously, throwing nightmarish shadows down the corridor. "How do you know my name?"

"Everyone here knows your name. I simply had to ask the barkeep." He holds up his hands again as though displaying their weaponless state makes them harmless. "I'm here to warn you. The Vampire King got wind of a sunblood among the Elite Wing. He knows it's you."

I stare, my heart pounding. "What's a sunblood?"

"Those vampires that went into a frenzy over you? A few escaped and went back to Rannigan Bloodthief—with stories about how your blood smells like liquid sunlight and the sunshine we can never walk in. If that's the scent, it's the taste too."

We? I guess I was right about him being a vampire.

Unsteady, I brace my hand against the wall. "Escaped?" Fear and confusion clash in my stomach along with too much dragon's brew.

He cocks his head. "Didn't your precious Dragon King tell you?"

Bristling, I straighten. Bale told me about the captives. I don't remember him mentioning escapees. "There was a lot of chaos that night." Bale probably suspects some vampires got away. *I* should've suspected. "How do *you* know any of this? Were you there? Do you work for the Vampire King?"

The disgust on his face can't possibly be faked. "I have spies in Blackrock Keep." His strong features pinching, he adds, "I watch Rannigan Bloodthief as carefully as Bale Cinderheart *should.*"

Whatever this man has against Bale isn't my concern. "What's a sunblood?" I ask more forcefully, my nerves starting to calm. The recent bites remain hot and achy, though, reminding me of every second of that horrific fight.

The vampire's dark eyes dip over me, leaving me both worried and annoyingly warm. I shift uneasily, taking him in with a cooler gaze than he offers me. Neatly cut, wavy dark hair hugs his scalp. Fine clothing fits a powerful, athletic frame. His shoes don't show a hint of scuffs or mud. He's clearly rich, confident, and knowledgeable about things that concern me too much.

His roving gaze stops on my throat, making my pulse leap again. "A sunblood is someone who shouldn't exist. And it doesn't matter unless the rarity applies to you. Let me taste you, and I can tell you more."

A harsh noise erupts from me. "No fucking way." Words in

Bale's deep voice suddenly echo in my head. *Sunshine. Idallia. Behold the sun.*

Sometimes unlocking full potential is dangerous. And changes everything.

What the fuck does Bale know? And why hasn't he told me?

Another tremor works its way through me, and it's all I can do not to show this man how much I quake.

"Don't you want to know?" His brow furrows. "If it's true, I'll tell you all about how a sunblood is made." Steady, commanding eyes bore into mine. He looks like a man in his prime, but I see age in those granite-cut eyes.

I shake my head, my heavy heartbeat resonating like a hundred drums in the hollow of my chest. I'm not nearly as clear-headed as I should be after all that dragon's brew, but there's no way I'm taking him at his word and letting him drink my blood. It was easy for him to learn my name in this place, and it would be easy to obtain other information as well. That I'm not a dragon shifter like the others. That I was adopted and don't know where I come from. Maybe even that I'd just been set upon by vampires who went berserk—though that's less likely news to have already gotten out.

Doubt scratches at my flushed skin. "You're full of shit, and if you think you're going to trick me into letting you suck my blood, you're wrong. There's no such thing as a sunblood."

"I won't hurt you." His expression turns sympathetic, his gentle smile almost convincing. "I'll only take a sip, and with your consent, I promise it'll feel good."

I swallow hard, warmth flooding me. His voice turns velvety, full of promise, and tension gathers low inside me despite not inviting it—or him—at all. The tightening of my breasts and the unexpected pulse of desire mix horribly with the remembered terror of the feral attack on me. The battle is still alive and screaming in my mind, and I don't want this vampire anywhere near me.

"Those others couldn't control themselves," I say. Vivid

flashes of wild eyes, grasping hands, and murderous fangs drive all flickers of arousal away. "You can't either."

His brows snap together. "I'm *nothing* like those vampires." More calmly, he adds, "I'm trying to help you."

"I don't need your help. *Avoid getting bitten by vampires* seems pretty intuitive to me."

"You don't understand. Sunbloods simply don't happen. If you *are* one, there's a story behind it, something big."

"If they don't happen," I shoot back, "then your whole spiel here is a waste of time."

"They *shouldn't* happen," he corrects. "Which is why you have to hide—or change."

Change? "Hide where? In your own personal lodgings where I can be your blood host, and you can drink from me whenever you want?" I snort. "Nice try, asshole."

"I'm from Fanghaven. I don't drink without permission. And you're making a huge mistake. Rannigan Bloodthief will come for you. He'll want everything he can take from you—for *centuries*. Nowhere will be safe, not even your mountain with your Dragon King."

"If sunbloods don't exist, then I have nothing to worry about." I shove past him and don't look back.

"Idallia!" he calls after me, his voice low and urgent. "Stay out of the sun. The taste of the forbidden light will fade in time, and you'll be safer."

Goose bumps cascade over me as I hurry away from him. *Behold the sun.* Who in all the blazing stars named me? And what did they know that I don't?

Get some sun.

Stay out of the sun.

A landslide of contradictions buries me, and I shake my head, trying to fling them away and see clearly for once as I speed back to my friends.

I reach the main room and plow my way toward Maia and Arran. Wade already left. Danica's gone now too.

"Can we go home?" I ask, poised to sprint out the door. "I think I had one too many brews and need to rest."

They both get up immediately. "We were hoping you'd say that." Arran drops a handful of coins onto the table, covering the night for all of us and then some. "Not about having one too many, but about going home."

I nod, darting a look at the dark-haired, dark-eyed vampire who emerges from the back of the tavern. From a distance, I can take him in better. His clothing is truly impeccable and screams prosperity without anything ostentatious to pull him toward a garish display of wealth. His physique is flawless, tall, muscled, and strong. I don't want to think he's attractive, but he definitely is, with his marble-cut jaw, thick brown hair, and brooding eyes.

I yank my gaze away before he sees me watching him. A Fanghaven vampire who looks like that shouldn't have to lie just to get a taste of blood.

"Do either of you recognize that vampire?" I ask quietly, nodding subtly to show them who I mean. "He followed me to the washroom."

Looking over, they both suck in a breath. "Bloodpit," Maia mutters.

"What?" My heart dives straight off a cliff. "Who is he?"

"That's Rexton Hale, the pretender to the Fanghaven throne." She shields me from his view, turning back to me with worried eyes. "The one always trying to get in on Ellonrift Councils and take Fanghaven's vote back from Rannigan Bloodthief."

I blink stupidly at her. I don't think it's the brew. "The cousin who survived?"

"Did he talk to you?" Arran asks warily. "What did he say?"

"He wanted to drink my blood." Numbness rushes through me, with a chill so deep it freezes my bones. "But he stayed civil." Thank the stars.

"Let's go." Her face thunderous, Maia urges me toward the door. I let her push me in front of her. Arran takes up the rear.

We burst into the street, leaving the loud, stuffy tavern behind. The cold night air shocks a shudder from me, and I rub my bare arms. "How do you know who he is?"

"He shows up every time Bale hosts the Ellonrift Council—uninvited, as usual," she says. "He wants the Council to legitimize his claim to Fanghaven and its vote."

So that's how they recognize Rexton Hale and I don't. He's only been here when I'm gone. "Why won't Bale listen to his claim? Wouldn't it help?"

She shrugs, her puff of breath visible in the lamp-lit air. "Bale shuts him out, just like everyone else. But that doesn't stop Hale from hanging around Drayke and Drayke Mountain all week."

"He's a little early." I shiver, wishing I had a cloak. "I guess to see me."

"Why would he approach you?" Arran asks. "He could get blood from almost anyone."

"He said he heard how good I taste." Chilled and covered in goose bumps, I hug my arms around my chest. "I guess a few of those vampires escaped and told the tale." I can't imagine what importance I'd have to Rexton Hale other than him wanting to gulp down some of my drug-like blood. But why offer up dubious information in return?

Stay out of the sun. The taste of the forbidden light will fade in time, and you'll be safer.

Bale tells me to get some sunshine.

Rexton Hale tells me the opposite.

"I'm not surprised a few got away, but they'd better not start coming into Torridaig to find you," Arran growls.

Fear ripples through me from top to bottom, more relentless than ever. "One already did."

"He's different," Maia says in a steady tone meant to reassure. "Very controlled, and he knows what he wants."

"Fanghaven?"

She nods. "And he might get it one day unless Rannigan's

wife finally comes out of the woodwork to truly claim her throne."

"Even if he's not starborn?" I ask.

Her expression stiffens with worry, the tension in her jaw making the old scar on her cheek stand out and shine a pale silver in the lamplight. "What will starborn matter when Cealastra's light fades?"

When. Not *if.*

My heart drops like a stone. Does Maia already think the Star of Ellonrift is gone? Magic will be next. No more healers like Sybil. No more protective spells. No more everlife to spark the warbirds' rebirth.

Heat crawls toward my eyes. How long does a phoenix naturally live, without battle deaths getting in the way? I don't think any of us knows.

Maia shifts, and Arran helps me onto her back for the flight home. I'm desperate to see my birds, and I can't help wondering about Bale's intentions for this Council as we leave Drayke behind and angle up the mountain toward home. There's still time for Bale to send me and some others of the Elite Wing away before the Council starts. I never felt singled out in the past because I wasn't the only one to go, but now I have to wonder…

Were those missions Bale sent me on truly necessary? Or was he hiding me from Rexton Hale?

CHAPTER TWENTY-THREE
IDALLIA

It's surely not my best decision, especially with all that dragon's brew still heating my blood, but after quickly checking on my birds, I leave again without letting Fyrestar's golden-eyed observation, Rim's rumpled confusion, or Sol's sleepy little warble stop me. It's a long, steep climb up the stairs to Bale's lair, especially with brew-heavy legs weighing me down. Unfortunately for him—and my burning muscles—I'm on a mission to get answers, and I want them now.

The first time I stop to actually consider what I'm doing is when I'm right in front of Bale's door. I've never been here before.

I draw back, my hand poised to knock. After a long pause, I let it fall. I'm troubled, confused, a bit drunk, and intensely attracted to the man on the other side of the door. I should definitely walk back down the stairs.

The door swings open, startling me. Bale stands there, one

hand still on the doorknob and the other holding a towel he uses to scrub vigorously at his wet hair.

A fire surges to life inside me. He's shirtless, his trousers only half tied and riding low on his hips. The line of dark-red tattoos racing down his left side from his neck to his waist pops out at me as his arm moves to swipe the towel over his hair again, catching more drips. I stare, stupid with dragon's brew. I don't think I've ever seen this much of his inked-on series of stars, moons, and eclipses before, the straight line broken and puckered where it mixes with the scars over his heart.

"I could hear you breathing behind the door. What's wrong?" He slings the towel over his shoulder.

My eyes snap to his face, his muscled chest still imprinted on my vision. "How did you know it was me?" He just chuckles, something heating in his expression. When I realize he's not going to answer, I ask, "Are you alone?"

"I'm always alone." His gaze slides over me, taking in my flushed skin and revealing clothes.

Nervous, I wet my lips. "Not if you invite me in."

For a long moment, I don't think he'll accept my challenge. His hesitation is so palpable that I start to feel like a fool. But then he steps back, making room for me.

As soon as I'm inside, he shuts the door. I look around, curious. So, this is where Bale lives—or part of it. I see a tunnel off to one side that probably leads to a bedroom since there's no bed in here, and another that must lead to some sort of hot bath, considering the moss and condensation on the tunnel walls. Here, it's more of a large study, with bookshelves, a weapons display, tall, mullioned-glass windows, plenty of thick rugs, and a comfortable-looking set of armchairs in front of a roaring fireplace.

I spin on him. "What's a sunblood?"

He turns away, tossing the towel aside. He reaches for a billowing white shirt draped over the back of one of the chairs and pulls it over his head. His expression is neutral when he turns back around. "A sunblood?" I don't know if his lack of reaction is true confusion or the best evasion I've ever seen.

"Don't lie to me." The strong brew makes me bolder than usual, and I step forward, poking a finger at him. "They're not supposed to exist, and yet someone just told me I am one."

He looks me over more thoroughly, taking in my tight leather pants and corset-like top. His gaze hitches on the now-askew bow at my cleavage, and heat swells in my veins. His eyes flare. Shadows coat his skin. "Where were you tonight?" he growls.

"Out in Drayke with the team." I shouldn't feel like I have to justify anything, but more tumbles out. "We popped down to the tavern and back. Nothing special."

His jaw tight, he scrutinizes me. "You're the last person I'd expect to be cavorting with vampires right now."

"I didn't say he was a vampire," I answer warily.

"You didn't say it was a *he*," Bale rumbles ominously.

I narrow my eyes. "Why did you automatically assume vampire? What do vampires have to do with sunbloods?"

"I have no idea what a sunblood is." He sits, waving me toward the other chair in front of the fire.

I swallow. Sitting with Bale in his lair is a whole new level of intimacy. Too bad I'm here to interrogate, not seduce.

Or obviously, it's for the better.

"Who named me?" I ask.

"Sit," he snarls.

I sit. "Who fucking named me, Bale?"

"How would I know?" he snaps.

Clenching my teeth, I take in the cavernous space as I inhale a deep, calming breath through my nose. This is a home, not just a room. Except, there's no roosting wall. But why would there be? Bale gave all the phoenixes to the Elite Wing.

No matter how mad I am, the heat of Bale's fire soaks into my autumn-chilled skin and feels homey in a way I've missed out on all my life. I almost never light my fireplace, relying on my birds for warmth, and the space in front of the hearth at Glarraden

House was just like under the tidy little awning in the rose garden. There wasn't a chair for me.

I bring my gaze back to him. "You knew what my name meant."

"So does anyone with any familiarity with Cealastra's chosen tongue."

I deflate a little. That makes sense.

Steepling his fingers, he watches me. "Who was the vampire?"

I shrug. "Someone from Fanghaven." I don't say who. For some reason, I think mentioning Rexton Hale might result in fewer answers than I'm already getting. "He wanted a sip of my blood to confirm what Rannigan Bloodthief is apparently spreading around his court—that the non-dragon shifter of the Elite Wing is some strange creature whose blood tastes like basking in sunshine."

Bale tenses from head to foot. "Rannigan said that?"

"I guess some of the blood traffickers escaped the battle at Draywood and ran back to the Vampire King with tales of my blood smelling like everything a vampire wants but can never have. Apparently, smell goes with taste. Now Rannigan wants me."

Bale stares at me in shock. There's no faking that. "Bloodpit," he finally growls.

I sigh loudly. "My thoughts exactly."

His features darken with fury. Suddenly, he's in front of me before I even see him move. He grabs my nape with one hand, tilts my chin up with the other, and rips the leather choker off. "Did he bite you?"

I gasp, my pulse racing under Bale's hand. His heat washes over me, and his grip feels like fire branding my skin. "Of course he didn't bite me. I said no."

He slowly releases me and backs away, standing in front of the hearth. "Fanghaven. Good."

I shiver now that Bale isn't touching me anymore, and his

body blocks some of the heat and light from the fire. "They have a code," I say hoarsely. "They could be allies."

"There's no one to ally with." He slides my choker into his pocket. My belly clenches as I watch his now-empty hand press against the slight bulge of the stolen necklace. Heat washes through me.

"What about the pretender king?" I ask, trying to focus on what's important—and get some answers. "Would he be so bad?"

"He doesn't have the magic in his blood to keep, hold, and protect a kingdom."

"Neither does the new Fae Queen, and she's starborn."

"She's *young*. Her parents were killed in that earthquake, and she came along so late in their lives that magic was already waning. Look at the result. She's weak." Bale spears a hand through his hair and sits again. "All any fae noble wants to do now is get her pregnant so their bloodline produces the next legitimate heir."

"Would they kill her as soon as an heir appeared?"

Bale huffs. "Possibly."

"So, you can make your shadow dragon solid, be part man and part beast, and create phoenixes from torn-up scales because you're from a starborn bloodline, and you were born while magic was still strong?"

Bale turns a dark look on me. "Are you calling me old?"

"You are old." I move my booted feet toward the fire. "And I'm a sunblood."

"You don't know that."

"I might...if you'd tell me what it is."

"Why would you believe what some vampire said? Who is this man?"

"Someone from Fanghaven," I remind him. "Pay attention, Your Royal Forgetfulness."

His jaw ticks. "You've obviously been drinking, and I'm patient." I snort, and he adds, "But not without my limits."

"Well, what are you going to do to me, Bale Cinderheart?" I lean back in the armchair, closing my eyes. The warmth of the fire makes my limbs even heavier, and my head still spins. "Ten days in the dungeon for insubordination?" When he doesn't answer, I finally open my eyes. Bale is staring at me, and he's so close that I can see the yellow and russet pigments illuminating his amber eyes.

I don't move, staring back at him. I know we're mostly arguing, but longing still sinks through me like a wish on a star, desire mixed with feeling safe and warm and *seen*. How can I have utter confidence in a man I suspect is lying to me? I can't reconcile my own feelings, and I'm too tipsy and tired to try.

"The right time will come to ally with Fanghaven," he finally says. "You'll see."

"Will I?" I smile without humor. "If I live that long. Didn't you hear? Rannigan and his goons are after me."

Bale's fists clench in his lap, the fingers of one hand tightening over the pocketed necklace. For all I know, my hair is also in that pocket. Dragon shifters are hoarders, and when Kellan was falling in love with me, he kept things too.

Despite my heavy lids, my eyes widen and my heart thuds in my chest. I know things are changing, but *falling in love*?

Half standing, his face a thunderstorm, Bale leans forward and places big, heavy hands on the arms of my chair. "They touch you. They die."

I gaze into his burning stare, a riptide of emotion dragging a heated shiver up from deep inside. If I'd had one more dragon's brew at the tavern, I'd stretch up and kiss him. Fortunately, I'm not that drunk. "Good luck keeping a sunblood alive."

He doesn't move, so close his breath stirs my hair. "Don't buy into everything you hear."

"The source was pretty good." I shrug.

A muscle pinches near his eye. "Who?"

I bite my tongue. "I just meant he looked reputable."

Bale stops pressing and slowly sits back in his chair. He wants answers from me but won't give any himself, so I slough off my guilt at keeping secrets from him.

He's quiet for so long that I get sleepy, the pleasant crackle of the fire and the heat of the blaze relaxing me. I finally curl up, pulling my feet under me, and shut my eyes. The brightness of the flames still dances behind my closed lids. The warmth feels amazing. Or maybe that's Bale's inner heat, seeping into my bones.

"Idallia?" he rumbles.

I wish he'd called me Sunshine. "Mmm?" The fire is lovely, the room safe and warm. I still like my quarters better. My birds are there. There's the roosting wall.

"Don't fall asleep here."

"Why not?" I murmur. "You have plenty of room."

"I don't usually have...guests." His words trail away, the loneliness in his voice definitely not my imagination.

"Not really a surprise. Your lair is at the tippy top of the mountain and about a million steps up."

He clears his throat. "If you stay here, I'll..."

It takes effort, but I crack open my eyes. "You'll what?"

The way he stares at me wakes my whole body up like embers popping to life in the hearth. He finally drags in a breath that lifts his chest. "I'll go somewhere else."

Disappointment is the worst weight on a heart, and I don't even know what I was expecting. I'm not supposed to want anything.

Sighing, I force myself out of the comfortable chair and move toward the door. "Cealastra forbid the Dragon King leaves his lair. Have fun all alone," I toss over my shoulder, stumbling a little as I reach for the doorknob.

CHAPTER TWENTY-FOUR

BALE

"Stop." I leap after Idallia like a lovestruck fool. She turns bleary eyes on me. "You'll break your neck falling down the stairs." I crook my fingers at her. "Come back here." She just stares at me, swaying a little, so I move forward, lightly take her hand, and tug her toward a window. It's the better way down.

"I think I'll break more than my neck if I go out the window." Her hand curls against mine, and my whole chest tightens with the need to pull her into my arms and pretend that nothing else exists in the world.

"And I think you know very well I'm not about to toss you out the window."

"Debatable," she mutters, staggering into me. She rights herself just as fast.

My lips jerk up in an involuntary smile, but real humor escapes me. I just had the perfect opportunity to tell her everything, and I still didn't. My current excuse is that she's been

256

drinking. What will tomorrow's excuse be? That the wind blows from the east?

I've never felt like the villain in any of the happenings of Ellonrift before. But that's because I was never selfish about anything until the time to give up Idallia started breathing down my neck.

Still holding her hand in one of mine, I unlatch the window with the other and spread the panes wide.

With only a few words, I could change everything at the next Ellonrift Council. I could rip Rannigan's double vote away. I could maybe avoid a war.

Instead, I ask her, "What do you see when you look out this window?"

She takes a moment to breathe, steadying herself. I can smell dragon's brew on her lips and have the acute urge to lick it off, even though I don't even like the drink that much. She's tipsy and sleepy, and I should've just walked her down the stairs.

"The night sky," she finally answers. "Too many stars to count."

"You look up instead of down?" She nods, and I can't help asking, "Why?"

A breeze caresses her shoulders and lifts her loose hair. She turns her face into it, savoring the mountain air, even though I can tell she's cold, her skin tensing and pebbling with goose bumps. I drink her in—her fierce beauty, her bright sunshine on hard ice scent—and feel as intoxicated as she is. "Because that's where we all soar together."

Happiness jerks a lightning-bolt path across my chest. "You like flying?" *Together.*

She turns to me, the chill air slapping pink into her cheeks. Her smile makes the floor open beneath my feet, and I feel like I'm falling so fast and hard that not even my wings can catch me. "I love it. The freedom. The thin air. I can see everything from up there, and all the things that have seemed...difficult in my life can't touch me from way down here."

"It's an escape?"

Looking thoughtful, she shakes her head. "Not exactly. Just... a moment apart. When joy defeats everything else." Her muted, self-conscious laugh tugs at my heart.

"Are you not happy otherwise?" I can't help squeezing her hand a little harder.

"That's not what I mean. Flying just makes everything else go away because there's no room to think about anything but how special it is." Her brow creases. "But maybe you can't understand because you've had flight ever since you could shift. For me, it's an unexpected gift."

"Even after all this time?" Why am I still holding her hand? Why has she not pulled hers away yet?

"I think a million years couldn't change how special it is."

My chuckle makes her golden eyes flick to me. "We won't live a million years. A few thousand, if we're lucky." Natality among Ellonrift's long-lived peoples is very low—nature's way of balancing our populations. One of the few exceptions was the last royal family of Fanghaven. But then, that was a love match like I've rarely seen.

"You're more than halfway done with your first millennium. Does that ever scare you?"

The only thing scaring me right now is the terrifying need for *more* that this private moment stirs inside me. "Not really. I think life will have seemed very long by the time I'm old and gray."

Idallia reaches up, her fingers lightly brushing the hair near my temple. "No gray yet."

Sensation shudders through me, a roar of fire and desire that makes me desperately want to kiss her. "What else do you like about flying with the Elite Wing?" Maybe keeping her here isn't just good for me, even if it's not good for my kingdom. Maybe it's good for Idallia. What *she* needs.

"The friendships. The belonging." A soft smile breaks over her face. "My birds," she adds with even more feeling, love sparking in her eyes like starbursts.

"Are we friends then?" I rasp.

Her brows arch in delicate irony. "You declared yourself friendless."

"Maybe I don't want to be friends." My heart clenches violently as the potentially ruinous words leave my mouth.

Her lips part on a startled breath. Her eyes roam my face, looking for clues to my meaning. It could be that I want more from her. It could also be that I want to continue my friendless existence.

My pulse pounds hard. Hers does too. She finally turns away, her gaze fixing out the window again. "You say you don't want friends because you've never actually been alone. You isolated yourself plenty, but you had a choice, which makes all the difference. Loneliness wasn't imposed on you."

"Could you not have gone into Glarraden?" I ask, still holding her hand like a prize I won and won't relinquish. "There must've been potential companions there."

"All they did was point fingers and call me the gildenfae-gold kid in loud enough whispers for me to hear. I used to wish the gold would stop coming. Then maybe they'd all forget." Her sigh feels like a mountain sitting on my chest.

"There's nothing wrong with the gildenfae," I say stiffly.

She scoffs. "It wasn't about them. It was about the sheer amount of gold every year, which even you have to admit was a lot."

No more than any queen of Ellonrift would have at her fingertips. "Do you think Rita and Gerard would've kicked you out if the gold stopped coming?"

She laughs, the sound like ice cracking on a lake. "That would've required them noticing I was there to begin with."

I squeeze her hand, trying to convey an apology I should be free to say aloud. "I'm sorry," I still tell her, though she can't know why or how much.

Shrugging, she pulls her hand from mine. "Your plan to sober me up with frigid night air worked. I'm pretty sure I can make it down the stairs intact now."

"You're not going down the stairs, Sunshine."

Her suspicious gaze snaps to mine. "So you *are* tossing me out the window?"

Grinning, I step up onto the low window frame and reach out a hand. She looks at me warily but slips her hand back into mine. I haul her up with me.

"You said you like to fly." I grab her around the waist and fall backward, tipping us both into the void.

She gasps my name in a way that makes me want to devour her whole. As she clutches my shoulders, I turn in the air and let my shadow wings unfurl and solidify. We glide, the dragon in me heating us both, and she throws her legs around my waist, holding on with a grip so strong it pulls a low groan from my throat.

"This feels dangerous," she whispers in my ear.

It feels disastrous. "Don't worry. I've got you." Her hair flies into my face, the scent of it filling my lungs. I pull her flush against me, bury my face in her neck, and breathe.

Her heartbeat thunders in my ears. My own echoes it. I slowly circle in wide arcs to prolong the moment, dreading her window coming into sight.

"Is this what it's like to be starborn?" she asks huskily. Her hand slides to my neck, holding my face to her throat. Heat ripples down my spine. "A man and a dragon in one."

I think the dragon is about to take over. It wants to claim, keep, *mate*.

So does the man. There's no denying it, and I don't even try. "Yes...for me." And Idallia should know what it feels like to be starborn for her, except I'm keeping her from it. Or at least, from the *choice*.

"Why don't you ever show this to anyone else?" she asks as her perpetually open window slides by. I let it pass.

"I don't like to use this kind of power too often. Magic is waning, and I don't want to waste mine."

She pulls back a little, looking curiously into my face. "But you've shown me plenty of times."

My wry chuckle is almost pained. She's so close that it would take just the slightest dip of my head to kiss her. Would she welcome my lips? "I want you to know me."

Color rises in her cheeks, the deeper flush visible even in the dark. "For what it's worth, I think it's beautiful. You're everything at once. You don't have to choose."

Her words remind me of the secrets between us and help quell my crushing desire to fly her back up the mountain, lay her on my bed, and slake this fierce passion I've tried so hard to ignore.

I pump my wings, bringing us back up and through her window. Her legs drop from my waist, and I force myself to let her go. Her arms slowly fall from my shoulders, lingering just long enough to make me doubt my choice.

Her room is dark, though light starts glowing from inside the roosting wall almost immediately. Three twinkling lanterns to welcome her home.

My chest collapses with loneliness.

I back toward the window and hop onto the ledge. Standing there, I take her in.

Starborn.

Sunblood.

Idallia of Glarraden.

Which part of her will win?

She shivers, and I immediately want to warm her again.

"For what it's worth, I think *you're* beautiful," I rasp.

Her eyes widen as I drop backward off the ledge.

CHAPTER TWENTY-FIVE
IDALLIA

As usual, life ignores my inner turmoil, and everything goes back to normal over the next few days. We train without Bale, and I stay out of sight to avoid any potential run-ins with Bloodwold vampires as Council delegations begin arriving in Drayke and hovering around the mountain. I haven't heard about Rannigan Bloodthief appearing yet, but it could happen any day now.

Bale still hasn't sent any of us away, and I don't think he's going to. From everything he's said to me lately, this is the make-or-break Council—either things radically change, or he'll splinter off and no longer adhere to a broken system initiated by a missing goddess.

My hands turn cold and clammy every time I think about Cealastra's continuing absence, but if I'm honest with myself, when I look at the eye of the great phoenix in the sky, I know the Star of Ellonrift is fading. How long until its light snuffs out entirely? Cealastra's constellation will still exist, but the eye will go dark, and she'll no longer be watching us.

Maybe she's dead. Maybe she's turned her light elsewhere. Either way, I'm convinced she's gone from Ellonrift.

When Bale's staff starts putting out calls for in-mountain blood hosts to feed the Vampire King and his entourage while they're here, I start having even worse nightmares. There's no shortage of people willing to sell their blood for money, but my persistent fear of Bloodwold vampires becoming violent or going too far as they drink turns my stomach.

Even safe in my own room, I shudder, phantom pains bursting beneath fading wounds. I've never been scared like this in my life, and I hate it. Battles are hard and terrifying, but then I leave them behind and just think about the next one, not the one before. This time is different. I can't leave the battle at Draywood behind. It lives inside me now.

Since according to Rexton Hale, Rannigan Bloodthief will be looking for me, I decide to test out Hale's advice and avoid the sun entirely. If Rannigan wants a bite of me, he won't ask—he'll take, so the smartest thing I can do is try to taste normal.

We've been left to our own devices for training, so I just stop going. The team questions me, and I tell them I'm feeling under the weather. That becomes truer by the day. I don't notice much of a difference at first, but by the third day, my energy wanes and my stomach puts up even more of a protest to meals than usual. The following day, it's hard to get out of bed, the clear, bright morning mocking me. A splash of sunlight comes through the open window, and it almost physically hurts to not get up and move into the warm light puddling on my floor. By the next afternoon, I ache like humans do when they're sick with a fever, shivering in my bed, my skin chilled and sensitive, and my teeth clacking together.

Fyrestar flutters down from the roosting wall. Concern furrows the feathers on his brow. *"Should I get Sybil?"*

Trembling in the shadows, I look out my window. The

sunshine calls to me as though it has an actual voice. "She can't fix this."

"Hale's theory is making you sick." Of course I told my birds everything, and now they're worried and decidedly anti-Rexton Hale. I might be, too, considering his suggestion is making me feel and look like death.

"Let's go for a flight," Fyrestar suggests, moving toward the window. He hops right into the sunlight, and longing swells in me. *"Get outside for a while."*

I look yearningly at the blue sky as Sol flutters down next to me. *"Pale,"* she chirps. *"Need sunshine."*

"You sound like Bale," I say sourly.

"Dad's right."

I give her the side-eye. She hasn't stopped with the *Dad* thing since she started. "*Dad* might be," I agree. I can't help humoring her. "But I'm always pale."

She clicks her beak. *"Not like this."*

"It's a little like your winter blues," Rim says, joining Fyrestar at the big window. *"When the days are short and dark."*

I nod. He's right. I get listless in the winter if there are too many cloudy days in a row, but I go outside, and there's still some sunlight on me. This is much worse. "Do you think a sunblood *feeds* off the sun? Like a vampire feeds off blood?"

Fyrestar tilts his head toward the emptiness outside my window, the invitation clear. *"I think you're happier in the sunlight —happier and stronger—and that's all that matters."*

I huff at the simplicity of it after all these days of questioning myself. I have two options: stay out of the sunshine so vampires don't find me as delectable, or soak up as much sunshine as possible so I can be stronger and faster if they come after me again.

The choice is easier than I thought. I throw off my covers, stagger toward my south-facing window, and tilt my face to the rays.

The light and heat shock me. I gasp, the sunshine on my face and neck scorching me like a blast of fire—a sudden, fierce burn. But then it soaks in, wonderful, and I sigh, basking in the warmth.

"I needed this." Oh great stars, how did I ever let a stranger convince me to *weaken* myself? "I need a whole day of this. Or ten."

"I guess you're done with your experiment." Rim sounds relieved. Sol joins us all at the window, squeezing herself between Rim and Fyrestar.

"If I want a witch's hope of being able to fight off vampires, I need some sunshine again. Let's go for a flight around the lake."

I hurry to change into warmer clothes and tie my hair back. It's chilly outside, but I roll up my sleeves to get more sunshine on my skin. I already feel stronger just from standing at the window, and I want to absorb as much as I can before dusk.

"Off you go." I flick my fingers, encouraging the phoenixes to take off. Fyrestar leads the way off the window frame. When they all drop below my line of sight, I take a few running steps and dive out the window after them.

Wind pulls at me, cool air battering my skin. Sunshine coats me all over. Grinning, I spread my arms and soar. Sensation rushes through me, my laughter snatched away by the wind and left to echo against the granite. There's nothing like leaping out my window, the sheer mountainside a blur, the weather magnificent.

Drayke is a sprawling pattern of buildings and streets below, the river a shining ribbon winding through the middle of it. My phoenixes fly with just as much joy, their bright plumage glowing. A weight slides off my shoulders. Too soon, Fyrestar swoops underneath me. I clamp my legs around his body and plunge my already chilled fingers into his warm, black neck feathers, holding on. Rim and Sol flank us, my wing guards.

I can't help my shout of excitement as we bank hard, heading for the lake.

"Feeling better already?" Fyrestar trills a chuckle.

I laugh. "It's like magic."

"Magic!" Sol caws.

"A sunblood must need sun." Rim's dry comment fills my head as his amber eyes glint over at me.

I smile wryly. "You'd think we'd have been smart enough to figure that out a few days ago."

"It's never a bad thing to heed advice and see where it takes you." Fyrestar is far wiser than I am most of the time but, right now, I don't agree with him. For all I know, Rexton Hale is a liar. Unfortunately, I'm worried that Bale is too.

"I didn't know the source. I shouldn't have given him five seconds in the tavern, let alone five beautiful autumn days cooped up inside instead of enjoying the sunshine with all of you."

"You can't believe Rexton Hale about you being a sunblood—which no one's ever heard of—but disregard everything else he says," Fyrestar tells me.

"Well, aren't you the annoying voice of reason?" I say without heat or malice.

He warbles a chuckle. *"Look, even Embersol is nodding her agreement."*

I glance off our left wing. Sol is bobbing to her own merry tune and not even listening. Her playful zigging and zagging makes me grin. She'll fly circles around all the other warbirds once she's fully grown again.

"Since you're probably right, as usual, let's go to the library after our flight and see if we can find any books that mention sunbloods. We can recruit Sybil if she's not too busy." I already told Sybil about the Fanghaven vampire in the tavern and his warning. She'd never heard of sunbloods, either.

"I'm not sure how much help we'll be with books," Rim chirps.

"Moral support," I tell him with a wink.

"Support!" Sol tweets.

I laugh, new purpose piling on top of the deepest love and filling me completely.

Sybil and I descend the many levels to the Drayke Mountain library and head toward the vampire section, my birds lighting the way. We both carry a lantern as well. It's cold and dark in the preservation caverns, and I already miss the sunshine.

"Why does Bale keep the books down here?" Sybil's voice holds an audible shiver, and she pulls her cloak more firmly around her.

"He must think they're safest here."

"Along with all his gold?" She flashes me a grin.

"That's locked up." I grin back at her. On the way here, we passed the tunnels leading to the many vaults and treasure troves of the residents of Drayke Mountain, mine included. "Everyone has access to the library."

"I bet he'd show you his gold if you asked him to," she says suggestively.

I snort. "You're incorrigible." A snap of heat still warms me to the core, despite the frigid cavern.

"I'm romantic."

"There's nothing romantic about shoving gold at someone."

"Says someone who's never lacked for gold."

"Have you?" I counter. Sybil comes from a wealthy family in Ruthinock, and Bale pays her generously.

She tosses me an exasperated look. "Would you rather have flowers?"

I shudder. "And cut the poor things in their prime? Never."

"Then what *would* make you swoon?" she asks.

I laugh. "Nothing, I hope. I prefer to stand on my own two feet, not keel over unconscious."

"*You're* incorrigible."

"I'm realistic."

Rolling her eyes, she clucks her tongue at me.

"What made you fall for Stuart?" I ask, suddenly curious. "Besides him being the most handsome of the new recruits."

Her expression softens as she thinks back to their courtship. "I always felt safe with him. Comfortable. We were here, in this new place, doing and seeing all these new things..." A smile brightens her face in the lanternlight. "But with him, I felt at home. *He* was home. I didn't regret leaving anything behind because I already had what I needed."

"Home," I echo wistfully. I'm thinking of my room several levels up from here, but when I close my eyes on a blink, I see a mountain. It's a high peak that sits at the intersection of Torridaig, Fanghaven, and Bloodwold, the last in the chain of the lush and river-gorged Silver Moon Range that runs the length of Torridaig's border with Fanghaven. Shaking off the odd vision, I say, "I think that's Drayke Mountain for me."

"Not Glarraden House?" she asks.

I shrug. "One day, maybe. Not now, though." Bale's burning eyes and his warm, strong arms around me suddenly burst forth like the most vivid memory. Woodsmoke and wind tease my senses even though there's only cold rock down here. I look over my shoulder, half expecting to see Bale striding toward us, but there's only darkness beyond my phoenixes.

"Here's the vampire section. Anything to look for in particular?" Sybil asks.

"Old?" I hazard a guess. "Since no one seems to have heard of sunbloods."

She rubs her gloved hands together, her eyes already searching the shelves. "All right, then. Let's dive into some old books."

WE SEARCH FOR MORE THAN AN HOUR BEFORE I HEAR Sybil's teeth start to chatter. I'm frozen to the bone, too, and barely hide it better. My thoughts start to stray as the texts blend together. Why did Rexton Hale bother coming early to warn me? What's it to him?

Clearly, he wanted a taste of me. Only to verify the rumor? Or because he wanted his turn with the sunblood? Or something else I haven't thought of?

And what would he have done next if I'd let him bite me and he'd found me delicious? Try to convince me to become his blood buddy? Attempt to sweep me away to Fanghaven to live with him and his dark, brooding eyes, and show me what consensual bites feel like?

The thought isn't as repulsive as it should be, though my scars still prickle.

But then—not that it would *ever* happen—we'd both be a target for the Vampire King. There's no way the pretender to the Fanghaven throne would risk that, not even to get himself a sunblood. *If* sunbloods even exist—which no book in the vampire section has proven so far, and we've paged through most of them.

Admittedly, we're going quickly. It's cold down here.

I close another old, fragile tome and gently slip it back onto the shelf. "Nothing, either?"

Sybil shakes her head. "Though this is interesting, and I didn't have any idea." She points to a passage in the volume she's holding. "Then again, I don't meet enough vampires for the conversation to turn to child-rearing."

"What is it?" Frowning, I move toward her. My birds crowd in, too, helping to warm us and brighten the pages.

"This says that vampire babies don't drink blood right away. They nurse from their mother's breasts—or a wet nurse's, I assume—just like any other people until their teeth come in. Once teeth are established, it still takes a few months for fangs to be strong enough to descend from the upper gums and pierce flesh. Once they are, the parents offer up their own veins to tempt the hungry child, the little fangs instinctively pop out for the first time, the child bites, drinks, and becomes a bloodsucker for life."

I grimace. "I guess that makes sense about nursing first. But then they have about as much choice in the matter as werechildren stolen from places like Muirvale. Indoctrinated before they understand the implications."

She nods. "But this is where it gets really interesting." Her finger lightly traces the tight, angular handwriting on the parchment as she reads: "*Until vampire children take their first sip of blood, daylight cannot harm them. Only after drinking from a vein can they no longer behold the sun.*"

A chill surges over me. *Behold the sun.* I inhale sharply, a deep shiver icing my bones. My pulse suddenly racing, I discreetly run my tongue over my upper gums. It *does* feel like there's something solid, a subtle something extra I've never thought to look for, tucked in there above my canines.

Cold sweat needles my skin as I swallow hard, abruptly nauseous, but also so fucking hungry for something that could finally satisfy me. Most foods make me sick, and it's even worse when I don't get regular sunlight.

Mute with horror, I back toward my birds, barely feeling their warmth as shock and panic numb my limbs.

I think I might be a vampire.

A vampire who has never tasted blood.

CHAPTER TWENTY-SIX
IDALLIA

Torridaig's battle horn wakes me from a fitful sleep. I sit bolt upright, my pulse pounding wildly, then leap out of bed.

"Fyrestar!" Reaching for the clothes I dumped on a chair last night, I get dressed as fast as possible and brutally pin up my hair. I add an extra layer, a thick, fur-lined, long-sleeved tunic to protect me from the night-cold air I know is about to bite me as hard as a weretiger. "Hurry! I want right wing!"

Fyrestar swoops down from the roosting wall. *"It's not even dawn."* His golden gaze shifts to the window.

"Good. Maybe Kellan will be slow to wake up." If he's even here. No one's seen him in days.

I shove a foot into one boot and then hop, pulling on the other. Rim and Sol poke their heads out of the roosting wall. While Fyrestar flutters to the unlocked window and uses his talons to pull it open, I leap for my swords and strap them on. "Go!"

He takes off with a sharp caw. I'm about to run after him, then remember I want a dagger. I sprint across the room, grab one off my dresser, and slip it into my boot, leaving just the hilt accessible. Whirling, I race for the window, leap headfirst through the opening, somersault in the air, and open my arms and legs when I see the ground beneath me.

I fall like a star, my limbs splayed, the wind buffeting me. Fyrestar's big body partially replaces my view of a still-sleeping Drayke. The city lamps are turned down low, and barely a wisp of smoke curls from a chimney. I clutch Fyrestar's feathers and settle myself onto his back. He angles up immediately.

"Are you sure you have everything you need?"

"Yes!" Then I remember my vampire-repelling torque from Stuart. A sudden ache hits my neck, my thigh, my breast. Fangs. Pain. Shock. I suck in a breath.

"Idallia?"

"All good." We might not even be going toward vampire territory.

Except, nine times out of ten, it's a Bloodwold problem.

We climb toward the war room, growing dread coating my mouth with the bitter tang of fear. I try to swallow it down and can't, my throat closing over. The vampire bites that are just small marks now seem to scream at me with deafening voices. I don't know how they can throb like this when there's barely anything there.

Maia joins the race, her leathery wings darker blotches against the granite cliffside.

"Hurry," I urge. "We've got company."

Fyrestar moves impossibly faster, and we blast into the war room first. He drops me at the right-wing pillar, and I leap onto it. Maia soars across the room practically on Fyrestar's flaming tail feathers and transforms in the air, dropping her booted feet onto the front-left pillar with a force that rattles the dais.

She looks over at me with a grin. "Kellan's going to have a fit."

I smile too. "Is he back?"

She shrugs. "Don't know."

Kellan barrels into the room next, answering the question for us. His wing nearly brushes my shoulder as he circles tightly and drops, settling behind me as he shifts into his common form to fit on the column.

I turn to gloat, cutting off my snide remark when I see how terrible he looks. "You're back."

"I guess you got right wing," he says tonelessly.

"What's wrong with you?" Frowning, I look him over. "Are you drunk?"

He shakes his head, his blue eyes the dullest I've ever seen them. "You should know me better than that," he growls.

He sinks enough heat into his words to scald my face with regret. "I *do* know you, so what's wrong?"

Arran flies in, taking the column behind Maia. Kellan doesn't answer even though I wait, watching him. Danica and Wade arrive at the same time, and he gives her the right-side pillar without even going for it. Now *that's* friendship. Everyone's wing guards circle the cavernous room. Fyrestar circles with them. We wait for Bale. He never watches our race to the pillars. He times his arrival to see the result.

Bale swoops in, wrapped in shadows. He's a thundercloud, and my heart jolts as if struck by lightning. It's the first time I've seen him since that night in his lair, and my whole body ignites with awareness. He shifts and strides toward us. His amber eyes burn into me first, then sweep over the others.

"Did you settle the Fae Queen into the quarters we talked about?" Bale directs the question at Kellan. I whip around again, seeing the end of Kellan's nod.

My eyes narrow. That's what he was doing?

"She's here now and awaiting your formal welcome. The journey from Tanturriff took longer than I expected because she refused to fly," Kellan rumbles.

He would have *carried* her? Dragon shifters don't just carry anyone. They're not horses or wagons. They only carry someone if there's a connection.

Kellan's eyes flick to mine. His usual smirk infiltrates his weary expression when he sees me staring, and I snap my mouth shut, pivoting back around.

"What's the battle horn about?" Wade asks from the back pillar on the left.

"Vampires," Bale practically snarls. Anxiety grips my stomach so fast it's like a fist grabbing and twisting my insides. My palms start to sweat, and I shuffle on my pillar. "They went all the way to Ruthinock for this batch of humans and are making their way back through *our* land." He starts to pace, furious strides snapping against stone. "They're west of Fanghaven now, which means they're stuck on our side of the border until they can find a usable pass through the Silver Moon Mountains."

My skin feels hot and cold at the same time. Numb on top. Feverish beneath. "How many?" I ask hoarsely.

"A good dozen," Bale answers swiftly. "Nothing we can't handle."

A dozen vampires against the whole Elite Wing shouldn't scare me. My pulse still races, and my body locks tight. I've fought vampires for nearly two centuries, and yet the thought of going back into battle with them now fills me with spine-icing dread.

"Rannigan Bloodthief must be on his way to the Ellonrift Council as we speak," Maia snarls furiously. "He'll walk in here with claims of Torridaig being the aggressor while he waits for his raiders to haul their spoils back to his blood markets."

"What's new?" Danica snorts her disgust. "It's been that way for ages."

"We could kill him. He'll be right here," I say softly.

Everyone still hears me, and all eyes turn to me. I do my best to hide that I'm shaking, my body still telling me to flee.

"You're talking about murdering a starborn king," Bale says

with so little inflection that I don't know if he likes the idea or thinks it's utter madness.

I lift my chin. For all I know, Bloodwold could be my native home. My family could have been blood traffickers. "So? He murdered the Fanghaven royals in cold blood, then got everything he wanted and has been spreading his blood violence for two hundred years."

"So we should do the same?" Bale asks warily. "And during a recognized moment of non-aggression between Ellonrift's rulers?"

"We should if we want any hope of keeping diplomacy alive. We take his kingdom and his vote. Then we get Fanghaven's too."

Bale watches me from under lowered brows. "How do you figure?"

"She's dead—the last of the Fanghaven line. Rannigan doesn't have a wife, or else someone who doesn't live under Rannigan's thumb would've seen her by now. Fanghaven is without a true ruler, and we either take it or give it to Rexton Hale in return for an alliance."

"Let's put Idallia on the Council," Wade jokes from behind. "We'll control half of Ellonrift in no time *and* put an end to blood trafficking."

A muscle jerks in Bale's jaw. Smoky shadows darken the air around him. "Cealastra might impose consequences."

"What consequences did she impose on Rannigan Bloodthief?" I shoot back. "None. Not a *fucking* one. And now she's gone anyway."

"We don't know that," Bale says sharply.

Somehow, I do. I know deep down in my heart that she's gone. Magic will keep waning. The fae will die out entirely unless they start intermarrying with other populations or organizing full-on people-thieving like Bloodwold. Shifters will still be able to shift because that's physical, not magical, but accelerated healing might disappear, and no one will be able to create healing spells or protective torques or everlife-infused firebirds.

Loss crushes my heart, and nothing has even happened yet. I will *never* let Rim or Sol back on the battlefield. And Fyrestar...If something happens to him, I'll die of grief, so at least we'll return to the stars together.

"So...what's the plan right now?" Arran asks after a tense silence. "How much time until these vampires make it to safety?"

"They're only a day out of Ruthinock now. They couldn't move up the mountains on the Fanghaven side because the passes were blocked by an early snowfall the night of their raid," Bale answers. "They had to veer into Torridaig, and it'll be their fatal mistake. It's close to dawn now, and they'll be forced to take cover. They'll be on the move and out of hiding again at sunset, which is just about when we should reach them if we leave now and fly fast. If they get in another full night of travel, they could reach a potential passageway into Fanghaven. We can't let that happen." Bale turns and motions everyone toward the tall, wide windows. "Let's go! Move!"

The others shift and take off, whooshing past me. Their wing guards follow. Fyrestar angles low and sweeps by next to me at pillar level. I tense to spring onto his back.

And don't move.

Fyrestar flies on, but his head whips around, his golden eyes questioning. He circles the room and comes back the same way. Bale is watching, too, and I try to take the leap onto my warbird this time. I really do.

Fyrestar sweeps past me again and then circles higher, waiting near the rough stone ceiling. My heart thuds. Dread curdles everything in my stomach. Rooted in place, I can barely breathe. Cold washes over me. Everything feels vague and distant but still intensely awful, just like in my nightmares.

"Idallia?" Bale strides over to me, a slash between his brows. His amber eyes hover between disbelief and worry. "What's wrong?"

I know I'm slowing him down. The tremor that shakes my hands slides like poison through the rest of me. "I'd never been bitten by a vampire before." *That I knew of.* Those old, small marks on my inner wrist burn along with the new ones. The pillar seems to sway, and I try to find my balance.

Bale reaches up to steady me. "Are you afraid?"

I swallow hard. "They were all over me."

"This isn't the time to go soft on me. People need our help." His words are hard, but his voice is gentle.

Biting my lip, I shake my head. "If it's nothing you can't handle, then I think you should handle it without me."

"It's nothing *we* can't handle. As a team. I didn't say it would be easy. We'll still be outnumbered."

"Not with the wing guards."

"We never know what we'll find when we get there. Draywood was proof of that."

My eyes snap to his. "Not helping." Anger rises to mix with fear. Maybe I'd have gotten over my dread if he'd told me the truth and helped me understand what I am. All I have are questions and speculation, and piecing things together has only scared me more. Instead of helping me, Bale said he didn't know anything and then distracted me with his shadow wings, broad chest, and strong arms.

If what Rexton Hale says is true, and I bleed even a little, this could be Draywood all over again.

"Get on your phoenix," Bale says steadily, "and fly."

I dig in my heels. "You don't need me."

His expression hardens. "There are six pillars for a reason, Idallia. I need my whole Elite Wing."

Duty yanks at me. Kellan wasn't himself, and I'm worried the Fae Queen used what little magic she has to drain some of his lifeforce from him. As a dragon shifter, he shouldn't feel the effects too much unless she got greedy. Maybe he's just tired. Everyone else is in top form.

Except for me. I can't make myself move.

"The sixth pillar was empty until I came along. If you really needed six fighters for this kind of thing, you would've filled it from the beginning."

"I didn't want just anyone, Sunshine." He grips my waist and lifts me down from the pillar. Startled by the unexpected touch, I brace my hands on his shoulders, some heat sneaking back into my frozen limbs.

"I'm the only one gravely injured on a regular basis. I'm a liability, not an asset." I let my hands drop away from Bale.

"If I thought that, I wouldn't let you fly out."

Bitterness and fear stir inside me again. "*I* think it."

He lightly squeezes my waist. "That doesn't make it true."

"Doesn't it?" We're only as strong as we believe we are, and right now, I feel like one hit could shatter all my bones. I back out of his hands, the weight and heat of them imprinted on my sides. "No fire. No flight." I laugh like daggers cutting into skin. "And now I'm worried about my own neck like never before."

"Stop. You're good. You're fast. You're worth fifteen vampires in a fight if you can just get your head in the right place."

"Maybe if you'd tell me the truth about things when I ask, I *could* get my head in the right place," I snap.

He doesn't move, doesn't flinch, doesn't even react. My heart beats heavily, waiting for something to give it hope. The thudding weight sinks into the pit of my stomach at Bale's silence.

"Do I have to drag you out of here?" he finally growls.

"Try it," I growl back.

"That's when you'll fight? *Against* me?" He looks shocked, almost sick. "So ready to turn on me. Just like that." The angry snap of his fingers echoes loudly in the war room.

"What are you talking about?" Bale is our rock. Our starborn king. The constellation we circle, and my dread only grows at seeing him look so unsteady.

He reaches out again and grips my shoulders, his urgent gaze blazing into mine. "If you're loyal to me, then you'll get on Fyrestar and fight."

I shut my eyes to block out the fire in his. I want to lean into him and take comfort in his arms as much as I want to savagely lash out, and not only because I'm scared.

"I know you lied to me." I open my eyes so I can burn *him* with my gaze.

"Don't make this about something else."

Fuck him and his evasive nonanswers. "I'm not like the others. I don't fight like them. I don't eat like them. I don't fly like them."

"What are you saying?" His fingers tighten, drawing me in.

His warmth and strength are almost too hard to resist, but I turn away from him. "I don't think I belong here." My voice hitches. "Maybe I never did."

He turns me back and grasps my chin, lifting my face to his. His eyes like a volcanic eruption, he thunders, "If you go, I will chase you down and bring you back. This is your home. These are your people."

Tears sting my eyes. "Lying to me again?" I spit a laugh at him and wrench my chin free. "I have no people."

"And Fyrestar?" His seething gaze swings to my warbird. "Rimblaze? Embersol? *They're* where you belong." His short, harsh laugh is vicious enough to rival mine. "You love them so much the rest of us are fucking jealous!"

I blink at that. I've never seen any jealousy from the team over my phoenixes. Not even from Kellan.

My throat thickens with impulsive words that surge up and spill over. "You're right. They are my home. I want to go and take them with me."

Bale takes a sudden step back as though I've slapped him, his eyes flaring, though I didn't raise a hand. "None of you are going anywhere—except to the Silver Moon Range."

"You don't dictate what I do. You can't stop me."

"Get on your phoenix and fly," he orders, low and hard.

"*No.*" It's the first refusal of my life directed straight at Bale.

His fists clench at his sides. "If you don't come with us, I'm taking Fyrestar anyway."

My eyes shoot wide, and my heart spasms violently. "Don't."

"I have to. And I know if I ask, he'll come." Bale's whole face transforms into something I don't even recognize. Is this what his enemies see right before he rips them in half? I shudder as the next horrible words leave his mouth. "I'll take Rimblaze too. I'll need him to replace you."

My insides hollow in dread. "No! He hasn't passed his tests."

"This *is* his test." He looks at me harshly. "And yours."

I start to shake all over, rage and fear so mixed together that I don't know which is which. "Fine." My nostrils flare, my breath storming in and out. "But leave Rim out of this. It will be your fault when I'm dead. And if Fyrestar dies, I'll kill *you*."

Bale doesn't look triumphant at all as he wraps his arms around my waist and takes off, only his shadow wings lifting us both. Locking me against his chest, he flies out the huge, soaring window, calling for Fyrestar to join us as dawn cracks the night darkness over the spiny mountaintops like a jagged rip in the sky.

I grab Bale's shoulders and hold on, but I refuse to throw my legs around him, this time letting them dangle. Drayke Mountain slips past us, the rough granite walls and carved terraces glowing pink and orange with first light. The wind scrapes over me from one side, the rest of me sheltered by Bale. I feel even more powerless in this position, torso to torso, his fiery, windblown scent surrounding me, and his warm arms infuriatingly reassuring, despite it all.

My voice trembles with wrath. "I fucking hate you right now."

"Good," he growls. "Because right now, I fucking hate you too." His gaze tracks Fyrestar, watching my phoenix speed up and angle down. "I saved the best for you," he mutters. "Closest to the heart."

My eyes jerk up, too close to his chin. He doesn't look at me, his flat mouth and granite-hewn jaw seeming to brutally hold in anything else he might say and then regret. I don't fully understand, although I'm certain he's talking about my warbirds.

"What do you mean? The damaged scales?" He doesn't answer. "Bale!" How could he have saved anything for me? He didn't even know I existed until decades after he created the phoenixes and the Elite Wing.

His grip tightens, sending a shock of sensation up my spine and down my legs.

"Why are you doing this?" I grind out. "If you have answers, I want them." I wanted them centuries ago.

"When did life suddenly give us what we want?" Something in his voice slices at my heart. Such bleakness. Eons of it hollow out his words.

I don't let sympathy steal my fury. "I'm not talking about life. I'm talking about *you*."

The wind snatches his dry huff almost before I hear it. "Maybe I'm talking about you too."

His low words explode inside me in a tangle of heat and confusion. They barely have time to penetrate before he opens his arms and drops me. I fall, watching Bale shift above me in a roar of fire and wind. All dragon now, he dives but stays close, huge and dark beside me as I flip over to find Fyrestar flying in.

I settle onto Fyrestar's back, and we soar over the rooftops of Drayke alongside Bale. I'm out of the mountain now, my choice taken from me the second Bale threatened to bring Fyrestar and Rim in my stead. They'd want to go if he asked, and the thought of making them choose between us makes me sicker than I already am.

Bale's other words still rattle around inside me like a discordant note from an unexpected tune, but I find myself just as unexpectedly readjusting my mindset. I start hardening my fear into strength and siphoning my emotions into that place inside me that'll wake up like a thunderclap and turn me into a force almost as deadly and formidable as Bale.

If I'm going to fight vampires, I'm going to fight them like a rabid animal and cut through them so fast they won't have a chance to bite.

We join the rest of the team on the southern outskirts of Drayke and leave the city behind. The faster we fly, dawn pouring over me in a splash of sunlight, the more I *want* to fight. My heartbeat settles into a new, vengeful rhythm, and my dread-filled hesitation in the war room starts to feel like it came from a different person.

These vampires want blood? I'll make them bleed. And then I'll deal with the Dragon King.

CHAPTER TWENTY-SEVEN
IDALLIA

With the wind against us, it takes longer than it should to reach the southern peaks of the Silver Moon Mountains. We left at dawn and made two quick stops to eat, but even at dragon and phoenix speed, it takes us the entire day and then some to reach where the vampires might be. At least we're not bound by roads and can fly straight as an arrow. The only resistance to our direct path southeast across Torridaig is the cold east wind coming out of Fanghaven.

"It's past dusk," Bale calls out to us. *"They'll be on the move but blending into the mountains and shadows. Keep your eyes peeled!"*

I'd wanted to find the vampires still hiding from sunlight, though spotting them in a cave or under a deep overhang from this high up would be nearly impossible. It would've made for an easier fight. They'd have been hemmed in, and we could've plowed through them like summer hay. I even started fantasizing about catching some and forcing them into the daylight.

Sadly, my vicious daydream set with the sun.

Kellan pipes up from behind me for the first time all day. *"Watch those slopes on the left. There's a cart road at the base and a deer track higher up. They could be on either."*

I scowl at him over my shoulder. What does he think I'm doing? Snoozing on Fyrestar's back?

"I'm glad to see your obvious fatigue isn't affecting your ability to annoy me." Kellan's not so far from me that I have to shout, especially with his dragon ears doing the hearing. He still speeds up to fly beside me, and I glance over, asking, "Did that fae girl make you work to keep her safe? Or did she use her glamour magic on you and steal some lifeforce with a touch and a kiss?"

His eyes flash to mine, ice blue and striking. I see teeth. *"Jealous?"*

I instantly regret this conversation. "Worried," I answer truthfully. I have been since the moment he showed up in the war room, looking exhausted and like he didn't even care about winning right wing.

Or that I won it.

He might look disappointed by my answer, though it's hard to tell under his iridescent scales and burning eyes. Kellan's hide is dark overall, but when the light hits him in a certain way, he's every color in the world. *"You'd be surprised by how many fae have zero scruples and want a starborn royal to spring from their loins."*

My brows lift, mocking. "Spring from their loins?"

"You wouldn't think it was funny if you were the one constantly running or hiding from attempts at forced marriage. Or forced anything," he mutters.

I sober. No, I definitely would not. "Is she nice?" I hope I won't have to make small talk with her next week inside Drayke Mountain.

And how in the holy stars am I going to avoid running into Rannigan Bloodthief?

"She's scared." Kellan faces forward again. *"Small and weak and scared."*

So Bale sent Kellan to escort her. I should be grateful. If

there's one thing that'll distract Kellan away from me, it's someone who needs him.

Sudden suspicion hits me along with a cold gust of wind. Was this Bale helping me? Or helping himself? Maybe both, but I'll bet the Fae Queen came last in the calculation.

"How did you get back so fast if she refused to fly?" I ask. Secretly, I'm glad she didn't ride Kellan. He's never carried anyone but me on his back.

The thought is utterly unfair since I've now flown with Bale. If anyone broke that special link between Kellan and me, it was me. Just like I broke the rest.

"*We rode.*" His dragon's voice rumbles with disgust, and he shakes his big, elongated head, his nostrils emitting enough heat to make the air around his snout waver. "*And it wasn't fast. It took fucking forever.*"

I grin. "Because she was bad company?"

He turns a blazing look on me, fire rolling between his jaws. "*Because she was terrified of me.*"

My brows fly up. Kellan is the quintessential knight in shining armor—except when he's plaguing me. He'd probably let the helpless queen walk across his body rather than let her step in mud, and she was *afraid* of him?

I bite back an incredulous snort. "Did Stuart at least coat you with fae-resistant magic so she wouldn't try to trick you out of some years and strength?"

"*No. But she didn't try.*"

I frown over at him. "How do you know?" A fleeting touch could siphon off little enough lifeforce that Kellan might not notice. She could have done it twenty times, leaving him just a tiny bit more tired and haggard with each brush of her fingertips.

"*Because I saw her pay handsomely for a burst of vigor partway into Torridaig.*"

I huff. What a hero. "She's going to have to coax more gildenfae back into Tanturriff if she's going to keep that up, but at least she's paying. But who would sell their life away?"

Kellan swings a critical look at me. *"Not everyone has endless chests of gold, Idallia. I saw a mother sheer years off her life so her children would never be hungry again."*

"Is that why you look so harrowed?" I shoot back, stung. "Because you stood there and watched a leech steal someone's future?"

"How is it different from Fanghaven vampires? They pay for blood."

"Blood regenerates." Just look at me, strong again. "But years don't. Once they're gone, they're gone."

"The mother was a dragon shifter," he says tonelessly. *"Her years are long."*

That makes me feel a little better about the Fae Queen's strength-gaining and life-prolonging snack. A human doesn't have years to spare. A werebeast, even less. But dragon shifters and vampires...Sometimes, they live so long they grow bored and weary with their days.

The fae age faster than dragon shifters or vampires, but their ability to siphon years from others puts their lifespan on par with the other long-lived peoples of Ellonrift.

"There! On the road with two wagons." Bale is the first to see the vampires moving along the cart road. I squint in the same direction but don't see them at all. Fyrestar angles down with the others. Once we're lower, I finally spot the raiders, cursing my probably vampire eyes for not seeing as well.

The entire group is dressed in hooded, granite-colored cloaks. They're well hidden, especially in the near dark. I count fifteen in all.

"They're hard to see," Kellan remarks, maybe as an excuse for not spotting them first. We were talking when we should have been looking. We used to bring out the best in each other. Now we seem to bring out the worst.

I don't respond, focused on the blood traffickers. Even the two wagons and the horses pulling them are the color of stone. Everything is gray on gray. They move at night and sink straight into the base of the craggy mountains during the day. If a routine patrol of dragon shifters near the border with Ruthinock hadn't spotted them before they hit the granite and shale lining the base of the mountain range, the vampires could easily have taken this batch of humans all the way to Bloodwold.

We descend. There'll be no surprise attack. We're several huge, winged blotches, unmissable, even against the darkening sky.

I glance at Kellan again. "Are you sure you're up for a fight?" I'm worried he's not in any shape to engage.

"Not with you." He drifts away from me. *"I'm tired of that."*

I press my mouth flat, my throat growing hot as I watch him lengthen the distance between us. He falls behind me, honoring the formation the race to the pillars dictated this morning. Turning back around, I stay my course with Fyrestar. If Kellan and I don't have fighting, I guess we don't have anything anymore.

Or maybe we can finally be friends.

"They're sticking with the wagons," Bale growls. *"We need to drive them away from the humans."*

"Do we try to take prisoners?" Maia asks.

"Kill," Bale says darkly. *"Danica, Wade—get the humans to safety before anything else. The rest of you—no quarter!"*

We dive, wind whistling, wings burning, and battle lust rising in my veins. Even if we can't do anything about the blood slaves already in Bloodwold—or the farming of people there like livestock to feed the population's lust for crimson gold—here, Bale is king and can stick each of these vampires on a pike and watch them burn with the morning sun if he wants to.

Personally, I don't have the patience for that. Heads are about to roll.

"Fyrestar." He cocks an ear toward me. "Do you remember the battle at Sinjar Hill?"

"That was werebeasts. A lot of bears."

"But do you remember that move we pulled?" He trills a *yes.* "Don't get too low. You have to stay out of striking distance." The first volley of arrows arcs toward us. Fyrestar pivots expertly, avoiding the bolts. Hatred burns through me. Like all blood traffickers for nearly two hundred years, they're going to force dragon shifters out of the sky and into skin.

"Swords out?" Fyrestar snarls.

"They are now." The ring of my blades harmonizes with the whistle of the wind, a melody that belongs in nightmares. Tonight, they won't be *my* nightmares.

Fyrestar banks left and right, avoiding the near-constant barrage. A spear hurtles past us. Fyrestar must sense my need to start—and end—this fight, because he flies so fast we outpace the others. I tighten my grip on my blades as we head straight for the back of the caravan. The wagons are in front with only their drivers. Vampires take up the rear.

"Hey, bloodsuckers!" I want my revenge for the holes in my flesh and the blood I lost. For my nightmares. Did I really resist flying out this morning? Now I want their deaths all over me. I'm going to slice them to ribbons and swim in their stolen blood.

Grinning like a knife-opened throat, I reach for all my hard-packed emotions from this morning, setting them loose in their altered form. Fury, not fear. Resolve instead of reluctance. They detonate inside me with a roar only I can hear. Strength rushes through me. My senses come alive. My focus sharpens. I can make out every fang glinting in the low light. I can see the whites of their flaring eyes as I arrive like a shooting star on my blazing warbird.

"Now!" I shout, clamping my legs so hard around Fyrestar's body that I won't move as he rolls. Blood rushes to my head as he flies upside down above two vampires, and my outstretched blades cut through their unsuspecting necks like warm butter. We kill the two just behind them in the same way before Fyrestar rolls back over, pumping his wings hard to regain the elevation we lost. Leaning over, I swing low and decapitate another as we wheel around.

The rest of the team arrives on our heels and shifts as they crash down and plunge into the battle. Wade and Danica head straight for the wagon drivers. Bale and Arran attack from the side while Maia and Kellan slice into the back of the group where I entered and carved my way toward the middle.

I vault off Fyrestar, slamming feet first into the face of a vampire. The blood trafficker keels over, my boots crushing his head. I spring off him, and Fyrestar pounds his beak down on the vampire's neck and tears out his throat. We fight side by side. Every head I sever feeds my fury and starves the fear that's been living like a parasite in my stomach ever since Draywood.

I move faster than ever before, avoiding hits, sliding away from swords, and dodging arrows. I move so fast that I barely see myself, my ability to recognize friend from foe in this accelerated state stretching far beyond my usual limits. Skin opens, blood sprays, and bones crack under my blades. Fyrestar guards my back, allowing me to plow ruthlessly forward. I revel in my victory—over these vampires, over my fear, over that thunderclap of strength and speed that ignited the moment I asked for it.

I kill without mercy until suddenly, there's silence.

Breathing hard, I look around. All the vampires lay dead on the ground.

The Elite Wing stares at me, Bale's amber gaze heaviest of all. Half escaping its pins, my hair drips crimson beads, the blood-soaked mass heavy on my shoulders. My chest heaves as I gulp down air that tastes of clashing blades, fresh kills, pine boughs, and shale-tumbled mountains. The first stars appear and shine down on me. My warbird glows beside me, his inner heat drying villainous entrails right onto his feathers. We're both covered in blood, and some savage part of me wants to lick my arm and taste the death of my enemies.

I swallow down the impulse along with my own saliva. What if I truly am a vampire? That might be too close to drinking from a vein.

I lift my chin as Bale looks at me, his eyes wary. The team

stares at me in shock from across a slew of mangled bodies. I don't know how many they killed. I killed a lot of them.

As the team takes me in like I'm something different from before, I start to realize that I might not be able to shift like they can, but there's just as much of a beast inside me. The difference is that it doesn't come out on command.

Except, I was in control tonight—of my senses, my speed, my focus. For the first time, *I* chose.

And just as I promised myself, heads rolled, and I swam in the death of the Vampire King's soldiers.

CHAPTER TWENTY-EIGHT

BALE

After leaving Idallia enough time to clean up and eat something, I summon her to my chambers at the inn. We stayed in the southeast, securing rooms for ourselves and the human captives in the town closest to where we intercepted the vampires. We already flew a whole day and fought a battle, though most of us barely got in a kill. The humans will be on their way home tomorrow under the protection of dragon shifters from the local garrison. They're taken care of. The rest of the Elite Wing can take care of itself. The warbirds too. But Idallia and I need to have a conversation.

My heart turns over hard.

The knock comes faster than I anticipate, barely giving me time to finish dressing after a bath. I open the door, half expecting to see the blood-covered tornado from earlier.

There's no gore, but the sight of Idallia still arrests me, a punch in the chest that stops my breath and shocks an explosive heartbeat from me. Straight black hair frames a face with delicate, pale features that give the impression of a moonlit sprite sliding like mist out of a forest. Then the sheer whiplike strength of her, the power vibrating under her skin, belie that impression entirely. She's iron disguised as silk. I never want to be her enemy. Someone who loves as intensely as Idallia can hate just as powerfully.

We stare at each other, her golden eyes guarded in a way they never used to be. "Bale?" she says sharply when I don't move from the doorframe.

I unlock my limbs and step back, inviting her in. After a moment's hesitation, she sweeps past me, teasing my senses with the subtle scents of sunshine and ice and the softer, flowery perfume of the inn's soap. Her hair is still damp, the thick, heavy mass holding the floral fragrance like a bouquet under my nose.

I steady my breathing and shut the door, the snick of the latch far quieter than either of our hammering heartbeats. Turning to her, I ask dryly, "Are you here for my blood too?"

She swings around, scowling. "I might be."

Despite her obvious hostility, the prospect of a challenge excites me and stirs the shadowy beast lurking under my skin. "I'd like to clear the air between us."

Her sour huff is astonishment incarnate. I deserve it after lying through my teeth. She crosses her arms, creating a barrier between us—or a shield for herself. "You told me I was worth fifteen vampires in a fight." Her lips curve in a small, tight smile. "Looks like you were right."

I can only agree. "What changed?"

She shrugs. "Once I was flying, all I wanted was revenge."

"I think you got it."

She nods, a hard glint in her eyes. With her big heart and special connection with her firebirds, she's kept something innocent about her all these years. It was something to protect and preserve, but I see it fading now. Idallia is on the cusp of change—like everything else, I suppose.

"So I was right to push you?" I ask.

Her expression ices over. "Don't *ever* threaten Rim again."

Shock renders me speechless. I love Rimblaze. I love all the phoenixes. They're my flesh and blood and made of more magic than even a starborn king should pull from his deepest inner wells and give away. "I didn't threaten Rimblaze. He's a warbird. He's trained for war."

"And that was all right when rebirth was a guarantee. We both know it isn't anymore."

"So what, then?" I scowl at her from under lowered brows. "What are you saying?"

"I'm saying that Rim and Sol are off limits. If you care about me at all, or *them*, you will never put them near a battlefield again."

A flush of anger rises in me. "That's not your choice," I say stiffly. "It's theirs."

"Then you don't get to make it, either!" she snaps in fury. "Like you tried to today."

We stare at each other in a standoff. I eventually nod. I can agree to that, especially because I know what the phoenixes will do. They'll choose Idallia. If she's fighting, they will too.

She slowly exhales, seeming to evacuate some of her anger along with the air. "What exactly did you want to talk to me about?" Her tone remains accusing, as if I've already lost my chance to say anything else that matters to her.

I open my mouth, but no sound comes out. Finally, like I'm unlocking a vault, the hinges squealing in protest as they creak open on a lifetime of secrets, I say hoarsely, "A sunblood is a vampire who has never drunk blood. They can eat regular food and walk in the sunlight. But the moment they drink blood from a vein—or even a cup, I think—they're confined to the night and a diet of blood."

Her expression doesn't show a hint of horror or surprise, astounding me. If anything, that hard glint sharpens. "Thanks, Bale, but you know what? I figured that out for myself."

Her new bitterness feels like a hundred arrows piercing my skin. "Then you know you're a vampire?"

"I do *now*. And I thought so." Her nostrils flaring, she turns and picks up the knife I left on the table. "I would rather have found out from you, but since you chose to lie, I found some pretty convincing information on my own."

"I didn't think you'd like hearing you were a vampire."

She digs a hole in the wooden table with my knife, dulling the tip. "I don't. I fucking hate it." She swings furious eyes on me. "But at least I know where I come from now."

"Do you?" I ask warily.

Her mouth turns down in distaste. "Somewhere with vampires."

"Torridaig has vampires."

She drops the knife with a clatter. "Is this why sometimes I can't speed up? Focus? Because I'm not drinking blood and sustaining myself the way I should?"

"You're better and faster than almost anyone, even without that. You don't need to drink blood to be the best."

Rage visibly builds inside her again, her golden eyes heating. "You talk about choices, but isn't that *my* choice? How long have you known? Forever?"

"And what would you choose?" Dread-fueled urgency roughens my voice. I step toward her. "To be a creature of the night? To never fly out or go into battle with us during the day? To never take your birds out under the sun?"

Her flinch hits me like a blow to the chest. "I didn't say I'd *choose* to drink."

I can't help reaching out and gripping her arms. She stiffens but doesn't pull away. "You don't need that. You're smart, you're fast, you're skilled." Her lips part on a sharp breath. My gaze riveted to her mouth, I murmur, "I wouldn't change a thing about you."

"What if I could be better? *Do* better?" Anger and hard-pumping blood paint her cheeks the color of a winter sunset. "Maybe I should take Rexton Hale up on his offer."

Cold shock and a hot surge of jealousy collide violently inside me. "What the fuck does Rexton Hale have to do with anything?"

She shrugs out of my grip, half turning from me. "He's the vampire from the tavern who told me I'm a sunblood. He wanted to drink my blood. Little did I know I could do the same to him and"—her narrow-eyed gaze swings back to me—"unlock my full potential."

I recognize my own words on her biting tongue. *Sometimes unlocking full potential is dangerous. And changes everything.*

I turn her back to me. She doesn't resist, despite the angry hiss of air through her teeth. If anyone is going to finish what we all started more than two hundred years ago, it's going to be me.

"If you want to drink from someone, you can fucking drink from me," I thunder like a low storm rolling over the mountains. I pull her against me, our hips meeting with a thud. "Is that what you want? Blood and darkness. Only the cold stars and never the hot sun." I lower my head so her mouth brushes my neck. Despair twists my stomach. Desire heats it. "I give you my consent. Do it, if that's the path you want to take."

She shudders under my hands, her breath a ragged caress against my throat. She leans into me, pressing against my swelling cock. Liquid fire roars in my veins. I haul her closer, and her lips open against my neck. I feel a cool scrape of teeth. It turns into the sharper prick of fangs. Her sudden gasp heats my skin, and my willing blood surges to meet her bite. I don't know what she'll do, but right then, I know I could very well die on the flaming pyre of my ruin that is Idallia.

"Wait." She abruptly pulls back. "I need to think." Her hand flies to her mouth. Her face scrunches up, and she shakes her head. She cautiously touches what appears to be a normal tooth again, then swallows hard. "Should it be that easy? Out one second, in the next?"

"I think so." My heart pounds in relief. As much as I started to crave her bite, I wanted her to resist more. The thought of Idallia losing daylight forever makes my throat heat and my eyes burn. "Letting down or retracting your fangs are physical actions, just like any other. You just never knew to ask your body before, or to even think about it at all." I gaze down at her, arousal still driving half my words. Low, almost desperate, I say, "If you don't want to bite me, then kiss me. Your choice, Sunshine."

Her pulse accelerates with a fierce leap, and she stares at me, her eyes huge. "I don't want everything to change."

"Hasn't it already?" My blood rushes as violently as hers.

"When did this happen?" She sways toward me. Lifting her hands to my sides, she anchors herself. She doesn't push or pull. She just holds on, locking us face-to-face. I revel in her deliberate touch. It's new, and yet somehow, I've already been locked here for years, just waiting for her to click into place.

"Does it matter?" I'm not sure I even know. Two hundred years is long, even for me. "You're vital to me now."

She tilts her head back, her lips slowly parting. My dragon roars in anticipation, and I dip my head, hope and need surging inside me, but then I hold still at the last second, our mouths nearly touching. My pulse thunders as I wait for her to close the final distance. This has to be her choice.

Her eyes flutter closed. After what feels like eternity, she reaches up and her soft, warm lips press against mine. Sensation ripples through me. Her kiss is the sweetest thing I've ever felt. Though sweet isn't the half of it. There's an intoxicating tension inside her that jumps straight into me. She brims with passion and intensity, the slightly bolder brush of her lips already burning me alive. Groaning, I slide my hands into her hair, kissing her back the only way I know how—like I worship her. I could fall to my knees right now.

She softens against me even as the kiss turns harder, hotter. My blood rushes like a swollen river. My cock stiffens, growing impossibly rigid as the scent of her arousal fills my nostrils. With barely any coaxing, she opens her mouth for me, and I take every bit of space she offers. This...this is my eternity.

The thought jars me even as her moan warms my lips and her fingers dig into my sides, pulling me closer. She rolls her tongue over mine, and lust rises like heat from a volcano. As we kiss, doors slam shut inside me, keeping the feel and taste of Idallia safe and flourishing and *mine*, like I'm the vault and she's the treasure. My dragon agrees, and my possessive thoughts, tight stomach, and nearly trembling hands tell me this is more than simple desire. I finally have Idallia in my arms—the woman I never dreamed would become the one thing I wouldn't be willing to give up, even for my kingdom.

We breathe raggedly, our mouths and bodies fusing. Her leg slides over my hip, and she rocks into me. I rock back, showing her how much I want her. The sounds we make, loud and rough and urgent, set off sparks inside me. She feels like a sunburst in my arms, one I could both consume and let burn me. We kiss each other like this will never end. So, why does this searing moment suddenly feel like the road to losing Idallia, rather than keeping her?

A cold serpentine of fear tangles through the heat and desire just as she abruptly rips herself away from me.

Eyes wide, she backs away. She holds out a hand when I try to follow. Arousal still perfumes the air like a delectable meal we haven't been able to share yet. My gut sinks at her distrustful expression, two centuries of lies a sizable anchor.

"This isn't a good idea." She shakes her head, biting a lower lip still plump and shiny from our kisses.

It's a disastrous idea. But I've tasted her now. Smelled her passion. Felt her hands and mouth on me and swallowed down her moans to keep them locked deep inside. Bad idea or not, the man in me doesn't have any intention of letting her go, and the dragon in me will have to be tied down in chains to give her up now. "You want me. I can hear it. Scent it. *Taste* it."

"Want isn't the problem." The color drains from her face. "I've already been down this path. It didn't end well."

I gape in disbelief. "Are you comparing me to Kellan?" Shadows swirl around me, taking form. A solidifying talon grows too long and scrapes the floor. "Did my kiss taste like his?" I pulse with jealousy, skin and scales.

Her gaze darts to the scratch in the wood before bouncing back to my face. "Not to Kellan, to the situation. But this is worse. You give the orders. My job depends on you, my home. My birds."

I tense, offended. Nothing she's said is wrong, and yet there's nothing right about it at all. Doesn't she know me? If Idallia doesn't know me, no one does. "Does any part of you honestly believe I would kick you out and take back your birds if you don't *sleep* with me?" The fucking nerve. Flames build in my throat. Smoke seeps from my nostrils.

"How do I know what you'll do, Bale?" she asks sharply. "Everything changes when intimacy is involved."

"And you know this because of one failed relationship?"

She flushes angrily again. "It's one more relationship than you've had in the last two hundred years."

"That's because all I could see was you!"

She rears back, shock stamping across her features. "No. You just liked being alone." Her brow creases. "And then..."

"And then I wasn't anymore. Because you showed up, and I was drawn into your orbit over and over."

Her face pinches, her expression unsure. "Well, you were so subtle about it that I didn't even notice."

I chuckle roughly. "I didn't want to impose. Kellan is still clearly an issue, and all you ever need are your birds."

Her tongue darts out, wetting her lips. My eyes track the pretty pink tip like prey. Lust thumps inside me again, sweeping low and hot toward my groin.

"Kellan's not an issue." She doesn't say anything about her birds.

"Does *he* know that?"

Her eyes flash brighter than all the golden coins in my treasure vault. "Does that matter? I can't change what he does."

I can. Which is why I sent him to pick up a helpless little fae package. Unfortunately, from what I hear, she arrived in tears. I have no idea what happened and don't care, but Marissa Turin is going to remain Kellan's problem so he can stop being *mine*.

"Let's not fight anymore." I take a cautious step toward her. "I want to kiss you, not argue."

Heat rolls off her, flushing her chest and neck a summer pink I want to fly straight into and savor. She clears her throat. "Why did you lie to me the other night? What was the point?" The sudden tremble in her voice stops me in my tracks. "I came to you for answers. I was scared. I didn't know what to think."

Remorse heavy in me, I scrub a hand down my face. "I'm sorry. I made a mistake." My mind whispers to me to tell her the rest, and my dragon tells me to shut up. The dragon in me has never been in charge before, but I listen to it tonight.

I'll wait to see how the Council goes. I'll keep Idallia close this time instead of sending her away. If things take a turn for the worse, maybe I'll finally find it in me to pull my ace out of my sleeve.

Worry rips through me like a tear in my soul. But then my ace will become a wildcard, and I could lose everything—Idallia and the vote I need.

She nods, but instead of coming back, she moves toward the door. With a last look at me, half longing and half suspicion, she leaves.

CHAPTER TWENTY-NINE

IDALLIA

I can't stop thinking about Bale. That scorching kiss. His simple apology. And he came clean about me being a sunblood. Late is better than never...isn't it?

I wanted to stay with him so badly back at the inn, to just give in to our heat and connection. Walking away was the hardest thing I've ever done.

Because what's really changed? I might suddenly know I'm a vampire who doesn't drink blood—and resisting Bale's offer to pierce his vein and drink from him was the second hardest thing I've ever done—but I still don't want to jeopardize everything I've worked for.

An evening bath does little to ease my tension. I step out of the cooling water and dry off in the screened alcove at the back of my room. Fyrestar, Rim, and Sol are out hunting and won't be back for a while, so I simply tie a towel around myself and move toward the dresser to untangle my hair.

My comb and brush set is the only thing from Glarraden

House that means anything to me. In an uncharacteristic moment of thoughtfulness, Rita gave them to me. They were her mother's —a woman I never knew. But her name was Imogen, so an ornate *I* is carved into each silver handle. If they'd been carved with an *R*, I probably wouldn't have been allowed to touch them.

I pick up the comb and start working it through my wet hair, drips rolling down my shoulders and soaking into the towel. Besides this silver set, I don't really have fancy things. Maybe being the gildenfae-gold kid made me never want to display wealth, or even truly accept my own. The inherited comb and brush are the nicest things I possess, and I wouldn't have treated myself to them. They always make me wonder if Imogen of Glarraden would've made me feel welcome. Old Gus used to talk about her with more fondness than he ever did Rita or Gerard, so maybe she would've been a decent grandmother.

My feet sink into the thick, soft rug in front of my dresser. There are three new rugs in my room, which are now the second nicest things in my possession. They showed up yesterday. I didn't buy them myself, though I'd meant to get some.

My chest tightens uncomfortably. I guess Bale can't resist giving things any more than he can resist stealing them. My hair first, then the choker. And probably my heart.

I roll my lips in, pressing. Nothing's really changed, but hasn't everything? Going backward is impossible, and ignoring things rarely works. There's no way I can ignore that kiss, and I don't think Bale will, either. I also worry about his ability to listen when my words don't match his perception of things.

I look around at the evidence. Didn't I specifically say I'd buy my own rugs?

But no...

Idallia needs rugs. Provide rugs.

I hear the words in the deeper, raspier rumble of his dragon. Even imagined, that dark-velvet voice carries an underlying swell of fire, heating me from the inside out.

Sighing loudly, I shake my head at my own hopelessness. One

kiss and I'm still a bonfire two days later. How does life simply go on after the most scorching kiss of my existence? The one I've been secretly craving for decades.

My toes curl into the plush rug just thinking about it, and I feel the pressure of Bale's lips against mine again. His hands on my back, sliding into my hair. His body, his breath, his groan as he deepened the kiss and gave me exactly what I wanted.

Longing tugs sharply inside me. I haven't seen Bale since we flew home as a group. I both want to seek him out and escape him. I might come away scathed and hurt and wanting if I see him, but *not* seeing him might hurt even worse.

A knock at the door startles me from my thoughts. I told Sybil I'd come down to her before dinner, but she must've found some free time to meet me instead. We haven't had a chance to talk in private, and I have so much to tell her. I need advice—or maybe someone to talk me off this fragile limb I'm climbing out on.

I hurry to the door, cold stone attacking my bare feet as I leave the rugs behind. I throw it open and find Bale standing there. Shock slams into me. I pull up short. He takes up the whole starsdamned doorway, and my entire body suddenly feels charged like the air before a lightning storm. His amber eyes widen, gleaming with inner fire, then drop to my chest. I tighten my hold on the towel, my pulse beating so wildly it steals my breath.

"I thought you were Sybil," I say in a mumbling rush. It's the second time I've made the mistake recently, but in all fairness, aside from when I've been badly injured, Bale didn't ever knock on my door before.

"I'm not." His voice comes out hoarse, the gravelly abrasion against my heightened senses kindling an instant fire inside me. My belly tightens, and warmth sinks heavily through my most intimate parts. Bale's nostrils flare as he inhales deeply. His expression darkens with desire, and I slam the door shut, leaving the Dragon King on the other side.

My heart jumping like a startled rabbit against my ribs, I race to my dresser and pull out the first thing I find. A dress. How in the blazing stars did that happen? I only own one, and it's the first thing I grab?

I pull it over my head anyway. It's tight and hard to get on, the white fabric sticking to my still-damp skin. I yank it down, wiggling frantically to get it over my hips. My wet hair is cold against my back, making my skin pucker with goose bumps, and my nipples stand out.

Another, more tentative knock comes as I twist the damn thing into place. "Idallia?"

"Just a minute!" Shaking with alarm and anticipation in equal measures, I stare at the door as if it's my nemesis. I force calming breaths. When I can picture the man on the other side without my heart thrashing like a wild animal, I walk back to the door, open it, and offer Bale a bland smile. "Hello."

He arches dark brows, his eyes glinting. "Hello."

Belatedly, I realize I forgot to put on any underthings. Or shoes. I'm just standing there in a white dress I've only worn once before, and there's a very good chance Bale can see my nipples through it. *Great.* "Did you need something?"

"Going somewhere?" he asks at the same time.

I shake my head. "Just...panic dressing," I admit. "It was the first thing I grabbed."

His mouth lifts in a crooked smile. "Do I make you panic, Sunshine?"

Sunshine. My whole chest tightens and heats. *You're special.* Isn't that what having a nickname means?

A soul-deep want seeps into my bones. How can Bale look like decadent lust and fiery passion all mixed into one with his sleek black clothing and burning eyes? And more than that. He's safety. Home. Even knowing he kept something vital from me for so long, I still want to put my trust in him and sink into his arms.

"You surprised me. I wasn't expecting you." And when Bale looks at me like I'm a feast and calls me Sunshine, yes, I panic a little.

"You should start expecting me. It won't only be Sybil knocking on your door."

I stare at him, absorbing his words. It's a clear message of intent, and my resolve to remain sensible tumbles away like he's the downpour and I'm the mudslide. Panicking again, I pivot and stride back to the rug to put some distance between us and save my bare feet from the stone floor. When I turn again, I find Bale's gaze sliding up my body, hugged to indecency in this ridiculous dress.

Voice low, intimate, he rasps, "You look amazing."

Well, that doesn't help.

"Thank you." I glance away, shifting nervously. "And thank you for the rugs—even though I didn't ask for them."

"You don't have to ask for the things you need."

Because a dragon shifter gathers, keeps, provides. *Sees.* I clear my throat. "Come in if you want, but close the door. There's a draft."

"Are you suddenly *un*immune to the cold?"

"You put ideas in my head," I grumble. "Now I can't get them out."

"Are you only talking about the rugs? Or something else?" His voice lowers to a heated purr that settles right between my legs.

Steeling my spine, I do what Bale always does: answer a question with a question. "You saved the best for me? Closest to the heart?" His gaze instantly turns guarded, his expression closing off. "How about you stop lying to me and tell me what you know?"

"Why didn't you tell me it was Rexton Hale who approached you in Drayke?" he counters.

"Because I didn't want to," I snap, already annoyed.

"He's here now," Bale says sourly. "Taking up my time and going on and on about what a great ally he'd make if I'd only support his claim."

"Maybe he would." I spread my hands, inadvertently pulling

the low-cut dress tight across my chest.

Bale's gaze dips again. His hands curl into fists. "Were you tempted to let him drink from you?"

I stare in shock. "No."

"Would you drink from him?"

"No," I practically snarl. "What's wrong with you? Why would I do that?" But then the remembered temptation of Bale's hot blood just beneath his skin, my mouth over his vein, sends a shocking pulse of hunger through me. I take a step back.

Bale cocks his head, his eyes narrowing. "It's different now that you know, isn't it? You'll never *not* wonder again. Never not think *what if*."

I swallow, hating how right that sounds and how saliva floods my mouth. I usually have little appetite. I'm ravenous now, but not for anything I've ever tasted. "You shouldn't have kept the truth from me."

His jaw tics as his eyes scrape over my body, looking as though they want to burn off my dress and scorch me alive. "I can't offer you what a vampire can. I can't take your neck in a consensual bite and make you shatter with just one touch."

The flood of wet warmth between my legs is mortifyingly quick. "It can't always be like that," I murmur.

"Only if that's the intent. Otherwise, it's just a pleasurable moment, leaving the host without worry or pain."

"I've never delved into the specifics of consensual bites." Suspicion blooms, and I frown. "Have you?"

"Did you want Hale's fangs here? Penetrating you?" Moving closer, he lifts his hand. Heat and tension overwhelm me before he even touches my neck, his strong fingers pressing against my hammering pulse.

A shiver races up my spine, making my nipples pucker even more visibly under my dress. I can barely answer, overwhelmed by the most demanding arousal I've ever felt. "No," I finally rasp.

Bale's gaze holds mine, his hand still on my neck. "Good."

My breathing shallows. My senses burn. I want him to yank

up my dress and touch me between my legs so badly that I barely hold back a moan. "Why?"

His voice is low and dangerous, simmering with violence. The rough rumble washes over me like summer thunder as he stares at me with stark hunger in his eyes. "Because if he touches you, I'll rip off his head."

My knees weaken. I tilt toward him. "That wouldn't be very diplomatic of you."

"You're more important than diplomacy." He curls his hand around my neck, gripping my nape. "You know that, don't you?"

I gaze up at him, dazed. "You don't break a kingdom over a woman."

His eyes drop to my mouth. "I'll break whatever the fuck I want. I'm done playing by the rules."

"Bale." His name whispers past my lips. "Why are you doing this?"

His other hand rises, his fingers twining into my hair. "Doing what we both want?"

"Changing things." My voice wavers, betraying my fears. My body heats, betraying my desire. I'm split down the middle, and I don't know which part of me should win.

His brow creases. "Are you worried about your position? Your birds?"

My hazy eyes focus. He never answers questions, only asks them. So I do the same. "How can I not?"

He gently grips my head, his features suddenly serious enough to rival the death of stars. "I will *never* separate you from Fyrestar, Rimblaze, and Embersol. Whatever you do, wherever you go, if they want to follow you, that's their choice. I swear it on my kingdom. I swear it on my life. They are yours, and you are theirs. That's all there is to it. Forever."

My breath catches. Tears sear my eyes. Forever...or until death. I think Sol's rebirth will be the last for the warbirds. "You promise? Even if"—I motion between us—"this goes wrong?"

"The last thing I want is for this to go wrong, but I swear it. No matter what," he vows.

Tears on my lashes, I do what was unthinkable just weeks ago. I lift up on my toes and kiss Bale.

He kisses me back with a low groan. All the heat in me rushes to the surface in a blaze of desire. He deepens the kiss, slanting his mouth over mine and exploring with heady, savoring intensity and heated strokes of his tongue. We move as one, pressing closer and pulling each other in. My head spins as Bale devours me like he's never tasted anything so divine. I kiss him back just as passionately, sliding my body against his. I want more, harder, now. I want this dress off me and Bale in. My body aches for him.

His hands drop to my waist, his fingers clamping down. He holds our hips together, and I grip his shoulders while our breath mingles and our tongues spar. His hard shaft presses against my lower belly, the significant promise of it amplifying my desire. Sensation rushes through me, and I press back, desperately craving more.

With a low sound of need, Bale locks me tightly against him, his mouth never leaving mine. He's in control of how we move, how soft or savage we are, and his dominant, starving-for-me ferocity is shockingly thrilling. I gasp in air between kisses and touches that leave me hot and slick at my aching core. His thigh slips between mine, lifting a little, and the sudden pressure where I already throb for him pulls a ragged moan from me.

"Bale." I claw nearer, kiss deeper. Now that I've surrendered to my feelings, I can't get enough, and I grab his shoulders, jump, and hook my legs around his waist. He holds me up, his big hands sliding around my thighs. I push my heated sex against the hardness settled right between my legs and kiss him with years of secret longing and pent-up lust.

His hands glide toward my ass, my dress now bunched around my waist. A guttural sound tears from his throat. "You're bare underneath." His breath pounds my lips. His voice is rough, *wrecked.* Exploring fingers lightly graze my slit, and I shudder in pleasure.

"No time to get dressed." I breathe as hard as he does. His big, strong body trembles, and I feel like we're two shooting stars hurtling toward an explosive collision. "This works out better anyway."

His deep groan is a chasm opening in my world. I fall straight in. "I want you naked under my bed furs for weeks." He roughly palms both my ass cheeks, and I quiver in anticipation. "I can smell your wet heat," he rasps. "It's driving me insane."

"It's all yours. All for you. Just take me to your lair." I glance over his shoulder toward my open window. "I don't know how long we'll be alone here."

He backs toward the window, his fingers teasing the damp outline of my folds. I gasp into his mouth, arousal jolting me and need shivering all the way to my toes.

"Anyone could see us fly up the mountain," he cautions.

I draw back. "Do you care?" If he plans on keeping me a secret, then I don't plan on giving him a secret to keep, no matter how desperately I want him right now.

"Only if you don't pull that dress down enough to cover your beautiful ass." He squeezes me possessively, and I exhale in a rush, growing even wetter and more aroused. He scents the difference, and his eyes ignite. "Fuck, Idallia. I'm so hard for you. I want you. I've wanted you for so long."

His raw admission feels like I just won a war. I unhook my legs from around his waist and get my feet under me. Bale steadies me as I tug my dress down. The second I'm decently covered, he swings me up into his arms, leaps onto the window ledge, and launches us into the void.

The free fall excites me even more. Almost too soon, Bale's shadow wings unfurl and solidify. A first solid pump stops our descent. Then we rise, heading for the top of the mountain. My arms around Bale's neck, I turn in to his chest and rub my thighs together.

Nuzzling his jaw, I whisper, "I want you inside me."

"You're going to make me crash." His throaty reply adds fuel to my fire.

"Then crash into *me*." I think he understands my meaning, but just in case, I open my mouth and breathe a hot, "Fuck me, Bale," right into his ear.

His inner heat blazes, almost burning me. The scents of dry leaves, wind-whipped forests, and embers about to ignite surround us, and he breathes out smoke, his dragon close to the surface.

Bale climbs the mountain dizzyingly fast. We burst through his open study window as dusk splashes the bright, fiery colors of phoenix wings across the darkening sky. He lands smoothly, reabsorbing his wings. He nudges the window shut and turns down a tunnel, striding toward what must be his bedroom. It takes just seconds to reach a large chamber with a huge bed. He tosses me onto it and starts stripping.

Breathless with anticipation, I push up on my elbows, watching him. My white dress stretches tightly across my chest, my dark nipples straining against the material. The hem is around my hips again, and I let Bale look his fill. His searing gaze riveted to me, he drops his shirt to the floor. My eyes dip, his muscled torso suddenly commanding all my attention. That long crimson line of tattoos. The chiseled ridges. I bite my lip and squeeze my inner muscles. I could climax just looking at him.

His voice almost violent, he rasps, "When you look at me like that, I want to mark you as mine."

I shiver. "Territorial."

His boots come off. "If Rexton Hale even looks at you this week, I'll kill him."

I arch a brow. "Jealous already?"

"I've been jealous for a century."

Heat swoops through me on burning wings. "How would you mark me?" I ask with primal interest, though I'm not about to let him tattoo his name across my chest.

He pulls at the laces of his pants. "My scent. All over you. No one will touch you."

"You promise?" I ask with a silky smile.

"I promise to mark you inside and out."

A thrill ripples through me. My lips part, and I open my legs in invitation. I can barely stand another second without Bale inside me. "I almost want to skip the foreplay," I murmur.

He groans. Then suddenly, he's naked before me—and the most magnificent thing I've ever seen. My gaze roams over him, snagging on his erection.

"And how will you mark *me*?" he asks, stalking forward.

I wet my lips, entranced by the way he moves, the sheer power, the control, the potential to leave me both sated and destroyed. "Not by biting."

Bale clearly doesn't find that amusing. "Idallia—*behold the sun*." His amber eyes hold mine, suddenly serious. "Be careful in the throes of passion."

Just from a few words, I almost taste the blood I never craved until the idea of *vampire* came along. "You're promising *throes of passion*." I swallow the imagined flavor, my still-retracted fangs aching to descend. "You'd better live up to it."

He sets a knee on the bed, then another, and crawls forward like a predator, looming over me. He runs a big hand down the center of my body from my throat to the juncture between my thighs, pressing his wide palm against my bare skin where it's already slick and throbbing with need. I exhale raggedly, watching his every move.

His gaze molten amber, he straddles my legs. "Do you like this dress?"

I shake my head. "Not at all."

He grips the material at the hem and rips it clean in half. Cool air hits me all over, and my skin pebbles. My nipples practically reach for him, begging for his mouth.

Bale's eyes fix on my breasts. "You're perfection." He slides a finger through my folds. Shocks pop inside me like starbursts, and

I lift into his touch for more. He strokes me again, lightly increasing the pressure.

"Yes, this," I pant, clenching my belly. He deftly teases the most sensitive part of me. Sparks of sensation radiate from his touch, and my vision grows hazy. "Bale."

Leaning over me, he plunders my mouth. "What was that about skipping the foreplay? Seems like you're enjoying it." He caresses me, spreading my dampness. His other hand fondles my breast.

"You're torturing me," I groan.

His possessively dark chuckle warms my lips. "If that were true, you'd be screaming."

"Bale!"

"Better," he rumbles in a voice that sounds just like when he's a beast. Then he works a finger inside me.

Moaning, I let my head fall back and move my hips. He trails his lips down my neck to my breast, taking a nipple into his mouth. Arching my back, I free my arms from what's left of my dress and spear my fingers into his thick hair as he turns his attention to the other breast. Lavish kisses and searing words melt my skin and bones as desire turns into a drumming pulse right between my legs.

"Bale, I want you. *Now*." We've already waited so long for this.

"I feel like I'm dreaming those words." His kisses scorch my throat. He takes my mouth again, his tongue dominating mine in that way he dominates everything. Born to rule. His hands clamp down on my head, and he angles me for an even deeper kiss, a low groan building in his throat. "Are you ready?"

"I was ready the second you knocked on my door." I pull my knees up and reach down, giving his thick shaft a few long, firm strokes. His jaw bulging, he inhales roughly. Our eyes lock as I guide him toward my opening. "All you have to do is push."

He slowly thrusts, his eyes never leaving mine. It's been so long that the hot stretch takes me off guard. He's gentle but relentless, then suddenly, we're fully joined.

With our bodies locked together, our next kiss feels completely different, like a promise. Bale moves, and my world tilts. I moan, pleasure sweeping through me. He thrusts, the shudder in his breath making me feel powerful and desperately wanted. I grip him close, our mouths still fused, and rock to meet his hips.

"Are you protected from pregnancy?" he murmurs against my lips.

"I'll get something tomorrow." Though with the low birth rate among our kinds, conceiving is rare.

"I'll pull out," he rasps.

"Don't. I know what to take. It'll be safe." Just because I thought about having children recently doesn't mean I want to start trying for them now. "You promised to mark me inside and out. Don't disappoint me, Bale."

Groaning, he dips his head into the curve of my neck as he holds me close and pushes into me with steady strokes. We both breathe raggedly. He kisses my shoulder. I feel a brief scrape of teeth and, in response, my fangs ache again. I'm too distracted by all the other amazing sensations to stop them from descending this time. Bale grips my hip, moving faster, and I tighten, ready to burst.

Emotion stings my eyes. All the longing. The reality of *this*. Every stroke brings me closer to completion. I rise to meet his thrusts, and white-hot sparks snap between my legs. My body trembles. My lungs are filled with Bale. My tongue thirsts for his blood, and I gasp, angling my head away from his hard-beating pulse.

"Stay with me," he murmurs. "Never go."

I barely hear his whispered plea or understand what he means. My mind is a blur, all my concentration arrowing to where his hard length pumps in and out. Climax rushes toward me, a flare igniting fast and hard. My breath hitches, and I tumble over the edge, my body convulsing around his. Stars streak my vision. I clench my muscles, gripping him so tightly that I pull every last sensation from my body and his.

Bale groans above me. His hot release thumps powerfully inside me, driving a second wave of tremors through my core.

We gradually uncoil our muscles and sink into the mattress with matching moans. My breathing is still a reckless hurricane, and Bale rolls to the side, leaving me more air. I curl into his body, and he cradles me there. I inhale woodsmoke and wind and know I smell the same now, his scent coating my skin.

A low sound hums in my throat, thirst still taunting me with the possibility of blood. Bale's warm, delicious chest is right in front of my face, and I want to open my mouth and bite. Stemming the reckless urge, I fight my fangs back into place. We haven't talked about consent again, and I have no intention of giving up sunlight. More tension leaves me once the sharp tips retract, and I prove to myself once again that I'm in control.

Bale's breathing settles faster than mine. He strokes my shoulder. He idly kisses the top of my head, and I barely keep my heart from leaping straight out of my body and offering itself to him.

"What does this mean for us?" he eventually asks. "I don't want you to feel...pressured in any way."

My chest spasms like a muscle cramp. "What do you mean?"

His pause is too long, worrying me. "I mean I want to continue this, but I don't want you to feel obligated. Nothing has to change if you don't want it to. Your home, your position...I swear to you that nothing depends on *this*."

A knot somewhere deep inside me unravels. Despite his earlier assurances about my birds, I still needed those words. I also still know for a fact that if this doesn't work out, it won't be easy, and everything *will* change. But whatever decisions I make will be mine. I trust Bale not to make them for me or my birds.

Leaning my head back to look at him, I draw a light line over his sculpted chest with my fingertip, lingering on the edge of a red crescent moon near the scars above his heart. He never did answer my questions. I'll just have to keep asking until he does. "Didn't you say you wanted me naked under your bed furs for weeks? I'll be very disappointed if you don't make good on that."

Happiness flashes across his face before a wolfish grin replaces the quick shot of joy. "We're on top of the furs."

I smile back. I want to see his joy regularly. Bale's smile is my new goal. "Then by all means, Dragon King, get me under them. Or better yet," I say suggestively, "under *you*."

I'm rewarded with a grin that'll carry my buoyant heart straight into the next century as Bale rolls me onto my back and covers my body with his.

CHAPTER THIRTY

BALE

For three blissful, sex-filled days, Idallia barely leaves my lair. We're rarely dressed in more than robes and can't stop touching each other. We do everything together—eat, bathe, talk, plan, make love, sleep—and then start all over. It's idyllic in a way I didn't know existed.

Sometimes we fuck, and I love that too. It's harder, faster, more urgent. My cock stirs just thinking about it. About her. About us, because there's such a solid *us* now that I don't know how we circled each other for so long without one of us cracking. I used to smell her arousal and think it couldn't be for me. It was just a physical response to the action or the danger or the fury—or stars forbid, Kellan—but now I know. She wants *me*.

Primal desires grip me in their iron fist. *Keep. Protect. Mate.* Heat thumps in my abdomen, but ice slides through my veins, raising a chill on the back of my neck. I can't do any of that unless Idallia knows the whole truth. And then, will she still want me?

Idallia left our mountaintop lair only once to speak to Sybil about protection against pregnancy. I could barely stand to be without her, pacing like a caged animal. The second she returned, I tossed her onto the bed and devoured her. She devours me too. Sometimes I feel fangs scrape my skin, and we both tense. I call her Sunshine in a soothing voice, and she controls her nascent urges. I make sure her food is more satisfying than it used to be, resembling blood in ways, and fill her plates with figs and blueberries.

We've been outside together, flying with Fyrestar, Rimblaze, and Embersol. She chooses to ride Fyrestar instead of me, and I can accept that. No part of me wants to come between them.

But now, everything is about to change. It's the opening meeting of the Ellonrift Council, and I have to spend my entire night with people I only see once a year if I'm lucky, one of whom I hate with the intensity of a thousand erupting volcanoes.

Rannigan Bloodthief. I keep my growl low, not wanting to wake Idallia. I gaze down at her as she sleeps, sated from our lovemaking. I have mere minutes before I have to leave for the first of the week's meetings, and my gut instinct tells me to grab her, her birds, and get out of here.

But I can't do that. I'm the fucking Dragon King.

Every ruler of Ellonrift—legitimate and illegitimate—is currently inside my mountain, and their proximity to Idallia makes my skin itch. The Vampire King's presence grates on me from levels away. The treacherous bastard is always the one to worry about. I've individually welcomed the kings and queens of Ellonrift and settled them into their guest chambers, but I haven't dined with any of them or singled anyone out for conversation. I should've been making nice with the new Fae Queen in the hopes of an alliance, but I couldn't bring myself to give up any of this precious time with Idallia before Council duties rip me away from her.

I used to simply find Rexton Hale irritating, but now his requests make my stomach pitch. He's been sending me letters from *inside* my own fortress. I gave him a room at Idallia's insistence but refused to meet with him personally or accept his endless petitions to join the Council. The more he wants in on the voting, the more I want to shove the truth in his face.

But I can't do that without my own walls crumbling.

Every breath I take as I back away from a stunning, sleeping Idallia feels like my last to bask in this extraordinary happiness. And maybe I deserve to lose it, since everything is built on a lie.

I GO TO THE ELLONRIFT COUNCIL EACH NIGHT AND return to Idallia during the day. The meetings have always taken place at night so Cealastra can guide us with her light or appear in her starlit form—though the daunting yet dazzling latter hasn't happened since we drew the kingdom borders near the start of my reign. Now the Vampire King is the only one benefiting from night meetings, infinitely safer for him, and we haven't seen evidence of the Star of Ellonrift since Rannigan brutally killed the Fanghaven rulers.

The Torridaig, Ruthinock, Fanghaven block ceased to exist, and so did tied votes.

Idallia talked about there not being consequences after Rannigan's brutal murders. Maybe not directly for him, but what about Cealastra fading from our lives? The Council going from useful to a farce? Magic waning more than ever? Rannigan might've gotten exactly what he wanted, but all of Ellonrift lost.

I think about killing him now, like Idallia suggested. I dream about it while he drones on about sanctions and aggression, seeing myself bite right through him like I'd meant to all those years ago.

But something in me hesitates. I still need him to attack first so I can justifiably kill him in my own Council room, and so far, he's all talk.

Rannigan wants the other rulers to believe—or at least profess to believe—that Torridaig is constantly attacking Bloodwold. I want them to do the opposite. And since penalties can only be imposed by a vote, we'll eventually vote on it, and there's a good chance Rannigan will win.

That's the moment I'll be done with the Ellonrift Council after more than five hundred years. That's the moment I won't just kill blood raiders on my soil anymore. I'll kill them on Rannigan's and keep going until Blackrock Keep is mine and Rannigan is dead.

And that's the moment Idallia will finally be safe and free. I can confess everything, and then hopefully, this life we've already started can soar just like we do over Torridaig.

For Idallia and me, bright, mid-autumn sunshine defines our time together during this week full of arguing, posturing, and threats. She's my light in the dark. She's my reason to keep listening and debating when I'm so starsdamned sick of everything and everyone and already know how this will end.

Every day, I go over what happened during the previous night's meeting with her, and we strategize. She helps me see more clearly and maintain patience, but we both agree it's time to pull out my Bloodwold prisoners and see if the bald-faced evidence of Rannigan's lies can help sway his usual allies away from him.

But even if that works, I doubt Rannigan will respect a vote against him or accept sanctions. He'll keep sending raiders, and blood prisoners already in Bloodwold will continue to suffer. Starborn or not, it's time to eliminate him. Unfortunately, his population is used to doing things a certain way, and getting rid of Rannigan won't stop the majority of his people from thirsting for blood violence. The undertaking to control the entirety of Bloodwold and its vampires will be enormous.

It's late in the day but not yet dark, and I shut my mind off to the Council. Another night of the same useless arguing is coming up, but right now, I'm going to make love to Idallia and savor every moan and touch she offers.

We move into the bedroom with just a look, no words needed

between us. She welcomes me into her body, and all the bad tension drains away to leave only the good. Fading afternoon light filters through the colored-glass window as I rock inside her, her head in my hands and my mouth on hers. She draws shudders of pleasure from me. I'm already so addicted to her taste and touch and feel that I have wild thoughts about keeping her in my lair and never letting her out.

I drive into her more powerfully, asserting the only control I have. Her excitement builds, her fingertips pressing into my back, her thighs hugging my hips, and her passion burning us both. She gasps my name, and I catch the sound right out of her throat. I want to be the air she breathes. I want to give her every fucking thing she'll ever need.

"Mine." The gruff word is out of my mouth and against hers before I even think. "Be mine."

She lifts into me and squeezes her inner muscles so tightly that I nearly lose myself. "I am yours," she breathes out, writhing against me as she reaches for her climax. Her nails score my shoulders, leaving me a mark to carry into battle tonight.

"I love you," I rasp against her lips. She's my guiding star and everything that makes me happy. Our days together. Our flights over the mountain forests and glittering lakes. Our endless lovemaking. Talking through issues and hearing her advice.

Her golden eyes open, holding mine. "I love you, too, Bale."

My heart swells to fill my entire chest. It barely leaves room for the fear that this could all come crashing down and leave me burned to ash. Fear that once Idallia knows everything, she'll look at me in absolute shock, *betrayal*, and turn her back.

Kissing her with fevered passion, I lift her to meet my increasingly savage thrusts. Her breasts rub my chest. Her legs lock around my waist, spurring me on. Her arms hold me close, and her body fits perfectly with mine.

She tips over the edge with a groan, and I follow her so fast and utterly that I shake with the force of the aftershocks.

Rolling her on top of me, I hold her close. "I want this to last a lifetime." My murmured words stir her hair, and she looks up.

A slow, happy, almost surprised smile spreads across her face. "I do too. Why wouldn't it?"

I tuck her head back under my chin so she can't see the abject terror on my face. "Let's bring the birds out for a picnic dinner by the lake. They can hunt, and we'll bring food." We'll fly together and talk and laugh and just *be*, which is something I didn't even know how to do a week ago.

Idallia has brought me her family, and it's a gift I didn't know I wanted or needed. Fyrestar will stick to my wing with composed strength and wisdom, ever sensing what Idallia needs even before she does. Rimblaze will swing between moments of maturity and spurts of youthful dauntlessness that still need a firm word and heavy look to rein in. And Embersol will fly circles around us, her sharp little beak piercing the sky like an arrow, and her fluffy yellow head crest leaving a trail of sparks on the wind.

Sudden heat sears my eyes. Embersol has been calling me *Dad* lately. I can't help encouraging her.

My heart grows impossibly bigger, my chest tighter. I exhale unsteadily. I haven't had a family in so long that I forgot what it was like—or what I'd *wished* it was like. I never had siblings, and frankly, I didn't like my parents much. Now I have Idallia and her phoenixes, and I want to spend every waking hour with them and keep them all tucked safely under my wings.

But that feels frighteningly impossible. There's no peace until Rannigan Bloodthief is off my doorstep. And there's no peace when I know the end of my happiness could very well be my own damn fault.

INSIDE THE MEETING ROOM, THE ARGUING IS INCESSANT and always on the edge of violence. My head pounds, and all I want is to leave this big round cavern with its big round table and its five totally different people who will never get along. I want to walk away and go back to Idallia.

The irony is, she should be here.

Even if I tell her the truth the very next time I see her, it'll be too late for this year's Council. Too late for her to help me and Torridaig as I always intended her to. Too late for her to decide if she even wants to.

The chasm in the pit of my stomach widens. It's going to swallow me whole soon.

The Were King steeples his fingers, listening to the Vampire King complain. This week, we've already negotiated updated prices for the metals, fabrics, and wood products coming out of Torridaig, increased efforts on the Were King's part to control the kidnapping fanatics in his kingdom, harsher penalties on any fae caught using their glamour magic on people instead of paying for what they need, and sharing of the southern lake waters near Glarraden via new aqueducts. The increasingly dry agricultural plains of northern Ruthinock will receive irrigation and, in return, Torridaig will receive first pick of the human sorcerers willing to leave home. It's a better deal for Ruthinock. They'll still have water, even as magic fades.

What's left is the fucking Vampire King and his completely illegal blood raids. Rannigan tries to paint everything as my fault, inventing utter bullshit left and right in a way he's never dared before. No one feels even a shiver of Cealastra's light, which just spurs him on. After hours of this, the Human Queen barely listens to his tirades anymore. The Were King already knows his vote—it's always the same because he's more scared of Rannigan than he is of me. The little Fae Queen tries to make herself as small as possible in her great, big chair. The fierce dispute barely concerns her. She's got my whole kingdom between her and Rannigan.

"My people are in *his* dungeon." Rannigan jabs a sharp-nailed, permanently bloodstained finger at me. "I demand justice."

"And what would your justice look like?" I ask, seething.

"Blood debt," he immediately answers.

I laugh in his face. I'm not giving him people to eat. Not mine or anyone else's. "I *do* have vampires in my dungeon. Because *his* raiders"—I jab a finger back at him—"were stealing *my* people straight from *my* towns."

"And mine," the Human Queen launches from across the table in a hard voice. Her eyes narrow. Isabella Varlo is my kind of ally. Quiet and still until she can punch someone in the throat with only a few words. "*I* demand justice for all the humans you've dragged into your blood markets and sold to your vampire horde."

Rannigan stands, slamming both hands on the table. The Fae Queen squeaks and makes herself even smaller. The Were King leans back. Isabella holds her ground. "My justice is a life for a life," Rannigan grinds out, ignoring us both like we never even spoke. "Between you, you've killed a hundred vampires in the last weeks. I want a hundred of yours now. And I want dragon shifters, not weakling humans." Rannigan swings a blistering look at Isabella.

She stares back at him with a lifetime of hatred in her eyes.

"So, you admit to sending at least a hundred raiders into our sovereign territories in the last weeks?" I say smoothly.

His shoulders stiffen. "You crossed the border and took prisoners. I have witnesses."

"Where are your witnesses?" I ask with lethal impatience. "Oh wait, I have mine."

I stride to the door and open it. I gave orders to bring up the Bloodwold prisoners earlier. They're lined up against the wall outside, and I pull the first one from the guards holding his chains and shut the door.

Shoving him in front of me to show him to the Council, I demand, "Where did I capture you?"

The vampire sees Rannigan and flinches. He knows he's dead either way and lies through his fangs. "You crossed the border." He jerks his head at me and then turns back to the table. "I was minding my own business in Hellwood Forest when the Dragon King and his Elite Wing flew in and massacred the entire village."

"Just as I said!" Rannigan cries in triumph. "I demand justice."

I snort in disbelief. If I was known for massacres, that might be believable. And where the fuck is Cealastra? The only reason the Ellonrift Council has ever functioned is because she doesn't let lies pass or violence erupt between rulers in the meeting room. There are stars out the window, but there's not even a hint of divine light hitting the table or any of us here. The eye of her bird-shaped constellation looks weaker than ever, and the primordial star seems to flicker before my eyes.

My gut clenches. I'd held out hope that she'd return, that she was still watching, and that my attempts to do the right thing would somehow balance out Rannigan's constant crimes. No more. I'm done. If killing is how I get results, then I'll kill.

"This one lied. Let's try again." I open the door so the other captives see everything and incinerate the one I hold with one focused firebreath. I'm the only dragon shifter in the world who can breathe fire without shifting, just like I can form wings or a tail or talons. "Next," I snarl.

The vampire's agonized scream still echoes in the room. Bones and bloody muck dirty my floor. Marissa Turin leans over in her chair and retches. I grab the next vampire in line and haul him inside.

"This is coercion!" Rannigan hisses. "Violence to get what he wants."

I wrap my hands around the vampire's shoulders, my heavy touch creeping toward his throat. "Where did I capture you?" I ask in a dangerously soft voice.

He trembles, because I'm suddenly the scariest beast in Ellonrift again.

"Draywood," he chokes out. "We set fire to Draywood and took people for the blood markets. Humans and dragon shifters."

"Draywood is within *my* border," I say, searing a hard look toward the people around the Council table.

"Lies!" Rannigan spits.

"Cealastra knows the truth," I shoot back, still hoping against hope that her starlight will fall on me right now, definitively marking my words as truth and revealing Rannigan as the liar he is.

The Vampire King sits again, throws his head back, and laughs. It starts out slowly and builds until worry and anger coat my insides in a layer of ice. "Cealastra is *gone*. Can't you tell? That's the light of a dead star still reaching us. There's no one there, and when the light finally fades, magic will die in Ellonrift."

Deep in my twisting belly, I know it's true. We've been at this argument for hours, nearly coming to blade-point more times than I can count, and Cealastra has been nothing but silent. I'm more certain than ever that Rannigan either killed her or drove her away when he murdered a whole family she painstakingly created from her own starlight, then viciously turned his forefather's kingdom into the blood pit it is now. Rannigan cut down Cealastra at the same time he cut down my friend, his wife, and all but one of their children. And now the Star of Ellonrift is gone.

The Fae Queen starts quietly crying in her chair. Her people will be the first to die out unless a population that conceives children as infrequently as dragon shifters suddenly starts reproducing like rabbits. Magic is their survival.

I inhale deeply. The goddess is gone, and I have no reason to play by the rules. I open my mouth and coat Rannigan Bloodthief in flames.

He doesn't burn.

Rannigan chuckles, the sound making me want to tear out his throat. My fangs ache to sink into his flesh and rip, but he gets a sword between us fast. "Do you really think I wouldn't protect myself? Come now, Bale. Everyone knows you're a bleeding heart, but now we know you're stupid too."

My nostrils still flame as I stare at him. "So what does it come to?" I ask bitingly. "We fight to the death and the winner takes three kingdoms?"

Rannigan's cold laughter betrays a hint of nervousness. One-on-one, he knows I'd decimate him, magically protected or not. "We're at the Ellonrift Council for a reason. Let's put it to a vote. I win, and you hand over a hundred dragon shifters. They'll feed my people for years. We don't raid your kingdom, but if we did, raids would...lessen with the bounty you'd give."

Never. Not a chance. "And if I win?" I ask with so much rage that I can barely keep my inner fire from seeping out, let alone the shadow of my dragon. My dragon wants to grow into a hard, dark monster and rip this despot's head from his neck.

"You can keep the sunblood, and I won't try to take her back."

My blood goes hot, then cold. I stand unnaturally still. *Take her back?* Does he know who Idallia is? *Really* is?

The Were King thumps the hilt of his dagger on the table, denting the wood. "Do you agree to the terms?" he asks me.

My teeth clamp together so tightly that my jaw hurts. I nod, but it's a lie. I will never turn over my people, and I will never let Rannigan have Idallia. But I can lie with impunity now, just like Rannigan.

"Then let's vote," the Were King says. "Who supports the Dragon King?" Isabella, Marissa, and I lift our hands. "And who supports the Vampire King?" The Were King lifts a hand, and Rannigan lifts two.

"Fanghaven vote. My poor wife couldn't be here." He smirks at me, and rage erupts in my chest. I should've killed him centuries ago.

Our hands fall, the votes cast. It's a tie, and we all wait a few tight breaths, but Cealastra doesn't intervene. If I'd played my cards differently, the way I'd always intended, the vote would have been mine.

"Where does this leave us?" Isabella asks.

"A fight to the death is still on the table." I narrow my eyes at my enemy. "Unless you're too much of a coward."

Rannigan stands. Something in his eyes, his tiny smile, scrapes deep furrows of worry through me. "Your war room seems like a fitting place for a final confrontation. Say your prayers to your dead goddess, gather whoever you want, and meet me there. We'll need witnesses." He looks around the table. The others all nod.

"The war room," I growl.

And so ends what I assume is the final Ellonrift Council. From now on, we either maintain our alliances without any star to guide us, or go to war.

CHAPTER THIRTY-ONE

IDALLIA

I wake up in the small hours of the night, tucked under a mountain of furs and still warm and a little achy from our lovemaking. I smell like Bale, his scent imprinted into me. I stretch in bed, smiling and recalling memories from the previous day.

We slept all morning so Bale could rest after another full night at the Council. Then the five of us flew beyond Drayke, heading southeast with the sun high above us. While my phoenixes hunted in the nearby woods, Bale and I had lunch in a town by a roaring waterfall, the autumn colors at their peak and brilliant all around us. After, just the two of us again, we bathed in Bale's dragon-breath heated pool, his hands and mouth hotter on me than the water. We were hungrier for each other than for dinner and raced, still dripping, to the bedroom. It took a long time, but we finally exhausted each other. I fell asleep before dark, but Bale had to leave again.

I try to go back to sleep, but it's a useless endeavor. I slept too much during the day to be tired now. Bale will be at the final Council meeting until sunrise, and I'd rather be with my birds than alone in his lair, even if they're sleeping. I dress quickly, brush my hair, and slip a dagger into my boot. My swords are downstairs. I leave Bale a note telling him I'll be in my quarters in case he gets back before I do, then slip out the door.

A chill hits me the second I leave Bale's lair. The inner mountain is cold and dark this late into the night, and I shiver as I make my way down the endless stairs and corridors. Some of the torches lining the walls have already guttered and died. Shadows seem to reach out at me from everywhere, and for the first time, I start worrying about what's around corners I know as well as the back of my hand.

Slowing as I start down a particularly dark and silent staircase, I think about turning around. Bale's lair is warm, comfortable, and there are still embers in the hearth. I could build up the fire again. It's also an empty set of rooms until Bale gets back. Shaking my head at my hesitation, I keep going toward the Elite Wing level. It might be cozy in Bale's lair, but there's no roosting wall, and my birds aren't there.

I don't understand this troubled feeling as I make my way to my quarters, and while I don't ignore it, I try to push through. There shouldn't be any danger right now. During the Ellonrift Council, there's a code of peace, even among rulers who hate each other. Rannigan will be holed up in the Council room with Bale. His entourage and guards will be in rooms far down the mountain from here. I doubt Rexton Hale is wandering around where he doesn't belong, and even if he is, I don't think he's a danger to me. I'm just nervous because I've never been here during a Council before, and Bloodwold vampires are suddenly a much bigger threat to me.

With logic on my side, I keep going. Despite my giddy happiness and focus on getting to know Bale in a whole new way, I miss my birds. I haven't seen them as much as usual, and I've barely seen any of the Elite Wing since that first night with Bale.

Kellan has avoided me altogether, but I've spent some evening time in our lounge with the others this week, when Bale's been unavailable. They don't quite seem to know what to say to me right now, but it's not as uncomfortable as I feared.

As for my phoenixes, I know Fyrestar has been doing what he can to give Bale and me privacy, keeping the younger birds busy and happy and sometimes taking them to the training sessions that Bale and I are missing so we can spend our days together before he goes to the Council. My birds won't come up to me even if they know I'm alone in Bale's high lair, not quite daring yet to simply push through his windows.

More than halfway there, a warning prickle skitters over my skin. I get the oddest feeling of being disconnected from the foreboding sensation, as if I'm not the one in danger, and yet fear makes my stomach clench. Tensing, I stop, listening carefully. There's not a scuff of a boot or a flicker of light beyond the usual torches, but something in my gut tells me that everything just went horribly wrong.

Panic grips me. *My birds.*

My heart in my throat, I start to run, pounding down the stairs and careening around corners. I see the last bend in the corridor leading to my room and don't slow. I race around the corner, and rough, unforgiving rope cuts into my skin. I flinch, my face scraping against coarse mesh. Dark figures pounce. Gasping, I struggle against hard hands and the net closing tightly around me. I grope for my dagger. The strike comes from the side before I can grab the blade or scream for help.

Pain flares, hot blood seeps from my temple, and I drop like a stone to the faint echo of little Embersol screeching in terror behind my closed door.

I WAKE IN THE WAR ROOM, WOOZY AND STIFF. I'M TIED to one of the Elite Wing pillars, my legs folded uncomfortably underneath me, and my arms and torso strapped so tightly to the column behind me that I can barely draw breath. My hands are numb from cold and lack of circulation. At least a dozen booted feet move in my lowered vision. A sharp pain pounds in my head, and the ambush rushes back to me with sickening clarity. Nausea roils in my stomach as I lift my head. *Where are my birds?*

"Ah. She wakes." A man steps in front of me, blocking my view of the room. He's tall, lanky but strong, objectively handsome with blue eyes and dark hair, and subjectively my personal nightmare.

Cold fear swamps me as Rannigan Bloodthief squats in front of me. Even though we've never met, I'd recognize him anywhere.

Maybe it's the sharp, black nails. I swallow the flash of acid in my throat. No, not black. *Bloodstained.*

I lift my gaze from his chilling hands and glare at him. "This is a huge breach of diplomacy." I don't know how I form the words. They feel fuzzy in my head and thick on my tongue.

"We're both too smart to pretend that matters anymore."

"You don't know anything about me," I grind out. But my stomach sinks. Something terrible must've happened during the last night of the Council, and Cealastra didn't show up, confirming our worst fears. It's the only reason Rannigan would dare this.

"Idallia!" Fyrestar's frantic caw helps clear the cobwebs from my head. My pulse takes off with a surge, and I struggle to see around Rannigan.

"Looking for them?" Rannigan moves to the side, and my heart crumbles and dies in my chest. Fyrestar and Embersol are across the room, bound from head to tail in netting that must be coated in Rannigan's infamous magic to ensure it won't burn. I see them trying, but their fire is Bale's fire. It won't work.

Tears sear my eyes. My breath shudders, but otherwise, I don't move or make a sound. I have to think. Vampires hold swords to my birds' flaming throats. Rim isn't here.

"Let them go, Rannigan." My hard, wintery voice holds all the stone-cold ways I'm going to kill this bastard the second I have the chance.

"I'm glad you know who I am, since we'll be getting much better acquainted soon." He smirks, and rage explodes in me. It turns into icy terror when he leans in and opens his mouth against my face. He sweeps a long, slow lick from my cheek to my temple, and I shudder, turning away from him. He grips my jaw, forcing me back to his mouth for another taste. I can't move, his pointed nails digging into my chin as he swirls his tongue over the cut on my temple.

"Get your disgusting tongue off me." I wrench out of his hold, and his blood-covered nails claw my skin. His gaze dips to the fresh scratches, hunger flaring in his eyes.

"You have no idea what I had to threaten to keep my men from devouring you if they managed to catch you. They were going for the birds—to hold for ransom and force you into the open. But you walked straight into the trap. So convenient. And you spared me from having to fight Bale. Bravo. You're already so useful."

I stare at him in shock. "Fight Bale?"

"That was the official plan, but I made an alternate one while he wasn't looking." Rannigan smacks his lips, his cheeks flushed and his eyes gleaming. "You *are* truly delicious. The sunblood scent from that cut is making me ravenous. I'm surprised my soldiers resisted."

Cold sweat pricks my skin, and Draywood stabs at my memory and senses again. I fight my rising panic, desperately hoping Rim isn't here because he escaped and went for help. Bale will come. The team and the warbirds will come. I'm not alone. I'm never alone here.

"Breathe, child. I prefer you conscious." Dropping his hungry gaze, Rannigan lifts my right hand and inspects my inner wrist.

"Good. You still bear my mark." Sharp fangs descend from his upper gums, and panic spikes so hard that my vision darkens. "Let's renew our vows."

I don't know what the fuck he's talking about, and all I can do is scream in pain when he bends his head to my wrist and pierces my flesh, sucking with a deep groan of pleasure.

"Idallia!" Fyrestar's desperate screech breaks my heart. Sol chirps wildly, and it's not even words. It's pure fear.

Pain and devastation rattle a hoarse shout from me as my pounding heartbeats launch my blood into Rannigan's mouth. I struggle savagely against the ropes, and Rannigan's free hand shoots out, roughly circling my neck and pinning my head to the column with a hard thud.

I wince. My head rings, and gray colors my vision. Deprived of air, deprived of blood, I feel my strength slipping away. My mind dulls, and a chill creeps over me. A sob works its way up my throat, but before I let it out, Rannigan ends his bite and lifts his head.

The sight of him sickens me. My blood coats his lips. He licks it off with a slow, deliberate show of tongue that makes my skin crawl. "My first sunblood. Scrumptious. But unlike mindless soldiers, I can control myself. It's a shame I have to turn you. It would be sublime to sip from your sun-filled veins for centuries."

I spit in his face. "Fuck you, you revolting bastard."

"What a little brute. I love it." He smiles cruelly. "You'll fit right in back in Bloodwold."

"I will *never* go to Bloodwold."

His chuckle terrifies me. Then Bale's roar thunders through my fear as the Dragon King dives through a window and lands in a crash of fire.

"Get your hands off her," Bale snarls, already in skin. Rim is by his side. I exhale sharply. *Thank the stars.* Rim caws my name, and I look back at him.

Rannigan whips around as the rest of the Elite Wing swoops into the war room with their wing guards. "On the contrary. It's *my* hands that belong on her." He pulls out a knife and slices through my bindings. Roughly, he hauls me to my feet. I sway unsteadily, my head swimming, my muscles cold and stiff. Spinning me, he jerks my back against his front and holds me there, inhaling loudly against my neck. "I smell you all over her, Bale Cinderheart. Not only did you steal my wife, but you're fucking her," he growls.

My mind slowly catches up with his words as I find my balance. "Your *wife*?"

Rannigan wraps a hard arm around my ribs, pinning me to his corded body. His other arm locks tightly around my throat, forcing my chin up. "Shall you tell her? Or shall I?" The challenge is for Bale.

I turn to Bale in desperation, terrified by how guilty he looks, stock-still and pale and not meeting my frantic gaze. I still don't understand, but horror sinks into my bones on a whole new level.

Bale's eyes burn a furious amber. He still doesn't look at me, his entire focus on Rannigan.

The other members of the Ellonrift Council suddenly burst into the room from the stairway. Rannigan swings us toward them, and I see who I now know is the Human Queen and the Were King. The new Fae Queen slips in with them, hiding behind their shoulders. Rexton Hale emerges behind her, and my lips part in disbelief. Even *he's* here to witness this?

Bale stalks forward from the window side, forcing Rannigan to turn us back to him. His voice dangerously low, fire-filled and grating, Bale says, "Tell her how you massacred her entire family? Or how you left her alive so you could steal her destiny from her?"

"You stole her destiny more effectively than I ever did. I'd have put her on the Council two hundred years ago," Rannigan snarls.

"After turning her into *you*!" Bale snarls back at him.

"You're no better, on your high mountain, lording over the world. You turned her into *you*, and then you didn't even give her a seat at the table."

Bale flinches. My heart thrashes in my chest, my pulse beating like a storm that'll break down all the walls of my body. These words…I think I know what they mean, but it can't be true. My family—massacred. My destiny—taken.

"I'm the Vampire Queen," I whisper.

"Glad to see she's smarter than you," Rannigan snaps in Bale's direction.

Bale stares at me, spine stiff, shoulders back, eyes blazing. I stare back at him, the feel of him on me, *inside* me, still vividly immediate and so intimate that I'll never recover. My love for him implodes like a dying star, crushed inward by a force so powerful it shrinks to a burning pinpoint. He had so many chances to tell me the truth. Lifetimes of them.

My gaze hardens. His softens, pleading. I shake my head, his betrayal stabbing me in the heart over and over. He's a fucking liar, and he stole my life from me.

My gaze slides to Kellan. He's pale, visibly shaken. I wish I could tell him I'm sorry. I'm sorry that I didn't know the truth to tell him. I'm sorry that I broke his heart, because now I know what it feels like.

"How am I your wife?" I grate through clenched teeth. "I think I'd remember that." I remember almost everything.

Rannigan sniffs my neck again. His fangs scrape my skin but don't penetrate. I shudder in revulsion. "You were floundering in the remains of your family. I picked you up, drank your blood, and declared you my wife. You didn't have teeth or fangs and couldn't drink from me yet, so we took your wail as a *yes*, and the Bloodwold scribe wrote it into the royal books. It's law, and it cannot be undone."

My eyes widen. My breath saws in and out. "I didn't give my consent!" I wrench against him.

He laughs darkly, strengthening his grip to keep me still. "That doesn't matter in Bloodwold."

I stop thrashing and take a measured breath, forcing myself to calm down, to think. To be stronger, smarter. "I'm the starborn ruler of Fanghaven and the legitimate queen of Bloodwold."

"That's right, precious," he confirms loudly enough for everyone to hear. He nods against my head, rubbing our cheeks together. "Welcome to the family."

My hard swallow bumps painfully against Rannigan's tight arm around my neck. "So how did I end up here?" My eyes find Bale's, the question for him.

Bale takes a cautious step forward, his expression still begging me to understand. "I learned of the coming massacre before it happened. I tried to get there in time to stop it, but I was too late. Everyone was dead. Soldiers. Staff. Advisors. The royal family."

Bale inches closer. Rim sticks to his side, and my eyes drop to my bird. The look I give him screams at him to go, to get out of here. My heart pounds like phoenix wings on a flight to war, and Rim clicks his beak at me, his amber gaze flicking to Fyrestar and Sol. I look at them, too, then back at Rim. I don't know how, but I'll save them. I silently promise with every drop of blood still inside me that they'll make it out of here alive, and so will Rim.

"I was in scales. I charged Rannigan, ready to bite him in half for murdering a family I called friends, and do you know what he dragged out of his cloak to shield himself with?" Bale's gaze holds mine. "You. A tiny, limp, bleeding *you*. I pulled up short so I wouldn't swallow you along with half of him. I had to throw my head up to keep my fangs and fire from hitting you."

Dizziness strikes me again. I see it in my darkest, faintest, most confusing memories and piece the rest together. Nightmares about black-nailed hands and blood against scales that look just like Bale's. "That's how he sliced through your chest and nearly killed you?"

Bale nods. It was because of me. He almost died for me, the infant daughter of his Fanghaven friends. "I swiped you from him and gripped you in my talons while he sliced into me and ripped a scale from my chest. The injury slowed me down. He ran, and I had you to protect. There were Bloodwold soldiers everywhere. Instead of chasing him down, I flew you out of there as fast as I could."

"So there *was* a fourteenth scale," I murmur. "He ripped it off."

It's Rannigan who answers. "Very useful. My sorcerers used its protective magic to discover a way to shield us from firebreath. Raiding became so much easier after that."

Sickness washes over me. *Because of me.* Torridaigans and Ruthinock humans hunted more easily for two hundred years *because of me.*

I straighten my spine, hatred and disgust an iron spike keeping me ramrod straight and hiding the tremors trying to shake me. "What do you want, Rannigan? What happens now?"

"Drink from me. This arm, right here." He lifts the forearm he'd had banded around my neck, shoving the softer underside right against my mouth and under my nose. With his other hand, he quickly cuts a line with his own sharp, blood-dark fingernail, then grips me tightly around the middle again.

The scent of blood hits me hard and fast, but revulsion doesn't follow. My mouth starts to water. My fangs grow.

"Once you're a real vampire, you'll come back to Bloodwold with me. The Council and its useless votes won't even exist after this, so all I really need now is an heir to both kingdoms."

My stomach heaves in disgust. "Never." I angle my face away from his blood.

"Never?" He nods to the vampires holding swords to my birds' necks. "Drink, or they die."

"No!" I thrash wildly. His blood smears my chin. He's strong, stronger than I am, and reels me back in.

"We'll collect their blood in goblets and toast to how marvelous they taste. We'll drain them straight down to their everlife. There'll be nothing but bones and feathers left."

"You sick bastard," I hiss in rage. "If you harm them, I will kill you. You won't get an heir from me. You'll get fucking torn in half."

Rannigan rubs his face against the side of my head again. His chuckle raises goose bumps on my neck. "You're a delight."

"Idallia!" Fyrestar speaks to me urgently, not moving a muscle to give himself away. *"Let them kill us and fight your way out. He doesn't want to kill you, and once he can't use us against you, the Elite Wing can take them down. They won't have time to steal our everlife. We'll be reborn, right here in the mountain. We'll be together again."*

I shake my head so little I barely move. My eyes swim. My love burns brighter than a phoenix, and I will *never* sacrifice them for me. Cealastra is gone, an empty light fading from the night sky, and everything Bale has said over the course of the week confirms it. If Fyrestar and Embersol die, they won't come back. Rebirth is done.

Sol chitters in fear. *"Love you. Love you,"* she chants over and over. It's her goodbye. She knows there's no spark that can bring her back to me. Fyrestar knows it, too, but he'd still die for me.

Bale must hear Sol. Maybe she can't control her thoughts with fear snapping through her like wildfire. He steps forward, pushing Rim behind him. "Take me. I'll name a successor for Torridaig. Right here. Right now. Starborn or not doesn't matter anymore. The Council is over. Let Idallia and the phoenixes go, and I'll step down and come with you."

My eyes widen in horror, my heart clogging my throat. I don't want that, either. Bale a blood slave to Rannigan and his cohorts? Drained over and over? Powerless after being the most powerful man in the world?

"Idallia. Behold the sun." Rannigan blows hot breath against my cheek as he laughs mirthlessly. *"He* named you that. It's not your birth name. See how he controlled your fate from day one?"

Thoughts riot through my head. Bale set me on a path. There's no denying that. And he lied. But would I rather have been carted off to Bloodwold as the Vampire King's infant bride and brought up to hate and take and send blood raiders into sovereign lands?

"What's my name?" I rasp.

"Clara Bruhane," Rannigan tells me.

"How fucking boring," I spit.

Rannigan laughs. "Like I said...a delight. I can't wait to see what kind of child we make."

"Take me," Bale repeats, moving closer and holding out his weaponless hands.

"So you're not just fucking her. You love her. How sweet." Rannigan drags me back a step. "It makes me even more excited to take her from you. Now my dear," he says, squeezing me until my ribs ache, "drink, or the little one dies. Then we'll see about the other bird."

My hard, ragged breaths ricochet back to me from against Rannigan's bloody arm. Rim starts squawking, his frantic gaze swinging back and forth between me and the captive birds. Sol is still chanting her love, her little croak like a dying fire. Fyrestar caws to me, his violent *no* pounding soundlessly into my head like the sunlight that will never stab my eyes again when I first leap out the window.

I block out the sounds of their desperate, fear-filled cries. My fangs are already out, sharp and ready, and no matter how much Rannigan repulses me, they ache for the hot wash of blood I know is coming.

"Don't!" Bale shouts roughly. He lunges for me, and Sol squawks in pain as Rannigan's man cuts into her neck.

Panic catapults an unhinged howl from me. Bale stops, shock freezing him solid. Rim and Fyrestar screech in terror. Several blood-wet, partial feathers drop to the floor, sliced through. Blood gushes down Sol's chest, hissing against her flickering plumage. She wobbles and stops chanting, her amber eyes glazing over.

I forget to struggle against Rannigan and watch in helpless horror, dread destroying me. Sol somehow stays upright as her feathers dim. There's a deep gash in her neck. She breathes hard, looking focused and furious, and the magic left in her and in Ellonrift seems to start working. After long seconds of abject terror, I see Sol's eyes start to brighten, and begin to hope that maybe the worst won't happen. She's fighting, pulling through, and relief weakens me so fast that I slump against Rannigan.

Bale watches me, his eyes wide with fright. He looks like he's about to step toward me again, and I shake my head, standing as tall as I can with Rannigan clamping me against him. My expression already colder than a snow-capped peak, I harden my eyes even more, hoping they glitter with hostility. I'll never forgive Bale for any of this, but if Sol dies because he takes one more step, I'll kill him.

I see his reluctant capitulation. He holds still even as he pleads with me. "You'll never walk in the sun again. Never fly under a blue sky. Never fight a battle with us in the daytime. Everything will change."

It will anyway. It already has. And I don't care about flying or fighting if I can't do it with my phoenixes.

"Maybe I'll finally reach my true potential," I say tonelessly. His eyes flare in panic as I lower my head to the Vampire King's arm, open my mouth, and bite.

Rannigan drags in a loud breath, half obscuring Bale's choked-out denial. I seal my lips around Rannigan's punctured skin and suck. The first hot wash of blood into my mouth and down my throat is ecstasy. Moaning, I gulp down another. The Vampire King slackens in pleasure, his hold on me loosening. I feel his cock hardening against the small of my back. This is a consensual bite, after all.

I drink again, strength infusing me. Another long sip, and my senses sharpen until every little sound and smell in the space around me makes perfect sense. Everything's clearer and more intense. I can smell Bale on me like never before. I can smell the stale blood on Rannigan and hear his heartbeat as loudly as my own. Taste is suddenly exquisite, Rannigan's blood a powerful flavor on my tongue and an even more powerful force in my veins. I drink long and deep, building myself up for what's to come.

"Don't get too greedy, wife." Rannigan starts pushing against me. "Leave some for the marriage bed."

Still drinking, I grip his arm in a caress, both my hands sliding over his smooth, cool skin. His grasp on me loosens even more. The hand at my waist simply holds my hip like a lover would. I slide my body against his, and he softens behind me. Encouraging him with a slow push of my backside into his crotch, I take a last, deep swallow and lift my head.

"Delicious, right?" he purrs in my ear. His thumb caresses my hip. He clearly already sees us making that heir. I already see him dead.

"Useful." Still holding his forearm in a solid grip, I whip around, kick him in the middle, and yank so violently that I pull Rannigan's arm clean off.

He stumbles back, gaping. Pain and shock slash across his features as blood spurts from the ragged gap of his open shoulder. I cock his severed arm back and crack him across the face with the full force of my newly unlocked potential. He falls, sliding in his own blood.

"I guess starborn strength really is different." Looming over him, I stab the exposed bone of his torn-off limb at his throat. It takes three brutal hits to pulverize the skin, reach his spine, and break his neck. Savage, full of hate and hurt, loss and residual fear, I finish off the flesh and bone with the knife from my boot, then lift Rannigan's severed head.

My gory prize swings in my grip and leaves a wide spray of blood as I spin around with a sharp hiss of breath. My feral gaze slams into a battle already in progress. Wade, Danica, and their wing guards take down the vampires holding Fyrestar and Sol, then they start freeing my birds from the nets. The rest of the Elite Wing and their warbirds are picking off Bloodwold soldiers and Rannigan's royal entourage alike. Rexton Hale streaks forward from the other side and joins the fight. From the look he gives Rannigan's severed head as he passes me, I think he'd have killed the king again if he could.

The combat is already well in hand, and I don't move. Bale doesn't, either. He just stares at me as I hold my enemy's severed head in my fist, true starborn strength coursing through me for the first time in my life, and sunshine forever out of my reach. He starts to move, and I give him a look that says he'd better not come near me, or I'll claim *his* head next.

The battle quickly calms. Vampires lie dead in the war room. The leaders of Ellonrift gather round, and I realize that for the first time in Bale's reign, they don't look at him to see what comes next. They're looking at me now.

"I have no quarrel with any of you." I look at each of them in turn, including Bale, even though the sight of him yanks my stomach to the floor. "I have two kingdoms to rule, and one that needs drastic changes. I'll put an end to raids. To blood markets. Bloodwold vampires will heed me or die." I lift Rannigan's head as proof of intention. "I'll bring my *husband's* head back as evidence of my rightful succession—and that I mean what I say."

Rexton Hale lifts his voice from the middle of the crowd. "And Fanghaven?"

"I'm hoping you'll work with me," I answer. "Help me keep Fanghaven running smoothly while I deal with Bloodwold."

A dangerous sound rattles in Bale's chest. Shadows seep from him, but he doesn't let them take form. "You can't be serious."

My attention whips back to him. "Starborn doesn't matter anymore. Cealastra is gone, and we all know it."

"So you're giving him a kingdom?" Bale growls.

"I'm giving him a job," I snap. "I'm the Vampire Queen. The entire east is mine."

"Idallia..." He reaches out a hand, too far from me to make contact. It's supplication, not touch.

"Don't you mean *Clara*?" I ask harshly.

"No, I mean Idallia. Please." His hand still reaches for me. I can't take my eyes from it. How I once longed for that hand, that invitation. For *him*.

Hardening my heart, I rip my gaze from Bale and look around the room for what I need. I see a satchel and grab it off a felled vampire. Blood all over me, I stuff Rannigan's dead-eyed head inside, then sling the strap over my shoulder and walk to Fyrestar.

"If anyone needs me, I'll be in my castle in Bloodwold. I'm its queen, and Rannigan has no heir." Fanghaven doesn't truly need me, but I can change Bloodwold. I won't rest until I eradicate the blood violence there. "Everyone is free to visit except Bale Cinderheart." I say the last looking straight at Bale. I might never see him again, and I refuse to acknowledge how much that hurts.

He looks pierced by a hundred daggers, and I'm the throwing hand. His eyes. That mouth. His feet slide backward, taking him away from me. Bale has never retreated from anything, but I just blew him wide open. I crushed him like he crushed me.

Fyrestar gets low near my side. I climb onto his back and then pull an injured Sol into my lap. "Rim!" I call sharply.

Rim looks once at Bale and then hops toward us. *"Forever and always,"* he says just for me. I swallow thickly. I have my family with me.

I turn to Kellan. Then to the rest of the Elite Wing. "Thank you for being my friends. I hope I'll see you again."

They all look devastated, but no one asks me to stay. They know I can't. I see the promise to visit in their eyes, and that's enough for now.

"Kellan?" He steps forward despite Bale's low growl, and I ask, "Will you please give Sybil and Stuart enough of my gold for five lifetimes? You know where my vault key is, right?" He nods. "Tell them goodbye for me and send the rest of my gold on to Bloodwold. I'll probably need it there."

"Sybil would want you to say goodbye yourself," Bale says softly.

I turn to him, tears crawling toward my eyes on burning spikes. "We don't always get what we want, do we?" My words seem to flay him alive. *Good.* I'm raw and bleeding too.

I look away, swallowing the thick heat in my throat. I won't see Sybil grow old and go blind after all. I've never had a premonition that didn't come true, but I guess there's a first time for everything.

Like finding out I'm a starborn queen.

I don't ask Bale for permission to take my birds. He gave me his promise. And no matter what else he's done, I know that wasn't a lie.

I can't look at the team again. I miss them too much already, the closeness, the fun, the danger, the having-my-back no matter what, no matter when. The wing guards are a flash of glowing feathers in my periphery, and I keep my head low, unable to find the courage to watch them circle the war room like Rim and Sol and Fyrestar used to. I'll miss the rest of the warbirds too. My phoenixes will miss them more.

"Let's go," I say roughly, my throat a tangle of tears. It's a long way to Bloodwold, but I'm pretty sure we can get a good start on the journey before the sunrise forces me inside.

We take off, and Bale's lips part on a sharp breath I hear all too clearly now with my heightened senses as we sweep past him, speed across the cavern, and soar into the night.

CHAPTER THIRTY-TWO
IDALLIA

I sit on my throne, Rannigan's decomposing head on a spike next to me. It stinks and oozes, but I keep it there as a reminder. *Don't fuck with me.*

I killed all his advisors. His courtiers fled, so at least I didn't have to put their heads on spikes. My outer walls are already covered with them.

Fyrestar sits at my right hand. Rim sits at my left. Sol warms my feet, because this place is bloody cold and awful. Sol's neck healed, but the severed feathers are a blunt reminder of how close she came to death. Her unmarked skin is another reminder—of how, for the moment, magic endures in Ellonrift. I've kept most of Rannigan's sorcerers on hand, and I'm even starting to rely on some. He had a legion of magic users, many of them as skilled and powerful as any at Drayke Mountain.

There were a few rotten apples among the sorcerers. Their heads had to go on spikes, but mostly, they were just terrified humans doing their best to survive in the bloodiest court in Ellonrift.

It's still bloody, but not for the same reasons.

I had the new edicts read in every town and village across the east, from the border with Torridaig to the wild, windblown edge of the continent where I saw the thrashing sea for the first time. I go back sometimes and turn my face into the hard wind and salt air. It feels cleansing somehow.

Bloodwold has a new ruler and new laws.

Blood feeding without consent will be punishable by death.

I had to execute four thousand six hundred and ninety-two of my own barbaric people before they decided I was serious.

All blood hosts are to be freed and allowed to go where they wish.

I'm still working on that, combing the kingdom from household to household with the help of Rexton Hale and the combined Bloodwold and Fanghaven armies under our command. We're finding fewer people chained in basements now that dissenters realize I'll personally grind Stuart's torque into their fangs and make it so they can never feed directly from a vein again.

Sybil and Stuart came to visit almost immediately after I left Torridaig. They brought my torque and all my belongings. I threw out the rugs Bale gave me, but it made me sick to my stomach. While they were here, they switched from day dwellers to night walkers so we could be together. They didn't like the heads on spikes. Sybil called it unsanitary, and I'm sure it is. Effective, though.

Don't fuck with me.

Stuart enchanted several golden rings with the same fang-disintegrating magic. I gave them to Rexton and our army commanders. Our zero-tolerance, kingdom-wide campaign is steering even the most recalcitrant Bloodwold vampires toward a consensual blood commerce like in Fanghaven.

Surprisingly—or maybe not—people from all over Ellonrift

have been flooding into Bloodwold, looking to make their fortune selling blood. Ruthinock is in a drought, both magical and agricultural. Humans need a new source of income. And not everyone in Torridaig is satisfied with their lives and fortunes. This new opportunity tempts more people than I would've guessed.

The fae have been making their own game plan for survival as the Star of Ellonrift fades—an exchange. Caravans of them are crossing northern Torridaig now. They bring the sweet blood coursing through their veins to Bloodwold, and vampires want a taste of it enough to trade years off their extended lifespans. Everyone leaves satisfied. Some even stay. Vampire and fae couples can feed off each other for centuries.

There used to be no one in this kingdom except Bloodwold vampires and those who were coerced and enslaved. Now there's a bit of everyone. I wouldn't be surprised if midway trading establishments start cropping up in Torridaig, but I guess that's Bale's decision.

Pain lances my chest. I wish my heart didn't feel scored by razor-sharp talons every time I think about him.

And I think about him too much. Sometimes with utter, betrayed hatred that burns in my veins and sometimes with heartbroken, anguished adoration that slingshots right back to me every word, every kiss, every touch we ever shared.

But even in my most somber, violent moments—my perfect memory more of a curse than ever now—the person I used to be isn't really gone. I still love my birds more than anything, and their love keeps my broken heart beating strong.

We fly at night now. I don't have the expansive views of green mountains and wildflower moors or sunshine on my face, but I have freedom from my heavy throne and all the heads on spikes. My birds and I have the dark, open sky, and we streak across it like shooting stars.

Fyrestar is my rock. I feel like we're the same being sometimes, so linked I could have his burning wings and he could have my starborn blood. Rim matured too quickly after that last night at Drayke Mountain. He never complains and finds ways to help, but he's sad he won't get to fight alongside the Elite Wing and the other warbirds again. It was his dream since rebirth. Sol is my tender happiness, the one I need to snuggle during daytime sleep and who burrows right into me instead of using the roosting wall I had built. She doesn't fly as fast or as joyously anymore. I know she misses *Dad*.

Just like any vampire, I exclusively drink blood now, and it satisfies my hunger and my body in a way that food never could. I never drink from a vein. Rannigan's was my first and only bite. I drink from goblets filled by humans who I know are treated well and live comfortably at Blackrock Keep. I don't want dragon-shifter blood. Someone handed it to me once, and I could smell the difference. The old, fire-dry scent, the strength and power. Woodsmoke and wind. I threw the cup across the room, both craving Bale and hating him so much that I shook for an hour. No one offered me dragon-shifter blood again.

Except for when I fly with my birds, the only times I'm even close to happy are when the team shows up. They must know I need them, because they start coming around so regularly that I quickly set aside permanent rooms for them. They don't usually arrive all at once, but everyone except Kellan comes and goes. I don't think his absence has anything to do with hard feelings. Maia told me he took Grambolt and Featherspear and went west to Tanturriff to be Marissa Turin's bodyguard. I knew the Fae Queen had enchanted him. She looked harmless enough, but I'll bet her little claws sink deep and that Kellan won't live as long as the rest of us.

My phoenixes are always ecstatic to see the other warbirds. We're all sad when they leave, and Blackrock Keep goes back to being cold and dark and lonely.

I write to Rita and Gerard sometimes. They haven't answered yet. I still daydream about retiring to Glarraden House one day with my birds and sitting in the rose garden with a hundred chairs if I want to. But you can't really see a garden at night, and queens don't retire, do they?

I'm stuck in Bloodwold. This place needs an economy that's not based on blood trafficking. There's work to do. I invited gildenfae in to look at the now safe-for-them land, and they quickly struck gold in northern Bloodwold. The mines are still new and a work in progress, but even with the gildenfae taking their generous cut to do with as they please, I'm starting to gather enough funds to finance bigger projects.

Maia and Danica arrive one day and tell me Bale disbanded the Elite Wing. It's the first time I've seen tears in Maia's eyes. They don't know what to do with themselves. I'm hollowed out and devastated to see a past I loved die, even though I hide it better than they do. I guess I'm doing such a good job of putting heads on spikes that Torridaig is safe in the east, and more of the regular forces have been moved north to block werebeast incursions.

I learn from them that Bale invited everyone to continue living inside Drayke Mountain with their warbirds. He even keeps paying them, even though the battle horn never blows, and the team doesn't fly out to fight for the kingdom. Kellan's gone, and Maia, Arran, Danica, and Wade are restless and unhappy, but they don't know what to do. They don't want to leave Bale alone, even though he rarely seeks out their company and never trains with them anymore.

Learning all this sends me into a dark spiral, and I slip into my chambers and cry into my pillow. I miss my old room with the roosting wall and all the empty space so my friends could see me. I miss the leap into the void below with Fyrestar. I miss dinners with the team, and Sybil knocking on my door. I miss Bale, even though I hate him.

But when they say he's miserable, devastated, *lonely*, my tears dry and anger rebirths just like my phoenixes once did. Bale had two hundred and twenty-six years to tell me the truth, to give me my history, my story, my place. Instead, he made me love him and then ripped my heart from my chest.

Maia and Danica cautiously remind me of the same things the night air tells me when I fly out with my birds. Bale gave me a home, taught me to fight, protected me, and cultivated my mind as a leader. Would I be ready for this awful throne without what he gave me?

Probably not.

But I still hate him.

Wade and Arran show up on the heels of Maia and Danica. I'm surprised by the pairings, even though I don't say anything. Why aren't Maia and Arran flying together? And Wade and Danica? That's the way it always was when I was there, which left me with Kellan.

Wade can't keep the smile off his face, looking so happy and satisfied that I have to ask what's different. He flashes his new ring —mated to the older dragon shifter he met that night at the tavern.

I jump up, squealing, and throw my arms around his big, strong body. I squeeze him tight and feel the first moment of true joy since I woke up tied to that pillar.

Their visit ends without the same joy. Before they leave, they give me a note from Bale.

I'm eternally sorry. Please talk to me. I'll meet you anywhere.

I fold the parchment back up, rip it in half, and return the pieces to them to give to Bale, pierced through with Embersol's severed feathers. They didn't regenerate, so her body finally dropped them. There's a hole now in her colorful neck plumage.

I hope Bale sees the broken, bright-yellow feathers and weeps. I hope he somehow knows that Sol doesn't make cute little huffing, warbling noises in her sleep anymore but wakes up squawking with nightmares, just like me.

Exactly one year into my blood reign, I give the Fanghaven crown to Rexton Hale. We make a whole ceremony of it at our mutual border, the audience huge, the stars brighter than usual, but I walk through it numb, barely hearing a word. We work closely together, and I know and rely on him now. He's helped me build an army I can trust for Bloodwold and root out the rot that made crimson gold worth more than people's lives here.

But no more. Trafficking is done. Raids are over. There's blood commerce, not blood violence. And I still hate my new home.

Maybe I'd like Fanghaven better, but I don't feel that it's mine. Rannigan Bloodthief only wanted the vote he stole from me and an eventual heir to dominate the entire east. He wasn't truly interested in Fanghaven or its strong, determined people who hated him and his ways. Rexton kept Fanghaven together and safe for two centuries and defended its borders, its traditions, and its vampires. He's their king more than I'm their queen. Besides, the idea of living in the house where my parents and siblings were murdered makes my already cold blood run like ice through my veins.

I know it now, that corridor from my dream with the billowing drapes and the ballroom at the end of the long hallway. I've walked down it several times and had to force my feet forward, the echo of a happy past I barely got to taste layered over with the grisly memory of the massacre. I wish I didn't remember, but I've learned that's part of my starborn power.

Rexton asks me to marry him not long after the ceremony, wanting to join the vampire kingdoms in truth and in peace and rule equally. He suggests calling the new land Bloodhaven. I decline. We're only vaguely related, so that's not the problem. I'm pretty sure feeding off each other and fucking wouldn't be a problem, either, but I don't love him.

Sybil and Stuart arrive one rainy evening and don't leave. They bring everything they own and sweep into my night-cold castle like it's a perfectly fine home. It's my second moment of true happiness since I woke up tied to that pillar. Now that they're here, I don't hate these black walls as much, and I take all the severed heads down. Rannigan's is barely recognizable, and the flies are driving me crazy. I set up my chosen family in lavish quarters and make them head healer and head sorcerer immediately.

I guess I will see Sybil grow old and go blind. My premonitions don't lie. They're another aspect of my starborn magic and growing stronger by the day.

Which is why when I start to dream more and more often about making love to Bale in a room I don't recognize, his strong arms around me, his body moving inside mine, and his amber eyes burning with passion, I can't quite convince myself it's a memory and not a glimpse of the future.

His betrayal constantly aches in me, cold like a winter night and hot like a blazing sun. I wish I didn't love him still.

I see the night of the Fanghaven massacre and things from before it more clearly now. My too-good memory, even from my earliest days, shows me royal parties, laughing older brothers and sisters, and a beautiful mother smiling down at me. She had golden eyes and blood-red lips. My father had jet-black hair, just like me and my siblings.

The recollections are vague—I was tiny after all—but my starborn magic helps me understand how that awful night went, and sometimes, I still feel the blood of my family on me, the pain of Rannigan's wedding bite, and the warmth of Bale's inner fire turning utter terror into safe, exhausted sleep as we flew through the night. He held me close, far above the ravaged land as Bloodwold vampires looted, pillaged, and stole free people to keep or sell as blood hosts.

I know now that Rexton rallied forces and drove them out. It took years. But I was safe, high above it all in the thin air, rocked to sleep by the motion of flight, Bale's body and blood keeping me warm.

Bale chose me and let the kingdom burn.

My fang-punctured arm must've bled on Bale's damaged scales, maybe on one more than the others, giving Fyrestar my golden eyes. Bale could've healed instantly if he'd shifted, but enemy forces crawled below, he had me in his talons, and a long flight ahead. *I'm* the reason for his only scars. He waited until we were safely into Torridaig before he shifted, and by then, it was too late. His skin never perfectly healed, and neither did his scales.

And then he made our firebirds.

I saved the best for you. Closest to the heart.

Tears well in my eyes every time I hear his voice in my head. He planned it all. He created the Elite Wing for me—to teach me how to fight and protect me right under Rannigan's nose. No wonder he took me straight out of school, trained harder with me than with anyone else, talked the strategies of monarchs with me and only me, and made sure I could think like a starborn queen.

Because I am.

For decades, if not centuries, I could've been helping Bale and Torridaig and innocent people in ways that had more impact than individual battles against fanatical werebeasts or blood-trafficking vampires. I would never have voted with Rannigan, even without knowing what he did to my family or how he forced marriage on me before I could speak.

But when Bale Cinderheart could've given me my seat at the Council table, right there in our own Drayke Mountain, he didn't. He kept me in his bed instead.

CHAPTER THIRTY-THREE

BALE

Days are long and dull without Idallia. Nights are torture. It takes months for her unique scent to fade from my bedroom, and even then, I still think she's around every corner. It was especially hard that first spring after a cold winter. Sunshine hit the cracking ice on the lake and threw off a brilliant glare along with the essence of Idallia about to burst into action.

She sent my first letter back impaled by Embersol's broken feathers. My chest caved in, my limbs turned heavy, and for weeks, I could barely drag myself through the daily routine of ruling.

Then ruling got easier. It didn't happen overnight, but Idallia is so effective that blood trafficking went from my biggest problem to nonexistent. The separatist faction of werebeasts is still an issue, but I have more than enough soldiers to deter them, and if prevention doesn't work, to fight them.

Fae have started trundling across my land to get to Bloodwold so frequently that they've created a flatter, wider road across northern Torridaig just from wagon wheels, footprints, and hooves. The southern roads were already in better shape, but are requiring more upkeep now that they're being so widely used. I don't care if fae pass through my land as long as they're not trying to glamour anyone. Towns along their frequented routes are profiting. Inns filled, food and products purchased. I've stopped referring to them as parasites and am trying to guide my people to do the same.

It was a gut-wrenching decision, but I dissolved the Elite Wing. I made the team—and in some ways the warbirds—for Idallia, and she's not here anymore. But except for Kellan, no one left. Hearing them laugh in the dining hall or fly out to Drayke at night as a group sometimes makes it feel like nothing has changed.

I don't join them anymore. Being with them, or even with Stuart, is a too-painful reminder of what I lost, and how I destroyed it.

I sit in my study, staring blindly and wordlessly into my fire for days after the woman I love gives a kingdom to Rexton Hale. For all those years, I refused to hear him out because I wouldn't give him Idallia's birthright, no matter how much he'd earned it. But she took Bloodwold and gave him Fanghaven when I didn't give her anything, not even the truth she asked for so many times.

What if I'd told her years ago when I'd meant to? When she could keep herself safe, and the necessary secrecy could've given way to the partnership I'd always intended. Would everything have been different?

I hear she and Hale are close. If they're sleeping together, I might throw myself from my mountain and not open my wings.

Not too long ago, Sybil and Stuart packed up and left. They went to her. Good. Seeing them makes me sad, but it will make Idallia happy.

That night in the war room, Idallia told everyone, including me, that I'm not welcome to visit. I won't darken her doorstep without an invitation, but I can't help eventually writing to her again.

I'm sorry. I love you. There's so much to say. Please hear me out.

She doesn't answer, and life seems endless and gray. I'm not anywhere near done with mine, so how long until this pain ends?

Probably never.

I write to her again, sending the note with Cinderblaze and Glimmerwing because Maia and Arran are off somewhere, doing something. Strange that they went without their phoenixes.

I miss you so much that I face each day with dread. Please talk to me.

Her reply comes back with the birds eight days later.

I'd rather jump into the mouth of an erupting volcano than be anywhere near you.

I hold the note to my chest. At least she answered this time.

I did this to myself. I know that. Nothing is Idallia's fault, and I'm just thankful that my lies and selfishness didn't get her killed, or her birds killed, or her stuck with Rannigan Bloodthief. Reliving the memory of her killing him with his own arm actually makes me smile sometimes, which I never do otherwise. I knew she'd be something incredible with her true power coursing through her veins. She was already so much stronger than Rannigan in so many ways.

I wish she could understand why I held back from handing her over to everyone else so I could keep her with me. I desperately fought one change because I desperately wanted another, even before I knew it enough to put it into words.

I wish I could tell her how sorry I am that I kept her from her rightful place for so long. I try writing again. I don't know what else to do.

I didn't do it to hold you back. I did it because I couldn't let you go.

She doesn't answer this time.

I send my next letter with a dragon scale pulled straight from my chest. I don't shift afterward, making sure it scars and grows back crooked and lighter than the rest.

My heart beats for you. I'm sorry.

I don't hear anything back for so long that I figure she must've thrown the scale into one of the tunnels along the border she's having filled in and buried it along with her love.

But then, one late summer day, almost two years since she left, Rimblaze shows up at my window. At first, I think he's a mirage. My imagination. My frantic hope.

I walk toward him and touch his warm, radiant feathers. When I'm sure he's real, I bend my head to his and shudder. I can barely breathe.

"Is she all right?" I ask roughly.

"She's lonely and miserable."

My heart both expands and breaks. "She has you. She has Fyrestar and Embersol. She has Sybil and Stuart."

"She needs you. She just won't admit it."

Tears sting my eyes and spill over. "Does she know you're here?"

He chirps a sound I can't decipher. It sounds maybe like a yes, but that she didn't like it.

"What does this mean?" I ask. He unfolds his talon and gives me back the scale I offered. Misery tears me in half. "She didn't want it?"

"She said you shouldn't waste your starborn magic on useless healing for no reason."

No reason? She's the only reason I do anything anymore. I keep ruling so her kingdom is safe from mine dissolving. I fight werebeast fanatics so they won't even look in her direction, especially now that weres are trickling into Bloodwold to live, work, and raise families. I continue to send gold to Rita and

Gerard so she'll have a magnificent mansion and a huge fortune one day if she wants it. I rip scales from my chest and give them to her because it's the only way I can think of to prove how much I love her.

I stare at the scale in my hand, remembering the one Rannigan took from me so long ago. The piece of me is cold and dark compared to Rimblaze's glowing feathers in my peripheral vision.

An idea flits across my mind and sinks into my stomach, clenching my insides in a sudden, tight fist. I meet Rimblaze's eyes, my heart suddenly pounding like a hammer against my ribs. "I think I know how to do it."

Rimblaze's eyes look just like mine. He cocks his head. *"Do what?"*

"Give her back the sunlight. The daytime. Her life. With the help of you, Fyrestar, and Embersol, I think Idallia can behold the sun again. She'll be able to walk out in the day. She can fly in the light."

WHATEVER RIMBLAZE TELLS IDALLIA ABOUT OUR conversation convinces her to meet me this time. I feel like two opposing generals on a battlefield instead of a man who loves this woman so much that my life doesn't feel worth living without her in it. I remember her complaints about Rita and Gerard—how they saw only each other. I believe love can expand with family, but I understand the owners of Glarraden House better now. All I see is Idallia. Everything else could fall into ruin, and I'm not sure I'd care.

She lifts her chin, her eyes hard but glistening with tears. I did that to her. Hard and unhappy. The legacy from the best week of my life.

My chest folds in like a book closing on a chapter I wasn't

finished with. It wasn't just a week, either. Our physical intimacy lasted a week, but friendship, teamwork, and admiration began from the very start. As for the yearning, I don't remember when it started. Only that it became everything and pushed me to make choices I never should have.

We stand on the rocky plateau of the first peak of the Silver Moon Range. An autumn chill laces the night air with the scents of turning leaves, cold granite, and woodsmoke from the hamlet to the east. Everything reminds me of autumn two years ago, when all this started in earnest. The mountain has a foot in Torridaig, a foot in Bloodwold, and views to the southeast over Fanghaven. At the juncture of two kingdoms and nearly three, Idallia chose it as neutral ground, but nothing between us is neutral.

Her birds flank her. They look at me with kindness. Maybe pity. She lays a hand on Fyrestar. He stays by her side, but the younger two both come forward to greet me, Embersol with an affectionate head bump against my thigh that makes me smile softly, sadly. I stroke their warm, glowing feathers.

"Embersol's grown so much," I say hoarsely, my voice grating like it hasn't been used in a decade. "She's twice the size she was when I last saw her."

"Blackrock Keep has a lot of rats," Idallia says flatly. "She likes them."

"Pest control?" If that's humor, I fail miserably. Idallia doesn't soften.

"The fields around the keep are terrible for hunting. The city rats are fat, at least."

Do they miss the mountains of central Torridaig? The pines and cliffs and cold, blue lakes? The gusting winds and secret, emerald meadows tucked between soaring, snow-capped peaks? "Are you all well otherwise?" I ask.

She ignores that, saying sharply, "You have something to tell me?"

I swallow the hot ache in my throat. "I'm sorry."

By the light of her warbirds, I see her shoulders stiffen. "I know. It doesn't change what happened. Or what you did."

"I know it doesn't." Would getting on my knees help? I don't think so. Idallia responds to strength, but my strength feels gone. "I didn't want to lose you. I was scared you'd leave, and everything would change."

She huffs a sound so dry it sucks the damp sheen right from her eyes. "That's where you made the mistake, Bale. If you'd told me, I would've stayed."

My name on her lips is both everything I want to hear and a dagger to my ears. "I always meant to tell you everything a long time ago. I taught you to protect yourself and a people. I trained you to lead." I shake my head, hardly understanding myself and my choices. It was all instinct. "But every year that went by, every Council meeting, I'd think...next year. I'll tell her next year. We'll all be together just a little longer. A team. A family." My voice cracks, and she inhales with a shudder, her eyes gleaming. "And then..." I swallow. "I didn't really understand it yet, but I needed you in my life. To talk to. To train with. To protect." I wave a self-deprecating hand at myself. "Dragon shifter, you know...We gather and keep and safeguard. It's against our nature to give anything up."

"I'm not a thing, Bale. I'm a person."

Her emotion-shredded voice makes mine even rougher. "You were the first person in centuries I wanted to spend time with and confide in. And that brought me other people too. The Elite Wing. Stuart and Sybil. You gave me that." I clear my throat, the words sticking. "I don't even know when I fell in love with you—over the course of decades, probably—but as soon as I started thinking you might have feelings for me, too, it was like an avalanche inside me. Powerful, unstoppable, and so incredibly dangerous for us both because it made me hold on to you tighter when I knew I was supposed to let you go."

She rolls her lips in, her mouth trembling. "Your groveling isn't terrible," she says with a sniffle. Her back is still stiff, her expression hard, but hope jerks painfully inside me for the first time in nearly two years.

"It's all my fault. You asked for your story so many times, and I didn't give it to you. I pretended I didn't know. I did fear your reaction for your sake too. The facts are awful, violent and full of loss, and I didn't know if living with the truth would be harder than living without any truth at all. But now I know that wasn't my choice to make. I'm sorry, Sunshine. I was selfish—*am* selfish. I kept you from your kingdom so I could keep you in mine."

A sad smile lifts her lips. "Sunshine." She sighs. "Not anymore."

I take a cautious step forward. The cold wind snaps my cloak around my legs as it whips over the mountain, and Idallia shivers, moving closer to Fyrestar. Rimblaze and Embersol close in, phoenix warmth for her and a barrier against me. I created them, but they've been hers since the day I put them in the same room together and the place instantly turned incandescent with devotion like I've never seen.

Maybe she and Fyrestar somehow knew they carried the same blood. Hers was all over that scale.

My breath shudders audibly. I love them so. I love them all. "Did Rimblaze tell you what I said?"

She shakes her head. "He just told me I should listen to you and meet you this time. That I'd want to hear what you said."

My heart starts to pound. What if I give her false hope? It'll be like lying to her all over again. I still have to try. "Do you still have Rannigan's sorcerers who used the magic in my scale to protect his raiders against firebreath?"

Her eyes narrow. "Most of them. Some had to go on spikes."

I'm well aware of her propensity for heads on spikes. Incongruent with the Idallia I knew, but she brought the entire population of Bloodwold to heel in a year. I would've tried diplomacy and failed. "They did something to coat raiders individually and temporarily. It worked, but it would wear off. It was just the magic from one scale for sometimes dozens of vampires. And the sorcerers had to keep the enchantment going from a distance."

"We know this." She shakes her head, starlight splashing across her furrowed brow. "What are you getting at?"

"Do you think it would be possible to take the magic from a phoenix feather—maybe one from each of yours—and imbue it with the same kind of spell? Your birds' magic is still strong, even if rebirth is probably gone forever, and they'd shield you with their lives. There's love in that magic—for you. To protect you. If just one of my scales could protect dozens of vampires I'd have rather seen dead, maybe three feathers from birds who adore you could let you walk in the sun."

She stares at me. I hear her swallow even above the whistle of the wind. "I don't know if that would work, but it's not up to me to take my birds' feathers."

"*I would give you any feather,*" Rimblaze tells her, letting me hear. "*A hundred if you needed them.*"

"*Love you.*" Embersol simply leans into her hip.

"*Only the best for you. Closest to the heart,*" Fyrestar says.

She drops to her knees in the middle of them, gathering them close. Her sob breaks my heart. Tears flood my eyes.

"Will you try it?" I beg her.

She looks up, her beautiful face streaked with tears. "I'll try it. I'll let you know if it works."

All I can do is nod. It sounds like she'll send me a letter when my ardent hope was that she'd come to me herself and we'd fly out over the mountains again, all five of us in the sun.

A fool's hope.

She doesn't approach me, and I don't think she wants me to come closer. "Can you ever forgive me?" I rasp. "I love you. I would do anything to regain your trust."

She stands, wiping the dampness from her cheeks. She climbs onto Fyrestar's back, something about it so final that my heart grows heavy and sinks. "I don't know, Bale. And if this spell idea doesn't help, you live in the day, and I live in the night. It doesn't work."

"I'd make it work. I'd rather never see the sun again than never see you."

Do her features soften? I almost think so.

"You live in Drayke Mountain. You're the Dragon King. I live in Blackrock Keep. I'm the Vampire Queen." There's no part of her voice that says she likes her Bloodwold home, and I have a sudden idea.

"We can live here. *This* can be our mountain. We'll build a new home for both of us that touches both our kingdoms."

She looks around, seeming a little shock-dazed by my bold suggestion. The landscape isn't as wild and jagged as in central Torridaig, but the peaks are high, the forests are green, the lakes are plentiful, and the rivers run with frothing rapids and jumping fish. The hunting is good.

"There's no city here," she murmurs.

"Then we'll build that too." I dare a step closer. "I've got a lot of out-of-work soldiers these days. I have more gold than I know what to do with, thanks to the skills and needs of the gildenfae. Torridaig is rich in stone, in timber, in strong people looking for employment. A mountain to hollow out and turn into a stronghold will bring in droves of people looking for a new beginning. A city will grow from there. It'll probably be done in a year."

"You'd leave Drayke Mountain? For me?"

"I would die for you."

Her lips part. Her stare is golden starlight in the dead of night. Magnetic, almost hypnotic. It draws me to her, and her birds let me in. Idallia watches me warily. "You don't even know me anymore," she murmurs. "It's been two years."

"Two years don't erase two hundred." I reach toward her on Fyrestar's back, offering my hand. "I *know* you."

She swallows hard. "Do I know *you*?"

"The only secret I had was yours. You know everything now."

My hand still hovers between us. *Reach for me.*

She grips Fyrestar's feathers instead of my hand. "Meet me here on the first day of the next full moon. Come at midday but wait until dark."

I drop my hand to my side, my skin still aching for the touch she didn't give. "I'll wait. Noon. Dark. Forever. I'm not giving up on us."

She turns from me, but not before I see the anguish on her face and the tears in her eyes. Fyrestar lifts off without her signal, knowing it's time.

CHAPTER THIRTY-FOUR

IDALLIA

This is it. The test. My birds watch me with encouraging but slightly anxious expressions. Sybil and Stuart are with me. Danica's here, too, but that's just a coincidence. She visits a lot. She's bored without Wade. He lives in Drayke now with his husband, Brian. They make the most fantastic carvings out of birchwood and red cedar and juniper trees that hold details down to the thousandth-layered dragon scale or the tiniest shivering leaf on an autumn tree.

They bring new pieces to me every so often, and contrary to the cold, classic statues all over Glarraden House, I only see the light and joy in this artwork and don't mind it decorating my home. I see the improvements in Wade's work every time they visit. He's learning from Brian, and their business is booming. Not that they need the gold.

"Just a little sunlight won't do too much damage, will it?" Danica asks nervously. "You know, if the magic doesn't work?"

I shrug. "I'll get some nasty burns, but I can jump back into the shadows before anything too awful happens."

Dawn isn't far off. Light already limns the horizon in bright gold and blood red. When the sun rises, I'll step into its light for the first time in two years and test the combined magic of Stuart, my best sorcerers, and the earnest, endless love of my birds. Everyone's been working nonstop for nearly a month. Today is the deadline—the day I'm to meet Bale on the mountain where our kingdoms join.

My heart swoops, free-falling into the void of my chest with maybe no one to catch it. I almost hate Bale more for giving me this hope—of sunlight, of a new home we build together, of *us*.

But love is stronger than hatred, and mine feels like it's climbed the endless steps of Drayke Mountain, one foot at a time, until it reached the top and pushed hate out the window. I've wondered these last weeks who I'm really punishing at this point. Continuing to punish Bale feels a lot like punishing myself now.

I needed time. Bale gave it to me.

Now I think I need *him*.

I swallow hard, tears blurring my eyes. Hope and dread. Fear and elation. I wouldn't change anything about my choices, but I never expected to have *this* choice again—to move around outside, both during the day and at night. I would drink from Rannigan, pull off his arm, and pound him to death with it again in a heartbeat, even if it ended my time as a sunblood. His blood made me truly starborn, a queen, and the scourge of Bloodwold —until the kingdom finally turned the corner I wanted.

And now...maybe I can live again.

The sorcerers only just finished, and most of the residents of this keep are heading to bed right now as the sun rises in the east. If the Bloodwold sorcerers hadn't already had a base spell to modify, it would probably have taken years, not weeks. The first one did, and those human sorcerers are long dead. Creating Rannigan's firebreath shield from Bale's stolen scale took most of the decades I lived at Glarraden House. It was done by the time I reached school, giving me equal footing to fight Torridaig's greatest enemy. Fire and flight didn't necessarily crush vampires anymore.

My bound breasts are covered, and I take my shirt off. For this magic to work, for it to be safe and not something someone can take from me in broad daylight or that'll wear off with time, it needs to merge with my skin. A tattoo would only be inked on. This will be fused with my very being.

Fyrestar's feather is soft, medium-sized, and fiery orange. He plucked it himself straight from his chest. Closest to the heart, just as he promised.

Rim's came from his reddish-gold wing. It probably won't grow back, but it was so long and beautiful that he wanted me to have it. It's still warm with inner fire, even weeks after he pulled it out and gave it to Stuart.

Sol's gift to me was a little feather from her bright-yellow head crest. It might be small, but it's one of the feathers that always brought me the most joy as I watched it fly in the wind, trailing sparks like a ray of sunshine in this endless dark.

I take a deep, steadying breath. "Here goes."

I turn my back to Sybil, and she tucks Rim's long feather into the cloth binding my breasts, laying it flat against my spine from the small of my back to my neck. The tip brushes my nape, tickling a little.

I hold the other feathers myself, pressing Sol's offering to the right side of my neck and Fyrestar's against my hard-beating heart, the angle of it forming a line from the inner curve of my breast to the top of my left shoulder.

Idallia. I'm meant for this. *Behold the sun.* It's in my name— the one Bale chose for me, knowing my story and hoping I'd turn to the light in my life instead of the dark.

It's been dark lately. I'm ready for the light again. I might live for centuries, but two years is already enough time to waste on bitterness and doubt.

With my phoenixes' spell-imbued feathers against my skin, I pull my shoulders back, lift my gaze to the east, and step into the rising sun, praying to a dead goddess that I don't burn with the dawn.

CHAPTER THIRTY-FIVE
IDALLIA

Autumn has truly set in now, and the snap in the air is even harsher as we fly toward the first peak of the Silver Moon Mountains. I haven't stopped smiling for hours. I bask in the sunshine, three phoenix feathers a permanent part of me now, brilliant yellow, firelit orange, and reddish-gold brushstrokes painting my skin with protective love and the strongest threads of magic that could still be woven from the fading light of a dying star. My birds are as happy as I am.

"Are you going to forgive Dad now?"

My heart tumbles wildly. Laughing, I shake my head at Sol. "Do you think I should?"

Hugging our left wing, she nods into the wind, her crest a little less thick now but as jaunty and sparking as ever.

"And what do the rest of you think?" I ask.

Rim angles a little closer to our right wing. *"You don't seem as angry anymore."*

I glance over at him. That was a nonanswer if I've ever heard one. I understand him, though. He chose me, but I know he misses Bale.

"If you're ready to forgive, then forgive." Fyrestar pauses. *"Or maybe you already have."*

I have, haven't I? I don't think I'd be flying toward this mountain otherwise.

I finally see Bale, a dark, powerful dragon on a granite cliffside. He turns and stares in our direction, his amber eyes reflecting the afternoon sun, and his reddish-black scales absorbing the light until he looks like a shadow cast against the wall. Preternaturally still, he waits, watching. He doesn't track me like I'm prey. He tracks me like I'm *everything*.

We speed past him and up, landing on the summit. Huge wings flap, talons send stones cascading down the sheer rock face of the mountainside, and then he's with us, seamlessly shifting into skin as he strides forward.

Voice rough, awed, he says, "It worked." Stopping a few steps from me, he stares at me so hard that his gaze both burns my skin and makes me shiver. "Is it permanent?"

I loosen my cloak and tunic enough to show him at least part of each of the three feathers, ending with the one at my nape as I turn, lift my wind-tangled hair, and look over my shoulder at him. "They're bonded to my body. I can't lose them, and no one can take them from me." I turn back around, pulling my cloak closed against the thin, cold air. "The shielding magic was infused into the feathers and then into me when they hit daylight. It's done, Bale. I can walk in the sun."

His face a wreck, his hands already reaching for me, he closes the distance between us and folds me into his arms, pulling me against him. I stiffen on reflex, then close my eyes, sigh, and sink into his warm body. Woodsmoke and wind. Autumn leaves and pine-scented forests. Inhaling his scent, I lift my arms and hold him back. It's not as hard as I thought it would be.

"I'm so proud of you," he murmurs against my hair. "Is there anything you can't do?"

"I can't live in Blackrock Keep anymore. I hate it." I lift my gaze to his. "I want high mountains and furious updrafts, wild spaces and shining lakes, and..." My breath hitches. I can barely get the word out, my throat clogging with tears. "You."

His eyes widen. A low groan sounds in his chest, then his mouth is on mine, his hands in my hair, and his kiss is everything I've been terrified to think about for the last two years.

I kiss him back, fiercely, passionately, and for the first time since I left Drayke Mountain, I can't wait to see what tomorrow brings.

CHAPTER THIRTY-SIX

IDALLIA

"You weren't wrong about having labor and resources to spare." I look around the finalized interior of our new lair, satisfied and impressed. The outside of the new stronghold carved into our mountain is just as magnificent. It's as much a palace as a fortress, with wide terraces, high, arching windows, and crenellated walkways atop towers and lookout points protecting the summit. I can't believe how quickly even the finishing touches went on, and now the town in the river-cut valley below is growing by the day, houses and businesses sprouting like mushrooms.

"I was motivated." Bale brings my wrist to his lips and kisses the sensitive inside. "You said you wouldn't marry me unless it was in our new home." He smiles seductively, and heat snaps in my belly. "Here we are."

Here we are. My heart flutters like a vortex of autumn leaves swept up and around in happy circles. "I think you could fit a horse in that fireplace. And there are a lot of rugs."

He chuckles. "You should see the bed I chose."

I arch my brows. "Over the top?"

"You told me to pick the furnishings. Now you have to live with my extravagant choices."

I smile, laughter bubbling up so easily these days. "If it were up to me, you'd hate it. I'd have a bed and some swords."

"That's a little minimal, but I swear there's no clutter. Just nice pieces and what we need." Grinning, Bale sweeps me into his arms and carries me toward what I know is our bedroom, though I haven't seen the finished version yet. "The roosting wall is separate from the bedroom for obvious reasons." He flashes me a wolfish grin. "But it's right on the other side of the living room, so your birds will never be far."

"Our birds."

His arms tighten around me, and I'm pretty sure a flush of pleasure deepens the color in his cheeks. "Now that this is done, what are we going to do with ourselves? Even the werebeast incursions are settling down."

I roll my eyes, knowing he's not serious, except about the werebeasts. "More schools in both kingdoms. Housing for the disadvantaged and displaced. Medical training, since magical healing is dying out. Social integration—there are more fae and vampires mixing with dragon shifters and weres than ever before. Infrastructure! We need more and better roads. Not everyone in Torridaig can fly, and there are more and more people around that can't these days."

"Ah. I knew you'd have plans."

I laugh. "And if all else fails, sex for days and days."

Bale's inner heat sears me through my clothing, and his low growl is all I need for a pulse of arousal to thump between my legs.

"Before we get to that—which we will," he promises in a husky voice, "I have a surprise for you."

He veers off before reaching the bedroom, heading down a corridor I'm convinced was hidden before. Curious, I sit up straighter in his arms. "What's this?"

"Patience, Sunshine." I huff loudly, and he dryly adds, "That's the spirit."

Laughing, I bite his neck with little fangs. Not enough to draw blood. We'll save that for later. Bale is delicious, and he finds my bites delicious too.

With me still in his arms, Bale strides into a huge bathing chamber, natural runoff pooling in a wide, deep basin carved into the rock. "Amazing." Grinning in surprise, I take in the large, rough-walled, stalactite-hung room. "This cavern must've already existed."

He nods. "Right here at the peak of the mountain. I was thrilled when the workers broke down a rock wall to expand our chambers, and there it was, already half ready to go."

"Fantastic." I beam. "How starsdamned cold is that water, though?"

He chuckles. "Very. Unless I heat it up."

"Promising," I murmur. I can't wait.

"I have another promise for you." He sets me on my feet and drops to one knee.

My eyes widen, and my heartbeat accelerates, taking off with an excited jolt. As if by magic, Fyrestar, Rim, and Sol swoop down from previously dark corners, brightening the big room as their feathers heat and glow.

"I lay my kingdom at your feet," Bale rumbles, and Fyrestar hops closer, pushing a pine bough toward me. Its fresh, sharp, woodsy scent anchors me home in the mountains of Torridaig.

My breath shudders. I lift my gaze back to Bale.

"I give you my heart, my body, my strength." After Bale's words, Rim moves forward and opens one clawed foot. He drops the scale Bale sent me all those months ago at my feet.

Tears crawl toward my eyes, fogging my vision. I swallow hard.

"I give you the rest of my days, all my nights. Will you marry me now that we have our home? Live here with me and be my mate and my partner in all things?" I can barely tear my eyes from

Bale, but Sol draws my attention as she flutters in. She has a ring in her beak, and I hold out my hand. She puts the golden jewel into my palm. The ruby is gigantic. Bale knew I'd want something red.

My breathing unsteady, my pulse a joyous riot, I turn to the man I love. "I think those are three promises. Maybe more." He looks worried when I hand him the ring. "Don't just stand there. Put it on." I offer my hand, fingers splayed.

A wide grin splits his handsome face. His eyes glitter with inner fire as he slips the ring onto my finger, the metal band warm and a perfect fit.

I step into Bale's arms and smile up at him. "Yes, I will be your mate, and we'll live in this amazing home you had built for us. We'll take care of our people and our land. We'll keep our friends close and love our birds." I sweep an adoring gaze over our phoenixes before turning back to Bale. "Yes to everything. I love you, and I love the life we've started here."

I hadn't seen our fully finished lair until now, but we've already been living inside the new mountain for weeks. Sybil and Stuart moved in at the same time as we did, and I took any of the Bloodwold sorcerers who wanted to follow me, just like Bale did with his. Maia, Arran, and Danica will all live here with their birds, giving mine some of their brothers and sisters to hunt and play and argue with again. Wade is staying in Drayke with his phoenixes, but I'm sure he and Brian will visit often. I've already commissioned wood carvings to decorate the different levels of the mountain, ones filled with life and nature and beauty that will only add to the warmth here and not hide anyone.

"This almost feels unreal." Bale lets his big shadow wings unfold and solidify, wrapping them around all of us at once. "Like a dream."

Even this chilly cavern feels warm in the shelter of Bale's arms and with my birds giving off a happy, heated glow under the leathery tent of Bale's wings. "It's real, and I'll love you until more stars die and others are born. We don't need magic or the Star of

Ellonrift. We have each other, and we'll forge whatever new paths we need to—together."

"I love you." He cradles my head in his hands, his fingers threading through my hair. "And if our family expands one day, I promise I'll never leave anyone out of the rose garden."

A sudden, unexpected sob hitches in my throat. It's not grief. It's trust. Love. Faith in Bale and our future. "I know you won't." But I'm grateful that he said it. I glance at the clear mountain water. "Should we give that a try?"

Looking eager, Bale pulls his wings back inside and tips his head toward the exit, inviting our birds to find somewhere else to be for a while. They fly out with backward glances that range from satisfied to cheeky to sparklingly gleeful, leaving us alone in the chamber. Bale shifts quickly, heats the water to near boiling with firebreath, then shifts back to skin.

"You could've lost the clothing," I say archly.

He chuckles. "You know it doesn't work like that." He starts undressing. "Hop to it, or I'm tossing you in fully clothed," he threatens with a red-hot gaze that sizzles over me.

Grinning, I lose my clothing and carefully tuck the gifted scale into a pocket for safekeeping.

Both of us naked except for my new ring, we slip into the hot pool together. Bale hooks an arm around my waist and pulls me against him. Anticipation coursing through me, I loop my arms around his neck and my legs around his waist and kiss him deeply. Our lips and tongues brush and meld. A needy ache builds in my core. I slide against him, and we savor each other as steam rises around us, slicking our skin and dampening our hair until Bale's curls and mine glistens.

Water gently laps at the edges of the basin, and drips echo in the background, natural music to join our heated moans. I grip Bale tighter, rolling my hips. Our kisses turn hotter, our touches more urgent. Bale's erection nudges my belly, and I desperately crave the exquisite pressure of him between my legs and the hot wash of his blood in my mouth. Not wanting to resist and knowing I don't have to, I lower my head and sink my fangs into the curve of his neck, taking small, suckling sips that excite us both.

Bale tilts his head back with a deep groan, his fingers digging into my backside as he rocks me against him. His erection grows impossibly harder, and his breathing turns ragged and fast. Releasing the bite, I slowly lick a drop of blood from his skin with a hot swirl of my tongue, then lift my head, my eyes meeting his.

His voice a low rasp, he says, "Every single thing of beauty in this world pales in comparison to you." He hitches me higher against him and slides a hand toward my core. His fingers glide between my folds, stroking and teasing and making sure I'm ready for him.

I quiver in pleasure, his touch my utter weakness. "I want you, Bale." I can't stand another second without him inside me. If he's the lightning strike, then I'm the thunder. We need each other to be whole.

He kisses me like there's no end to his hunger, and I kiss him back like there's no end to my thirst. When we join, his thrusts filling me completely as our moans echo around the chamber, I know this is my new favorite place in my new favorite home and that I could live happily here until the end of my days.

And I will.

I have everything I want and need right here in Firebird Mountain.

ACKNOWLEDGMENTS

Every book seems to be a different beast with its own ups and downs that help me learn and evolve as a writer. I am so grateful to friends and family who support me throughout the process and are understanding about the long hours and deadlines.

After ten years of being traditionally published, I'm striking out on my own with this series, but I quickly learned that I'm not alone. I'm infinitely grateful to my author friends who immediately reached out with offers to answer questions about self-publishing and share their knowledge. It made taking this leap so much easier to know that I have an amazing support system in the author community. I would especially like to thank Jennifer Estep, Adriana Anders, and Clare Sager, who have been so generous with their time and expertise. I also want to thank my editor and formatter, Shelly, for helping me make this book shine to its fullest and for so patiently guiding me through parts of the publishing process that I hadn't been involved in previously.

And to my readers—thank you from the bottom of my heart. You're the reason I get to tell stories for a living and connect with people all over the world. I'm forever grateful.

ABOUT THE AUTHOR

Amanda Bouchet grew up in New England where she spent much of her time tromping around in the woods and making up grand adventures in her head. It was inevitable that one day she would start writing them down. She writes what she loves to read: epic exploits, steamy romance, and characters that make you laugh and cry.

Amanda is a *USA Today* bestselling author of romantasy and sci-fi fantasy romance. She was a Goodreads Choice Awards top 10 finalist for Best Debut in 2016 with her first novel, *A Promise of Fire*.

For more about Amanda's books with equal parts adventure and romance, sign up for her newsletter and connect with her online:

www.amandabouchet.com

ALSO BY AMANDA BOUCHET

THE KINGMAKER CHRONICLES

A Promise of Fire

Breath of Fire

Heart on Fire

Of Fate and Fire

A Curse of Queens

Beneath the Burning Sea

NIGHTCHASER SERIES

Nightchaser

Starbreaker

STANDALONE NOVELLA

A Curse for Spring

HEIRS OF THE SECOND DAWN

The Light Under the Shadow Wing

AMANDA BOUCHET

CAPTIVATING
ROMANTASY

www.ingramcontent.com/pod-product-compliance
Lightning Source LLC
Chambersburg PA
CBHW020544120726
47903CB00001B/122